Letras Secretas

The Secret Linkage
of the
Archidux & Catalí

Julien Vandenbroeck

authorHOUSE®

AuthorHouse™ UK
1663 Liberty Drive
Bloomington, IN 47403 USA
www.authorhouse.co.uk
Phone: UK TFN: 0800 0148641 (Toll Free inside the UK)
*   UK Local: 02036 956322 (+44 20 3695 6322 from outside the UK)*

Published by AuthorHouse 10/16/2020

ISBN: 978-1-7283-5582-5 (sc)
ISBN: 978-1-7283-5580-1 (hc)
ISBN: 978-1-7283-5581-8 (e)

1

She was already slightly balding and in a vain attempt to camouflage the pale friar's crown on her cranium, she wore her scarce grey tresses tightly combed backwards, in a small knot. Between the wrinkles grown from frustration, however, there was something of ageless beauty still shining through. Of a Greek tragedienne rather than a thoroughbred Spanish fury, Dugal thought.

"You can only get those documents on presentation of a proxy, sir," she said wryly. "And with a member card." It was no use obtruding oneself. In the mean time she went on typing, without looking up, on a keyboard that had also seen better days, with one finger and the mortal contempt of a pianist giving his last concert. *You remind me of Irene Papas, as Iphigenia, or of Maria Callas at her best,* he meant to say, but he was just able to bite his lips. "You look a bit like my wife." She was working on unrelentingly, as if there were nobody there. "La Ionès." Even now the clerk did not turn a hair, but around the corner of her mouth he thought he could sense a slight quiver. "Catarina Ionès. Don't you know h- …?"

Suddenly she gazed at him, straight in the face, without blushing at all: an eagle face to face with a big prey. *You don't say so. Catarina? La grande Ionès, and you are …? No!* He was close to blushing himself, the way she was examining him from top to toe. Which imbued him with the feeling as if an utterly strange lady-doctor were undressing him, to check whether he was still fit for a role in a picture where he had to show up just so, in his nudie.

"The code is: L.S., and the authorizing person: Prof. Marquez," he finally said to break the painful silence. With the chick who had served him last time, all that seemed to be superfluous. That young thing had jumped to her feet at once: "Oh, mister Mikes! Of course, señor." All adoration, she had fetched him the desired reading matter, coming back as quickly as lightning. With red ears, as though backstage she had relived Bernini's ecstasy of Teresa from Ávila. In a jiffy.

"That'll be all right!" To his surprise the elderly desk-worker in her turn went right to the rear now, without further comment. But still a bit dryly. Or had he just caught a flicker of recognition in her glance? At the door she wavered for a moment and turning halfway round, she said with a wink: "But perhaps an autograph won't be a big deal for you, afterwards?"

That takes the cake! Open-mouthed he stood there, gaping at that woman. Somehow she touched a tender string in him. After all, such a restrained roguish hint could be more useful than some far too exuberant aficionados. While that herring in vinegar was setting off to snoop about in the entrails of Palmera's university library, he was getting a bit anxious about his 'imago' after all. Was it possible that, within this short incubation period on Marcaio, his star was already fading pretty fast? Alright, he was no longer that Greek god of yesteryear, but if you see more and more rarely a light shining up in people's eyes: *Oh, isn't that …?* At the apex of your glory you can't set a foot anywhere but they cling to you like leeches. Then it may be a relief to slip off incognito once in a while.

But this? To an actor, withdrawal from the public is like permanent abstinence for a bull on a meadow full of cows. But all the same, he comforted himself, perhaps the secret worshipping of a withering rose gives you more satisfaction in the end than turning randy about one of those lewd chicks bursting to frolic around with you ~ just a matter of putting your name on her record of achievements. *Plato or the bliss of getting to maturity*, he grimaced.

"Here it is, señor Maïks, at your service!" The grey-haired lady put the pile down in front of him and a smile slid over her worried face. "Your signature, please?" He jotted down a scrawl on the paper while she slipped a second one under his pen. "For private use," she said. "By the way, I appreciate what you are doing for our Archidux. I 'm sure to read your publications in the Diario."

That hit home. Darn! How could this crossbreed of Greta Garbo and Mary Magdalen know about his Letras Secretas? Or rather: the Dux' apocryphal scripts. While he was already half on his way to the reading hall with his bibliographic reading stuff, he lingered a bit, wondering whether to return on his steps and ask her straightforward: *has professor Marquez himself blabbed … or is there anything going on between you and the editor of that newspaper?* But he had better act possum or soon all Palmera would know what he had in mind with those secret letters. If you start stirring in a cesspit …

No, from the prof himself she could not have got the information and editor Mortado's lips were surely sealed, for else, the effect of the sensation would have gone in advance. On the other hand, this was insiders' information after all and who else could have leaked it? About his Catarí he was dead certain; she would not trumpet about things like that, and after all, they were just four of them. Unless … Maybe this clerk was just a stand-by for her younger colleague. In case of menstrual migraine e.g. they would get her from the reserves' bench and for the rest she worked behind the curtains in Roberto's department. That way the old hand had probably intercepted a talk between the Prof and an assistant. *God-damn, a she-assistant!* Something about some spicy Dolly knocking about there flashed across his mind. Such an intellectual stunner who made a lightning leap forward in the academic circles, as the right hand of a professor. You see! And who said this grey mouse was not a relative of that nice piece of skirt with brains?

Ah, what did he care? Such rumours could only arouse people's fantasy, as a kind of appetizer. In the movie business that was not a bit different. Anyhow, later that day he could possibly drop in at the editor's office ~ this news should not spread like wildfire after all, or else the fun was gone. Before pushing open the swing door to the reading hall, though, he changed his mind and walked into the cafeteria a bit further down. Over a cup of cortado he first wanted to browse through the first epistle once again, to make sure. Out of anxiety whether this might really be an absolute hit all at once, or with the diffidence of the film producer whether he could soon throw his baby to the lions just like that ~ exposed to ruthless nitpickers? Catarí had voiced her objections enough and his friend Marquez played the devil's advocate. *This has the potential for a world success, amigo, but yeah … ~ for the same reason this whole island is going to tumble over you before long.*

Yet, from the very first letter out of don Lois's pen (even though this was but a retyped copy of the Dux' intimate secrets), it gripped him again and quite soon he lost every sense of place and time …

Brendais, October 13

Dearest Catalí,
Send you all my love from Bohemia. In the oriel where I am writing here ~ in some way also my dungeon ~ I am wrapping for you my most intimate wishes: the happiness that I myself was never able to give you.

Forgive me, I was a bad lover. Like most men, I suppose, who are always so much engrossed in themselves and their honour, and only realize how boorish they have been, when it is too late. Forgive me for that, if you can.

It is true, remorse comes after the sin. But I beg you, Cariña, to grant me this last chance. Herewith I offer you, in the deepest corner of my heart, all the flowers, the most ravishing gowns and jewels which I failed to bestow on you during my long sojourn on Maremira. If there were a flowermail-from-a-distance, every day I would have the most beautiful bunch delivered to you from the gardens of La Granja. With a lot of arums, for those were your favourites. Ses Taca swarmed with it, every time I passed by, seeking some repose under that shadowy carob tree. The 'algorrobo', as you used to call it, with those whirring rr's of yours.

From the first time I saw you, Catalí, when you poured me a rummer of the local wine out of a cool stone jar, one day in October, just like now, but then in the blazing sun, under a mulberry tree on a terrace in Valle de Muša, there already the pure white of that rich arum lily stood out as a symbol to me of your whole person: pure in body and soul. Believe me, never on all my rambles, even among the noblest spirits who crossed my path ~ nowhere in the aristocratic circles either, the 'pick of the people' (as far as one finds the true nobility in there), have I found that serene chastity thus, in all its intensity.

But no, I don't want to coax you. You, more than anyone else, know what a genuine dislike I have always had of adulators and lickspittles. Here they shower praise on you and toady you, and there, they would stab a dagger in your back. Therefore I admired you at once - you and your father, God rest his soul. Though of simple stock, you bore a natural kind of nobility about your person; that indefinable touch of mental peace which cannot be acquired by means of a grandiloquent title or fortune. A magnanimity which many high-born families have vainly strained after, to include it in their banner or escutcheon. Yes, even murdered, schemed, robbed ... And you, you simply had got it, in your way of being and thinking. 'Duc in altum'. I am not sure whether your father quite understood that Latin proverb, but he had chiselled it on every couch or wash-stand: aspire to highness!

And that is something I had not learnt yet either, until I came here (oh, again and again I catch myself thinking 'here' still, while I am hundreds of miles away from you) : to look up at the sky, the steely blue sky above the Teix; or between the myriads of stars that remind us of our insignificance. After seeing you, Cariña, all the emperors of the Holy German-Roman Empire, all my illustrious ancestors, deep back in our Teutonic veins, may get up from their tombs, to call upon me to follow my destination: "this and no other woman" ... I should not have been able to.

Our absolutely ungodly, unpredicted meeting has made me immune against all princesses, countesses and other valuable nubile candidates. Regardless of the treasure of precious stones and ducats which are hidden behind the marvellously attired hair, diadems and immaculately aligned features. Maremira, Ses Taca - that is, you, Catalí, and all that was dear to you - have cured me for ever of that vain grandeur.

Whether it was pure coincidence that our paths crossed each other there, on what was to become the most magical spot on earth to me, at the most intense moment in my nobiliary, yet not so happy existence? For you, a simple daily route, from the parental home to some small earnings; to

5

me a blind choice, inspired by señor Herreros ? Oh, I do not think so. When he ~ one of the few grandes whom I really held in esteem ~ had recommended to me that wonderful piece of land between heaven and earth (as it seemed to me; and to him: that accidental crossing of the 39°27' northern latitude and 2°14' eastern longitude), it was love at first sight. Indisputably, I knew, I felt: this was the place that matched my soul perfectly.

For you see, Cariña, this is mankind's misfortune: that most starvelings are deprived of this choice. A swallow builds its nest where it suits him, where it feels is the best dwelling for him, in the land where the wind, nay, its instinct has driven him. On the wings of freedom which the wise man, the homo sapiens, has clipped with himself and his kin.

And what prevents us then from being ourselves in the Promised Land? Our reason. No, not our common sense, but man's foolish craving for power and possession. So, all that I, my futile self, stand for. Very soon, however, I understood, owing to my expulsion, that it was not my own spirit that wanted things to be like that. Namely, this is my tragedy: to be the scion of a condemned lineage. A pedigree of mediaeval, rapacious knights, plotters and falsifiers …, emperors.

I hear you saying now: an impecunious creature cannot choose ~ you, however, belong to the select company who are able to buy their freedom. Or rather: were, until that bloody war came. Only now do I realize how lucky I was when señor Herreros threw that piece of land into my lap ~ for a scanty sum of ducats.

Here, at Castle Brandeis, I am 'privileged ' enough, as you would call it, to while away my days far away from the turmoil of battle. Requisitioned by my country (my 'homeland '?), I am sitting here, in this golden cage, pining away like a parakeet that tears off its feathers while abiding in vain the return of its mistress. It drives me mad.

Oh yes, I try to console myself by the thought that many people must bear some hardships, much worse than that. But waiting, this senseless idleness, is a greater torture to me than getting squashed at the side of others, by that ruthless, absurd war machinery which tramples thousands and thousands of humans, all in the name of God and fatherland. As if any god would openly align himself on the side of one of the parties, where in fact the same creatures stand together as those across that imaginary frontier – in the end, brothers as they are. But truly, the people and their leaders have always been so blinded that they attribute the same short-sightedness to their God – their greediness. Rather would I be shovelled into a mass grave, together with nameless soldiers slain in battle: pulchrum est pro patriam mori. To die for one's fatherland – how noble, indeed, but for which fatherland: the empire, Bohemia … or yours, Cariña, under whose sky I felt more at home than anywhere else?

2

<hr/>

That morning the Palmera city library permeated a hectic ambience, as usual. *How queer,* Dugal thought, a little drowsy, *nowhere in town you'll find such silence. While here the air buzzes with feverish activity.* Maybe it was all due to those heavily charged ideas circling around one - hyper-intensive atoms generating a vibrating strain field between themselves. With some imagination you could almost hear the electrons crackling.

But the annoying clicking of the fan was more likely to be the cause. Turning rounds rather for fancy, the poor thing. *Am I going crackers too?* he grinned about himself. He, a theatre flea from the cradle, began to get some of those visions of a physicist, of late. *A fizzkiss,* he nearly said. One like Caves, ages ago - Mister Cavy, as they used to call him by his nickname. "A disaster, Mikes," he had roared. "Dugal Mikes, you are a real …!" "I know."

This time, it did slip out of his mouth. But fortunately, no one had an eye for the laurelled actor bent over a pile of yellowed books. By and about the Archidux.

The poor chap should have known how far one can rank up despite an inbred loathing for all that smells of chemistry and physics. *The world is ruthless,* he chuckled. However, the Cavy had been a sneaky fan of Mikes Sr.'s. Or rather of ma Daniela Mikes'? Whose gorgeous couple of legs and ditto bosom were also worth a sin, at the time, and … *which added to Daniela's acting talent,* Dugal mused. *And by now you have become a living legend yourself, ready for the Hall of fame. Or Madame Tussaud's, dear me! Not as the scion of …, but 'as one of the most striking character actors of the last decades'. Caves should have lived to witness this.* Even for his dad it had been hard to stomach that he, the icon from the great Hollywood era himself, was not awarded the long-awaited prize until the end of his career. *And yet, daddy, I haven't got that sturdy chest and that dimple in the macho chin, which was your trade mark.*

He tried to shake off the memories by plunging passionately into his documents. Without any system at all he worked on, blindly like a mole, yet in utter concentration sometimes. Jotting down scraps of notes here and there, in the old-fashioned way …

"Señor Mikes." A sonorous baritone threatened to shatter his daydreaming; Dugal however wanted to repel every disturbance whatsoever. A dark shadow glided over the paper, startling him out of his exalted concentration. Only now he felt the cramp in his fingers.

It took a while until it came home to him it was not the twilight that brought him back to reality, but Roberto Marquez's shadow, between the window and the paper in front of him. "Dju-gââl!"

"Oh, you. I didn't recognize my own name at once." Obviously, with that Marcaian accent it rather sounded like 'Ma-ïks'.

"Odd," mumbled the stout, somewhat boorish figure, with the posture of a rural chief constable rather than an armchair scholar. "What spiritual dedication a vegetating Hollywood divo is up to! This is getting some mystical proportions, amigo!"

Pertly Dugal spread the article from the Diario de Marcaio out on the table, clearing his throat. "And what's on the professor's mind?" His voice sounded hoarse, as though he had unlearnt to use it for months ~ save for some guttural murmur and a few monosyllabic sounds to the servants who, at intervals, brought him a titbit or a cup of black stuff.

"That you'll get out of here like an utterly dazed dope, before long. Hey man, what possesses you? For days on end you have been living like the count of Montecristo, on stale tea and shrivelled coca de verduras. You don't even notice that spicy skirt I sneaked in here to clean up your mess. The poor chick is exhibiting the best of her hip and tit sway to perk you up a bit … All in vain."

"Which hair colour?" Dugal grinned, leaning back on the two hind legs of his chair.

"Fair-haired. Dyed, of course."

"That's it. Dumb or false blonde, I only lust after mahogany or jet-black, ever since Catarí."

9

"Look!" The professor, leaning with his two bear-claws on Dugal's armchair, pushed him back down.

"I am looking." But the bent-over body-mass with gorilla airs seemed more convincing than ever. By and by one forgot that prof. Marquez was also a dab at old manuscripts, Germanic literary history and some more of those bizarre things. "Either you dash like blazes to your poor homebound Penelope, or ..."

"Or?"

"Or a Roberto Marquez in person is pacing to your love-nest, and then I am not liable for the consequences."

Dugal burst into Homeric laughter. " 'Heavily scratched and clawed Prof slinks off from Casa Ses Taca, tail between his legs'~ I can see it smeared out all over the local tabloids, ha ha ha ... But no, joking apart ... To the point now: what are your first impressions?"

"Well ..." Professor Marquez sat down before him, ponderously. "I must say, señor Mikes ... This does not look like the greatest masterpiece at once or ... the discovery of this century. But, seeing the circumstances in which this scribbling did come into existence, or precisely the man's background ~ I am not sure. There's something about it, something captivating that I haven't come across since my childhood."

"Ha háá ... The salt herring that finds out there is a soul after all behind his own academic façade."

"Mind it, don't underrate our race's imaginative power! You actors could even pick up something from us there."

"It's just a pity that epistle did not flow from my own pen. If only to baffle my dear Cathy. 'That's at least something else than those few quickies you scrawled together at our early courtship,' she reminded me this very morning, just by the way."

Roberto sniggered sardonically. "This belonged to another epoch anyway, my friend. And you can't compare the style of that spiritual nobility with the level of today's heroes of the silver screen."

"Or even with that of the present-day professorial race," Dugal parried wittily. That fell on deaf ears, however. Dugal's erudite friend paced up and down a few times throughout the room. *Just like the Panther, as Rainer Maria Rilke described him*, Dougal thought.

Meanwhile Roberto kept mustering that star from across the Big

Pond, with obscure European roots, who had got it into his head to wash ashore, notably here, on the isle of Marcaio, for a (provisionally) premature Goodbye-to-all-that cure … With a calculating glance, implying: *What shall we do with that curiosum ~ up to the flea market with it, or is he still fit for the local star circus?*

"There's one thing I ought to tell you." Roberto Marquez, leaning on his elbows, lowered his imposing athletic torso on the opposite chair.

Procumbit humi bōs ~ that image of the felled bull flashed upon Dugal's mind, one of those kaleidoscopic fragments from his entangled store of school knowledge: 'and the bull sank down on the earth'. That old verse by Virgil seemed so apposite now, but he could hardly tell the Prof, could he?

"You have made a marvellous find, in a most wonderful setting: Ses Taca, that must be said to your credit. For it is greatly your personal merit that the old Moresque hacienda has finally got restored to its … truly fairy-like Arabian Nights dimens- …"

"Pro-fessor!" Dugal interrupted, emphatically. "What were you going to tell me?"

"Oh yeah, precisely. I meant: for myself and connoisseurs who would see the document, its originality is beyond dispute. But now you have let this sample of immortal prose, if I may say so, go to press, and notably in the popular Diario de Marcaio …"

"Wow, what are we up to now? The old pedant tacking on the left, never averse from a vulgarised publication himself, and suddenly turning so elitist ~ or may it be so that in this small world blood is thicker than water?"

When Dugal took that wry tone, the celebrated character player arose in him: the he-man of cynical politician and tycoon roles, Oscar-greedy and target of lechery with the female fans.

The philanderer type hardly seemed to impose on his academic counterpart, though. "Just suppose you had published this in some Anglo-Saxon paper. Without any frills or so, just your proper name under it. Probably some would think: 'Hey, Mister Mikes on the literary tack, what a lost talent!' Or ~ …"

"Or: 'He wants to try a side-line, as his star is fading?'"

"Those are your words. But … that's L.A., or London. On this island, however, things don't work that way, amigo. Many will regard it as a blasphemy, or a mystification. Those who do see through it …"

"…would rather clench their jaws? Because otherwise another sacred chapel might topple over, which they hate here as much as a toothache. Don't you think I can grasp that as well, don Marquez?"

Roberto spread the palms of his hands, in a cryptic gesture, without changing his countenance. As he always did, Dugal had noticed, when someone tried to tag a noble twist to his surname.

"In other words, Marcaio's cunning intelligentsia will wash their Pilate hands whilst observing how those morons are shedding the blood of that decadent actor …, that trashy, petty actor who endeavours to slander their coryphaeus! And among that select club of cynical miscreants I may count a marquise Roberto, right?"

The Prof slowly clapped his hands: "Gracias, señor Mikes. Thanks for the gentle words, and the strong performance - I mean, the way you can act the outraged innocence. But look."

"I am looking, And what do I see in front of me? An extraordinary Prof."

"Professor in ordinary - editorial correction. That means: I have a steady nook at the Palmera Univ."

He was doing his utmost not to burst into laughter at the sight of Dugal's grim face: that oblique distorted mouth, his sullen aloofness concealing a supreme scorn of his race - the muzzy quill-drivers, as Dugal used to call them, wizened under the dust of tons of yellowed parchment. Steam seemed to come out of his ears. As a counter reaction, also Roberto's suppressed cramp in the belly seemed to act contagiously on his sulky friend's laughing muscles and soon after they were both sitting there, shaking with laughter.

"Listen, amigo. I am but a fatuous little Prof at a provincial institute and, it's true, the arbiters of taste in the movie-biz rail at such a dabbler's opinion. But still, if you ask for my expertise … Well, the objective value of such a piece depends on a few factors. First, the contemporary criteria; secondly, the vision of our era on the personality, the place etc … And tertio: the geographical/social restrictions. Thus, a certain work can develop into a hype in this or that country, but get little or no echo outside that epicentre. Or even collide with the norms in an area where it was once published."

Simply because for some bigots it's hard to swallow, Dugal growled, *and all those fawning lackeys of the old Habiger clan are mortally afraid the gossip papers are craving to line up with the Mikes couple to lead sainted don Lois and his lovey-dovey by the hand and thus saddle the watch-dogs of the Marcaian heritage with a scandal.*

"Thank you, Professor, for your relativity theory, but don't you think it's about time the Marcaian establishment deserves a thrashing? Supposing the old fogeyish patrician circles here get all the hullabaloo over their heads, in their turn they will cry for vendetta. You know, first they fiercely kick around themselves, whip it all up in a scandal column, but what happens is …"

"…that the reader's attention is steeply aroused, but the whole shindy will abate just as fast, as the reading public smells a rat and savvies it is merely a storm in a tea-cup. So you believe then the tide will turn against them? But don't underrate the chameleon's tricks of that old guard, dear friend. They might as well mobilize all their flunkeys, from the pulpit down to the youth movement."

"Oh, well … After all, half this island would gorge me skin and all, I'm afraid. Let's hope the soup is never eaten as hot as it's served. What does my very learned friend say to that?"

The latter, an extinguished cigar between his lips, blew an imaginary cloud away, with slightly narrowed eyes as he watched it hovering above them.

"There is a chance to that. Yet, we may not forget what this figure meant to Marcaio. And still does. So you can't expect them to clasp you in their arms all at once, can you?"

"You ought to have gone into politics, Professor," Dugal suddenly nagged his diplomatic friend, still wavering though, whether to get on first-name terms with him. "But then you couldn't have stuck out your neck either, for such a self-conceited arsehole who confuses the film world with reality."

Roberto was glad his famous friend put it himself like that and he also told him so. When Dugal instantly flared up again, he noticed how that bodyguard-with-brains was sitting there, chuckling over his fit of anger.

13

That's the second time now I let myself get hoodwinked like that, he thought, and that annoyed him all the more so: to see how the other was laughing up his sleeve when the tartar arose in him.

"Okay," he waved aside his own sullenness. "Why am I always egged on by … bookworms of your type?"

"Maybe that tells something about the superiority of the race." While saying so, Prof. Marquez recoiled and, the doorknob already in his hand, he winked: "Go in peace, hermano, and enjoy your warm nest. Tomorrow there is little else left to us but assessing the first damage. Let us keep our fingers crossed."

3

Less than half a day later he was sitting there again: ibid., on the edge of his chair, enwrapped in the act of sifting through don Lois's writings. And those were legion, Dugal found out, and hefty, like the author himself, in his later days.

'Alboran', 'Serbs at the Adriatic', 'In the gulf of Syrte', 'A winter in Ithaka', 'Song of the trees in Ramleh', 'Djebel Esdoum ~ Sodoma's salt mountain' … In a way, you felt getting small again while going through the whole list of that deuced Dux's brainchildren. Three full sheets! Okay, some just seemed to be travel reports ('Skizzen', sketches like that one about Helgoland e. g. ~ *what the heck was he up to there? Queer customers still, those Teutons)*. Or feuilles volantes, like that specimen on the pile beside him. 'Abbazia'? You even had to ferret out that name stood for Opitija in Italian, or else he even put you on the wrong track. So, keep atlas and encyclopaedia at hand!

But then there were also bulky tomes among them to knock over an aurochs. Take those seven volumes of the 'Bailares' e.g.. So to say a vade-mecum about Marcaio and co. . Dull whackers, one would think, but who reads them still? Until you started to leaf through them and then you were lost. Impressions about tiny spots, the flora and fauna and their connection with crafts and trade, the economic background … He told things with a painter's hand and before you realized, he dragged you deeper into the picture. The couleur locale, the fragrances, you could taste them like that. You simply were there, a century back or more.

And what things the old man was not enthralled by! That other standard work of his: about the Liparian islands and volcanism ~ a passion you also found again in a study about the Kaimenes. The Caymans, yeah, they were familiar to Dugal, but he had been fascinated by don Lois's description of those islands in the crater-bay of Santorini. And thus it went on: 'The Mediterranean pearl' ~ Venice? Not at all! The Algerian Bougie is what he meant. 'Coleopterae' then proved to be some bug species on Marcaio. Nothing was strange to him or beneath his dignity, not even the fairy-tales on Marcaio. Good gracious, he would even outvie good old Goethe.

Dugal had already been browsing in his 'Tabulae Ludovicianae' too. If ever it came to a movie about this fellow (*why not, they have dug up so many éminences grises from their graves, of late, even Leonardo*) ~ well, then he would interweave those scientific gimmicks, 'Spielereien', in it. *Damn it, they are a match for the Codex Atlanticus. 'Decoding the last Archduke's Tables'*, he already saw it figuring in the headlines. One could also brood over another title: 'the last homo universalis' or something to that effect. Don Lois wás a versatile spirit, anyway, and a dab at languages. That was something to come out with. He even gibbered a bit of Marcaian, and when Dugal watched down the list … Karavanska cesta z Egypta do Syrie', edited in Prague. At the age of 17 his Highness had not only picked up some Slavonic in what was then the second Vienna; probably he had already dreamt too about the caravan routes and seraglios. Boy, what a duffer you felt, in comparison, as an exponent of thé universal lingo of this era. About that he had already raved to Roberto as well as his Cathy: "That man was an ace, really. Just fancy: don Lois crossed the Mediterranean, with his certificate for ocean-going trade and with quite a bizarre crew; charted quasi unknown coasts, even discovered some new islands, and just in passing, he wrote booklets about it. And all that on the part of a self-alleged hedonist too."

Byzerte, Tunis, Tripolitania, Alexandria, The Holy Land, Alexandrette … The latter was also an item he had been obliged to ferret out: the antique Iskanderia, along the Turkish coast, near Troy. The Dux had made a splendid lithopanorama about it, scroll-shaped, with comments on the backside. "That on top of it. This chap was even a match for Schliemann, owing to his 'aesthetic archaeology'".

And this way you plunged into the Greek world with him. So many pearls in the Aegean Sea for which Zeus had once spilled his seed (*hey, that confounding mythology,* Dugal grinned), and then: the Ionian islands, Xanthe and the like. A new world opened before his eyes. *To dive into that crystal-blue water, as he used to do, that's something you ought to try at least, professor. So you too might learn to chat with the birds, in thirteen languages nota bene.*

Of course, the fellow had been pushed on quite a bit by his mixed background: dad being duke of Tuscany (and half Viennese) and mum a Bourbon ~ there's the advantage of migrants' marriages. His first booklet, about Venice and thereabouts, had been dedicated to mummy Antonietta, and in French at that! Whereas his second last dealt with Friulian pet names, from the area in question.

As Catarí and Roberto were apt to modify don Lois' linguistic virtuosity, Dugal recited to them his description of Opatija: "His comparison with a painting by Lorrain and the way he depicts that with words …, sublime! Just try yourself, proffy!

For hours on end they would rattle on about it, until his Cathy got fed up with it. "Can you talk about anything else yet?" Ouch, but then they had not even got to the wider rambles of the Dux, with that 'Nymphe' of his. Just fine for sailing up the Nile, that yacht, but scouring the oceans in such a barge? Therefore you ought to be nothing daunted. 'Um die Welt ohne zu wollen', here it was, on his desk. Something like: 'globetrotter willy-nilly'. *What may have possessed that chap to sail as far as Tasmania, in those years? And after that, all the way up to California? Or had he achieved that some time before?* 'Eine Blume aus dem Goldenen Land', Dugal could hardly imagine L.A. in those days like that ~ a 'flower' from the gold country! *What was the high-born toff looking for over there, good heavens, without gold fever? And that just when the fine de fleur of his time used to flock together in steady haunts like Livorno, Amalfi or the Lido.* Indeed, some time before the Dux had already turned up in Philadelphia. Somehow Dugal got the feeling that some things did not tally. Soon he would go into that matter with Roberto.

Besides, if you took pains to dwell on the exhibitions and congresses the man frequented: Milan, Brussels and Paris, Venice and New York, Rome and Athens … Why? Just to shake hands with the noble smarties of his age and by the way grab along a medal here and there for his merits in the field of natural history, geography or philology? No, that would not go down with Dugal. Something told him that this avowed shirker, by turns represented as an a-political romanticist, a somewhat unworldly ego-tripper or a wayward dilettante, must have been damned well aware of the events of the moment. The way e.g. he anticipated the mischief while meeting archduke Franz Ferdinand in Trieste. Soon after followed the assault on that heir to the Austrian throne in Sarajevo and hell burst out over Europe.

"Maybe the old gent was a bit clairvoyant?" Catarí had suggested. *My foot, apparently don Lois knew better than the men in power what was seething in the world. But then he also wandered about everywhere, mixing among the people.* The frown on Prof. Marquez' forehead told him there was more to it with this lost son of the imperial house. But what? Had he played a surreptitious role behind the scenes after all or was he just dreaming about another blueprint of Europe and the world with his highbrow friends? But time had caught up with them and the fatal evolutions turned out to be irreversible. In a Kafkaian sense: *Einmal dem Fehlläuten der Nachtglocke gefolgt, … Once you have followed the false peals of the night bell ‑ it cannot be atoned for.* That was nearly the only literary German on Dugal's repertoire, but it happened to come true. Just like the Dux's unknown idiosyncrasies, his dark side perhaps. Who e.g. knew that L.S. had suffered from elephantiasis or that his Catalí had caught a leprosy-like affection in Egypt or Palestine?

But such 'human failures' had been rubbed out for a long time by the local folklore scamps in Marcaio. Even more than the custodians over the old Viennese protocol, they had stuffed up L.S., don Lois for the hoi polloi, and extolled him as a harmless, innocuous icon nobody could tamper with.

"Well, well, well!" Caught again! Prof. Marquez blew into the reading hall, sniggering: "Got out of bed with the chickens ‑ and your pretty chick at home couldn't keep you in it, could she?"

"Same as you then. Although … with an old chick in bed it must be easier, hey?" The beadle shuffled in to have a look. On other days nobody ever entered before ten.

"There is a reason for that, amigo, look." Ostentatiously he took the early morning paper from under his arm and tapped on it, before throwing it on Dugal's pile of books. "The gossip factory has already worked. Piping hot."

With growing disbelief Dugal looked up at the Chest. *Do you see him, sitting there in a fairground booth, with a black wig, looking in a glass globe: Roberta, the soothsayer?*

"No time for kidding. Here, read! About your publication, the town buzzes with it." The professor walked on to a backroom with an espresso-machine. *I had better make him a strong 'solo', he'll need it.*

Dugal nearly tumbled off his chair. 'Shocking forgery of documents in Marcaian publishing circles. Real scandalizing of archduke's private life by fictive letters. Unprecedented infringement by top-liner Mikes.'

There it was, in huge letters: his name next to his spiritual brother's nobiliary names, and pictures ditto. One could not overlook it.

"Why? Porquè, Roberto!" he shouted to the back.

A front page of the Diario, that's a feather in the cap for a cockerel or horny tomcat running across the field of Real Marcaio. But something like this! The refractory enfant terrible from Europe's noblest lineage who, with his hobby-like landed estates, was the envy of the small country potentates of old, who were still saddled with a marriageable daughter at home … But now, who cares?

"I haven't the haziest notion, but it was in the air, you bet!" Roberto's bear's paw pushed a comforting cup of coffee under his nose.

"A couple of zealots who look green with envy because of my success and cannot bear an outsider digging in the past of their saint's figurine. So what, why should I bother about such trifles?"

If he did not even deign to read the film criticisms below par by some of those moronic ninnies … The professor pushed the epistle back to him, though.

> '… and judging from these fictitious letters El Duque would still have sent some writings to Catalí d'Omar, the Maëstra on one of the manors of Maremira: Ses Taca. Harmless readers have already been able to peruse the first edition of those lyrical effusions in this very newspaper … Without accusing the publishers of malevolent intentions, we do assume that some people at least were aware of the lack of authenticity … that this is a mystification on behalf of the actor D.M., with cheap claptrap … who bought up the old mansion, considering this area as his private backyard … tries to appropriate the aureole of spiritual heir of the previous owner … to entwine old

secrets of the heart with fancy frills ... grievous for the living relatives ...

'D.M. ', Dugal groaned. As if it were about a manufacturer of washing-powder or fertilizers. And now - you could feel them coming along with real threats:

'... but Mr. Mikes should be warned: we will not have the peace on our island disturbed ... ' Etc., etc ...

Okay, and what of it? Dugal folded the pamphlet neatly and shoved it back to the professor's cup. The latter was looking glum for a while, producing a pulled-up roller blind across his brow.

"I don't know, Dugal, but I wouldn't just regard it as a macabre joke. I'm afraid those guys are deadly serious about it."

Oh yeah, what could they do then - shoot him in his legs, kidnap his wife ...?

"Come on, I have never given in to that sort of blackmailing. Not even with heavier calibre than this."

"Maybe you are right, maybe you aren't; still, if I were you ..."

What! Was this man like a bear already knuckling under, due to such a squib? Then they, actors, were used to worse things, with all those sensation hunters of the yellow press, a horde of photographers swarming around you like hornets. That vermin seemed to know better your agenda than you did yourself. *How quiet it is here, in Palmera. No Roberto, we won't let anybody filch that peace of mind from us, least of all by a bunch of doting sticklers for propriety.*

"OK. But they can be more headstrong than the worst of mafiosi over here."

The weight of Roberto's hand pressure on his shoulder was directly proportional to his sincere solicitude.

"How do you mean? Have you once collided with that pack of lodge brethren yourself? So they surely have urged you on to acquire a member card?"

"On my support you can rely, amigo," said Roberto with a hazy glance. "But mind it: circumspection is the mother of preservation of life."

"Thanks. What a reassurance! Now it's time to skedaddle and run errands," said Dugal and, already on his way out, grabbing his notes together under his arm, he cleared his throat: "Although …, let's just hope they don't hold you to be an accomplice, Robbie."

Dugal chortled while he watched Prof. Marquez go. This was the first time he had really been on such familiar terms with him. From behind the swing-door he saw in a flash how three men ran into the professor. They accosted him, aside and rather tensely. *If those chaps are colleagues of his, I am a nuncio of the pope's.* But Dugal did not have much time to think. No sooner had he got out, hopping down the imposing outdoor flight of stairs, than his mouth fell open with astonishment: "My ~ …"

His car! There it was, still. Or what remained of his dark green cabriolet: the door indented, the bumper bent down, the windowpanes shattered to shivers …

While he dashed around the wrecked vehicle, it flashed across his mind: *this is no collision but the work of a gigantic excavator which ~ 'erroneously'~ put its teeth into this tasty morsel.* What was the use of calling the police to it?

But if they thought that he, D. M., was going to yield because of this! For a bit of damage to such a shabby car as there were thousands of them ~ Jesus, Palmera was swamped with them. *No,* he muttered slit-eyed, *to subdue Duke, you'll have to turn up with something else, gentlemen. Tomorrow number two will go to press.*

4

Bohemia, October 18th

You could not believe, Cariña, how absurd all this sounds to me. I was born and bred in the city where Dante and Botticelli lived, and that is how I felt: a ragazzo, a Tuscan lad. As for my second mother-language, I did not learn to use it fulltime until I landed down in Prague, after our escape from Palazzo Pitti. All of a sudden, imperial Vienna discovered that petty nephew, and there I needs had to attend the Theresianum. A second exile for a boy who could only thrive under the silky Florentine light of Fra Angelico and Filippo Lippi.

I have never told you, my dear, but actually I was born into the infantry. Imagine: commander of the 58th regiment, from the cradle, what a birth right! In Vienna I began to realize where my destination was - Sankt Stephan. Probably means nothing to you, neither did it to me at the time, for I shunned the military academy like the plague. So back to Prague. At the Karlsuniversität, where I whiled away my time with Lady Jurisprudentia (do not be envious: that is just law), I tried to postpone the verdict all the time. With natural science, philosophy, ... archaeology. At long last, however, his Majesty, the kaiserliche Hoheit, began to see through my game, and little nephew flew back to Vienna, predestined for a splendid military career, for the greater glory of my Habiger homeland (?).

But Ludwig would not have been a Tuscan Ludovico, if he had not made, once again, a big twist there. So

I acquired my … certificate of 'Captain for ocean-going trade'. Particularly at the Danube, hundreds of miles away from the sea! You can imagine the incensed countenance of His Highness my nephew. As a punishment for that wilful behaviour the wanton enfant terrible was pitch-forked as 'regent of Bohemia and Moravia'. Magnifico, *you said as I told you about it: a country of woods and mountains! That is true, but to me, a child of the sun, it sounded like being expelled to some salt or tin mine.*

So you see, Cariña, the circle always closes itself. After so many years I have finally landed up at the place I have always been so much opposed to. A piece of wreckage that has loosened itself from the cracking mother-ship, bobbing up and down between the fitful waves, on its way to an island where it can look back on its odyssey, to be suddenly pulled back by the turbulent sea to the place of the disaster. May it be true after all that some spinsters - the moirae, as the Old Greek called them - are somewhere weaving the threads of our fate, without our being able to change much about its pattern?

Anyhow, if this is the place where I was predestined to moulder unto eternity, I do not grasp the sense of our own free will which the guardians of the Holy Truth have held out to us.

Perhaps it was an illusion to think I could trespass the rules of my own class. Choosing for freedom instead of rank and honour, it was my wish to reach a little happiness on the island of my preference and share it with the people who were dear to me. You in the first place, Catalí. In Vienna this must have seemed pure madness - self-chosen exile, the retirement of a refractory fool. And to you, folks? A whim of an unpredictable fantast or the umpteenth freak of a spoilt peer - something like a passing cloud maybe.

In that sense my honourable kinsmen at first were inclined to show some apprehension for my adventure ('Markaianisches Abenteuer', as they classified it over there).. After all, you know what had happened before, do you not?

Once I told you briefly : the 'self-incineration' of my bride Mathilde. You are the only one, Cariña, in whose presence I was ever able to let slip something about it. Writing about it is now easier to me, for missing you is much worse.

I daresay I truly loved her, although such marriages are a bit arranged, by definition. I had had the privilege ~ once again, I hear you saying ~ to select her from quite a series of princesses, as you see them lounging about at balls and receptions, prinked up by their mothers, like horses for a royal parade.

There was something about Mathilde that failed others: her unconstraint. Not that she was a dazzling beauty maybe, but I was not mother's prettiest of either. At once I felt we had a lot in common. Her genuine dislike of etiquette and protocol in the first place. "Have you got a fire for me?" was the first thing she asked me. As I rather sneered about ladies of noble birth who smoked, she said scornfully: "So you too are one of those moral preachers! I have no need of sermons."

At the same time, however, she let me feel she liked me, if only for my disdain towards those high-born ladies. "Why, actually I share your opinion about those bumptious marionettes dancing on a string." And we laughed simultaneously about just such a specimen from the Viennese aristocratic circles who happened to puff by, tightened up in a straight-jacket. "Countess Esterhazy," said a paunchy man behind us whom she looked at rather venomously. "Oh, forgive us our lack of tact," I said, "it was our fault." "Never mind," he answered. "My mistake. I am her husband."

That unforgettable scene created an unbreakable bond between us: one of spiritual relatives ~ as much as siblings. Even more than I, Mathilde loathed all the pompous caboodle at court.

Maybe it was precisely her dislike of conventional obligations that drove her to death. I can still see her standing there, on the kerb of the broad avenue where the tribune had been installed.

She refused to take her stand amongst the pick of the 'imperial harem', as she used to call them. Mathilde was there for my sake, but she made no bones about her spite that I had to comply with the higher directives. 'Commander of the 58th regiment,' *she must have thought,* 'accomplish your dismal duty,' *and lit a cigarette. Not that she was such a confirmed smoker, but simply in order to act shocking. To work off her own irritation ostentatiously.*

Had the match fallen on her dress or was it the cigarette-case that gave way? No one was able to tell. Suddenly I saw her there, beating about and tearing at her dresses. The bystanders hastened to help her, but in no time her gown and petticoat caught fire. A living torch, thus she faded out of my life.

5

Keep our fingers crossed? My foot! Dugal mumbled to himself, as he was halfway along the plane-lined avenues in the outskirts of Palmera city. It still gave him the hump when he thought of Prof. Marquez's words a couple of days before. On top of all those peripeteias, teasing games of anonymous stalkers. A fine support he had been! Besides, how pernickety that abortive gorilla would act about such trifling love letters in which a local notability effused his heart to a lady of a baser descent. Come on, it was public property in these parts. In every souvenir shop there lay a handful of books about that rather quaint esquire, and as for the alleged romance with his Catalí, they had polished it themselves glossily enough. Not with the kind of racy details they used for 'A winter in Marcaio', to get into the average tourist's wallet ~ the sneaky tête-à-tête of that other hackneyed couple with an even far more dubious fame: 'George' Aurore Sand and her consumptive piano tapper Fryderyk Shopen.

Dugal had only just driven into the town centre, for a few attentions ~ mere knickknacks, to coddle Catarí. An ensaimada too, just for fun: such a huge apple pie that you could put on your head like a sombrero. On the return trip, a little outside Palmera, right to the northern mountain chain, up to Valle de Muša, Dugal slowed down without a clear reason. Strange though, that tickling sensation, the thrill of 'the way back home' it used to give him, failed now. Whenever something thwarted him, a stone in his stomach, the speed merchant in him became a meek lamb. No compunction this time about a hog or a jay under a wheel. Neither was it that eschatological objection of his dad's ("Each speed fiend is a potential murderer, boy") that put a brake on him, but rather some poignant tang ...

Yet, all had gone off smoothly, after the vicissitudes of the previous day. "No problem, señor Mikes," they had reassured him at the editorial office. Surely one or another flaccid prankster who tried to drive him wild. Oh, really, and how could this have escaped the editors' vigilance? A riddle, Mr Mikes ~ nostra maxima culpa, all our excuses. All right, but what about that badly staged collision then?

It was a scanty consolation to Dugal that the gentlemen at the Diario tied themselves in knots, promising to take all discomforts off his shoulders. Such as the recalcitrant insurance agent and the slow service of the garage-keeper, and oh yes, in addition an extra rectification on the part of the editor.

So this time Catarí did not need to be frightened out of her wits. Nor did he have to open his jacket with a stalwart theatrical gesture: "They didn't riddle me with bullets, sweetie, look! Nor emasculate me." But still. Whence then did that shiver come when getting into his quasi unbattered cabriolet, equally dark-green again as it had been before?

Fate sometimes strikes when there is not a cloud in the sky. Here one drives through the almond orchards as carelessly as a chorister, and as you come home ... No tail-wagging dog that rushes out of the house, no answer in the patio, not even in the hall. Involuntarily he accelerated. *Rubbish*, he soothed his conscience, *if you already throw up the sponge because of a few specimens of that simplistic union who kick up a row about the lyrical outpourings of a withering oldie on behalf of an ingenuous country lass. Well, ingenuous?* Dugal grimaced. He halted for a moment where the road made a semi-circle, lined with oleanders. These gave the monastic village, clinging to the mountain wall over there, a surrealistic aspect. Here it must have happened, that coup de foudre, and Dugal tried to imagine the first meeting of the couple: the honourable guest and Catalí, the carpenter's daughter with the fiery eyes. Why must there always be carpenters in the game, depicted like a simple Joseph? And how came that each time Dugal thought of their own case?

Catarí at once dashed out into the yard, at his first hooting. "Dugal, where did you stay again!" Touching, wasn't it, a woman's excessive anxiety, and at the same time flattering for your ego. In fact, she seemed even more irresistible when she got so excited ~ a delight to the eye. *What a lucky dog you are, that such a beaut falls for you, unbelievable!* Whereas any sultan would offer a thousand elephants for her and an opulent oil sheikh his best choice of stallions, plus a twelve hundred race camels.

"I was afraid there was something wrong with the car again. You know, there is a man here who has been waiting for you for hours."

"Oh, a competitor, darling?" He pinched her cheek to stifle her, and his, growing annoyance. He had to make up a lot with her.

"Herr Mikes? Angenehm." A perky, straw-hatted dandy jumped up from his rattan chair like a jack-knife.

So so, ine Burliner, Dugal twaddled, and straight away he wanted to know what motive drove this oddball to their humble dwelling: an astronomical bid on Ses Taca? "Thanks, but that's no more subject to purchase than my wife."

"Nein nein, Herr Mikes, I am from the Universität zu Wien. Schnabel, at your service." Producing some credentials, he showed his boundless admiration for Dugal's find. "Sehr, seeehr interessant, mein Lieber. And by the way, a marvellous piece of literature. But apart from that, eh … Its importance, you see, as a document, in view of the writer's personality, undsoweiter." In his rapture the little man's pince-nez nearly fell off his nose. "We do not doubt at all the authenticity of your publication either. But that's just why …"

Yes yes, Mr Snappy, but how did they find out so soon? Dugal mused. *Ah, the world has become like a village, so small, and apparently the practices of the white-collar mob have penetrated into the musty Viennese professor closets. Funny, he thought, how one always remembers the droll words in a foreign language: Professorenkabinett, quite a decent chamber,* but he saw those learned fellows like this one brooding over their nefarious schemes on the privy: how to get to that valuable manuscript? A resonant academic title as a disguise for lucrative affairs? Who knows if Roberto Marquez too wasn't imbued with that gift of scraping together a fortune in that way?

"First allow me to let you enjoy a bit the grandeur of this spot," said Dugal, trying to distract the bespectacled scholar, and he ushered him promptly onto the terrace. Made Catarí come along with a big jar of treacherous sangria and one with a ditto alternative: fresh orange juice, looking harmless but with some dregs that scented suspiciously of gin and kirsch; ánd with an equally stunning pareo around her waist. "Splendid, this grandeza natural," Herr Schnabel whispered. "Hmm, of that bougainvillea, I mean," and he pointed at the rampant lilac flowers across the balcony and the crenels of the snow-white pavilion. "Ich gratuliere, gratulations, also for this find. You have a flair for hidden treasures, Herr Mikes."

Dugal turned his hand ironically in Catarí's direction, for Schnabel's sneaky glance at her stooping cleavage had not escaped his attention. "And … you do know what to do with it, eh, you make it show to advantage. A dream, wirklich, the way you had this gem restored."

Dugal let the Viennese visitor rave and coax. Now and then he even added some fuel to the fire and so Herr Schnabel was revelling in increasingly higher regions, as the jar of 'fruit-juice' advanced and Catarí refuelled it. "A Moresque Midsummer Night's dream, Herr Mikes? You just say so. A fata morgana, here above the azure blue sea, between the palm trees. Surrealistic!" He shivered with rapture, when Dugal made a comparison with an Arabian fairy-tale that the Dux had brought along from one of his sailing-tours. "Na wunderbar!"

If Dugal had wanted to, he could have finished him off. But something ~ the exuberant enthusiasm perhaps of this droll fellow, his baroque 'Begeisterung' which made him fall for all ~ particularly female ~ beauty, kept him back.

"Do you believe in coincidence, Herr Mikes? I do not. Somewhere there are threads running through time and the cosmos, spun by some mysterious Ariadnes, and they link us. Take yourself now. Your wife calls you 'Duke', wie ich höre, and a century before you, there was that Duque here. There must be a connection of some kind. This jewel of an inn e.g. from A Thousand and One Nights, really the acme of taste ~ your taste, nichtwahr … As though it were put down for you, here in this oasis of quietude." Professor Schnabel sniffed at two of his fingers, a gesture to take up that quiet in himself. The way one gets animation for enlightened dreams from a snuffbox. *My taste, I daresay, old scapegrace,* Dugal chortled because of the defenceless way Schnabel's narrowed eyes swept over Catarí's pareo, which by a jaunty movement, exposed her elegant leg for a moment.

"So, this way our liebenswürdige professor would like to dedicate a eulogy to his charming hostess," Dugal teased him. But the learned coxcomb did not get wise to it.

"Alas, Herr Mikes, we scientists envy you, film actors, for your sometimes gratuitous success and lifestyle. But alright, if you can use it thus, to surround yourself with grace and architectonic charm, with respect for the original … I tip my hat to that."

"Congratulate my wife then. Without Catarí Ses Taca would not look like this now."

"And without Catalí …" echoed the little Viennese, while his eyes wandered approvingly over the estate. How did he want to lay a transparent copy from the past over the image of the present?

To Catarí that seemed easy to visualize. Forgotten in overgrown woodland, where once vineyards had nestled up to the rock-face ~ that was how they had found the old tavern. Its paint peeling off, a decrepit diva past her prime. *Shall I once be like this, in the autumn of life: brooding over the glorious past?*

"An 'inn', what's in a name?" Schnabel whispered. His examining eyes, looking for some disharmonious note, swept to the swimming-pool, which they had got fitted in, in Ses Taca style as far as possible. Or to the stairs alongside which Catarí was retiring discreetly with her tray?

"To come back to your publication, Herr Mikes: we have no doubt whatsoever about the authenticity of those letters, but you understand …" Didn't Dugal understand! Now the bunny was going to come out of the hat. The learned clique in Vienna was clearly on edge. That he, monstre sacré of the white screen had not just made up that whole story, was as plain as a pikestaff. But where, and how, had he got at it? *They sure must have the jitters there*, Dugal smirked. *And I am not going to let the cat out of the bag at onc*e. By the way, Catarí's magic potion gradually began to get its desired effect and there she was again already to serve them some tapas ~ "our home-made speciality, Herr Schnabel, you can't refuse that, can you?"~, skilfully finished with a dash of jerez, enough to make even the driest old stick loose-lipped. In that foppish popinjay Catarí's domestic concoction was slowly awakening the facetious 'Wiener Gemütlichkeit'. After every roguish allusion of Dugal's he giggled to his heart's content.

"The secret of the house, genau, Herr Mikes. I expected to find it somewhere here hidden beneath the boarded floor or behind a dado …"

"But as you see, it's sometimes in a glass or a sauce, isn't it? The false bottoms, my dear fellow."

"…bottoms," hiccupped Schnabel. "Jaja, the truth under the lees, and …"

"Ah, the original often remains concealed behind a maze of figment, nursery rhymes for the ragtag, but that doesn't mean it wasn't there. How many mystifications haven't survived that way, Christianity first and foremost. And yet, many would spend a fortune to know THE truth, nichtwahr, Snappy?" Dugal enjoyed the moment, like a boxer the swoon of a dazed opponent. That one was tying himself in knots, without making a bid straight to Dugal's face. And there came the blow of the maul: "How much, Herr Snappy, how many millions are you allowed to bid - ten, twenty? How much scope have you been given?" Actually Dugal felt sorry for the poor fellow, a little shabby and whimpering now, crushed by the sneaky mixture from Catari's flasks.

Dusk had already entered when the factotum of the Viennese varsity finally crept into his unsightly car, by the entrance gate, sealing his own retreat with an even heavier tongue than on the terrace. "Yuer secrret, Frau Meiks, I've notte seen it, butte I knôo wheër it iss, hihihi ..."

Plastered he is, no, this is outrageous. Both looked at each other, raising their eyebrows. "Need we be apprehensive about that, because of some blackmail?" Catarina nodded compassionately, while their uninvited guest was chugging zigzag down the lane.

"I'm afraid they'll have to hire a real purse snatcher over there," Dugal mumbled. Besides, they were going to get what they were after, but ... by driblets. He had now made a definitive deal with the editorial staff of the newspaper and that gentleman's agreement suited him pretty well. He was going to follow the example of that Russian pole-vaulter who had made a little fortune in a similar way, that is, by planning his records in instalments. "And the secrret," he bantered, in a side-splitting parody of the envoy from Vienna, who had by now dissolved in the dark, "I'll take it into my grrave, if need be."

Making abuse of the situation, Dugal slipped his arm around her waist. Catarí tumbled to his tactics at once and tried to keep out of his grip, for it was so predictable what would follow. With all that sniggering of his and her laughing muscles put at trial, every amorous skid was bound to end in the swimming-pool. Suddenly however, his heart turned to ice. An invisible hand seemed to lead him to the telephone, in the hall.

There was a woman's voice at the other side. Whether he could not speak to Prof. Marquez? An urgent case, si si. Did that book-worm still live at his mother's, or was it a sis of his? Or perhaps an illustrious unknown Catalí whom the sneaky lecher scrupulously preferred to keep secluded from the world. "Hello, yes, Dugal speaking. Sorry about your night's rest, pal, but I absolutely had to …"

Dugal was so prompted by inquisitiveness that he skipped all his insipid jokes and ignored Roberto's. "Aha, from the Universität zu Wien, finally some high visit at your homestead," the latter said. Whether Roberto knew the beau monde over there? Well, about as much as Duke knew the celebs at Hollywood, and those were quite a few, no? "What! Snappy … professor Schnabel?"

You could see Roberto raising his eyebrows because of the way the excited duo at the other side tried to shade his pronunciation. "Jamás ~ never heard of." The Prof sounded apodictic but at the same time something seemed to dawn on him. "Unless … Schwabe perhaps. A thick-set, pedantic fellow with a little moustache?" Dugal and Catarí looked doubtfully at each other as they heard Prof. Marquez laughing uncontrollably. "A swindler, amigo. A failed professor who started working solo and now tries to cash in on all sorts of things. You … you haven't told him ~ …"

Of course not. But what if that phoney opera buffoon were just a scout, the harbinger of a much grimmer action? Then maybe this whole burlesque fitted in a trial round of a shrewd gang that had paid this Herr Schnabel to carry out his act.

"Hello, hello …?" Dugal slowly put down the receiver, leaving Prof. Marquez to his curiosity. He was staring through the window at an olive tree on the hill: an old geezer, worn out in the service, curved like a question-mark since the latter days of the Archidux.

6

Ever since the unsavoury protest article in the Diario and the troublesome complications resulting from that, it had remained quiet for some days. Flawless even. Dugal had some time left to spend on his wifey, taking her with him as far as Llosera, when he went to the library for a couple of hours. *Trite skirmishes,* he had mollified it all to her, *a storm in a teacup. Or maybe just an application of Murphy's law so that by and by you start to see 'signs': you see, those fellows mean it!* And yet, he kept a wry feeling about it. As though they were on the leeward and at any moment the storm could rise again.

At the next intersection he had to brake rather abruptly for red. Krrrrr …, he heard at the rear, and one moment there was a slight contact behind. *Fortunately, just a few Marcaian scratches,* he thought with closed eyes. Suddenly though, a heated face popped up beside his open window. A thick moustache, husky smoker's voice. Where had he seen such a mug before? Right, one of the walk-ons on the set. A look-alike, really. "Here is a ten-€P note, go and get a chilled San Miguel to cool down," he said curtly. Hadn't he given tit for tat to far heavier calibres than this one? Only on the set, okay, but one kept the airs from it. As the traffic lights changed to green, he dashed across the junction, but promptly a gesticulating cop made him stop: here, aside! Dammit, what was the matter again? A somewhat slender fellow, the Mastroianni type. "Señor. Seguro que no ha bebido?"

Course he had drunk. From Roberto's stale tea. And of course he understood the chap perfectly and he had noticed the 70/h sign, but he was not going to wise him up. "Sorry chap, no Español."

"Whatte speed yo thinke yo werr' drrivink? Thatte signpôst yo did not see? Whoë do yo sink yo arr?"

"Dugal Mikes," he said blandly. "How much do I owe you?"

While the bewildered limb of the law was writing the fine: 70 €P, Dugal at once produced a 200-note: "Round it up, so you've something left for yourself, by the time I return the other way tomorrow," and off he dashed from under his nose, chuckling. Something seemed to glance off at the rear, on the boot, and in his rear-view mirror he saw the policeman dancing a few rounds, one hand clasped around his other elbow. A mere graze? *By gum, that 'll teach you a lesson, fellow!* he snarled, but at the same moment he noticed a fashionable lady staring after him with raised eyebrows. George Sand, as two peas in a pod! *What a pity*, he sighed, *that's how life flashes away!*

"George Sand, eh," his Cathy had sniggered only yesterday. "That cigar-smoking lady-in-pants! O yeah, such a mascot from the beau monde who used to scour the Parish salons. Surely you 'd rather have found a few 'lettres confidentielles' from her ~ or dreamed up a version of your own?"

What, not jealous, was she, or did dear Catarí already dream of a part in a romanticized picture about that femme fatale of the 19th century belles-lettres? Hmm, who knows? she would act mysterious then, with those catlike eyes of hers. But … not with Mikes Jr. as a counterpart ~ at best as stage director of that fatal liaison.

"Aha, that's why: too virile still to personate that piano-caresser from Żelazowa Wola? Thanks. I'm flattered."

And he chuckled, thinking of his father's warning, the day he had introduced Catarí to him. "Oh, boy, I wouldn't like to be in your shoes." She did make an overwhelming impression on his old man, then, as she did anywhere she appeared with him the first time. Not just owing to her exuberant charisma (which brought a blush of shame to any infamous skirt chaser's cheeks, as if he were a stammering chorister). No, particularly her disarming humour made Mikes Sr. loosen up altogether.

"How much do you give me?" she laughed ad lib, and as pa kept sampling her from top to toe, she turned around with a pirouette and posed in front of him, arms spread: "On your veterinary inspection, I mean."

Upon which Spartan Mikes burst out laughing. His trademark, that rogue dimple in his chin, had never been so applicable. He had pressed both their heads against his cheeks, and said just as candidly: "Mikes, boy, you bet that Rubens, eh, Tiziano, Raphael and all notorious connoisseurs

34

of the lasses turn around in their graves, with pure envy? But mind it: look before you leap, for this is the most precious jewel in history."

The old rascal knew what he was talking about, with proverbial irony ~ even if sonny boy had a dozen box-office successes to show off with. And did pa think he couldn't support her with that revenue? "Her? Of course, you could. But what are yóu going to live on?" Sparto chortled with a snide grin.

Naughty! she had screamed. What did they think of her? "Everyone makes me compliments, that even in rags I look good. So … don't panic."

"Yes, rags from Valentino or Ricci," Dugal sighed. Which he had to pay for at once with a poke between his ribs. "You bastard, that's gratuitous show material then!"

Pa Mikes had to settle the squabbling with a toast: "To my primal diamond of a daughter-in-law and a destitute son then!"

"Hey, you old rake, am I courting her, or are you?"

In the meantime Dugal had reached again that loop-like strip around the 'industrial site' or whatever they called it: a handful of warehouses and depots they had pressed in behind some haciendas which had also seen better days. Horribile vistu! That much Latin he remembered from Prof. Marquez, for as far as that was concerned, they were on the same wavelength: both namely loathed the awfully bad taste of this era.

Besides, what did they produce here? Nada! Only the building mafia benefited from it. And all the while the vacant lots in the city were running riot. "Press all those monstrosities on a heap," he would plead to his friend, "reinvest that in the rehabilitation of old premises, and you will sow again bucolic wasteland full of poppies and coleseed into the suburbs. Between an idyllic mini windmill park, for all I care."

That was grist on Roberto's mill. Revaluation of his molinos de vela: those circular windmills equipped with sails and a Cupid-arrow ~ how lyrically he would rave about it in his touching way! His ancestors? They had been smarter than all those cunning technocrats nowadays. Moorish blood, boy! With their norias they had imported gratuitous irrigation ~ those paddle-wheels which once used to drive 4,000 wells on Marcaio. The Archidux had counted them and described them in 'Die Bailaren'.

Pure nostalgia with contemporary purposes. But there was plenty of lobbying in Marcaio, and they had already fought quite a scuffle with the bigwigs of ill taste. Preaching in the desert, yes, he scorned towards Roberto: holy prophet, redeem us from the Evil and all the epigones of Le Corbu!

One would become a terrorist in the end, if cowardice were not that easy, he grumbled to himself. Which made him think of Catarí again. "Take care you don't end up under a bridge, with a dagger between your shoulders."

Before the exit to Llosera there was a congestion. The road was covered with a load of coleseed from a canted lorry. "Madre de Díos, qué olfato!" shouted an infuriated booth-owner, hanging out of his window. "Garlic-bulb!" Dugal retorted, withdrawing his head. Man, look into your own bosom. But he knew better than that. They tried to pin the bad smell on the coleseed business, instead of the meat waste factory a little farther down.

And that reminded him. One quarter of the Marcaians already ran on bio-fuel ~ a thorn in the flesh of some importers. They knew how the wind blew. The city council needed more such wrangle about odour nuisance like a hole in the head. So … Typico Marcaín, all that tug-of-war. By the way, they had already suggested a couple of times to him that he had better not rub elbows with that green pack. And as for that kind of squabbles, it was no use appealing to the BMW's either ~ the Big Marcaian Worldfamous like the Schiffers, Brosnans, Nadals, Barcelo's, Montiels …

All those stars at the isle's firmament ~ models, actors, sports stars, painters, singers: real gold nuggets for Marcaio's tax-collectors and estate agents, but they kept their door at a chink's width, like for Jehovah's witnesses. "Who is going to stick one's neck out for such a knotty question? Rather a living coward than a dead lion," said Catarina: even at la reina's Palau he would have got the door slammed in his face.

Once past the toppled lorry, Dugal noticed the cause of the trouble. A wrecked car, a similar model as his, was buried under the pulp.

While driving on, Dugal saw a policeman looking in his direction and then making a sign to a colleague of his: *that one there!* Automatically Dugal tore away, slipping along a crowd of calamity-watching drivers.

Phew … Finally he glided onto that magnificent lane, well-nigh alone, for miles on end, between the olive groves and algarrobos: dark-green carobs with yellow undergrowth ~ what a foreground against the towering Sierra de Alfaiba! That was the difference. But he was still sweating down his spine. Whether that had, subconsciously, more to do with that crashed car, some minutes before, than with the sultry ballyhoo? How odd anyway, now that he was fretting over it, the behaviour of those cops! Suppose it had been a mishap and he the real target? Ah, he didn't care a hoot, but he got even warmer when thinking of home.

After all, behind that mountain range, his Catarí was waiting for him at Ses Taca, maybe not nail-biting and ... faithful like a dog, to say it in Roberto Marquez' words: worthy of a modern Penelope? That remained to be seen. "If you're in love with a beautiful woman," he began to whine that old tune spontaneously, "watch your friends ~ everybody tempts her, everybody tells her she's the most beautiful girl they know ..."

Hey, hey, bet they were all green with envy: damned Mikes, he could be her father! *What does she see in such a man: his money ~ although she is already so rich ~ what else? He does not look that fresh either ...*

Queer, he pondered, did he have any special bond with that confounded Archidux after all? The longer you dwelled on it, the more likenesses you believed to descry ... Catalí and Catarí, for a start. The couple of counterfeits he had seen of the fellow's sweetheart, were also worth admiring. And then there was the jealousy they aroused, or from another point of view: both of them as alleged connoisseurs of female pulchritude. What was the matter with that old inn? Was there a shade of truth after all about what that mister Vivot had whispered into his ear, at Llosera's town hall, the day he tumbled in there for that purchase? "Ses Tacas, señor? You know what you are talking about ~ un lugar encantado. Splendid, an enchanting location, but ..., yeah, enchanted." The man had gazed at him with a vacant, slightly squint eye. "It's sold!" Dugal had quickly snapped at it and looked aside, lest he should be magicked into a frog or so. For, who knows, otherwise Catarí could have flung him away as well, horrified like a Grimm's princess?

7

As usual the winding road, behind the gardens of Alfaiba, carried Dugal away, in pure ravishment. Sixty-five hairpin-bends and there, on top of the pass, those wonderful vistas: across Es Pla, the plain behind you, slumbering in sun-veils, down to Palmera and the wide bay, and then, ahead of you, unfurled the vast valley in which Llosera stretched its small tentacles up to the villages at the foot of the Orfe. He could not pass by without first tossing down a hierbas, that devilish herbal concoction Catarí was so wild about. "Rather than about men. With one scarce exception," she had sipped at the brim of her glass with naughty suggestiveness. A divine caress on the tongue it was, the first time they got out there, and many a time since then on the return trip from the capital. From the terrace behind the ever cool bar your view reached out just a bit farther. Gaudi's most classical church ~ "disculpe señor: our cathedral!" ~ seemed to take pains not to glide off into the bay of Porto Llosera.

"La Concha, Mr Maïks," elucidated the new waitress, with the diffident pride of a fan who dares to give a sign of recognition after all. "Si, señorita, he said, a little flattered after all. Nice piece, that girl, but he did not leave any tip, wittingly. Tomorrow Catarí was coming with him, and he did not want to tumble into the same trap as the Archidux once did. Without his Cathy the 'Oystershell' lacked the last touch: Fra Angelico's perfect celestial blue, as she had put it herself.

It was a peccadillo, sitting and working there, with such a vista, but on the other hand, it worked inspiring. *What a shame I haven't got the patience to paint. In perfect harmony with this scenery! And, top of the bill ~ this darned flavour of a hierbas: how poor a wretch Van Gogh was, with that miserable absinth of his.* Dugal shook off the tempting thought, closing his eyes for a moment. The first draught glided down his oesophagus ~ the same wonderful feeling which poured through his veins with the nectar from Catarí's lips. Or more or less like that.

Querída Catalí, he mumbled. Lately I wrote you about my descent and my youth … Those happy days under Tuscan sun, and afterwards, our expulsion from Palazzo Pitti and the Giardini di Boboli. An escape which was to turn me into an eternal rover, even down to my present place of exile. Hmm, 'our' castle … Brendais. Never have I felt more pitiful than in this beautiful Bohemian 'heimat' ~ certainly not *mý* homeland …

Wow, not too bad, he thought, *for a Hollywood star in retreat.* If that was not a smooth transition to those first instalments they had greedily intercalated in the Diario de Marcaio under the column: *LETRAS SECRETAS,* intimate confidences of the Archidux; by Duke (world-famous actor)! It was about time they were going to raise him to the peerage, he pondered. Sir Dugal, or Lord Mikes, that would add some more verve to his editorship, no?

Besides, what greater merit had such a mere Bond actor or a Kain Michael got than he? Suppose this would ever issue in a real scenario for a screen version: bý himself, in a production by him and, who knows, with him in the part of … the intrigued and ferreting digger in don Lois' clandestine biography. *Too crazy,* he chortled, *an actor who playbacks himself in the life of his precursor/landowner. You must be completely cracked to do something like that*! And what about the role of the high seignior himself? Unfortunately, there was no Mikes qualified for that. His figure was still a bit too slender. Or not broad-chested enough, he reflected, with mixed feelings of conceitedness and regret.

"Sorry," he said, to shake off the young barmaid, "I'm going to work for a moment."

"Si, señor." The Marcaian fire in her black peepers betrayed the veneration of the humble for the great of the earth ~ was that what don Lois had ever seen in Catalí d'Omar's eyes?

It worked. No living soul was going to disturb him here, and soon Dugal was sucked up in the eddy of the ducal prose, back into the past.

> Cara Catalí,
> I am not certain if you did receive my latest letter, let alone read it. Sometimes this reality seems a dreary

dream. I appear to myself as a pawn that has fallen off a chessboard and is forgotten, somewhere in a nook, by the diabolic powers by which it was staked on it. Is it this dreadful disease due to which I can hardly recognize my own body and limbs? The former court-physician they sent up to me, pretends that the cause of my chronic illness must be sought in one of our travels. Mysterious worms penetrating into the intestines, pave themselves a way through the lymph stream. There it becomes a breeding-place for those little monsters which transform my body into a stuffed manikin. Just as though a pair of bellows make my veins swell. I prefer the version of a local nature doctor. A mountebank who blames nostalgia and the lack of the sweet azáhar and orange-tree blossoms as the malefactors. When our soul is suffering, the body goes asunder …

However it may be, Cariña ~ if this is the place where I was predestined to

moulder away into eternity, I do not see the sense of man's own self-

determination which the guardians of the Holy truth held out to us.

I know, the man's tinctures, ointments and compresses are but a plaster on a

wooden leg. Nonetheless, they alleviate the therapy of incisions and pills the Viennese doctor was poisoning me with.

Yet, I sometimes think that all this is pure imagination and that I am living in a haze. A marshland from which only one person could rescue me. But that, querída Catalí, is something I want to spare you. Seeing me in this situation would be too heavy an ordeal. I will pinch my leg or arm and think: no, this cannot be true. And then I doubt whether I have ever really gone through all this, and shall I really see you again, my dear, in my lifetime? Often I am overcome by the feeling that you were no more than a phantasm, an angel that has nestled in my fantasy. I must cling to the scarce pictures that I smuggled with me between my books. When I see those pictures of Ses Taca with you and a few well-known faces, I can taste again the scent of the freshly tilted fields, and I know: it has not happened in vain.

"Anything else, señor ~ shall I refuel your dram, perhaps?

There the young waitress was again, beside him, bottle in hand. All admiration for this curiosum. *The way one stares at some artefact in a museum,* Dugal grinned, *or a fossil.* The sun, panting under her own ardour, was already leaning towards the summit of the Teix, bathing the Concha, that oyster bay down there in the depth, in a deep glow. It was as though he returned from another century and yet, this girl might as well have stood here, at his side, in a baize skirt and demure décolleté: *Catalí d'Omar, cut out from a picture,* it flashed through his mind.

"Interesting reading-matter, it seems." The young lady blushed slightly, rather because of her own pluck than of the film-star's intrusive look.

"Does that theme mean anything to you?"

She smiled subtly, while filling up his glass. "Which girl here wouldn't like to be in Catalí's place, mister Mikes?"

"Depends on how you look at it," he mused. *Good gracious, now that chick already knows what I'm up to,* he wondered. *Innocent? Who assures me she too doesn't want to … Trees have eyes here.* Ah, was he seeing spies everywhere again? On an island like this one could not vanish in the void, and this maid was not born yesterday either, you could tell from her keen eyes. A student probably who earned an extra on the side. He had a weak spot for her ~ without any by-ends, really. *She could have been a daughter of my own, this moonlighter,* he smacked over his hierbas, with a tinge of tenderness. Or regret?

'… not happened in vain … 'The letters danced a bit before his eyes.

Oh dear. Not in vain: did don Lois mean the whole affair about Ses Taca ~ the purchase of Maremira and its concept of a piece of nature in which man, and human activities, fitted like a beehive in a fruit plantation? His love-affair, or whatever it was, with a beauté pure of rural stock …

41

Or was there something more behind it all? Something you had to read between the lines maybe.

> ... so I just hope one thing: that you now feel secure, Cariña, in a homely setting, though not in your beloved bodega, but at the place we both conceived. After your illness and its aftermath we could hardly contrive anything better. How else could there have been life after death? With so much surveillance, on me and the activities of our secret alliance, there was no other possibility but taking that step, a rash step, I know: out of public life, the community that was so dear to you. After all, to you it meant separation from goods and chattels, from most friends and the world of your youth. From all that was dear to you. And that, sweetheart, you did only for my sake. Not merely to safeguard my 'reputation', but above all things on behalf of our common ideal. I am quite aware of the sacrifice that demanded of you. I am very grateful for that. But you must realize it was a bitter decision for me too to perform that feint. Acting towards the outer world as if you no longer existed, were banished from my life. As a matter of fact that was true, indeed. Or almost. Fortunately there were those few loyal people on whom we could thoroughly rely and who managed to take over my tasks: administering your medicines, ensuring the deliveries.
>
> It was nearly like the adoration for a secret beloved, secluded in a severe Carthusian cloister by hard-hearted parents.

Well, I never! Dugal muttered. *Was that wrecked piece of a nobleman totally daft, or am I going nuts myself?* He rubbed his eyes and stared at his glass, as if the hierbas were the culprit. *Now I really can't follow any longer,* he thought. *At the outbreak of the Great War Don Lois sneakily starts writing pitiful love letters in his Bohemian castle, where he considers himself a hostage. For himself, in fact, but he fancies they are meant for his Marcaian lovey, who, nota bene, is supposed to have passed on for about a decade (I've got to check that one, in the library). Quite a sublimated form of schizophrenia, if you ask me ~ where other privileged detainees would have idled away their time with crosswords or family albums, for my part.*

For a while he was thinking of his dad and what he was probably doing now: emailing with old fans of his and digital photo composing. And suddenly that uncrowned king of Marcaio turned up with a kind of post-mortem scenario. Conjuring up his old beloved, with a deft trick by the way. His Catalí might have caught some virulent affection, on an Egypt tour perhaps, but not of such a nature that she would posthaste have kicked the bucket, as the official versions tried to make the general public believe. Ranging from leprosy via cholera down to syphilis ~ dependent on how 'favourably' the respective sources were disposed towards them. One could read the wildest stories about that. Poor thing, I feel so sorry for that child, Catarí had said only yesterday. The way they would revile you, already at that time, long before the flatting-roller of the paparazzi had set off!

True, don Lois admitted he did not look that fresh any longer either, over there (also an aftermath of that memorable boat-trip?), but to Dugal's explicit impression, that mysterious swelling affection did not shackle the emperor's old aberrant cousin to such an extent that it really got him to hallucinate. *I wonder what Roberto has to say to that. And Catarí?* For she had let slip a remark like: "Wouldn't that old billy have been full of remorse? How many effusions of love haven't arisen after a blazing row? Just look at all those withering widows who daily shamble to the grave of their once so hated husband. Keep talking to him over the cutlery set for two." She did not even respond to his laconic teasing: "Ah, an anticipation of our own case?"

Resuscitating one's sweetie for the pangs of love? Pure wishful thinking, quite understandable with such distracted hearts. Yet, that did not explain why a crippled don Lois should link a resurrection theory to a rather dark motive so as to let his unrecognised bride go into hiding at a clandestine location. Where probably he was still able to reach her, alive or not. Hmm, pretty bizarre after all, Dugal thought, and upon rereading that passage about a 'bitter decision' and 'a fake performance', it all began to look as if that deuced Dux had participated in the staging of an apparent death of his beloved. Merely to let their forbidden love live on, beyond shame. But what was the old hippie drivelling then about ensuring the 'deliveries'? Wine perhaps or hierbas? A clandestine distillery at Maremira. Or drugs: Luigi Salvatore, the opium-smoker. Joking apart!

No, that did not hold water. Presently he would tell Roberto ~ ... *Hey, but suppose this is macabre joke. A game with posterity that the Archidux had contrived there, in his golden cage.*

"Everything okay, señor?" There the barmaid was again, with a slightly teasing smile: "Is that too suitable for publication, mister Mikes?" Caught out. Dugal flushed down his last sip of liquor and said: "I've got a better proposition than that: I will give you the part of Catalí to play. Sixty years of age."

8

How can you still get riled like this by sheer trifles? Simply because such a young chick sneakily has you taped, you are ill-tempered and once again you begin to believe in the first conspiracy theory you come across. Dugal tried to quell his frantic driving style, but the first couple of bends downwards he kept resenting the naughty twinkle he thought he had seen in the eyes of the young waitress. *What will that lassie now think of you, the big movie celeb she used to look up to?* A bit farther down he already started to snigger about that ludicrous pent-up anger of his. Until at long last he found himself shaking with laughter. *Idiot,* he thought aloud, *what are you busy with?* All the small events of that day ~ they just belonged to the daily vicissitudes on an island like this: the typically Marcaian chaotic oddities of the mañana culture. Not that these people were backwards, no, but simply, they were … different.

The therapeutic effect of his fit of laughter worked wonders. They still befell him, sometimes, such whimsical fluctuations of mood. Of course, Catarí found them pretty difficult to deal with and once in a while she would rage like a devil in a holy-water font. Just verbally, thank goodness, at least for the time being. Hurling pots and pans she had already demonstrated on the set, like in 'The Peace of the Pink', Dugal's most ferocious example of degenerated matrimonial happiness. No, by now he preferred seeing his sweetheart from her most lovely side: the dreamy, the tender one.

With Catarí's beatific smile before him on the road, the gliding landscapes merged into each other twice as softly and slowly, bend after bend. Seeing and living consciously, hic et nunc. Looking through the eyes of your beloved, was that the way to happiness?

'But on a day full of golden foliage,
and spring and gilt azure,
I pass over the last mountain ridge,
and live my most beautiful venture.
For, sitting under a cypress tree,
I behold with still eyes the town
from which I could not get free,
since I heard of her renown … '

He would like to tell her, sing it for her, up there, drunken like a skylark; she could only scream with laughter, in his face, what was there to lose? Better anyway than the silly whispering of those three trite syllables with which Cathy could always put you on the wrong track: I love you ‑ and your money too.

No, a full-carat diamond like Catarí ought to be re-conquered daily, helter-skelter, with handstands of another dimension. Even if those verses were from a long forgotten tome on Roberto Marquez' desk, by a Bertus Aafjes. A queer bird, that Flying Dutchman, to go to Rome on foot, god knows from where. *Totally wrested from its context, that strophe,* he thought, *but that does not matter.*

Or some tunes set by Granados or Rodrigo. Even De Falla, re-echoing in the patio at Sa Finca ‑ it cost you nothing and Catarí was randy about those vintage music-sorcerers. On top of that a surrealistic sunset above the palm-trees around Ses Taca, from one of the belvederes don Lois had devised at the time, and she would devour him. There was no Freud or Jung to scrutinize Catarina, one needed other norms for that. How else could he have conquered her where other, maybe smarter nobs had failed, including Jorge Clones?

And then in the manner of Botticelli: painting her, from that terrace, as a black-haired Aphrodite, emerging from Llosera's Oyster-shell. Over the inspiring fragrance of a hierbas and with Respighi's Nascitá di Venere as background music. That was going to cost him a bit indeed, for he did not want any priers on that occasion. At the risk of her railing at him, once she was in that bar he rented: "And, Pinturicchio, is that brush of yours equal to such a risky enterprise?" Yet, even in case of a flop, you had to persist, that made the difference with her. Sublimating things, with humour too. That most of all.

The difference was ~ Dugal had jested of late, playfully grabbing her at her haunches ~ that one 'very honourable' Rainer Maria Luigi Salvatore Zanobi and whatever the rest of his dozen names might be, had set his teeth in a girl of humble descent. Not just a ravishing crumpet; obviously this Catalí had lifted him to a level unparallelled by the ladies of his rank. And all the chimeras he had made up about such intercourse, got the charm of the forbidden on that mouldy paper.

Of the impossible, yes ~ as if all those flirtations with room-maids with which historians could fill several libraries, excluded genuine, sincere love.

To Catarí that seemed all pointless. Fiddlesticks, she thought: if a fellow really wanted to stand up for his sweetheart, he should not keep her on the sub bench. Why had Rafael counterfeited a baker's daughter, La Fornarina, on the sly? And Vivaldi ~ hé had even fallen into eternal sleep in the arms of his favourite female pupil … Hypocrites, whom it suited better that way, because they put their career at the first place. Things had not changed a bit, so far.

"How do you mean ~ that you suit me well once in while?" He had tickled her, until she screamed out, drumming on his breast.

That was Catarí from top to toe. She ~ protected chicken though she was ~ had had to start down on the ladder, without a push in the back ("neither of fumble-greedy impresarios, my friend," she would tease him then). Whereas hé at least had got a famous daddy behind him.

How often hadn't he told her he had never needed his dad's patents of nobility: he did not want to pass for the son of … "There you are again: 'nobility'!" she jeered coolly, and on seeing his choler running high: "Checkmate." After which he saw again the mocking twinkle in her dark eyes. "Caramba, you horrible imp, you 've chaffed me again!" The subsequent cushion fight could not have been staged better in front of the camera. But the other one, the kissing fight, was parried by her finger on his lips: blue blood always had to be distinguished from real nobility.

"Yet, the average reader of a bestseller doesn't feel it that way, my angel. If you want to transform lyrical effusions of that kind, you should do it in terms of a soap opera."

And as far as extra-marital scenes were concerned, he could turn in a word now, couldn't he? she bit peevishly. Hit below the belt!

About that Sparto Mikes was amply in the right: Catarí was quite a spitfire. Again and again she tackled him at every attempt to rehabilitate his male image, "ignominiously besmirched since Attractive Fate, isn't it, Duke?"

Whenever she coaxed him with that pet name, she was quite on edge; only with 'Mickey' he had to be even more on the qui vive. He simply knew she suspected his female counterparts of too much identification with their roles. His performance as a (less willing) victim of a nymphomaniac in 'Basic Senses' had added little to patch up his reputation of 'haunted game'. An employer of higher origin who wants to hook up her subordinate … Hard though he played the impeccable who did not yield to the advances of such a femme fatale, on the Golden Globes Cathy found that co-actress of his just a bit too strikingly close to him while waving with her trophy.

'Course, her nasty attitude tickled his vanity, he smirked. He had arrived on top of a secondary valley by now, at the 'umbrella' ~ that huge fir from where he used to look behind when Catarí was in his company too, across the Concha and Llosera, inland, with its splendid landed estates crawling up the flanks. And slowly he let the car glide down towards the grandiose amphitheatre in which Deió was embedded. The greatest triumph of his life, the first time he had turned around that winding: "There, your wedding-bouquet!"

Her unfeigned bewilderment, unforgettable that day! "Sold", she mumbled, and did not seem to grasp his further explanation: "Ses Taca lies opposite, over there, just around the corner; we are sleeping with the neighbours."

That's how things were to go on ever since that moment: he always had to share her with someone else ~ with Deió and the gardens in hotel Sa Molina, with the Archidux' guardians of virtue, the poet Ranke-Graves and his brand-new widow now, and a good deal of trendy painters who regularly infested Deió. Despite, or precisely due to, that bohemian-like retro atmosphere which permeated the little town with such a colony of enfants terribles, something remained there of the authentic, ancient Iberian. And Catarí was totally enraptured by it.

Whilst driving past there at a foot-pace, he peered up the sinuous streets leading to the top of the cone, right in the middle of the circular valley: a whim of the creator, it seemed, to put down a chapel high up there. As a matter of fact, she, Catarí, fitted altogether in this picture. *A thorough-bred Welshwoman? My foot!* With that dark hair, those bead-like eyes … Any ignorant passer-by would take her for a local painter's model.

Nothing of the sort, now! You could hardly spot a mongrel round about there, they were all at table: tomatoes-olives-garlic. No Catarí to pick up at Sa Molina either. But he hoped she had found inspiration - and time - enough to stew a tastier variation on that eternal theme from the Marcaian kitchen. Or … Or else she was fed up with waiting and then there was something in the offing. If she received him with a suave smile, oh dear … There would be a storm brewing then. "Now … that's - the – LIMIT!"

He did hear it as soon as he saw the silhouette of Ses Taca looming up between the trees. He still had to get around it, yet thought he could see the crenels and the palm-trees nearby trembling. *Because of her pent-up rage,* he grinned. Soon he would not dare to do so any longer, or else, the fat would be in the fire. With unusual haste he sped over the half-paved track. Not quite worthy of a Hollywood-star, that entry. So, another thing to rake up from the past.

He lingered a bit before getting out. Stay of execution, he thought. No sooner had he opened the door of his car, however, than she dashed towards him, without watching the steps. A half-cut cucumber in her hand. *Softer than a cake-roller anyway,* it ran through his mind.

"Dugal!" she shouted, flinging into his arms. He nearly toppled over. What had he done to deserve that? He was not going to be a father, was he? Or a Lord, like Shaun Conrey; or the boss of Bross Co., to offer themselves the main parts in a new serial about Eduard and his non-divorced American bride?

The expected reaction - "What, do I look ugly enough for that?" - did not follow, and her spasmodic way of clinging to him as well as her suppressed sobbing took him aback, more than her most vehement fit of temper could have done. "Eh, eh, what's the matter?"

She did not find her tongue again until he had ushered her in cautiously. "How … glad I am … you're here … alive." Her nails scratched down his back, as though to make sure he was not a phantom.

49

A phantom ~ ... of delight? he quoted Wordsworth, as a pretext for swaying her around. "No, Dugal, "They came down here for you, three of them, and ... and those assaults, they even said it on the radio."

Dugal tried to calm down her gibberish, but now his old girl, so strapping at other times, completely freaked out.

"This is no screenplay, Duke! Those blokes asked for the editor of that 'blasphemous' piece about don Lois and they said they would come back."

And what about those news items? On his way he had not put on the radio, for he was not in the mood for radio Marcaio's blend of euphoric hit parade and live zarzuela arias.

"An overturned lorry ... and the car that got under the load. At first they thought it was yours, Dugal; that there was some malevolence involved. Because just before that they had mentioned a shot aimed at the same cabriolet, but the bullet had grazed by, hitting a cop just behind it ... at his arm."

Dugal could not believe his ears. Had those pressmen been watching too much of Jamie Bond or read some Grishams?

"Hey, Carina, are you starting up too! You don't believe in conspiracy theories, I hope, here in this very outpost?"

"Du-uke," she sang, with the fearful patience of a housemother who has to call her rash son back to reality. " Those fellows didn't look like softies."

What they did look like then ~ like Dugal Mikes in a failed replay of the Godfather? he tried to curb her fear.

Still, she was likely to see the doubt in his eyes. That close-shave ramming from behind, the intimidation by that driver, AND the policeman hopping with his injured arm ... ; the incident with the load of rapeseed. Was it only a fortuitous concurrence of circumstances, indeed?

"Come, come, honeybun. Pure coincidence. Apparently those newsmongers today found me quite a succulent bone to gnaw at. Oh dear, sensation justifies the means. And yet, it's not even the slack season."

"No, Dugal. It was all about that Archidux, they did not beat about the bush." It tickled Catarí it did not seem to occur to her hero for a moment that she herself could have been the target as well: molesting, killing her, abducting her for a ransom ... That was possible after all, wasn't it? And now she dropped a hint ~ about one of those louts clutching her arm, his

50

garlic breath had caught her in her throat. One moment she thought her last hour had come.

Dugal was staring at her, the way a fellow does who is growing demented and starts doubting about himself. What that trio looked like then? He could not smother his curiosity any longer.

What! A foppish oddball with broad sunglasses; a close-cropped bulldog with frog's eyes, and a double of Al Pacino with a snappy voice …? "The Holy Trinity," he laughed. Those were the sticklers for proprieties Roberto Marquez so often had to contend with. Innocent local lore fanatics who wanted to keep everything here olde-worlde. But they would not hurt a fly.

He had got as far as her earlobes, in the vain hope of being able to massage Catarí's emotional life onto nicer tracks via some mysterious meridians.

"O, the phone!" She slipped from under his arms, as if she had been waiting for it, and held out the receiver towards him: you see, doubting Thomas!

It was Roberto, rather curt and upset, an unusual thing for him: "Hello? Marquez speaking." As Dugal put him at ease with waggish cynicism ("You speak to someone risen from the dead"), the professor's tone changed all over: "You Dugal? Good heavens, that takes a load off my mind. You know, it's said there was a double attempt on your life …?"

9

A double attempt on your life. Dugal still could not help chuckling about it. Nearly everyone had been bowled over that day. Catarí, Roberto Marquez, Jordi, the manager of Maremira. Also, in particular, their maidservant. The way she rushed up to him, flying around his neck, even worse than Catarí herself! The latter had been watching it, moved, with trembling lips. As if this were just her sister. "Okay, okay, I am resurrected," he had cautiously patted the upset girl on her back. Maybe she had a crush on him after all. But no trace of jealousy with his very dearest, this time. After all that had happened the past month. That juicy story of a false 'eyewitness' which, as a teaser, the daily vexing column in the Primera Hora, should have snatched away quite a morsel from the reading public of its big rival, the Diario. Fortunately the chief editor of the Diario, meanwhile a house-friend of the Mikeses', had stumbled over it, and he had tripped the rascal. Even extorted a public confession from him. Wasn't that a bit of luck! That there was still someone to watch over the internal chastity of Marcaio's press ~ one could hardly imagine anything like that in the Anglo-Saxon world. Besmeared though his reputation with the 'natives' might be, Catarí's opinion was much more sacred to him, of course.

And what about Ripoll then! Mister Ripoll of Sa Molina. The distinguished hotel manager had driven up the crunching gravel some minutes later, all anxiety. " You came to see the brand-new widow straight away!" Dugal could not desist from needling the poor chap each time about his very obvious weakness for señora Mikes. But then, which gent did not have a tender spot for her? Come on, that's just platonic, she defended the always well-groomed caballero.

"I should not underrate those things," Ripoll thought. And he told about former threats because Sa Molina had once sheltered a camera crew making an evocation of Dame Sand's sojourn on the island, and about the antipathetic attitude of the community at Valle de Muša because of her 'profligate' intercourse with 'a frail musician'.

"Times have changed, Mister Ripoll." Dugal confessed frankly that he had never thought much of what prof. Marquez had called 'the holy trio'. But those Knights of Virtue today could not be compared with 19th century hypocrisy, could they?

"Precisely, señor Dukes, that's it! You are searching in the wrong direction" *Slyboots*, he smirked, but he could never blame the hotelkeeper for that twist of his name. And Ripoll professed that the Holy Trinity had nothing to do with it. "Anachronistic image-guardians they are, indeed; but they would not hurt a fly. No, there are some other scamps behind all this."

Now, a few days after, the whole fuss about the case had abated again. Only Roberto Marquez kept insisting: "Let those two souls rest in peace, amigo. Bury your pride, and the documents under our wings, until time is ripe for it. There they'll be safer at least".

That's what you are after, hm! Dugal thought. For objective research, yeah yeah. "But who guarantees me that you're not hand in glove, all of you?"

One moment his academic pal was on the verge of exploding. "You, miserable …!" It was high time Dugal had bolted, but as a matter of fact … "Why, it's true, after all," he argued, in Catarí's presence, "always poking about here, and then snatching away the flowers under my very nose. You can already see it, in a few years, a de luxe volume edited by prof. Marquez: 'Secret letters of the Archidux.'"

Catarí's compassionate grin, those mocking lights in her eyes … It always reduced him to a swanky tartar, her 'old naughty boy' she had to appease over and over again. "So what? Just give me a milksop, rather than a post mortem celebrity."

However strongly he was mesmerized by her eyes (like, in fact, by all of her attributes), he would not be called Mikes if he let himself be hectored that easily, under the motto 'better safe than sorry'. No sooner had Catarí shown a clean pair of heels ("To the village shop, darling, can't I really get you jealous with that?"), than he plunged back into his 'treasure-chamber' where he had made his great find. An unsightly mezzanine room, to the left of the entrance hall. Ten steps, as it used to be in many old Marcaian houses. It still smelled of the herbs Catalí d'Omar had hung there for drying, five lifetimes ago. The ceiling and the walnut wardrobe were permeated by the fragrance of lavender and laurel, oregano and coriander. *The scent of a departed era, and here I have got the fluke of my life, the best concealed secret of the century. Maybe even Carter would have dropped Tutanchamon's mask for it, just fancy.*

Bet he would, he chuckled. The workmen who kept their tools stored in there during the restoration works, had left the wainscot a bit damaged. *What a shame!* he thought, and one day he had started mending it himself, in full competition with his Cathy, who wanted to work off her designer's skills on the overgrown patio garden. A cloakroom chest had been lifted off its hinges, and after a good deal of jerking and cursing (*Damned, you dilettante!*), suddenly he caught sight of a slanted board at the rear. After a bit of fiddling and knocking, a second one gave way. Hey, there won't be ... here? A heinous idea came to his mind: who knows whether a former inhabitant had not loosened it regularly? A primitive safe, no? Maybe even a hiding place to hoodwink the tax collectors, at the time when there was an inn here, the 'Weinstube' of doña d' Omar. A bit later he grabbed in it with his whole arm and ... gotcha, at once*!*

Alas, no suspender-stockings of the lady of the house, stuffed with ducats from a century ago. But yeah ... canes! Walking sticks belonging to the Archidux, three, six, ... a dozen. Quite a collection, caramba! *Not bad,* Dugal had groaned, but what a disillusion! If you expect to fish up an intimate garment of his mistress, in fact a winsome token of gratitude for the fruit from acres of wonderful Riesling, and then just this failed phallus symbol!

Now he was able to laugh with his greedy reflex of that moment. A linen chest with a false wall ~ it might have meant the turnover of a few film-productions, enough to cover the restoration costs of Ses Taca. Although ... The value of such old currency, he did not have the haziest notion about it. And besides, who would tell him how you could barter them without falling into the soup?

Even with those canes Dugal remained on the qui vive. His Prof/friend had already insisted more than enough: "But where have you found that manuscript?" "That's what you are after, eh? Well ..." he had whispered to him: "in a false bottom of a wardrobe in the vestibule. In some old tobacco pots. Or walking-sticks. And if you don't believe that, I'll make up another story for you." Roberto could not help roaring with laughter, but bet he thought to himself: *spoiled trumpery actor?*

No, nobody was going to get hold of don Lois's canes. For three days he had fumbled at it like daft. Screwing off the handle ~ gorgeous specimens, all of them, truly. With a copper grip, just like a world globe; a silver eagle's head; one with a cross engraved on it ~ no common oblong cross, however, no, but such a symmetrically shaped cross which reminded him of the Maltese Order. Weren't they emblems of …? Precisely. It had cost him some research work in Roberto's library, but now he was certain about it. The Archidux had used unique sticks with Habiger symbols; by the bye, one image showed clearly the profile of his imperial 'niece' Elisa. But what about the other ones? Even, all of them, with simple tools etched on them: a chisel, a pair of callipers, a protractor … Would he have got them from some craftsmen? One could hardly imagine his Highness displaying such practical affinities.

While Dugal was sliding one of those earthly, far too earthly, specimens through his hands, a stealthy skulker could have noticed the secret amusement on his face. With what canny naivety he had extracted the necessary expertise from Roberto! "Strange," he heard himself still mumbling, "there were such queer signs fixed on the inner walls. All day long those workers had to scour them off the wooden and plaster walls on Catari's order."

"What! The last few years there weren't any freemasons or so lodging in there, as far as I know." You could see the regret on señor Marquez's face that he had not gone to have a look at SesTaca beforehand.

Freemasons or so, hmm! Dugal hugged himself with the professor's harmlessness. But that's how it started to dawn on him: who could have delivered those rather prosaic specimens to Rainer Maria Lois? And that motto that was chiselled on the edge of the wardrobe door ~ like on all the chests and closets in the house: Duc in altum … It could not be from anybody else but the carpenter in charge. And who that was? Exactly: damsel d'Omars very own father. Dugal spat on his thumb to put an imaginary medal on his breast. If that was not a fine piece of detective work! A freemason, my foot! Nowadays they saw a corpse in every closet, very soon even John XXIII would have been a member of the lodge. No sir, those non-dynastic canes were a craftsman's gift for the favour of being allowed to work for such a highborn personality. Particularly in a swell Moorish dwelling where the Archidux employed the carpenter's daughter Catalí ~ not as his maidservant, but as the 'maestra', the manager of Ses Taca and mistress of his vineyards. So, a present of dad's to his unofficial son-in-law.

Dugal passed the walking-stick under his nose with a violinist's gesture: Could one still smell the noble hand, or had Catalí put it in there once, cherishing it as a token of honour? Dugal himself had always felt the lack of such a memento ~ a pipe-rack of his granddad's e.g. And after the finding of the canes that aromatic association had promptly got him to an idea. Such walking-sticks usually contained a liquor flask. And indeed, there they were! Not under the crutches of don Lois's own sticks, but under the others. And blast! Was it imagination or not, there still was a fragrance coming out of them. Of hierbas, unmistakably. Delicious, probably home-brewed liquor from Valle de Muša. *Typical,* Dugal thought. The nectar of the average poor Marcaian wretch. Not that a noble weirdo like the Archidux would sneeze at such a concoction ~ *hey, I begin to feel more and more familiar to that old lecher,* he chortled. But it was a public secret that even now many a pater familias kept distilling illicitly. And Catalí's dad will hardly have formed an exception to that, one could assume.

He had tried to visualize those scenes in his mind: how that rich esquire had stood here, clinking glasses with the local Joseph ~ oh, irony, how history repeats itself: a few days ago Dugal's own carpenter had let him in on the niceties of the licóres de hierbas. Only, that fellow had not brought a Catarina along for him.

And all at once he knew. Just as if a voice, a wink of the archduke had made it clear. He took a pocket torch out of the settee alongside and, acting on the spur of the moment, he pulled off the cap underneath. *Eureka!* Behind some fumbled paper (it still smelled of herring) the rolled-up paper scroll made a sign to him in the glaring lamplight: *'Hey, at last, that was about time!'* How big his surprise had been, however, when he saw the seal on the letter. So, no money, no deeds at all. Yet, who knows this discovery would not turn out to be of much greater importance than a few illegal millions.

Leave it! Everybody was imploring him, as though opening these intimate secrets of the heart would put a curse over them. *Scaredy-cats,* he laughed. While unfolding the first document (in cane n° V, with the chisel on it: he had put them back in the proper order), his decision seemed to be definitive, rock-solid. Carry it through! This was far too nice to have it 'classified', like so many a state secret or apocryphal document in the Vatican. Doomed to vanish into the archives, that is, into oblivion.

From where was he going to let the next part issue? He was going to play it shrewdly. Not the way hack writers such as Dumas or Dickens used to do, in daily instalments, no. Only in a good week or so, and then going on like that. In dribs and drabs, enough to fuel curiosity. So …

Querida Catalí, …

Or maybe another form of address, for a change? Cara mía …, or: Cariña … And some antedating as well, but apart from that: no falsification whatsoever. They would not get a chance of blaming him for that.

As Dugal started to read again, time seemed to take him back again, stripping off his modern cotton togs in exchange for the 'Mantelrock' and the striped trousers he had seen over there, at a stone's throw, in the museo del Archiduque. And, what with that small difference of a letter in their names, she, Catarína, would find it even less difficult to play the part of the carpenter's daughter. The role of her life ⁓ ¿ qué *lo* sabe?

10

Querída Catalí,

As I have already told you before: with the tragic death (as a matter of fact tragicomic, to the outsider) of Mathilda, my promessa sposa, light faded, literally, for me. I would have liked to explain to you some more about it, some time ago, but there are things that are easier to write than to tell about.

Without that tragedy I am not sure whether I should ever have stranded on Marcaio, and I refuse to see Mathilda as a piacular offer to appease my venerable family in Vienna. Even with her I cannot imagine my life would not have taken a special turn. A different one anyway than what had been drafted so neatly with an imperial pen. However, it is a fact that over there, at the Viennese court, they had become reconciled to my 'false step'. Temporarily, at least.

Yet, do not believe it was an easy step for me, Cariña. Really, as you said yourself: money is an old fogey, but one cannot redeem one's own freedom altogether. Now that slavery has been abolished, we are serfs to money.

The happiness that men of my rank are able to buy, floats on quicksand, for it is subject to the abuse of power. The sweat and blood of thousands of innocents ~ nobody can expiate such inheritance by abstinence. That is, the way I saw it ~ by simply renouncing from rights and duties.

Even if I had penetrated into the heart of Africa, in Livingstone's footsteps, Fate would have pursued me everywhere. The blood running through our veins cannot be replaced, and there is a curse that rests on our family. As though our original sin (whatever it may have been, for that is rather obscured in the chronicles of the Habichtsburg) is enacted in us, the last scions. A downfall no one of our spawn is able to escape from. However hard it is for me, in these days of insanity and the din of arms, to believe, in any sense, in this I do believe. Namely, that a spiral of despotism at its peak gyres down to the same urge of retaliation for which it all started at the basis. Usurpers are thrown over, avengers subjected to vengeance. To that generation of the reversal we belong now.

We are a final product of an evolution, condemned to be swallowed up in the whirl of times - as were the Romans before us, the Byzantines, the Arabians etc., etc ...

But I do not want to bore you with this dreary story, Cariña. What is done, is done, and if my ancestors had lived on your island, their spirit could have rested in peace. Maybe, however, it is our restless clinging to power that digs up all the sins in our descendants, thus preventing them from renouncing definitively. Oh, believe me, I would exchange my whole fortune - or what remains of it - for the life of a simple peasant. A humble farmer's son from Es Porles or Deió, without a grand pedigree and any patents of nobility, but with grit in his body (and smart looks on top of that) . How dearly I would have loved to sacrifice my name and origin for it, to fight for your hand, dearest Catalí, in fair competition with all the lads in Valle de Muša and thereabouts.

A name! How it can decide on a man's entire life - that too is such a typically human foolishness. What's in a name? the English say, and that is something I can confirm. I have seen the greatest jackanapes who could not by far come up to a simple commoner. Yet their title made dignified officials and ministers grovel before them;

changed headstrong arrivistes into demure lackeys. That filled me with silent laughter now and then. When some people did not recognize me, under a shabby cloak or so, thinking: 'what an impecunious noble', you should have seen their faces change all at once. Their haughty air suddenly became obsequious servility, so much that even I ~ oh, human weakness ~ on occasion could not suppress some unholy glee. 'Your Serenity' here and 'Your Highness' there, such that you cannot help feeling like serving them with the same sauce. But oh, noblesse oblige, and you act your part all the way along. "My name is Salvatore ~ Luigi Salvatore." One would do it just to upset all those conceited faces.

I wish I also had such a magic charm, many people think ~ as you once put it yourself: a name that works like a passkey, a kind of 'Open, Sesame!' Would be practical, no?

Indeed, at times it opens unsuspected doors, is able to grant you unbelievable prerogatives, truly. Often though it is a millstone around one's neck. Once in a while I tried to shake it off, to repudiate it. All in vain. I gave it a Spanish tinge, abridged it, transformed it, disavowed it ... But all of you persisted in calling me 'duke'. Not out of servile docility, I know. It is that typical mix of esteem and confidentiality, slight mockery almost, so inherent in countrymen, with which you try to give strange things an indigenous touch.

And from your mouth it sounded like a pet name sometimes ~ 'Archidúque'. "Archi," it rolled across your tongue with the endearment of a diminutive: "my sweetheart", quite the opposite of its meaning. And "dúque"? A soothing, somewhat teasing appendix for 'sweet'. For on your lips it got that by-sound of 'dulce'. So disarming, enough to put centuries of harsh history down as a boy's game. A title degraded to a caress.

At times it also sounded in all its grim gruffness, as if you were angry, and then it flopped like a dagger in my back. A revolt against the absolutistic injustice. So,

'Lois Salvator' gained over Ludwig ('lieberr Luddwik'), with which otherwise you would test my susceptibility to blandishments.

Salvatore ~ such another Christian name that has kept ringing in my ears. I carried it with me from the cradle. As if my distant ancestors had seen the portentous moment of my birth in their glass globe. At the turn of times, on the eve of the fall of the Occident, a new scion was to see daylight who could breathe new life into our dynasty. From the Southern Land, do you see? Zephyr, a kind of mythological animator, coming to sweep away all the feebleness of the previous generations. But you, Cariña, you know what a stigma that predestination threw over me. In vain I sought for that lighting star at the sky which ought to lead me to the lofty goal. Until you appeared in my sad existence and made it clear to me that for every human being, however poor or wretched, there is a spark of hope left. 'Duc in altum', your father's motto ~ I still remember what impression those elegantly chiselled letters made on me, the first time I came to Maremira to buy that wardrobe for the hall there. They were a sign to me. Really, at that moment I was struck by a strange feeling: there, at the very spot, the power of a lifelikeness pervaded me as I had never felt before in my surroundings. Or still …

Suddenly I felt again the tie with my youth. That afternoon ~ I was still a toddler ~ when I had strayed off with one of my sisters in the Boboli gardens. Foul weather had driven us to a small house outside the walls … Those simple neighbours who offered us shelter, I recalled their faces as if it were yesterday. I could smell again the fragrance of thyme and marjoram hanging in that room there; taste the delicious minestra we slurped like the best culinary masterpiece our chef the cuisine was able to dish up.

Zucchini, onions, celery, tomato, peppers and peas ...
The riches of the country folk. Well, those friendly people
did not exert themselves in cringing humility. We were
spontaneously taken up in that family, with the heartiness
of their unselfish hospitality. And when they had found
us and some servants came to pick us up, I felt ashamed
for our well-mannered lackeys, with their great gestures.

That scent, the same feelings now came back to me.
For the first time since many years I felt at home, and
those words ... They got the value of some letters carved
for a beloved in a tree. As for my part, it was a declaration
of love to your island, and to you ...

11

"Well, Cariño, what 's she writing? You almost look like the male counterpart of Bernini's Saint Teresa in Ecstasy."

"God-damn! It's just you, bless my soul."

Dugal could press his Catarina flat, with pure relief.

"Oh, oh, save me," she giggled, " but what if those stalkers of yours caught you in the act like this? Come on, I'm going to stew us a tumbet! For Land of Plenty hasn't passed by here, I guess. Here, look and admire yourself! That way you'll get on the front page again, maybe." In passing by she put all of the Marcaian press into his arms.

When she acted that way, he knew she was a bit miffed, and why. And wasn't she right! As he had cajoled her into coming along to this place, it all seemed to be a bed of roses. Finished, that hectic studio hullabaloo, the vain Hollywood merry-go-round. 'Goodbye to all that', a booklet by their precursor-neighbour Greeves–Ranke, was the first thing he had put into his bag. *There's my bible now.* They had visited his grave in the neighbouring village of Deió. A small tombstone under a cypress, some fresh flowers, and the epithet 'poeta' as a sole extra.

The island had conquered them. The 'Miques' (or'Maïks') started to breathe, to eat, to smell like real country-folk. They even began to jabber like them, in a smattering of Marcaian. One could not stamp them down to their properties any more. But that applied to a great deal of the natives here. A stray tourist would laugh compassionately and put some pocket money into their hands; but then those 'poor' Marcaians thought behind his back: *silly wretch.*

In a curiosity shop they had bought some fortune mottos to put up on the wall. One day for her: "*Real happiness costs little. If it is expensive, it is not the good kind.* Dixit Chateaubriand. Not referring to his beefsteak."

Another day for him: "*Happiness? A good bank account, a good cook, a good digestion. According to J.J. Rousseau.*"

Then it was her turn again: "*Happiness gives us a lot for loan, not in possession.*"

"Oh really, and who tells that poppycock? You yourself maybe? But then, I needn't have made you the heir of Ses Taca?"

With a catlike jump she had pulled him on to the floor then and, her bosom above him, she panted: "Si si, Cariño, that was symbolically meant, wasn't it? The most marvellous bridal present for a marvel of a girl."

And that way they teased each other: "Materialist," "Dreamer," "Sycophant," …

When in the end Catarí was lying under him, she wanted to have the last word after all: "A Publilius Syrus knew that two-thousand years before my time," and thus she knocked him over again.

Most difficult of all, however, had proved to be the change of rhythm. The real dolce far niente was not their cup of tea. Carpe diem, okay. No plans, nothing that urgently needed doing. Wonderful, that mañana culture, compared to German Pünktlichkeit. But after all, they did need something to do at least.

But since Duke had come across this Duque, there was no more holding him. His former grimness, which she knew had kept slumbering in him, suddenly flared up again. Less irksome than a fellow haunting the indigenous beauties?

A poor consolation, thought Catarí, as she realized he risked to slip away from her grasp due to that new passion. Truly, it had been their intention 'just' to dwell together here, hadn't it? Just live! Exempt from all deadlines and stress. And now she had to share him with an old, shunted-out dynast ~ and the man's local conquest. Catalí! Gradually she was feeling more and more kindred to her far predecessor in this house, *la dama de bodega*, daughter of a modest craftsman, raised to the status of the Dux's 'Rebegartendame': his lady of the vinery. How had things turned out for herself, Catarí, by the way? Little Welsh town-lass, she had been lauded to the skies, and there, at the acme of the filmbizz, long before her star got fading, she had been picked away by THE coryphaeus of the white screen. Her self-knighted Duke, who wanted to settle her in a ducal inn on this very island!

Dugal sighed. He could understand her wrath alright. She saw her Dukie, mesmerized by that chemistry of a secret love, slipping out of her web into that magnetic field between two sepulchres, miles away from each other. Probably she suspected him of digging up this grave secret so far that he could spin a ready-made screenplay out of it. Not just for the dough? Fiddlesticks!

And yet, that's what it is, babe: pure magic. How could he get that into her smart little head? A hell of a dilemma, for at the same time he did not want to lose her for all the money on earth.

Disconsolately he strolled round about the garden, her life-work, though still in statu nascendi. "There!" he smashed the newspapers on the pergola-table and angled a rattan chair in his direction. Hey, why had she bought all that reading stuff? Then he caught sight of his own face. Monstrously enlarged, in the *Primera Hora*.' Dugal Mikes in full action,' it was printed in huge letters. At the moment of his frenetic jump across that intersection, maybe. Fie, what if Catarí awoke with that in her eyesight? 'La belle et la bête, he could already see it standing out in the tabloids soon. And there: his own car tearing past the overwhelmed twin brother. On the front page of *La Isla*. And under that, the *Diario* ~ oh, nothing? Forget it ~ a gigantic headline: 'HERO OF THE WHITE SCREEN NEARLY TOPSY-TURVY HIMSELF, s. backpage. Yeah, there it was. A complete photo-report and a flashy eyewitness account reading like a page-turner: be ready for the big middle page! AND then the *Bailares*, the *Eco de Palmera*, and yet another and another one.

Dugal was swearing like a trooper. Nothing could have been further from his thoughts than this. A whole horde of paparazzi had shadowed him, without him noticing anything. Quite absurd! Somebody must have tipped off those guys, he mumbled. This looked like one great set-up. But why? Who wanted to scare him out of his wits here?

In a jiffy some cases from the past flashed through his mind. Attempts to intimidation from the part of ultra-conservative groupings, fanatic religious factions … What movie director, writer or actor did not have to cope with such things? Even smear campaigns by animal protection activists because in some seduction scene a fur coat had played the role of enticement. Thus La Share was once stoned as fur whore n° 1. The supplier of a piece of lingerie had expected a shindy with strict clergy circles, but got a punch on his nose from the Tax Office, because of clandestine publicity, *and* from feminists who feared abuse of the situation in it.

It came from the most unexpected corner sometimes. The worst that Dugal had experienced, was the hubbub about a kiss. The most chaste and volatile kiss even he had ever had to produce before the camera. On the cheek of an ex-Miss World namely who had had her share of Bollywood and took her chance in the Wild West. All at once he had got half of the Hindu community on his back, brahmans altogether unanimous for once with some Muslim radicals. Bodyguards, bomb letter checkers and quasi house arrest under CIA supervision ~ he had gone through it all. And laconically snapped his fingers at it.

Why should he goddamn care about this sort of folkloristic tomfoolery? Of course, some zealots would jump on it again and make him a target of some worst case scenario. *Look how our island is sullied by all those foreigners who buy up the prettiest nooks. Who wipe the floor with old values and our entity.* Nuts for the local nationalists and home-tied nincompoops, that was for sure.

"Well?" Catarina called him back to the kitchen. How it felt to be altogether back in the limelight? He ignored the irony behind which she hid her nasty mood.

"Oh my dear, it leaves me stone cold. Do you know what way I could do the greatest favour to those people? By reacting. And that's precisely what I grudge them. Let them just go on with their little schemes. You know, after Whitsunday they've got a real hangover at the editorial staff: no ETA-bombs, no political scandal or sensation about royals or sports heroes. They are slavering for some gooseberry season stories."

"And with you they happened to find a big bone to gnaw on.

Keep calm, Dugal, he said to himself and tried to get it across to her that he had not been after this kind of publicity. He only did so in admiration for the Duque.

"Oh, do you?" she said. "And why then did you link up your name to this publication? By the way, you're not going to tell me everything is peachy keen, are you?"

As if that thoroughgoing idea shed another light on the matter, for his part, he mused: "But who, Cariña, who may want to scare us into fits? That holy Trinity, no ~ softies, the professor and the boss of Ses Molinas say. Hardcore extremists? They don't shoot with blank cartridges; and nostalgic zealots make no scrap-heaps for a deterrent effect. IF those single coincidences were meant for me after all, I only see two valuable candidates."

"*?*" He replied to her sceptical glance with an equally laconic gesture. "Only two, yeah. Roberto Marquez … and you."

He had reckoned with two reactions: either a casual shrug of the shoulders ~ *hmm, you numskull!* ~ or a choleric outburst (one of those throw-and-kick scenes during which his Spanish fury looked most covetable. Instead she burst into an inextinguishable fit of laughter. "Marquez, you say! That you would suspect me, I could accept. Although … I would do it more thoroughly, wouldn't I, darling? With that saving pot of yours, and now this manor on top of it … Yeah, with me as the sole heir. You get me to think, y' know. But that poor professor, fie, shame on you!"

"Well, you would be able to hire those bogus killers to get me back on the right track and let that old scapegrace in Vienna quietly snooze on in his tomb. And Roberto? That's another matter. The more I'm brooding over it, the more plausible that line of thinking seems to become. Professor Marquez has been busy for years with a profound research about that mascot of Marcaio. He told me so himself, the first time he happened to pass by here, even before one stone had been laid. That's the way we made acquaintance. His idea, you know, to put up a new info centre about the Archidux. He was raving about it. And I laid the foundation stone for it. So far, so good."

"Academic envy? No Dugal, I don't know the professor like that."

"Oh no? Well, think how much energy the man had dedicated to it. Putting his students on that theme all the time. His shelves must be bulging with the final papers about Rainer Maria Zanobi."

"So what? As you say yourself: a passion."

"Precisely. And then I, an insignificant dilettante, is popping up with a find our learned fellow could only dream of from his cradle. Why do you think he was hanging around here all at once? Our private signpost 'Coto Privado' must have been like a red rag to a bull. His little scheme, you can see it from here: I, the moneylender-Maecenas, and he, the treasure-hunter who is going to snatch away a new Tutanchamon from behind the plaster."

"And there your wilful ego turns up with evidence about a forbidden love, and that stark jealous Tarzan with brains wants to make it disappear into the drawer as a mystification, and as for you …"

"To wrong-foot me? Yeah, but that failed, so he had to change his tack."

"Hmm, hmm. The safety therapy. But … my little bossy-boots won't let himself be fobbed off and keeps working on his own account: the fame of the discoverer, the Carter of the twenty-first century! Smart brain-work, Sherlock. But that's not how things work. A real historian like Roberto is only concerned about the protection of authentic documents, and …"

"Right. I had got them, but put them at risk. That protection instinct which drives collectors to murder."

"So, a bit afraid after all, my brave brat?" Now she was at her most seductive, his babe. How he would have liked, more than anything else, to press his lips on hers to silence her!

"Oh no, cause all on his own he would not have managed. That's why he needed you, and judging from your reaction I don't think you have made such a combine."

"What kind of twaddle is that?" Now he had to take care Mrs. Mikes's frenzy did not assume dangerous proportions. Then he would take the risk of burning himself at Brunnhilde's shield of flames. For weeks on end he would experience what it meant: silent pictures. Therefore he had to divert the tussle to a safer course.

"Well, those walking sticks." Indeed, he still had hesitated before letting her into it; everyone could make a slip of the tongue. "If you had really succumbed to the charms of that toff, he would already have tried to stage a burglary in that upper room ‒ with some help from within, you know: first putting asleep the alarm system and the dog. Now I'm at least sure my sweetheart hasn't got a weakness for intellectual teddy-bears."

Ugh, his tactics worked. With a lithe panther's leap she landed him down on the sofa, her hands around the scruff of his neck. " I'll kill you, I'll kill you!" To that kind of situations he was more equal, though, than to virulent strong-headedness, which overturns the strongest man after a couple of days. Less than ten seconds later the argument was settled. He pressed her head so strongly against his lips that, despite her spluttering resistance, her voluptuous head of hair beat fiercely to and fro across his head. Fortunately, no stray passer-by could observe the scene, or else he might have come to the wrong conclusion of witnessing an attempt to violation in the opposite sense.

12

That morning the whole world seemed to have reconciled itself with him: the sky was immaculate, the sun shining off in her Whitsun best. The cicadas were singing lustily ~ over-diligent pupils of a string players ensemble ending up in a grotesque orchestra pit. And yet there was a fresh fragrance hovering round about things, a whiff of the early primavera. After last night's drencher the naranjos gliding past them, were glaring in full morning gleam. The unrivalled orange trees, as inevitable on this island as the olive-yards, vendors of sun lotion and bikini worshippers … *Goethe,* he mumbled, and spontaneously the old poet's words came back to Catarí's mind. 'Kennst du das land, wo die Zitronen blühen …?' Dugal never got any further than that first verse, in fact the only one he knew from the Olympian's 'Mignon'. Once more she translated the rest of it: ' … in the dark foliage golden oranges glow … ' But also the oleanders along the road, the luscious tussocks over-hanging the rocks, the lizards basking in their gratuitous solarium … Everything brought an ode to the generous manufacturer of that celestial beeswax spray.

Even Dugal felt reborn, owing to the truce yesterday night and the clashing peace offensive that followed. Seldom had Catarina's amorous expressions and ditto yoga been so overwhelming. "Home peace? Heaven-ly," he still groaned now and stretched himself, mimicking the example of the lizards.

She suavely nestled up to him in the somewhat sagged front seats of the little Seat. Yet not without that ironic overtone that made her so ravenously charming: "Yeah. Such a period of bickering does have some advantages at least. By way of foreplay."

You daresay, he nodded. With an alternative breakfast served up in bed, by an unusually inventive Duke. Including freshly pressed fruit-juice from their own produce, her favourite croissants from Deió's only hot bread bakery, and that week's Paris Match flaunting a 'brand new' interview with Catarina Ionès, dating back to three months ago: "Catarí, c'est comment, la vie à Marcaio?"

The envelope beside the teapot had been particularly convincing. 'For a Whitsunday folly in Casa Vivot'. That knack always did it. Strolling along the seaport, the Moorish Palace, the cathedral was nice; even more so when doing it together. But sauntering between the aisles of Palmera's most classy fashion house, one had better do by oneself, with the contents of such a surprise envelope. Then, in exchange, the couple of hours in the hallway of Prof. Marquez's varsity were an acceptable deal.

"Through the Tunnel then, shall we?" she proposed. Was she going nuts? he thought. It was quite comfortable, for sure. Therefore they had carried out those protracted, gigantic excavation works right through the bowels of the mountain, so as to shortcut the zigzag road through the pass of Llosera. 'With a view to the opening up of the Concha', it sounded with political panache. And then, by accident, there was that hierbas factory, on the opposite side, called: Tunél. A happy coincidence. *But not quite the Dux's idea.* Now his motive was merely practical: just fancy some crank found inspiration in that? In the middle of such a mole-track ~ who could do anything against a … "A hand grenade for instance?" A flat tyre seemed already opportunistic enough to him. And that blue BMW in the rear-view mirror had been clinging on to their rear for quite a while. So better those 65 hairpin bends up and 63 down after all.

"Aha, whence that sudden superstition, my undaunted chaperon?"

"Just pillow your head on my shoulder. Now have a look in the mirror."

Catarí too found the company behind them a bit suspect.

"Eh, by no means draw attention, will you! Do you think they …?"

Dugal intentionally slowed down. Less than fifty yards further on their supposed pursuers were tired of it and … krrr, the BMW tyres squeaked and shot past them even before the bend. Aggravating!

Fortunately they had not entered the tunnel, Catarí sneered.

Beyond the little bridge he took the exit on the left, heading for Llosera-town instead of driving uphill. Ah, a change of plan, Dukie? Tomorrow, he promised, was going to be a day off in her favourite Oyster-shell, but now, just a quickie first in Café de Paris. Their weekly sin, that old village tavern: an horchata de chufas for her (groundnut milk, fancy!

His stomach turned at the very thought, but okay, there's no accounting for tastes), and for him his inseparable piña colada.

From the terrace you could see the stately palm-trees and mansions up there on the station-square, and a long row of cypresses behind it. Would the Duque also have enjoyed that picture back in his days? One moment Dugal was playing with the idea of taking the train, the oldest train in the world, so it seemed. But the month before a singer from the city had been potted on the way. Never mind, next week they would make a ride on it, disguised as a country couple! Catarina was crazy about such things ~ a bit typical, outdated, dingy …

Same with this road. Only each quarter of an hour you passed a car here that had missed the tunnel. Since the introduction of the new route you were more likely to cross a shepherd with his flock of sheep.

"A bit more slowly, please," asked Catarí, "I'd like to enjoy those landscapes gliding along." Dugal was constantly shifting between the second and third gear. A somehow clumsy feeling, in their gardener's old Seat. Let's just act as normally as possible, they had decided. Alpha Romeo nicely back at home; no jetsetters' airs in the streets of Palmera. "And especially, no eye-catching." Cause that's what you did soon enough there.

"Nine o'clock." Catarí turned off De Falla's 'En los jardines de España' for the newsreel. The crown prince's Whitsun visit to Palmera, the reopening of the orangery of the old Tesharon hotel, the start of the regatta at the seaport … And then, right at the end (as she wanted to switch over again): "And now some more news about the recent attempts at assaulting actor Mikes …"

Well, that takes the cake, Dugal muttered. Those guys were already pretending adamantly that the Marcaian CID (or whatever you might call it) had found the traces, as sure as death: "Hitmen who have already fled the island post-haste, after their failed mission."

"What did I tell you!" Dugal laughed. "I think those oblique shooters are sitting somewhere at the editorial office of a press agency, laughing up their sleeve; a generous bonus for that silly season stunt! As is also that 'detective force', namely."

Bingo! There it was. Near the fiftieth hairpin bend a bleating wool company were drawing a track of black pastilles over the road surface. As

Dugal was manoeuvring alongside at a footpace, the shepherd touched his straw hat, shouting: "Disculpe, señor Nikes."

"Señor Nikes. Did you hear that? You are a living legend already."

They did not give it a further thought. About fifty yards farther, however, it happened. "Watch it!" Dugal braked abruptly, a torrent of boulders and rubble came rolling down, sweeping over the asphalt, right in front of them. Followed by a heavy ruffle in the abyss beside them. Phew! And just when they wanted to take to their heels, on their guard for a hail of bullets, some late-coming stones flew in a wide curve over them. A few pebbles just hit their bonnet. Carefully they raised themselves up from their covering posture. No damage, save for some light scratches on the coachwork. They were spying upwards through the trees and ferns; no movement. "There!" hissed Catarí. "A blue ..."

"What, not a BMW, is it?"

Catarí would have sworn that ... But no, it might as well be a delivery van of a few bumpkins with hooligan tricks. Like blazes Dugal rushed on. An unequal fight? Supposing that was a BMW there, indeed: the tortoise against the hare. But even so. Amazing what one could get out of such a small Seat! Coming out of the bend and speeding up like the legendary Bahamontes ~ full throttle! From that point one could overlook three zigzag pieces. Nada. "But that's impossible!" Even IF there had been a race-car ahead of them, it still ought to be in sight.

They looked at each other. Well? "Do you think I'm seeing mirages? No, Duke!"

The rest of the drive they covered almost taciturnly. In a kind of trance. On entering the city, he stopped for a moment and asked: "Pinch my arm, will you? Am I dreaming all this, or what?"

By all means he wanted to put her down in the Calle Jaime; she did not want to let him drive on all by himself, though. "That salvo of meteors ~ that was also a sheer coincidence then? Wake up, Dugal! There really is something going on here."

What with all her resisting, he pulled her out of the car door at the corner of the main shopping street. "And take care that this envelope is empty later today."

"Don't act so heroic," she still shouted after him. That kind of scene he had already played once: in 'Attractive Fate' maybe?

Roberto Marquez was about to enter his office, when Dugal drove up along the curb. It was as if he could guess what was going on. "Mikes, hey man, you look a sight!" Instantly Dugal corrected his hairdo in the mirror.

"Better like that?"

"The bodywork of your vehicle, palurdo! Have you turned a somersault or how?"

The lady-assistant and secretary jumped to their feet as they saw him enter. A cup of coffee, wet cloths to dab his forehead, are you all right, señor Mikes?

Marquez even seemed to be more upset than he himself was. Who could be behind all this? Whether he had no suspicions at all?

"Well, eh, maybe I have …," he looked mysteriously. "You for instance." He ducked down for the professorial anger flaring up in Roberto's eyes. "Just a joke." "No es una broma," the learned gorilla grumbled.

This was certainly no longer an isolated action. No anti-tourist stunt or a boy's prank as happened to Sir Shaun Conrey last year. The figurehead of the British film world had almost been beheaded while driving back to his villa in Andalusia. Concrete blocks thrown from a bridge, you know?

"Venga!" The professor lured him away to a small hall behind the library where Dugal had settled down in the course of the last few weeks. "Look here, my ducal headquarters," he pointed at the beautiful tomes on the shelves, cases full of registers and files. Four long tables littered with yellowed documents and volumes, some of which were still tied up with thread, and, as Dugal noticed at once, printed in 'gothic' letters. Piles of periodicals and index card boxes. Five students were at work there, stooped over the piles of papers and clippings. *To create at least some order out of the chaos?* Dugal wondered.

"And my ducal staff," Roberto sniggered. "Last-year students working at a final paper." After that he also drew his guest's attention to the PC park at the opposite side. There too were some more students happily occupied. *Rabbits in front of the light box,* Dugal thought. They looked round, at that notorious face, frowning like *'Where have I seen that man before?'*

"The boffins of the Archidux," the host laughed.

"They too aren't …?" Dugal could not help saying incredulously. Prof. Marquez nodded, grinning in his imaginary beard.

"On some other occasion I'll take you to the archives of the theses.

There you'll find an impressive section dedicated to don Luigi Maria Ranieri Zanobi etc …, in short the Dux ~ say, your namesake, Duke," he winked, standing close to him, in a conspirator's tone. Almost as solemnly as an initiate who confides to some dolt or other that he is a far heir of the Davidic line. Dugal now slipped along the row of computer freaks and one of them, a lookalike of Jennie Lopez, showed him with a roguish smile the lists she had been bringing up to date. "The recent works. Of the last dozen years, Mister Mikes."

"Since this one here?" ~ "Si si, señor. From Prof. Marquez' time onwards."

Dugal examined the academician with a half-closed eye. Was he paid here to make a private study centre about a dissident of Europe's most renowned noble eyrie? Roberto invitingly pointed at a reading table at one side, with a couple of arm-chairs. "Isabella?"

A young student brought him a folder with some sheets of paper and put them on the table, for the special guest. It seemed to have been arranged beforehand.

"And?" the professor smiled. " A manzanilla or amontillado?"

"Oho! The hardboiled ascetic is familiar with the bon vivant's taste. But, if I may choose: a Pedro Ximenez, please, for a change."

"Aha, a piggy of Epicurus' that learns at least the more subtle nuances! Well, all right, so I'll change my water into your jerez. Just for once."

With a conspiratorial nod Roberto turned the fine cherry wood case, with a screen fitted-in, a 180 degrees around; and there, from a secret 'safe', the professor was rummaging between glasses and carafes, like a full-fledged shaker expert, until he reached, before Dugal's perplexed eyes, the correct liquor glass, with crossed arms: "No alcohol ban in Palmera ~ señor, to us!"

"And to the Archidux!"

And then, as he touched the tumbler, Dugal suddenly caught sight of it. It had the shape of a walking stick, and on closer inspection there proved to be a whole collection of such liquor glasses with the same shape in the little case. That is, all with a mouthpiece similar to the crutches on don Lois's canes. From the eagle's head and the globe to the chisel and the graduated arc. All of them were there and the longer he was staring at them, the more it was getting clear to him: this was the perfect miniature imitation, home-made, in Marcaian mouth-blown glass!

13

Dugal was staring at the sheaf of papers the spruce female student handed to him, with a mixture of bewilderment and suspicion. How was this possible?

"A copy, A.D. '88. Staggering, don't you think so?" Obviously Prof. Marquez was gloating over his consternation.

"But that would mean that ..." he stammered, his eyes turned upwards: a desperate friar on one of those Zurbaran paintings, searching for an explanation from above.

"Precisely." The academician, in a striped summer shirt and one hand leaning on the table, now looking more than ever like a hybrid of the Greek disc thrower and Rodin's thinker, nodded pitifully: "I'm sorry for you, my friend. You must feel like an Egyptologist digging up a new farao mask to find out that there is already a duplicate exhibited in the museum."

"But how ...? Where does this come from? And who ..."

"...cooked up all this, eh? That's the crux. I wish I could give you a proper answer."

The professor guessed, of course, what was spinning round in Dugal's head: which part he, Roberto himself, was playing in it; how that copy had got into their hands ... Besides, he had just noticed how Dugal had been staring, wide-eyed, at his strange collection of sherry-glasses. The suspicion had been aroused, he smirked.

"Disculpe, amigo." He apologized to his famous friend because he still had to settle something urgent himself. That was also opportune, he judged. He had to grant Dugal some time to get over the blow and compare the two versions.

"A copy, you said?" Dugal shouted after his professorial counterpart, who was already talking to another female student in the doorway. Or his assistant? The handsome chick cast a sidelong glance at him, as

75

incredulously as an Opus Dei member that sees the Pope passing by on skis on the square of the Vatican. "Jesus, if that isn't ..."

"Right. A copy, but not from the machine."

A handwritten one then?! Now it was for the graceful figure next to Roberto to grin, when seeing Dugal's bulging eyes. With a nod the Prof stretched his arm to show her out. Was she to go and brief his stalkers about the Operation Liquidation being a failure? *Stop it*, he thought aloud and smiled sheepishly at the girl lazing about near him.

Finally he was able to focus on the manuscript and was searching feverishly till he came to the passage where the next few days he wanted to go ahead with part four of the instalments in the Diario. The longer he gazed at it, the more strongly he got convinced that this manuscript was a nearly perfect imitation.

'Archiduque ... Salvatore, such another epithet ... 'There it was. The fragment was still sharply engraved in his memory. How it caught don Lois by the throat, the remembrance of their first meeting and then the association with another home-bound experience, from his early childhood, in that humble Tuscan dwelling, with a common country-folk family. The man's nostalgic exhilaration ~ no more for the daughter's sake than for the modest daddy-carpenter's? Dugal sniggered, and that made him think of his own Catarina. Fancy her too springing from such folk: no flashy career at all, no bucks to play ducks and drakes with, but ... what a peerless beauty, all the same! And he himself, mutatis mutandis, buried alive somewhere in such a clinically dead, luxurious flat in L.A. or S.F.. Damn it, he did not dare to think of it but he started whining like one of these howlers in the French hit parade.

Would it be opportune to let the old seignior chatter on and on with the same verve; but on the other hand ... Who gave someone a right just to trim in an old glory's secrets of the heart, to fool with the authenticity of a document for which he would like to set up to be the defender and shameless unveiler at the same time? *Who am I to ...,* Dugal wondered, and the answer came fast enough. A self-extolled actor beyond the apex of his glory ~ he could hear Catari's teasing. A macho on retreat who wants to elevate himself once more up to the level of a real aristocrat of the spirit. Cashing in on another person's bad luck, so as to put an organ-point behind his own career? Just at the moment even when Hollywood had almost shelved him: *let's give him a lifetime award and that's that.* Without any rancour; no fretful backbiting whatsoever.

That, however, was reckoning without one's host. *Hmm, how well my Cathy knows her urchin,* he reflected. *A Mikes does not let himself be ordered about, lobbied aside by a pack of meddlesome movie whoppers.* Dugal was groaning peevishly. But as the letters began penetrating into his mind, he thought: *shame on you, here you are, poking into the emotional life of a 'große Seele', and you are just thinking of how to save your bacon!* At once he decided to link up again with a copy that matched such another sheet, namely from His Highness' fourth cane. Which one was that again, with which symbol on it? Dugal assured himself that he was going to learn the sequence of those numbers by heart and the cryptic signs fitting with them. Something told him that might be useful one day.

"*Salvatore …*" he switched on again, quite attentively now. This time he hardly had to insert a few words as a way of connection. At that point, some days seemed to have passed until don Lois had again dipped his fountain-pen into the ink-pot.

> "*Dear Catalí,*
> I hope I did not exasperate you too much after all, in the latest products of my pen, with all those contemplations about my names and painful memories of my 'dynastic' past. I know what grief was brought over you: but you too know I myself never was a stickler for protocol and pomposity.

Splendid, Dugal thought. But whether the gullible reading public over here were going to swallow that mollified, somewhat polished prose of mister Rainer Maria Ludwig any longer? After the first shockwave of the scandal-mongering sphere that half of Marcaio had smelled, the enthusiasm was likely to fade, and how could you retrieve that blasé, soap-addicted public then? On the screen things were quite different. If need be, one could get the old gent in such a mellow soap opera to turn up in his birthday suit for once, running after the local country lasses – no decent citizen would take offence at it. But oh dear, if one should mention one word about some illicit love-tangles of a suchlike historic statuary! That

was set down on paper, man! They would fleece you alive. Or perhaps …
that was precisely the 'way to success'?

With that kind of thoughts still in mind, he felt a sudden shiver
running down his spine and his brains seemed to spin around like a top.
Had he read it correctly, or was he entirely confused because of his own
speculations? No, there it was, put down in black and white, last time it
had slipped his attention:

> *"…and even if you cannot answer me any longer, Catalí,
> we shall be united for ever, in soul and mind, beyond the
> limitations of space and time …"*

That's how it was written down there, literally: 'de alma y espíritu'.
Dugal rubbed his eyes, with the baffled look of a grinning Marcaian who
imagines señora Catarina Mikes sauntering down the Palmera boulevard
in monokini. *How can any reader skip over a thing like that?* While gazing
like magnetized at that little sentence, he grabbed distractedly at the sherry
glass one of the young computer boffins had brought him in the meantime
on Roberto's order. His eyes swerved back to the previous passage and
feverishly he resumed the thread:

> *Only once you asked for the meaning of my second name,*
> *and I remember you laughing at my elusive explanation. All*
> *right, as a lad I had always been a bit ashamed of it. Ah, you*
> *said, we have not been able to choose our names ourselves,*
> *and as I asked you what baptismal name you would have*
> *chosen, you said archly: "Cariña, maybe." "But … 'Darling',*
> *that's no proper name, is it?" I said. "Indeed. So, why then*
> *do you call me that way?" How you managed to checkmate*
> *me over and over again!*
>
> *I had at least plenty of choice, you thought: from ten*
> *names even. Oh yes, our father had seen everything tenfold:*
> *ten children, and for me, the ninth toddler, in Palazzo Pitti,*
> *also ten names. It was my pet aversion reciting them, all*
> *of them, and when later on one of the courtiers or visitors*
> *insisted if I could drone them one after the other, I jibbed at*

putting them in the proper order: 'Rainer Maria Ludwig ...
Ranieri', I reeled off a first series in one breath, and then, in a
casual way, switched to their Italian version at once: 'Giovan
Battista, Giuseppe Domenico, Carlo Fernando Zanobi ...
' *To the great annoyance of our Austrian family teacher,*
who was looking desperately at mother, clicking his tongue.
Whereupon she, a thoroughbred Neapolitan Bourbon with
Norman-Sicilian fire running down her veins, was looking
sternly, taking pains not to burst into laughter.

Maria Antonietta, could I but experience that scene
again! And father Luitpold too, looking on smirkingly. With
that frown above his eyebrows, just like a teasing pout, that
said: 'And the rest of it, figlio mío?'

"*Zanobi Antonio ... Salvatore ...*" *I let the whole lot of*
it fade out, with the sigh of a deflating concertina. Staring
at my shoe-tips, abashed.

I do not know who wanted to foist that epitheton ornans
on me, but as a child one gets stuck with it. 'The Saviour',
'The Redeemer'. As though our common Father up there,
whom we try to imagine as a bearded, gentle-minded
shepherd, had contrived some special plans for me.

"*Well, what was there for me to save? My fatherland.*
Human lives?" By the way, what does that mean: fatherland?
Your country of origin? In my case ~ the Austrian empire ~
that was already three generations ago. You must know, our
great Maria Theresia had paid by experience to the Duchy
of Tuscany. Namely, her consort Franz had once been grand
duke Francesco II there. And likewise, my elder brother would
have continued that Lotharengian tradition as Ferdinando
IV, normally, if those troubles of the Irredentism had not
intervened. More is the pity, for the people were very devoted
to our family, and so were we, to them.

Funny, but owing to that dynastic inheritance of titles,
the ten of us already belonged to the migrants of the fourth
generation, so to say. Our homeland however, la dolce
Toscana, was still too much kept at bay from us to offer us

that genuine homely feeling of shelter and security. Yet the lack of a nest's warmth was unknown to us. Therefore the ambience at our home was far too unconstrained. Vivace, in the southern fashion. What a difference indeed with the strict protocol in Vienna. But still. Secretly I would have liked to take part in the street life of Florence, the popular games of the ragazzi on the squares and along the Arno. Gambolling and frolicking about, with torn knees and elbows.

Ever since the Garibaldistic campaign and the rupture, in 1859, that feeling of being displaced, home-reft, got stuck in my memory for ever. Belonging nowhere and yet to the whole world. Whether that is just a disadvantage or conversely, the condition for a pure cosmopolitan spirit? Between the small world of our childhood and the wide world there is actually no factual national barrier. A child's soul, the natural broad spirit of an up-growing, budding citizen of the world does not recognize any artificial state borders, but experiences the contact with the outer world in circles, from human to human. As to me, this is beyond dispute, Cariña: that, as far as human solidarity is concerned, we have to stand beyond all nationalistic fanaticism, and make the world a home. How else can we acquire any real self-knowledge, let alone arise to the supernatural?

After all, in that sense there may have been a slight messianic trait in me, in the best Nazarene tradition. Yet, also in that respect I refuse to be put into a fixed compartment ...

14

"Mister Mikes ...?"

It took quite a while until it came home to him. The young lady next to Dugal, stooping rather conspicuously, had tried three, four times to call him back to reality. All in vain. Even her giddying décolleté, compared to which the spectacular rock mass of the Cornisa Tramontana paled into insignificance, was not able to work miracles. "Señor Mikès!"

The last sentences from don Lois' cosmopolitan reflections kept dancing persistently before his eyes.

"I had needs to bring you this tea, on professor Marquez' behalf. To perk you up, so to say."

"Oh, yes, yes" Dugal grimaced, and he took Roberto's approved substitute for a caffeine boost from her graceful hand. "I'm already feeling better this way."

This thoroughly non-academic appearance took the compliment as she ought to: with a modest smile, and she left it up to him to rate his own words at their true value, with a nearly perfect rotation on her heels and a condescending nod over her shoulder. *How does mister producer like me from my other side?*

Not too bad, the old stager of the silver screen clicked his tongue ~ that professional malformation tic he had got from Franky Copla during one of those selection sessions. His *'veterinary inspections'*, as the latter used to put it.

The tears sprang into his eyes at once, due to Roberto's all too zesty concoction, and yeah ~ there the Chest already straddled into his range of vision, in front of the occasional waitress's fine rear.

"Well, what does mister writer think of it?"

"?" ... Depends on what you mean: that crossbreed of absinth and sweet flag of yours; these mysterious copies here; or that peach over there from your harem collection."

"Oh, señorita Dolores?" the professor-muscleman smiled tenderly. "An assistant of my next-door colleague's. Who 's just turned emeritus."

"Prematurely, I assume, through the insistence of his over-jealous wife. Yep, there are some advantages about being devoted to the Alma Mater as a 'bachelor', eh?"

"Señorita Dolores has a passionate relation with the Archidux. In a purely platonic way, of course, if it may interest you." The 'full' professor produced his broadest smile. *One to one,* he seemed to think.

"So, for that reason that … transfer didn't prove to be so difficult at all? For her hobby-horse's sake that nice bit of stuff managed to join your ranks pretty smoothly then?"

"Oh, oh, mind it … The academic mobility is based on something quite different from purely opportunistic moves or hmm … call it a scramble for posts, my friend. This is no politics here."

No, maybe señorita Dolores had all trumps of a born diva in store, but she was completely proof against all bribes. Roberto certified that she had already refused a few offers for a role in a high-rate picture. Nota bene presented to her on a tray by the scouts of Almenabar. Yeah, the famous fashion king Rabaneda had even sued for her hand. But nada: that attempt went awry.

So she was no meat for her master either, teased Dugal, but his friend was imperturbable. "A marvel of a woman, believe me, Dugal. Gifted with an enviable cultural substance, really. And an exceptional IQ, as one seldom expects among women of such a star level, hmm, hmm … Something she hardly prides on, greatly to her credit."

Yes, yes, that sort of adoration was familiar to Dugal. "And before you realize it, you are sold, my dear."

"Hmm, mister president speaks from his own experience." It had taken a while, but whenever Roberto thus referred to his part in that movie in which the whole of the US had found out about Dugal's vulnerable Achilles tendon, he really took to self-defence.

"I only wanted to make clear that a charm offensive to urge Dolores to more than objective co-operation with regard to the Archidux file, makes little sense."

"Aha, now it's already 'Dolores', you're making a great deal of progress if you …"

"Have I heard my name? Can I be of any service to the gentlemen?"

During their squabble neither of them had noticed the assistant herself stealthily drawing up to them.

"Señorita, this is …" But Dugal cut the professor short: "We had just made acquaintance, hadn't we, Miss …?"

"Dolores Francisquita."

"Dol … Francisquita ~ well I never! But that's killing two birds with one stone! If only our dry academician here had said so before. Good gracious, two of the most well-known zarzuelas. Hey Roberto, I know my Spanish classics, you see!"

Spontaneously Dugal began to yelp an aria from Doña Francisquita. Totally off key, he realized. The students present turned around in surprise.

"How do you like my vocal skills, señor professor? You've got to admit, Chapí the composer would turn green with envy!"

"Or turn around in his tomb," Roberto grinned wryly. "By the way, mister expert is wrong: thát zarzuela was written by Vivès."

"Sin embargo. I'm flattered, thanks for the honour," the academic beauty ogled. "If you excuse me now, señor Mikes, duty calls me. Whenever you want to appeal to my ducal competence … Always at your service." And she slipped a visiting- card into his hand.

Phew, Dugal whistled between his teeth, while they watched her going. "That's different stuff, eh, friend. Look, that's what distinguishes an armchair scholar from a …"

"Presumptuous gigolo," anticipated Roberto. "But don't try to snatch this hot stuff away from us, or we'll pass it all on to Mrs Mikes, on the spot, and that wouldn't be your happiest day. And may I now lead the way …"

Dugal slinked off with his tail between his legs, after prof. Marquez. He simply enjoyed the amusement among the giggling eggheads. *It still works,* he smirked.

The musty cabinet Roberto now showed him into, made a glaring contrast with the adjacent computer room. Yet, however narrow and frowsty, it made all the more impression on him. Here the essays and theses were neatly displayed, back to back. "Mm, imposing," he growled.

His friend was revelling in Dugal's visible admiration for the industrious research work of so many young brains, devoted to this task with almost monastic patience. Their 'secret staff', as they used to call the team. And that was, to a great extent, the merit of señorita Dolores. He sensed what weak spot she had touched with Dugal, and that flattered his vanity. This star-like expert was a gold nugget, thrown into his lap just like that, he pondered with paternal endearment.

"If all of these are complimentary copies, I'm willing to relieve you a bit," Dugal said, without expecting any reaction from the Prof. The latter looked down at his watch. "Five o' clock, at the latest, okay? And mind it: one paper that is torn out and a sensor sets off the alarm."

"Don't worry, proffie, for this whole stack of niggling books you're getting none of my walking-sticks."

Ouch, what have you said now, he bit his tongue. *You had nearly betrayed yourself.* But there was Prof. Marquez, already closing the padded door behind himself. Feverishly Dugal began walking down the row of essays. All well-nigh identical as for the lay-out and titling.

"L.S. The Archidux as a writer." "L.S. The Archidux as an artist." "L.S. The Archidux as a pacifist." "L.S. The Archidux as a scientist." "L.S. The Archidux, a nature lover and conservationist." "L.S. The Archidux as a seafarer." "L.S. The Archidux as a traditionalist" …

There, there. Dugal blew between his teeth. And that whole package in one and the same person. They have nicely chopped up His Excellency here.

Of course, he knew the man's much praised versatility, but this really seemed an optimally executed dissection. And all of it so neatly standardized, a bit too priggish, in a schoolmaster's fashion. Just like clones of a prototype made up by a captious managerial secretary: the same size, the same font …, the subject in pseudo-gothic script. Communicants dressed up in the same kind of suit, that's what those neatly displayed theses looked like, to him.

"L.S. The Archidux as a globetrotter", " …as a visionary thinker", " …as a non-conformist" …

Well I never, he thought, *in the end they're going to make him a Saint, or what?* Amused, he turned around the corner of the table on which the series of scripts was displayed like a pack of cards. "L.S. The Archidux as a renegade." *That takes the cake!* Baffled, Dugal sank into an armchair alongside, looking down the nearly inexhaustible collection in order of succession. Hey, there was a small deflection there: " …dux and love" he read. What are we getting here? Next we'll get entangled in the secrets of the horoscope!

Suddenly a soft slender hand stroked over Dugal's chin. He startled out of his wits. "Caught you!" she laughed.

"Dolores Francisquita!" In his concentration he had not heard her stealing up to him. Obviously she had expected his reaction, for as he bounced up from his chair, her hip glided alongside his with a torero-act and her arms pulled him back down with her.

"And? No need yet of my expert help?"

It made him swallow for a moment, the way she was sitting there before him on the edge of the table ~ on one buttock and one leg pulled up aslant, enough to seduce even an inveterate ascetic to ruin. *The most beautiful one in the world maybe,* he estimated, *closely after my Catarí's. Lucky me.* That's what he had to clutch at now.

"Not yet by now," he faltered in a coarse voice.

And how mister Mikes liked this specialized script gallery?

"Sin par, really, this has no equal. Only ~ I've got the feeling I'm in a psychological dissection lab here. With all those split-offs of an infinitely diverging spirit. Or have they rather sprung from Prof. Marquez' brain? Or from a … señorita Dolores'?"

"?" The question-mark groove between her imminently tightened eyebrows formed an irresistible libido-point. *Nearly as irresistible as it is with Catarí,* he assured himself again. It could not escape her notice, though, how he kept watching it, mesmerized. *Not too badly, I hope, or she'd think I'm making risky parallels.*

"What can you say against that? We had to follow a certain procedure. And we …" (it sounded explicitly as if 'they' formed a regular tandem), "we have chosen for that incredible scope of personality features."

"I see. 'The archduke: the last universal spirit. A Da Vinci or Humboldt from the collapsing Occident.' An extinct race, *something like that?*"

"Algo así, indeed. Our intention is to remove a lot of misapprehensions about him. Alas," she sighed, "too often popularity leads to a stereotype image."

"And you're saying that to me? The price of fame! Take that gossiping for instance, like about myself. That's a heading that seems to fail here, or perhaps it's still bound to come: ' ... the Dux as a promiscuous libertine' or something similar. I myself can't go and have a drink with some lady or the press bulges with it: 'Mikes with his latest flame'. But my wife always says: 'Envy caused by fame seems to me like a virtue.'"

"Or vice versa? Then it would be a quote from ... Cicero."

"Exactly." Now Dugal felt even more daft, vis-á-vis such an erudite vamp. "And what stereotype image have you got of me?"

Señorita Dolores smiled evasively: "Here's another one like that: 'Virtue is vain if it asks fame for a reward.' Do you know that one?" she tested him subtly.

"Hmm ... Seneca perhaps? But that way you're also assessing me: 'Mikes the vain braggart' or ' ... the shallow rattle-pate'?"

"Montaigne," she just corrected him.

He would readily have played that joust with her for hours on end, according to the Faustian saying: 'Verweile doch, du bist so schön'. But she might have taken that too personally. Or giggled because of his shaky German. And secundo: at the same time he was keen on continuing his quest through this privy of L.S.

"Still, there's one question," he said. "Why that L.S. each time? Could as well be read Lectori Salutem, the reader be greeted, as if to pull the layman's leg. Particularly that S. You know Su Altezza loathed all those Saviour allusions?"

"Do you think so? Look at this then." Promptly she lifted him under his arm-pit, gliding down the row of scripts with her other hand. There! " ...the Dux and Christianity", and a bit further: " ...and messianic connotations": " ...Magdalen and the worship of the Blessed Virgin".

"Do you really believe you can see it so intimately?"

Unawares, Dugal had turned brusquely towards her and the señorita put a hand on his breast, only to adjust a clumsy position.

"Oho, I arrive at an inconvenient moment, methinks." There was Roberto Marquez, straddle-legged in the doorway, just too dark for both of them to see his countenance.

15

Once more Catarina Ionès was drawing up to her last bend; *the seventh time*, she had counted, passing by the same carob tree. Nicely drawing rounds, it was quite a help for one's condition, she assured herself. Or for your figure? Dugal would have sniggered. No sinecure anyway, on this toboggan course, jogging along above and under Ses Taca. Quite a difference with the smooth tracks on one of those beach esplanades along the Californian coast. The first time she had almost choked on the spot, but seven was her number, and giving up did not occur in her vocabulary. Otherwise, you could never reach the top. Already from birth a fortune-teller had forecast: Catarí was not going to be a softy. If not in the filmbiz, then it would have been in athletics - *aren't I a natural talent?* she chuckled.

Yet, each time it was a relief to her when the finish was within sight. But rather this self-chastisement, here on this very estate of the Dux (now her Duke's property), than such a parade trot on a sea-promenade where the whole world and his wife were staring after you. "Just do it every day, practice makes perfect," Dugal incited her regularly. "Phew, depends on what practice you mean," she would sneer then. Though many times in a heroic role himself, he was not so keen on that kind of training. "You can't have everything, mí amor. Extra or intra muros - where would you rather I played my athletic trumps?"

Boaster, she thought. *After such a day in that musty scholar's room, your boss will just be a little boy.* And he knew she loved it spicy. Wish-wash was not her cup of tea. Daily rehash spoils one's taste, a change of food whets the appetite, was her motto. *But ... within wedlock,* she was ready to bridle her better half at once.

Just trotting a little further, an ultimate sprint up to their yard and then ... She was already looking forward to the finishing touch: a dive into the cool water ~ father Kneipp's shock therapy, and there she would emerge like a reborn Aphrodite from the brand-new swimming-pool.

"Hello, Katrien!" The shock that ripped through her, came from another source. Jesus, she sighed, as she noticed the couple sitting at the pool. Gustl and Uschi, their Bavarian neighbours! Completely forgotten, that appointment she had made the day before. When Dugal picked her up in Palmera, one moment it had flashed upon her: *hadn't we been invited at the Shaeffers'?* That was the transcription for that bucolic Germanic name. Shepherd, the oldest profession in the world, as to good old Gustl. Oh, and I thought that was … eh, thingumajig, Dugal would banter.

And now they showed up here in full outfit: the old-Marcaian costumes of the pauperized land gentry. Grey and silver, complete with pocket-watch, bib and sundries; exactly as they had welcomed them lately in their orange-orchard, over a delicious Rivaner.

"Another one from the Dux's cellar," der Gustl had laughed so hard that his long thin, white head of hair was shaking with it. Sixty-five at the most, they had taken him to be. Until he pushed off about his sports career, about the time that 'clown in Berlin' had forced them to hook it. So off to cuckoo-clock country and thus, definitively, to 'Duxland' here, for the gouty devil's sake. Notwithstanding, that deuced all-but-centenarian had juggled plenty of Slovenian airs out of his violin for quite an hour. Peerless, they thought, the way Herr Schaefer jumped up the steps to those mezzanine rooms, as if time had no grip on his slim body.

"Totally forgotten." Catarí exhausted herself in excuses, for she did like those spongers after all ~ stateless migrants like themselves. They turned down her apology, under the motto: "Nothing must but may be done on this island ~ save for this delicious liquor". Which their bungling hostess then hastened to come out with.

They had marched out for their quasi daily mountain walk, but were 'haphazardly' passing along, rather out of concern. And all of a sudden, there had been no spunk left in him. "Some pain here between my ribs," he showed, "and if I dare to complain a bit, Uschi says: Don't be so weak-kneed!"

Chin up! *Incredible,* Catarí nodded. Though his wife was a quarter of a century younger than he was.

"Was ich sagen wollte ~ those guests here some minutes ago …"

Her neighbour-woman noticed how perplexed señora Mikes was looking. "Sorry, we didn't want to be immodest, but … A little removal or so?"

"What, a removal! What guests …?"

"Yes, eh … Two men in a delivery van, didn't you see them?" the woman said taken aback.

"What! And you're telling me just now?" So badly the old couple had not seen Catarí beside herself. Head over heels she dashed off in the direction mister Schaefer pointed to. No, not the wardrobe, really, with Dugal's hobby-horse: the collection of canes? Presently, around the corner of the inner court, she saw enough. The door of the room was open. Swinging round, she stared down the cobble-stoned path: there she thought she had seen in a flash the open back-door of a delivery van. A small dust cloud confirmed her worst suspicions.

Panicky like a miser who fears to find an empty pot of gold, Catarí flew up the stairs, pulled the clearly opened panels wholly aside …

Phew, all was intact, no single specimen had disappeared!

But what have those chaps been fumbling after out here? By Jove, I've just foiled a palace revolution at the Mikeses', she stuck a feather in her own cap. She refused to imagine what scene her better half would have made if … What a mercy the Schaefer couple were there!

"I've got to thank … ~ Well, I never!"

Those birds were flown too. She still wanted to run after the aged couple, but there was no Gustl or Uschi within eyeshot.

One moment she still wavered whether she would or would not ring up Dugal. But it was just two o'clock and then he would make off helter-skelter from Prof. Marquez's headquarters. No, her whole day was gone to the dogs, God save the mark!

Still a bit off her stroke, she was wobbling in her wicker-chair, but her craving for a swim was spoiled. In a brooding mind she walked back to the house. *I'll just thank our neighbours later. Hmm, my reactive faculties aren't too bad, after all; and my acting skills for that Zorrita movie came pat to the purpose, you see.* She would still chuckle over Duke's exasperation, because they had not proposed him for a role next to her as the girl-with-the-mask. "Save me from that honour," he had sneered, "such soppy stuff!"

Hey, those cadgers won't have rummaged our …? A good deal less

89

self-assured, she was pacing up and down the rooms; soon, however, feeling relieved again, she went on nagging about 'the little shepherds from Freising'. *Strange, though, why had they run off so suddenly? But maybe they were just fed up with my lousy mood; well, eh, Dugal would have been peeved too, in my place, and as for such oldies, they are keen on their mental peace after all.*

Inhaling deeply she admired herself in the mirror of the antique Spanish lavabo and involuntarily she groped for a comb to check her refractory curls. It lay a bit further than usually, though, and as she looked around, she noticed there was an envelope under it. A pink one even. Ay, how strange, that was not yet there a moment ago, was it? 'Señor D.Mikes, proprietario de Ses Taca … ', she mumbled, and when taking out the letter, she inquisitively turned the Biedermeier thing around. 'From your devoted ducal guide … ' *Female guide*, she corrected, and instinctively she half-closed her eyes, like a mischievous slit-eyed cat. 'Guia', yeah yeah, Dukie, I know that, but not with me..

Although the level of Catarí's Spanish grammar was still rather elementary, her female pheromones had been stirred. What with 'guía', obviously one of those hermaphrodite forms, female as it may be at the rear and yet male, that 'dedicada' before it did not lie any more than the pink packing.

Her woman's intuition was at its sharpest, and when la Ionès smelled a rat, she was kittle-cattle. Had her husband seen her that very moment, it would not have been his happiest day! As cool as a cucumber she kept standing there for a while, staring into space, while under that handsome skull a clear scheme started growing. Honey-sweet, that's what she wanted to look like presently. But her pores were permeated by a chemical cocktail of adrenaline, *stirred up* by hatred and jealousy, and a series of other stuff that science was hardly aware of.

"Professor!" As if there were not a cloud in the sky, señorita Dolores turned to the doorway, where Roberto Marquez kept watching them morosely. "I was putting Mister Mikes a bit up to the ropes about the less known aspects of our L.S. studies. I have just advised him not to precipitate in that matter."

"I can imagine."

Astonishing, with what sang-froid this highbrow prick would stalemate the gents. Even that hard-boiled academician. *Let him just not think now that I'm going to act the injured innocent*, Dugal thought sulkily. *'This is not what you think, Roberto, I can explain it all.'* No, it was not in his nature to squirm for anybody. And least of all for a fellow whose hands were not clean either, for it was as plain as a pike-staff: the Chest did have a soft corner in his heart for his assistant.

"Please, join us, professor. Our guest proves to have some objections in store."

"Some specific objections," echoed Dugal.

"You don't say so. Objections, eh?" Roberto Marquez walked up to the table, with that same resolute stride of his that Dugal was used to. "Such as?"

"Esto, señor Marquez, this for instance." Dugal held out one of the scripts he had hastily snatched out of the collection. 'El Archidux y sus bastones.' That was the specimen which had pertly caught his eye just before Roberto's lightning visit. So off-hand, really, that, in recoiling, he all but bumped up to Dolores Francisquita's winsome bosom. 'The Duke and his canes', 'Des Herzogs Wanderstäbe', etc ... Why had they needs taken pains to subtitle it in six, seven languages?

"For that His full professorship surely has such another irrational explanation of his ... It's definitely the work of some unknown treasure-hunters, isn't it? Nice eh, to be left out of matters in that way." Meanwhile Dugal was sulkily shaking his head at the thought. Just as if he had got a punch on the nose from one of those ducal sticks. From the hands of his own fine amigo, by the way. Dolores had to quell her laugh, at that droll scene.

"Dugal, this has nothing to do with your find or your publications. This work is based on documents that had been in our possession long before you ..."

Still, Roberto's sparring-partner was not groggy on the whole. Trying to bring this pig-headed actor to his senses was like ploughing the sands; soapy words had the effect of a red rag to a bull with him. And bawling at him? That was as much as blowing the coals and quenching them at the same time.

"Gentlemen!!!" Señorita Dolores' scream appeased the two refractory bantam cocks at once. Ever since her career as a juvenile tennis champion she had used it particularly when it came to separating rutting admirers. Which she had galore.

"Please! You behave like two choristers at fisticuffs or even better: dogs fighting for a bone." *Myself figuring again as the bone and the Duque as an alibi,* she was thinking phlegmatically.

"Yes but …" Dugal started jibbing.

"There's no yes-but at all. Please, let's deal with this matter in an adult way, d'acuerdo? You want to feature as exponents of the strong sex, or don't you?"

Especially that tone of hers did the trick. Half scourging, half abating, a pitbull would have jumped upon her lap. How smoothly she was tacking all the time between the formal and more familiar modes of conversing, did not elude the prof's notice.

Roberto Marquez knew how that flashy hot stuff was now revelling in the effect of her act, the way she managed to break through the current social patterns. Though precisely that resilience of hers no man was equal to, would make it hard to find a Mister Right for her. One who, in diffident respect for her psyche, could value her female qualities, without lusting after her with his divining-rod, and would not cover her with a glass bell either: sois belle, tais-toi.

For a moment the reading-room looked like a chapel, and in that icy silence a girl student dropped in: "Disculpe, professor, a call for señor Mikes."

Like paralysed Dugal was standing transfixed for a few ticks. A phone call for him, in here? That could be no one else but Catarí. Wittingly he had left his mobile phone in the car, *please, no tosh during working-time.* In case of an emergency he had given her the fixed office number.

With an ice-cube in his stomach he followed the co-ed. *An assault, Catarina kidnapped … The cabinet with the canes!* A constriction struck his chest, and remorse, about leaving her all by herself; just as if he had been philandering with that swell babe here. "Catarí?"

Phew, it wasn't that bad, after all. "Darling," she said smoothly, as if it were just the soup that had boiled over. "Will you come home, please? We have just had some uninvited guests …"

16

Quizas es un habíl actór, she sniggled. *This Mikes is quite a specimen. Evidently, if you keep figuring at that firmament of stars, with such an irresistible Adonis image like his. Pero, què palurdo ~ what a noodle!*

In señorita Dolores' vernacular that concept rather sounded like a petname. To a lady of her stature for whom the adorers are queuing up like the rows of tourists at the porch of Palmera's cathedral, not exactly every sample of the male species proved to be a hunk. Only, if Dugal Mikes had crossed her path under another constellation ... Somehow she felt pity for him. The way his better half watched the least movement of her jackanapes'.

On the other hand, though, if she were in La Ionès stilettos herself, she would not leave him either under the spell of a Dolores Francisquita's charms for too long. With a pitiful shrug of her shoulders the academician returned to the room where, together with Dugal, she had peeked into the scripts. *Palurdo,* she repeated. Would don Lois R.M. have despised such a stroke of godsend as well? She could not help envisaging some scenes of jealousy between the Dux and his cara Catalí which one of their students was trying to reconstruct. Ouch, what soap-like situations! That's what they called literary-historic criticism. As if ever *the* ideal couple had really existed. Love without suspicion, that was like a batida without coco.

Blind confidence in one's partner ~ a naïve soul who walked into that trap, was a potential cuckold. By the way, the ampler the occasions were, the bigger the temptation for the thief. It was easy after all to spew criticism on the rich and the celebs when one was ugly and penurious oneself and so, never exposed to that kind of seductions. Hence probably her bias towards the Archidux, faithful himself beyond the grave, yet with an eye for all the prettiness (including the female) that the Creator had put into his playground. For what a mess all those philistines of fundamentalist puritans had made out of it! *With all respect for W.B.Yeats' infinitely true swans, but such a poet mourning over his great love, is a piteous wretch after all.* That brought a passage to Dolores' mind in which don Lois showed his self-pity about the revendication on the part of his fatherland, in his case: Bohemia. Which he hardly knew, by the way, but which at the time had been annexed to the Holy Roman Empire - *the* precursor of the European unification, wasn't it?- by way of 'mariages de raison'. Diligently she groped for that part, wondering if 'Duke' Mikes had run across that one yet ... Here:

> ... in that way also this country was 'incorporated ', peacefully annexed by another liaison like that, in the 16th century. Such another jewel in the Habiger crown. Wooded hilly land, parcelled by brooks and rivers such as the Moldava. Not too bad, but where my spirit cannot thrive; even in peace time namely I could not settle down there. I am an algarrobo: a carob tree that only takes a firm root in southern soil, and its dry fruit releases its flavour solely to those who know its secret depth. You, Catalí, understood the art of breaking that black bean-pod and pick out the hard kernels from it, more deftly than a pearl-fisher would with an oyster-shell. 'There it is,' and you put down a split carob husk on the stone table in front of me. A disarming gesture, free from any cringing subservience, which made my last bit of class consciousness vanish like snow in the sun. I saw myself, lying there on the table, my inmost soul exposed and as sound as those rock-hard kernels. Title, descent, fortune - all that fell away from me: worn-off togs, gnawed to shreds by the moths. There I was sitting before you like the poorest starveling, because I felt that what only counted to us, was our pure being, human to human, touched by that secret ectoplasm that connects the hearts, beyond words.
>
> Up to now, my dearest, that moment in the patio when our souls were intertwined, keeps vibrating in my veins. That is the only perk that ties me up with this existence.

Knowing that, across hundreds of miles, nothing can separate us in our minds ~ to bear, in every grasp of breath, your soul in mine, and thus foster the memory of Maremira, the olive-green bosom at which my heart will beat for ever, over there by the steely blue sea.

Followed then again an enumeration of allotments and Riesling and Rivaner vines bound to be planted. *Wonder how our Yankee boy may tooth that*, doña Dolores smiled up her sleeve. Diffidently she turned over the leaves, like someone unwilling to pry into a couple's bed-table. With what ease the Dux was able to switch from the most matter-of-fact subjects to the most lyrical ones again. Down to pure sob-stuff, la Francisquita sometimes thought.

> *How long I lingered, Cariña, to write you that first letter! For months on end since my arrival here, an exile in my own nation, I have been wavering, weaving desperate thoughts … Rereading, frittering and coining new ideas ~ always full of suspicion they could put the pieces together again. It was just autumn, you see, and the hearth should not burn yet. Thus I was sitting here, entangled in self-compassion: stepchild of an imperial crown, orphaned in powerless delusion. With my swollen limbs not even able any longer to pace to and fro in my own cage.*
>
> *Until I rediscovered the 'inward eye', as an English poet put it, focusing on an impression of the homeland of my choice, on that screen under my brainpan. And with that, the most painful but most beautiful love poem ever written, namely by Rainer Maria. No, not your humble servant, Cariña, but my partial namesake. I do not remember it verbatim, but I hope my echo of it will touch you after all:*

Put out my eyes and I shall watch you.
Plug up my ears and still I can hear you.
Without feet I can creep to your village,
without a tongue I call up your image.

Tear off my arms, so I shall raise
you with my heart.
Cut out my heart and my brains
will beat and set my brainpan ablaze,
so I shall hide you in my veins …

It sounds rather pathetic, but only now I understand that poet. Do you know what I did here the first days of my internment? Turning rounds, like a crippled tiger in a cage, but then around my arm-chair. Gone was my former craving for liberty; just one thing I wanted still, the impossible, like a little child ~ to be with you. Gradually however, it came home to me: a man does not die when he wants. I felt so sorry for your parrot, which had thrown off his feathers, after your demarche with me to the Viennese court. In my cage, however, I cannot even lay a violent hand upon myself, I am not granted the Socratic goblet. After all, they will not just throw a symbol of the Ancien Régime into the lion's den, whatever a nuisance you are to them. Suppose there comes another kind of order (though it is unlikely to be the pax animae, as we had hoped), nobody will then blame them for disposing of us. With a Pilate's gesture they can extradite us: here they are, that anachronistic bunch, do with them as you like!

Perhaps I had better have fled into anonymity with you, Cariña. But then, how? Our congenial spirits would have understood, most certainly, and invited us to a hospitable country, but do you believe we could lead those sleuths from Vienna up the garden-path for a long while? They connived at my wayward conduct, but everywhere their shadow followed our steps, itching to interfere.

But even so. Supposing I had chosen an equivalent haunt in the Mediterranean, I should never have forgiven myself for tearing you away from the place to which you were attached with your umbilical cord.

Besides, my spirit could not have pervaded a landscape thus with the same feelings a second time in my life. Since that day when I perched in Valle de Muša (however desolate, in the lashing rain), I had been feeling that telluric bond with that stretch of mountainous country. The drops dripping from the bending foliage, seemed to be tears for the tragic occurrences in the past. All surged up in me again, the motives for my restless roaming, and in the background the verbal cascade of my companions, señores Ripoll and Herreros, trying to cheer me up. And right at that deepest point of my life a beam of light broke through the grey sky. At one blow the dreary valley was transformed, as if by magic, into a symphony of colours. That was my way of experiencing the conversion of Saint Paul. Before my eyes the small town, a rather dismal sight still just a while ago, with pock-marked walls and weathered roofs, was blown open as a symbol of arch vitality. An ode to beauty. The ochre houses snuggled up to the little church, climbing towards the stern and yet merciful complex beyond: a row of pilgrims, meekly bowing their heads to the miracle.

"La Cartuja de Valle de Muša," scanned one of the two gentlemen, relieved that at a fillip of God's fingers the sun expelled the clouds from my mind. "The Carthusian monastery where the Polish composer stayed for some time." With that naïve peacockish pride they had already shown whilst guiding me along the cathedral, the Moresque palace, the Arabian baths and the innumerable patios in Palmera.

Amid that revealing scene the great stage-manager above us swept the broad light beam across the road, where on the curb a family were staring with awe at our coach. That singular moment, Catalí, when our eyes crossed, will remain engraved in my memory for ever. During the last part of the climb to the Cartuja, the image of that intrusive glance, above the modest garment, was fixed in my mind and inwardly I felt a vacuum in which all my feelings seemed to be swallowed up.

"Let's have a look if the landlord of the tavern can prepare a warm tumbet for us." Little could the hungry gentlemen suspect of what was going on in my soul. But by the time the good old man put a big bowl with sopa marcaín on our table, I had become so talkative that, baffled by that metamorphosis, they could not help wondering whether all this was due to that steaming blend of vegetables that, soaking in their juice, were poured over a few toasts.

"Running a bit ahead of the facts," señor Ripoll broached the purpose of their journey, "as far as the Maremira estate is concerned ..."

"Vendido," I said: "Sold!" My hosts all but tumbled from their chairs. But I hardly noticed their bewilderment.

Yes, I was sold, Cariña. Owing to what I held to be a supernatural intervention in my existence, my peevish mood had turned into utter blissfulness. With that simple peasant's meal I seemed to have concluded peace with this island and myself.

17

Never before had Dugal covered this stretch of route so fast, with such self-contempt. And yet it all advanced vexingly slowly to him! Damned traffic lights, darned bends, blasted snails! For his part this whole island, with its backward bumpkins and the whole caboodle, could go to blazes. Actually he was cursing himself, though. Somehow like a half-baked lover who decries his adored, knowing however that he himself is a pathetic sucker.

Once away from the gran cintura – the circular road that held Palmera's heart strangled in an ouroboros grasp – he felt the hyperventilation ebbing out of his body. He turned up the slip-road to Valle de Muša. In fact, a lorry was blocking the main route in the direction of the 'Tunél'. *Hey, if that isn't exactly the same blue car over there that was close upon our heels yesterday! Coincidence or not,* he thought, *you had better make the best of a bad bargain!*

Come on, you should not start seeing a terrorist at every corner of the street either. A smoke-bomb in the tunnel, a cypress toppling across the road just in front of your bumper … It mustn't become an obsession! *But what about that incident yesterday? Bah, after all, every day somewhere there is some boulder rolling down here.* And that telephone call then just a moment ago? How could such a stupid call rattle him that much! Catari's voice had sounded pretty docile, icily collected even. *After a burglary or assault, no way! No my dear, your old girl has pulled your leg and you have been bamboozled. Like a simpleton you got browbeaten at once, dashed to that parking-site, jumped into your car panting for breath, without considering for a moment whether you shouldn't call back. Yeah, why didn't she do that herself? A mere dodge, of course, to get you there, otherwise she could have sent you an SMS, couldn't she?*

Dugal was now driving nearly at a foot-pace, considering whether he should make a U-turn or not. He flatly refused to ring her up still now.

How exactly had she put it again? *Unwanted visit,* or something like that. *Hurry back straight away!* On the other hand, Catarí was not quite the cocooning type in the sense of: cage a hubby in your house and garden. But all the same, perhaps she had got sick of being tied up with a gadabout celebrity who settled her in his last-purchased estate. As a female dog watching over his abandoned yard. She could not poke about in Deió all day long, could she, nosing among some ceramics, antiques and trinkets? On the petit beau monde of that retro-artists' commune one had pored one's eyes out soon enough. And could you see her sipping café sombras there the whole afternoon in a bar or merendero over a volume of poems by Greeves-Ranke? Catarina Ionès, the other day still celeb n° 1, at whose feet producers and film-managers were melting away, and now withering in the shadow of a mountain village amidst a bunch of crackpots, world reformers and daydreamers? Out of the question!

In her place he would have done the same: playing pranks on that ego-tripper of a partner. *Well done from her part and I swallowed the bait just like that,* he grumbled. But suppose there really was something about it and those extorters, still unknown so far, wanted some real hubbub. Course they had seen him drive off and waited for the right moment to score a hit. But then they would not have failed to filch away Mrs. Mikes as well. Which they did not, obviously. Yet, at that re-emerging thought Dugal gave full throttle again. Better a living coward than a dead lion.

By the time he reached the foot of the mountains he was reshuffling the cards a bit. That there was something in the wind, was beyond dispute. At once however, Dugal tried to minimize things again: *probably such a dabbler of a freelance reporter again who, hoping it might be bingo at last, has been pottering about at Ses Taca. Got wind of those letras secretas published in the Diario and all the fuss about it.* With a few compromising pictures and false links the fellow might find a small corner left open in some tabloid. Maybe even retail an article to a canny media magnate who could see some hot stuff in it after all. In his imagination such an arsehole surely dreamt of ever making it to the front page of the Sun or Bild. A photo report in the local Hola sometimes proved to yield some ten thousand europesas, one should not underrate those women's magazines. Fodder for chatterboxes and gossip mongers, yes sir. But that's what the world was turning on, wasn't it?

Oh dear, probably it's just such another misfit, unpalatable even for the amorphous populace whom they serve up the greatest pulp. The theme 'Mikes and libel' has been flogged to death that far that John Citizen is fed up with it. Besides, what photo material is still worth faking? Dugal put his tongue in his cheek, but at the same time he was aware of it: *you never can tell, with that ragtag.* Not that his lovey-dovey at home would be parading along the swimming-pool in mono- or nokini. And the postman in Deió was rather potty about a smooth bottleneck than about the loveliest lady's leg. *By the way, the first competitor-lady-killer who manages to pinch la Ionès away from me, isn't born yet,* he said aloud.

In a jiffy his car had torn through Valle de Muša. The mini town seemed to press itself against the mountain side, as if it had seen that crazy desperado approaching from a distance. The row of fiery-pink oleanders curled up their petals against the wreath of smoke and dust that Dugal left behind. In his rear-view mirror he noticed how a curious tattler's wide skirt was flying over her head.

Behind the last curve his heart started beating faster. *Badly enough, not for Catari's irresistible charms this time,* he puffed. What a relief it was again when he saw her standing there, on the driveway! Not quite upset at all, though, on the contrary: leaning against the pillar of the portico, she was waiting for him there, without a trace of emotion.

Also when he swung the car door open, shouting "Catarí, everything all right, what happened?", she kept staring at him stiffly, without uttering a word. The femme fatale, pur sang, couldn't have been cooler: Eris, the avenging goddess, the way she produced her most amiable smile, and he felt all life draining out of his body. "They did not do ~ didn't ill-treat you, I hope?"

She spun round on her heels, elegantly, and lured him in, ogling. If a woman of that calibre ushered you in, you knew what you were up to. Even a praying mantis being swallowed by his mating wifey seemed enviable compared to this Dugal Mikes. And the most embarrassing thing was that he was sure there would be the devil to pay. But not how or why.

"Catarí, my angel, what's the matter? Please, tell me." Any moment now the bomb could explode: the first jar she could get at, a vase inclusive the arum-lilies, a brand-new ashtray … Hitting his forehead, a shoulder; with a bit of luck skimming an ear, like last time, when she had grabbed a paperknife from his desk. All that she got into her hands, formed a deadly threat. In the least bad case she would use her knuckles, her neatly manicured nails. A silent witness of that: the scar above his eyebrow, from the penultimate time.

Dugal's eyes followed her right hand, how it glided over a magnificent Ainsley plate ~ oh no, one more second and the fine porcelain would fly against the wall, in smithereens. Or come into violent contact with his chin, umbilicus or other vital parts. While his face was still pulling a painful grimace, she took up a paper from the sideboard, saying very softly: "This."

No raging and raving, no ineluctable explosion. Why, Duke, why? Her eyes, so sorrowful suddenly, spoke volumes.

"How? What?" he jabbered, totally disconcerted as he saw a tear rolling down along her nose. *A terribly attractive nose,* he now realized, *for which Caesar or Charlemagne would have given up their whole empire.* Shocking. "A letter," she said, "by your sweetie."

Oh *no, not this time again. Say that it isn't the same old song once more!* The umpty-umpth attempt to taint their relation. Always was there going to loom up some miscreant wanting to intimidate or blackmail them, to arouse jealousy.

"Jesus, Cariña, we're not going to sing that old song, are we? How often have we gone through that scenario!" It was all very well for him to laugh it off like that now, the past year only she had flown at him for having three supposed bits on the side. One with the (frigid) wife of his business consultant; then his philandering with a lady-choreographer (lesbian, but all the same, a rejected dancing-girl had made her a target, and Dugal was the dupe); and last but not least, that flirtation with a chambermaid in London. As for the latter, there was something to it. That jolly nifty chick had been hired to perform a nice bowing act over the tub in the bathroom where Dugal was about to have a pee. Without her noticing, so to say, and he surely had not. Upon rotating brusquely, he had, hand at his zipper, stroked her just along her slack. A set-up of course, but just try to prove it. Fortunately the charlady had broken down, as it turned out that she had just 'borrowed' Catarí's suspenders and co. to add to her charms.

Nevertheless, it would take weeks until Cathy's suspicion was thawing.

"Come on, Catarí! With what hot-baked nymphomaniac do you think I have swept the couch again?"

"Here." Her veiled fumato made him mellow. Against an unchained fury you could brace yourself. But tears ... Even for crocodile tears Dugal would buckle under. Sceptically he turned the pink letter around:

> Querido amigo,
> Thank you for the wonderful moments we have shared so far. Remarkable, is it not, how our passion for don Lois has brought both of us closer together.
> Naturally, those scarce hours, the two of us together in the themes cabinet, hardly suffice to complete this experience ...
> Where shall we see each other, and when ...?

Incredible. He had just seen that woman for the first time today and this was already a lyrical effusion from her hand that left little to the imagination. And there it stood out in black and white: Su doña Dolores Francisquita.

"I can't believe my eyes," he mumbled.

"Neither can I," echoed Catarí.

"How impudent! And so naïve it just seems to come straight from the simpletons' club. And what a nerve to use such underhand tricks! Simply preposterous."

"I agree." She did not move a muscle. And though Dugal had saved his skin so far, he was not altogether out of range yet.

Acting the unimpeachable seminarian now might have a reverse effect. Stubbornly denying was no good, neither was swearing black and blue that this was a put-up job. The more he ranted like a devil in a holy-water font, the more she clammed up.

Until he caught sight of the envelope. Impossible, when was it postmarked? All of a sudden his destiny seemed to cant. "Look, it was marked yesterday!"

"So what?" she raised her eyebrows relentlessly.

"Don't you see what that means? Cara mía!" It meant it was all a set-up, undoubtedly. That courting letter was totally fake. Not even handwritten or personally signed for that matter. "Who types such a dating dodge so as to print it down on pink paper afterwards?"

Without her batting an eyelid, Catarí's sphinx-like glance kept fixating him. "Look," he threw his last trump on the table. "I'm looking," she said.

"I didn't know that creature until today. She is Roberto's assistant, ring him up, please. She happens to be THE pre-eminent Archidux expert. And admittedly, she is a bloodcurdling good-looker. If one hasn't seen you yet. But she isn't a randy play-kitten, no more than you are. Truly, Cariña, not for all the world would I dream of …

"I know," she said without turning a hair.

"You mean ~ how do you know …?"

"I have checked her. Double-checked. And I contacted professor Marquez."

She could not help laughing at him gawking open-mouthed.

"Well, where is now señor Mikès with his axiom for dumb chicks: sois belle, tais-toi?"

Every day she kept amazing him how many grey cells there must be hidden under that pretty scalp of hers. Obviously, she had called in all her channels ('telltales', she meant?) and till further notice she had to grant him the advantage of doubt. Conditionally though, she warned him: "I still want to see the test confirmed."

"?"

"A check-up of that potentiometer of yours tonight. And come along now, next door. I'll show you something."

18

As a matter of fact, the preceding hours la Ionès had not been idle at all. No sooner had her Duke rushed out of the big hall of Palmera's Alma Mater than the phone set at the office of Roberto Marquez was ringing once more.

"Hello, professor, Dugal's wife speaking. Have you got a moment for me?"

The Chest stood rooted to the spot. He had met Mrs Mikes only once in person. Enough though to feel again that shudder running down his spine. As her voice was sounding through the line, he changed at once into a stray iceberg melting at the vision of Copenhagen's little mermaid.

Whether he could pass on a few data to her concerning a doña Dolores Francisquita? The ace of Palmera's Faculty of Arts felt how the wind was blowing. With a short cough he began undressing his favourite assistant in a non-committal way: "Born and bred Palmerian, thirty-six, living at …"

"I know" she cut him off. "But I mean: as a person?"

She already knew? the professor mumbled, taken aback. Surely not via the faculty's intranet-site itself? "But, madam, how have you …?"

Resignedly Catarina explained to him, like to a child, how, as a seasoned actress, you contrive something like that. "You ring up the co-ordinator of your databank: 'Ah, is that the brand-new lecturer of historic criticism speaking?' 'Indeed, eh … how do you actually form your codename to get access to …? Oh, thank you, sir, that would be nice of you.' And the charmed chico harmlessly blabs out the secret house-key that enables you to open another person's sample-card."

Dol.franc./doc., in the correct frame, and at the first click doña Dolores had already appeared full length on the screen before her. In all weights and measures *and* with a whole batch of pictures.

"Nice folks around you, professor. But how close is her co-operation with my husband?"

Turning red like a lobster, the figurehead of the Marcaian intelligentsia defended his apprentice through thick and thin. "What, señora, a posted letter from her, at your house, so fast? *Imposíble!* I introduced the two to each other just this very morning, and you know how the post operates round about here ~ lentamente, lentamente."

Roberto argued what an impeccable, unimpeachable young lady his assistant was. "Oh no, madam, least of all a devious man-chaser full of whims. She is no match for señor Mikes, to be sure. By the way, he is not her type, and conversely she isn't his either. I … I'm speaking from my own experience."

"?" The dismayed professor had the feeling la Ionès could see him as it were through the apparatus. When a man of his standard exposed himself like that, in the nuddy, she could believe him. Reluctantly he called for the haunted assistant.

Anxiously he observed his Dolores, how she was answering the diva on the other side quietly, with raised eyebrows. *What a pity*, prof. Marquez thought, *don Lois knew neither of those two gorgeous specimens of the female species.* That, he pondered, was something he had in common with the Archidux: unfeigned admiration for all that the Creation procured. And there, surely, classy ladies featured in the front row, beside the most precious gems or butterflies in a collection. Who had, on any travels whatsoever, ever enjoyed that pleasure, like Dugal and he himself?

"Delighted to make acquaintance with you," he heard Dolores converse in nearly flawless English. Her imperturbability ~ such another property for which he envied her. Or could he notice a teeny-weeny aggravation in her attitude? "Perdón, señora ~ me having a crush on your husband? With all my respect, but I don't just fall for anyone I have just met for an hour, and least of all one with a wedding-ring around his finger."

Isn't she a specimen! reflected the academic pin-up herself while she heard la Ionès setting out her pawns on the chessboard … By and by, however, she began to appreciate the doggedness of her alleged rival. Somehow she could even feel some comprehension for the sneaky detours with which she managed to break through their privacy.

"Si si, I understand your concern and your cunning. And, ma'am, I hope to meet you once personally …"

Dolores Francisquita was staring at the Prof, wide-eyed as though she were standing face to face with a jaguar. *She looks like one herself too,* Roberto chuckled. *And I shouldn't like such one to jump on me. Although …*

"Wow, that Ionès doesn't sound like a meek lamb either."

"Either?" he said laconically. She didn't seem to hear him, though.

"What pluck, to hack our system like that! I'm afraid we'll have to guard ourselves a bit, professor, against some more of those cyber capers."

"I was not aware my wifey was such an adroit boffin." With increasing amazement Dugal was gaping at the results of Catarí's research-work. Leaning with one elbow on her shoulder, he scrolled down the personal particulars she had raked up on his laptop.

… Sección historica … nacional … Bailares … fichero de empleados …

Yeah, sure enough, there they turned up already, under prof. Marquez' name, in neat alphabetical order: his nearest co-workers. "Hello, his Lordship does know how to delegate things! But where is she ‑ Dol dot Franci …?"

"Well well, so blinded by the exterior!" Without turning a hair Catarí ticked off the fourth name: F.D. do Mar, and after a double click the data sheet of doña Dolores flashed on, complete with some very flattering photos.

"Yes, yes," Dugal whistled softly between his teeth: "Let's admit, for a promoter of the recruitment campaign for the Universidad Palmeriana, that means something, doesn't it?"

"O.K., but let your brains get to work a moment now instead of your hormonal stock." Catarí's finger went down all the possible details that threw doña Dolores F.'s professional and other qualities into sharp relief.

"This looks like a promotion-clip of a film producer to praise his latest movie to the skies." Duke was still enchanted; so: *as blind as a bat,* Catarina smiled scornfully, and she ticked with her nails on the place to be.

'… *F.D. do Mar … born in Palmera … spent a great part of her youth in Valle de Muša, where she also attended primary school for four years …*'

"Marvellous research work, Miss Marple," Dugal sneered, "but I assume a good deal of those niñas went to such a school somewhere over here."

"Most likely, and she exactly there, eh! Just wait, the best is still to come."

> '... *from landed gentry ... daughter of Pablo do Mar and Inès Shaeffer ...*
>
>   *when little Dolores' parents moved for the sake of their big furniture business, Muebles do Mar, which they wanted to expand ... with new outlet stores in town ...* '"

"With all my respect, Cariña, but this tedious story must have been dished up by a lady. Just reads like some sob-stuff for a women's magazine." In her pitying glance, though, he recognized her somewhat poor opinion of the strong sex. What had his she-wolf in sheep's clothing figured out? Go on, she showed condescendingly.

> '... *studied natural sciences, but very soon her passion for history became apparent, particularly of her own home-country ... Graduated, with the highest distinction, with a thesis about the genealogy of Marcaio's noble families and their crossbreeding with Moorish landowners ... soon acquired a doctor's degree with an ample study about 'L.S. Archidux, his role in Marcaio and his secret political vocation at the turn of the century.' She ~ ...*"

The whiny funereal voice in which Dugal had rattled off the text, broke down. "Political vocation? Fiddlesticks! What an academic twaddle that creature throws up. Don Lois was no more interested in politics than my aunt's dog. He, with his dislike of etiquette and protocol ... What?"

Catarí's smart-alecky air one uses to look at a choirboy, began to peeve him more and more. "Look, Cathy," he said at such moments, "I've been fiddling about in the chap's life for days on end, in those musty reading-rooms, like ..."

"Like a mole burrowing in his back garden to spy at him in secret?"

"Yes," he sighed. "Sorry for that, but I'm fed up with it, and I promise you solemnly ~ …" Her ironic smile would do to give every man a skid. "That's why I know, from all my sources, that the man was all but a world reformer or proselyte. Don Lois must simply, simply …" He gesticulated with the excitement of a peripatetic thinker who cannot get out of his own theories: " …have been an honest realist. Like myself, indeed. One who loathed all conventions and prejudices …, who saw people with their little shortcomings, beyond rank and class. Somewhat of a Nazarene."

"Aha. So, Dugal Mikes too appears to have some messianic traits himself?"

"How funny! I just mean: all the humbug of that 'scientific research', over there, in Roberto's headquarters. You should see that: 'L.S., the scientist, L.S. the polyglot, the liberator, the quitter, the … the freemason.' Presently they'll make him a half-baked Castro or Godfrey of Bouillon. As they made the living 'son of David' a supernatural saviour who, rather than brushing off the Roman occupant, was to wipe out all their cruel sins with his death. No my dear, that dynastic enfant terrible was by no means a saint. He only tried to find himself."

Catarí was clapping her hands. "You know, you look like a whizz kid when orating that way. But I see, after a thousand and one pages you don't catch any more *what* you're reading. Look what's written there."

They have eyes but do not see. Yes, yes, he knew, but he had never held with biblical fables. With a few Presbyterians in your family and hardcore preachers, all on mother's side, you've got the hang of it. Preaching nitpickers, one by one, who used to rant and rave at each other, bible in hand. *No, then I feel more akin to a half-heathen like don Lois,* he sighed, *even if he was not quite a champion of monogamy and petty-bourgeois prudery.*

"Yeah, and? What does miss telepathist see what I don't ~ …"

With a shock he started up, shaking his head. *And then the scales fell from their eyes, Acts of the Apostles 9:18.* Such another passage that was engraved in his mind. Now finally there was a haze sliding before his eyes.

"Well, darling, have you got it? At last!"

"Do you think what I'm thinking …?" Dugal mumbled, whilst he kept staring at that screen, as if he had just read an apocryphal gospel overwritten by a canonical version. *How dumb, that I haven't caught that at once! But … aren't we seeing ghosts?* Originating from Valle de Muša …

moved because of a furniture business … scientific studies and then suddenly her interest in genealogy and the local gentry … her passion for all that had anything to do with the Archidux … What, a minute ago, he had taken for endless drivel, gradually began to reveal a certain coherence, and if you could puzzle together piece by piece … The picture of 'doctor Dolores' was taking shape again before his eyes, as she conducted Prof. Marquez' study centre over there: his right hand or who knows even …? *The old lecher ~ would he combine business with pleasure*? "I already thought it was suspect, how those two …"

However, he did not get any further with such assumptions, for Catarina repudiated them as typical macho reasoning. "But that name!"

"F.D. do Mar? Downright Marcaian, isn't it? Damn it!"

"What?" Upon him saying it, Catarí seemed to guess his line of thought. Those Moorish connections ~ if you wrote it in a different way, you got: "One with a Moorish streak?"

"Of course: d'Omar! When she gave me her visiting card, I didn't give it a moment's thought, how stupid of me!" Same as he was unaware now of what his Cathy might think of that little card. Strange enough, it made her suspicion rather fade. "Or aren't we ferreting a bit too much for hidden meanings?"

"No … no, no, by Jove!" she said. What a pleasant surprise, to hear that her better half's acumen proved to be well-nigh unaffected despite all those temptations and Aphrodisiac charms. "I had twigged something that evidently escaped from your attention ~ the mother's name: Shaeffer."

Inès Shaeffer. Dugal scrolled a bit back with the mouse. *Nice Latin-American combination. Yeah, with us you get across such daft things too.* And then there was the writer's name, Peter Shaeffer..

"Dukie, I know that your Germanic roots are short, but try to spell it also like this: S,c,h, ä,f, e,r … What does that say to you?"

"Not the …? No, not the Schäfer ones! How are you going to link up those two old-timers with that?" Judging from her shrewd wink, he saw she meant it.

"I've got my channels, y' know." *Your eavesdroppers. Where else have I heard that?* Dugal wondered. "And if I tell you that those two witnessed that attempt to murder just a while ago …"

The house-breaking! Drat, he'd totally forgotten. And mind it, just after that, this letter had turned up … The power of an invisible magnet attracted Dugal, carried him across the patio, heading for the vestibule. With Catarí close upon his heels. He ran straight through the flowerbed, without chopping off any specimen. Jumped up the small stairs, pulled open the cupboard … Untouched, one, three, … six … ten!"

"Oh dear," Catarina was still panting, "already suffering from Alzheimer, sweetheart, or did you expect those guys to return so soon?"

19

There they were, archly flaunting in the regal mahogany closet: the bastónes del Archidux. "Extra polished by the Dama de la Casa," said Catarina, still a bit wheezy. Touching, the way he took one out of the row, almost fondling it, and carefully unscrewed the clutch with the flask. *EMPTY!*

One moment Catarí feared he would get petrified, like Orpheus, in the act of watching. "No panic, Dukie! The scrolls are hidden safe and sound. Ay, your wifey has got something more in store than a couple of boobs and buttocks, y' know."

Dugal did not seem to hear her and began fumbling hysterically at the shelves. "Du-uke!" she shook him at his shoulder to bring him back to his senses. "Follow me!"

A moment later he went up the attic stairs, after her: a docile poodle. *Great ~ what has my dear fairy conjured up here*! Gawking open-mouthed, he stepped along the trapdoor, all admiration for the metamorphosis his Cathy had brought about there, under the old rafters. A cosy reading nook, fitted out with rocking-chair, sitting areas and built-in shelves. Not just crammed with books, no; but delicately decorated with all kinds of Marcaian artefacts she had nabbed at some of the junk markets that she used to scour. Amongst others, a bust of don Lois, he noticed.

"As you can see, I haven't been idling during your escapades," she said, proud as a peacock. "Toodelidoo: premiere!" She pulled open an old closet.

No, don't say it's true! Again his heart seemed to falter. "Oh yes, it is," she nodded. "Perfect copies of those downstairs. Discovered here, while Cinderella was removing cobwebs, woodworm and Sleeping Beauty's rags."

Dugal could still recall the dusty attic as he had seen it once before: Velasquez' picture of Arachne at the spinning-wheel. "But what about the texts then?" He could not bear it any longer, watching Catarí with the impatience of a kidnapped baby's parent. Plop! sounded the clutch of the walking-cane that Catarí swiftly grabbed out of the row. With her dexterous forefinger she picked the letter roll out of it. "Numero cinco, por favor," she handed it to him.

The fifth one. Why not the fourth? Dugal seemed to wonder a bit awkwardly. "Cause this dumb non-blonde has skimmed through all of them already," she said as if by telepathic inkling, "and finally, this was something different from all that ingratiating and peevish self-pity that you've put into your Archidux column of the Diario so far."

"Oh, oh, mind it, you don't seem to have any notion of the poetic value attributed to such a soap story? Critics even make mention of unsuspected depth, even at the time of don Lois' half namesake: Rilke. Whereas his writings known up to the present, were rather held to be old-fogeyish."

"Rainer Maria …" Catarina spelled out dreamily. "The favourite poet of a prof of mine. Hmm, didn't know an iota of German. Would both those Ranieris have got into contact with each other? How coincidental it all seems today!"

You know more about it, sweetie, Dugal thought. And there it flashed through his mind again. *How queer, today I come across some duplicates of the old chap himself, and a complete study file plus ditto team, utterly under the spell of his venerable person, and then my better half proves to have swapped the letras secretas behind my back, just like that, nota bene in authentic clones of his walking-canes.* "And that very afternoon a couple of phoney burglars come and perform their act here, a pink dating-card falls out of heaven, right in our parlour, and ~ …"

"And our Teutonic neighbours are acting like peeping Tom. Besides, your Miss do Mar did know about those 'bastones'. So, is that scientific integrity so impeccable after all?"

"There we go again," Dugal sighed. "Conspiracy theories to spare. But suppose doña Dolores is a far relative, so what?"

"So, you trust that Chest without any reserve! But those two are hand in glove, aren't they, Duke? Why are they treating you as their buddy, fancy?"

Wild conjectures. By the way, can you really trust your own wife in the end? No, he thought, *before long we are both of us going nuts.*

"Meanwhile I've figured out my own 'cat peeps out' scenario."

"Oh yeah, and who'll get the honour of playing that part – not I myself?" She was watching him with those challenging eyes which had helped her to walk away with the main character in the first picture under Dugal's direction. Including himself on top of it.

"A columnist and/or photographer of a gossip paper who hopes to rake in the jackpot of his life. Quite possible, no? If he turns up with a juicy story about archducal dram sticks containing, so to say, mysterious letters smuggled to don Lois' decried lovey. A Maria Magdalen story, you can always cash in on that. And then declare it to be crap. Savvy?"

'The Mikes propping themselves up by the scrolls of Deió.' He already imagined seeing it on the front-pages. "If such a nosey parker merely suggests we want to force up the market value of those yellowed sheets and then barter them at an exorbitant price."

Catarí sceptically pursed her lips: "And then run the risk of a trial because of defamation, for they are no match at all for our lawyer? Forgery, not too bad as an accusation."

"Such trash papers readily take that for granted. If they just can hit the headlines with it for one week. You know how those guys tackle it. We, reviled for shameless mystification, desecration at the expense of a side-tracked peer … That will undoubtedly be whipped up for a few weeks by the yellow press … A horde of second-rate paparazzi jump upon it and with a stroke of luck some slyboots manages to pass the rights on to the American tabloids. There the thing will be smeared out for weeks on end, and thus it may grow into a real hype. You do realize that, don't you?" he tried to lend force to his plea by gesticulating. "If such a lout scores a direct hit in that way, maybe it will become a stepping stone for an overseas career. See the picture?"

"And you believe the general public is still going to put up with that?"

"Cariña, selling air, that's the caper, nobody cares about the truth. Just look at the success of all those Holy Blood thrillers and conspiracy mysteries!"

"Yeah, that's one line of thought," Catarina admitted reluctantly, "but I'm afraid, my dear, there is a little too much scent of a detective plot about it. By the way, where does the woman fit into the picture?"

He knew what she was hinting at. There needs had to be a female firebrand, a femme fatale as the pivot, like in his most famous movies. The

Helen, Electra or Cleopatra, ready to waylay and incite the harmless gents. "You see in what an antifeminist way you, women, reason yourselves! Why should doña Dolores be part of the scheme? And, as a matter of fact, who says there is a link between 'do Mar' and 'd'Omar' anyway?"

"Your Dad even had his name anglicised. And this one is so self-evident after all. But alright, it may as well be any other lady bounty-hunter. Maybe, there still is some role in store for me there ~ although …" (Catarí turned to look once more at the photos on the screen), "that academic stunner wouldn't be unfitting either in a film plot under your direction."

Dugal shook his head compassionately. But just then he realized how she was laughing up her sleeve. "You see," she chuckled, "my world star, my surrogate president is getting a co-actor in mind and already he's off his head."

From behind his back she produced the roll of sheets Dugal had left on the table. "I had thought you might be more interested in this."

"Ah yes, numero cinco. What then is so special about it compared to the previous letters?" She only granted him a shrug of the shoulders after that. *How short-sighted men can be!* Her significant laugh spoke volumes, though: *much reading fun, Dukie!*

As he unrolled the yellowed sheets of paper and settled himself in the rocking-chair, Roberto's reading chamber came across his mind again, with the whole bunch of essays displayed on long tables. Where was the connection? Damn it, she made him really curious. *What's she got after, my smart wifey, that has been dug up and unravelled by Professor Marquez' secret general Dux staff long before now?*

Could this part confirm what he had resolutely rejected just a little before: aspects of the old lord that one would tend to send off to the realm of academic phantasmagoria? And then, to think Roberto had been pulling him a leg all the time! He was still hopping mad when recalling how that whole lot of graduates were swooping down on the subject like hyenas. Dugal would readily have liked to pass off their theories as wild speculations ~ wishful thinking of juvenile word-splitters trying to force at least some breakthrough towards a pitiable career at the bosom of the Great Wise Mother. In fact, what difference was there with all those media-loving paparazzi who would relentlessly drag a man's good name through the mire? They too only wanted to blow up things a bit so as to boost their own name.

Reluctantly he set to reading:

Dearest Catalí,

At last I have got a sign! I cannot tell you how delighted I am. Perhaps this is the most wonderful moment in my life. As long as a human being, in all freedom, sees the good things on earth coming up to him, he takes them for granted. As a matter of fact, he deems himself the centre of the universe. Not until he is thrown back, however, upon his own futility ~ and the anima mundi is cut off from him ~ will he realize the value of the small terrestrial things.

As soon as I knew that all my writings here, from this small chamber, where I am granted the illusion of liberty, were not scattered in the wind (or, after being read by some ignoble scapegrace, end up in the fireplace), hope has flared up in me again. Not that we are likely to see each other again. There is little chance of that, you will realize. But to know that we can at least share these thoughts again ...! Is that not the bliss of blind people who once were able to see, and now can recall each other by means of their voice? Now that I am certain these words are not peeped at through a magnifying glass and not passed on to higher instances either, I am breathing more freely again. My chamberlain has reassured me: there are no imperial inspectors on our track ('sleuths', as my faithful Mathias calls them). Not even any customs officers who might intercept our exchanges of views. Henceforth, it will be just as if we can talk from face to face. Freely.

What a privilege, you will say again, and that is right. At a time when the whole mainland is bent under the insanity of suspicions and imputations, the relations between humans of different origin are shrivelling under the pressure of narrow-minded executioners of orders. Each word of humanity and charity may be interpreted in a wrong sense and used against yourself. Our state-leaders now think along the lines of self-conceit and petty 'national interest'. That is, against the interest of their own citizens at a long term.

This situation is totally contrary to my viewpoints, you know that, Cariña. It runs absolutely counter to the realm of thought of all our European cultures and great thinkers. But in that darkness you remain my sole point of light. The straw I am clutching at, in order to conserve our threatened values for posterity.

Where you are living now, you are safe. Do not go to Ses Taca with these notices, until the tide has changed. Probably I shall not live up to that day, but I pray that once our realm may come. Mathias the chamberlain is in direct contact with our couriers. Some of them you know. Really, you can build a cathedral on them. And even though I know how suspicious you are, after all those double check tests you had to endure so as to efface yourself, I tell you I trust those men more than my own self. They too have been double tested. They literally live on a knife-edge: no fire or dagger or any kind of torture whatsoever will get them to say one word too many. They have been trained to destroy any document, even at the most dicey moments. So we need not convert each phrase into coded images over and over again. Believe me, Catalí, our guides are devoted to our cause heart and soul and they know the smuggling route of the Vine thoroughly.

Therefore I can, with a clear conscience, transmit henceforward all our consignments and deliveries to you, without having to rely on other channels. The kind and origin of the specimens can be frankly notified. Do not worry, you will be no longer in a state of uncertainty about what creatures are dwelling in your backyard. As a matter of fact, these carrier pigeons no longer run the risk of being intercepted or shot down and being diddled out of their message. So, as this is settled, let me announce you at once the next collection: a few days after receiving this notice, you will receive eight more Rieslings; five Müller-Thurgaus; ten or eleven Gewürztraminers.

In the mean time you know: such specimens, tender greenhouse plants as they are, should not be transplanted just like that. On the road for days, suitably packed, deprived of the healthy open air ... They remind me of Egyptologists who have just come out of their musty study-rooms and bang, they are dumped into the blazing tropical sun. In other words, treat them gently, as they will be quite in need of assuaging and refreshing after such a long passage. And please, grant them some extras, the way you would take care of an exhausted, shabby traveller's appearance: having them trimmed and polished, fitting them out in a new jacket.

But I need not bother about that. I am sure they will be in good hands with you, the former landlady of Ses Taca. You know the tricks of the trade, do you not, like the best innkeeper. I had the same feeling with you myself: feeling secure, 'gut aufgehoben'. Besides, about wine and its treatment I cannot teach you anything any longer, familiar as you are with its whole genealogy ...

The letters of the last part began dancing before Dugal's eyes. Dazedly he lowered the epistle in his hands. If this was what he thought it was ... *This can't be true. Either I'm getting totally senile or I can't read any longer. Or ...*

20

From behind the door curtain Catarí had been watching him for quite a while, amused and at the same time anxious about his reaction. Stirring the fresh glass of naranja with a turn of her wrist, she made a wager with herself: *I'll bet you anything he is mad at himself. That he didn't grasp it any faster! And that humble spouse of his, as a matter of fact, did. Unforgivable! For women aren't any better than Christmas trees, only interested in what you can hang on them. Presently he is going to freak out and dash straight to his small car, destination Roberto Marquez. That underhand bastard, to leave him under such a delusion!*

All the time he had let him, Dugal Mikes, a celebrated actor, show off with don Lois's spiritual children ~ let him publish them openly, without first informing him thoroughly about it. Just vague warnings, yeah. But with no word whatsoever had Roberto mentioned this sort of connections. What a shame!

Maybe, though, he would change his mind in time and fly out against her, Catarina, to vent his fury a bit. And as usual, she was going to turn up her nose at it phlegmatically, and afterwards give him a good scolding. *That's what comes from running after your tail, Dukie. You've tried to impose on everybody and his dog with a great act. Under the calculation this might be a jump to a gigantic production of your own, sponsored by a few film magnates who always turn sensation to good account. A calculated risk, it's true, but in your wild zeal you have skipped a few steps again. Boys will be boys.*

To her astonishment, however, Dugal turned around quite composedly, walking to the open window, like in dream. Just a broken-winged Hamlet who mourns like a zombie over the ghost of his father. *Kids remain kids, damn it, my prediction won't hold,* thought Catarí. So the contents of the epistle had hit him worse than she had expected.

Suddenly he ran up to the other side of the room, got a gun from a drawer and said, without turning a hair: "See you tonight, darling."

Decisively, Catarí posted herself between him and the door. "What do you think you're doing, are you going mad ?"

With a lifeless glance he looked quite through her, but he would not get off so cheaply. "I'm going to catch Roberto and that nice piece of crumpet, you know, that assistant of his, in the act ..." ~ he grinned because of Catarí's bewildered eyes ~ and, no, not do them in, don't be afraid. I'm not going to play the hero, that pistol is just for the show. But in case of emergency ... You never can tell who those blokes are. Stop looking so glum, Cariña, all joking apart."

"I'm going with you," she reacted on first impulse. But Dugal seized her by the wrist, attempting to appease her. "No, you stay here, or do you want them to turn all our goods and chattels upside down ?"

Oh, really, and so they could molest or kidnap her just like that, so much he cared about his wife-as-a-status-symbol ?

Catarí noticed how he wavered for a moment. Whether he had read it all to the end? If he reacted like that, on the spur of a moment, he risked to make himself desperately ridiculous. OK, prof. Marquez could have initiated him more profoundly, as well as that gorgeous stunner ~ eh, Miss Dolores. "But would you have given them the chance to do so, Dugal ? No."

Bull's eye! His grouchy silence betrayed he was backing down. Catarí let him read on sulkily and withdrew in the kitchen among the ingredients for his favourite tapas. Not until he had found his feet again between basil, olives and artichokes, would he leave the Dux and his Catalí to their inner peace. *Or quite the reverse?* she sighed. *At which passage would he have switched in again now?* She could easily fancy.

Meanwhile I have learnt from my chamberlain that you try to take up again the thread with the past in a lighter mood. What a relief this is to me, Cariña! The way Mathias conveyed that joyful message to me, it was like hearing your own words, your own voice. Now you know : you could easily report your reflections yourself to me; yet, if it still seems safer to go on corresponding in this way ... Fine with me, it remains a double security. Notwithstanding, it is a load off my mind that you need not hide any longer from pillar to post, but that you have found a fixed abode at Keppler's. In a fine scenery, by the way. I myself cherish some good memories about that spot. Unequalled, that view of the small church, standing out against that wealth of wild flowers, yellow and white, at Easter. An undulating carpet that crawls up towards that fistful of houses - silent apostles, joining in devotion around their venerated master.

You are well-accomodated over there, Catalí, and secure. Besides, from that epicentre you have a good lookout on the falling stars. Owing to competent counselling you will be able to apply our planting advice easily. Each supply will be accompanied by the necessary instructions. Even if you can rely on your experience yourself, we had better exclude every possible error, had we not? Namely, it is vitally important on which lot our grafts are going to thrive. Anyway, not on the plantations of Maremira, but on the adjacent similar fields that we may consider to be equivalent experimental stations. However, should it turn out that they do not really take root there and are in danger of withering, another shelter ought to be thought of. But think of it: always after deliberation. You are wonderfully surrounded, Cariña, do not take too much responsibility on your shoulders. And beware of the waylayers : our competitors grudge us the harvest. Do not forget either : they are tender plants, those delivered specimens - do not expose them to the harsh Tramontana!

Hereabouts I am not surrounded by so many valuable things, my dear, but there is a picture of the Vine with all its tendrils and twigs which I foster as a sanctum. Therefore I pray every day : that at least I was granted the great bliss of having found such a great treasure like you. My vine-dresser, once, in better days, landlady of Ses Taca (what a disgrace, remember, at the time, as I did not appoint a major-domo) - history blotted you out and caged me like a bird. Nonetheless, a love like ours, cannot be hived up or erased. Hopefully it

> *will leave some traces in our 'children', with whom you feel*
> *so unified. As long as your days last, may you reign like a*
> *generous Persephone, over our piece of this Earth, which is,*
> *more than ever, threatened by randy rascals.*

It kept running on like that for a while; once again Dugal was staring in front of him, a bit dazed, with that cryptic document in his hands. *Persephone ..., young twigs on the Vine ... ~ in capitals, that is ~, ... do not expose them to the chilly north wind ..., accommodation, at Keppler's ... those hills with a symphony of dandelions, daisies etc ...*

Really, that description of the place seemed pretty familiar to him. Galileió: quite a picture like that, in full primavera; that was absolutely right. But Keppler ... could that be a hidden hint ~ to stay in the circle of the star wizards, so to say ? *Drat!* All of a sudden it flashed upon him: Kappeler, that sail-maker in Galileió, where they had gone a few times themselves already, for their failed adventure with an old-timer yacht that had been palmed off on him. Mister Capplèr ("of old Teutonic stock: Kappeler, in fact" the good man had admitted) was rooted in the tradition of the tree nurserymen who, ever since the era of the Moorish occupation, had regarded Marcaio as their new back-garden. Somewhere there must have been some cross-fertilization with the winegrowers, following in the wake of the Archidux.

Good gracious, that brought him back to the Shaeffers. Such another clan of marcaionized sauerkraut devourers whose path had crossed that Riesling aristocrat's. Their neighbours, those Biedermeiers from Freising and adherents of self-banishment, could confirm this. They had said goodbye to their homestead just like that because a few tree haters had deflowered the square where they lived; in order to patch up an idyllic dwelling of a Viconte (say simply: a Mister Viscount), unsuspecting about the kinship with those other Schäfers, five generations before.

No, it can't be all sheer coincidence, he grumbled. If you put two and two together, that code lingo that old mister Lois at first pretended to renounce, but then recurred to a moment later, did not prove to be so extravagant at all.

Hadn't he better return to Roberto and his racy pet, demure and doggo ~ a trip to Canossa, to join in with the intelligence pool of his general staff

? This ran counter to all his principles and gusto. Little by little a scheme began to develop in a backroom of Dugal's brain. It looked pretty finicky, indeed, but if he wanted to be sure about what things had been pulling together above the sky of Ses Taca more than a century ago ...

At the break of dawn they already left the long twisting path from Ses Taca for the asphalt road of the Cornisa. In a bend they halted, along a gap between the foliage, right above Ses Taca. The silhouette with tower and crenels stood out snow-white against the azure sea, under the slender palm-trees and the immaculate ethereal blue of the sky that one could only admire at that hour of the day. "Fra Angelico, thank you for this moment," whispered Catarí. "Eh ?" said Dugal, but she doubted if he felt the same magic of the surrealistic picture. What strange things had occurred there, in and around this Moresque fairy-spot? A century ago, or thereabouts. How much of it was fiction and what reality? Were those letters (to a dead person maybe) genuine or a mystification of an insipid wag; and who could still take offence at it now? Who by any means wanted to prevent it from arousing even more public interest ‿ and to silence him, Yankee meddler and vedette past his prime ? If need be, with god knows what means? Those, or at least some suchlike worries, must have been circling around in her Duke's stubborn head.

Maybe the old man had been totally out of his mind as he was writing that, about the imposed internment in that gloomy Bohemian castle ('claimed by the fatherland', as they call it). So, you just have to classify that whole code game as gibberish of a nearly demented oldie. Who, under better circumstances these days, would probably be sitting there, filling up crossword puzzles or whiling away his time with an old men's magazine .

"How?" Dugal asked, without really paying attention to her way of thinking aloud. Same as you hardly get annoyed any longer at your partner's belching or other disturbing noises after years of huddling together. Unusually slowly he drove on, as far as the first bar they passed along the road: 'At Pèpè's'.

"How about a desayuno?" That sounded like an expression of love in her ears, a long time ago. But this bonhommie would be rather due to Duke's need of reflection. *To proceed or to change tactics, that's the question.* Of course, he would persist. But as for his reading public (which, undoubtedly, he had: quite a bunch of soap fans of the Archidux; otherwise those editing guys would not let him occupy such a sensation column as if it were his back-garden) ... ~ how to propitiate those eternal swallowers of mellowy station novels at such a turnabout of 360 degrees ? *That's likely to give many a Marcaian the shock of his life.*

"What!" Catarina repeated that, if he published this letter to Catalí in that form, without any retouch, the opponents were going to swallow him whole. And the harmless reader? He was likely to feel taken in.

21

"And ? Do you know anything more now ?" Catarina examined him from aside. No reaction. Gradually she surrendered to her own reflections. Full of understanding for the small cares of such starvelings, this spectacular strip of landscape absorbed them in its deep crevasses and perilous bends with abysses, softened by green, overgrown rock masses. Dugal was driving at an exceptionally quiet pace, on the exceptionally quiet winding road of the Cornisa. Once Graves-Von Ranke had called this route, in a poetic way, 'Saint Francis' serpentine to Eden'. The fresh morning silence and the tremolos of various bird species exerted themselves to uphold that picture. In vain. The healing power of this natural cure slipped down from this couple. Lost in thought, they had no eye now for the majestic surroundings. *Once that feeling will come back, but god knows when.* That's what Catarí had also thought the night before. She had picked the most racy nightie from her box of tricks, but Duke looked right through that little nothing. At other times, though, he would not have let go of such a windfall. *And all that because of that deuced Archidux and his mascot,* she groused to herself. That couple had bewitched him ever since the day they had moved into Ses Taca. "What are you gibbering there ?"

Dugal seemed to have returned from the realm of spirits. "Oh, welcome back among the living," Catarí greeted him at his resurrection.

"I've been thinking." As if she hadn't noticed. A moment before she had still been playing with the idea: *shouldn't I give my mannie a decent brush-off? Threaten him with slipping off for a month or so? Back to the parents, if necessary, an approved pretext with couples that have to 'list all the points for a while'.*

"What things that petty chef was suggesting this very morning, Cariña! You know, instead of charging straight at the Chest with a battering ram, with Pépé's insinuations, we're going to catch up on all the news, just the two of us, over a snug cup of tea at Café de Paris."

On the market-place in Llosera there was already quite a bustle. *Jesus, market day. If only we don't get some of those inquisitive toadies on our backs.* Dugal loathed obtrusive voyeurs or autograph hunters. Still, at such an early hour there was no trace yet of any tourist cattle in ludicrous bermudas and T-shirts with ribald texts they hardly grasped. Just the locals, then: stocky mothers who had been laying in some new household goods and some stuff for the kids. They were shuffling around between the tables under the trees, while their lanky husbands were hanging about at the counter, sipping at an horchata or cortado.

Groundnut milk, bah, stuff that distorts your face, same as does that coffee-like poison here, he thought. "So, how about an horchata ?" asked Catarí, to see his peevish face.

The unsightly terrace of Café de Paris was chockfull again; otherwise they would have entered straight away as well. No sooner had they sat down than Dugal was accosted by one of those brownish louts that scoured the markets looking for a willing victim. And that's what Duke was. They did know him: Mister Maïks! One europesa, for yoh, a frend's price."

"Half the amount and the whole posy is for my wife." "Thrree quarrterrs, Mister Maïks, my fòòlk must also live."

As proud as Lucifer, Dugal pressed the whole bouquet of roses to her breast, humming an old Streisand hit: *You don't bring me flowers any more.*

"Now tell me I'm not a born haggler." Still, Catarí knew he had paid a quarter too much after all, and so did he. He simply could not brush them off like that; certainly when children were involved.

"Suppose I misused that weakness myself … as a real bounty-hunter," she teased him. In fact, that was a bit of kicking about in return for pa Mikes's suspicion at the time with regard to her.

The bar of Café de Paris was not quite in proportion to its name; however, it breathed a certain nostalgia that reminded Catarí of her childhood. "That smell of liquid bleach here all the time!" said Duke. Hey, that was it: the cleaning product of her grandparents! Same with their neighbours, a slight chlorine smell that softened her nostrils with a yearning for things gone by. "But that's it," Dugal muttered.

"What! Also a bleach fragrance from your toddler years?" she wondered.

"That tin in the shed at Ses Taca. On our arrival there was a can with exactly the same product. Really, I used it after clearing out all the rubbish there." "Yeah, so what?"

"Catarí," he almost whispered. "D' you know what was written on it? C. do Mar, 1915." "?" Catarí looked at him with pitying eyes. *Is he really turning dotty? Because of a tin of bleach, scary."*

"What! Don't you see? Catarí ～ oh!" Dugal all but burnt his lips at the té limón he had gulped at too hastily. "1915, and Catalí d'Omar officially died in '05. Ten years later she writes her name on something like that. And at Ses Taca, of all places: forbidden territory, according to don Lois' directives. So, after all, wouldn't that good old chap have been so …"

"Crackers, weak-minded? Hey, maybe that's a mere spoof of that opposite party: feigning not to want the Archidux to be depicted as mentally deficient. Unless … C. do Mar ～ well, suppose it is a variant of d'Omar, so professor Marquez' assistant might be kindred to … Good heavens!"

"What?" Dugal was hanging on her lips with narrowed eyes.

"I don't know. But what if she were a niece of hers. Or … a daughter!"

"Cariña, what ingenious ideas you have! I'm a lucky dog I didn't get a crush on a false or real blonde. Hey, that strapping Dolores is quite a bit younger than Roberto ～ or us ～ and the maëstra of Ses Taca …"

"Has been resting in the Lord for over a century ～ officially. Thanks, Dukie, I'm smart enough to see that myself," Catarí resumed, with an air. "By way of speaking, I meant. A grandniece or eh … great-granddaughter?"

Dugal seemed absorbed in thought again. That darned don Pépé had made their mouths water once more, with all the racy stories he had got from his grand-uncle, who had known another cook working at Maremira, and the latter … What speculations like that could lead to! *Namely, that implies there must have been a son, by her name! Ay, that happens in the best of families, and in that way the honourable donor kept out of harm's way. Good Lord!*

"Why, my dear, do you think we are going nuts ourselves?"

"No, but if you keep harping on the same string, then …"

"That hip doña Dolores might be the epicentre of a potential tsunami, is that what you're thinking?"

That cool grin with which she looked at him ～ typical, no, how it tickled the female vanity when you looked up, surprised at their clever anticipation to such a cryptic remark. *But aren't we a bit gone around the bend,* Dugal yarned on the same theme, *playing this detective game. Fancy: that Aphrodite, turned to flesh, in academic outfit: the brain behind all those nagging intimidations? Pull my other leg!*

"Alright, I see." Catarí's voice sounded exceptionally crabby, as she gulped down the last sip of her tea with the self-contempt of a whisky drinker. "That wily nymphomaniac has already wrapped you up so craftily you don't see any harm in it. Neither does that failed Chippendaler, I mean Marquez, who probably is dead gone on her as well. But accidentally she is close to the source, right? So she has a view on the tiniest details and secrets of the Dux's heart. The key to your 'manuscript cabinet', which you held to be top secret."

"Ah, so you think …" Dugal lashed out for what threatened to end in one of those vain attempts at self-defence against female jealousy. At that very moment, however, an alarm set off somewhere on the square. One of those yelling burglar alarms no car-driver whatsoever takes notice of any longer. But shortly afterwards they heard a small explosion. All terrace customers got up, some passers-by stopped. And then there was a series of short bangs. They saw people seeking cover behind a table or a shop rack. But after that nothing happened any more. No collapsing façades or terraces that were swept away. Someone shouted: Mira ahí! There it is!" At the same time they saw it too. "Goddamn, it can't be true!"

Dugal dashed outside, dead certain it was their car. Halfway on the terrace, though, he already noticed: the pale BMW right behind their car had got it hot. Boot and bonnet had flung up through excitement, the doors burst open. But apart from that, no direct signs of damage. No trace of devastation spread across the square. Only on the rear and front side of the car there were some smudges, like black-smoked. By the time Dugal got to the spot, the arm of the law was also there, assessing the situation with regained self-confidence. "Fortunately no Molotov cocktail … Seemingly a number of firecrackers or rockets … kind of firework … No terrorists anyway …"

All of a sudden the whole square was buzzing like a beehive. "Listen to that, they all must have their say," the cop shrugged his shoulders. "Afterwards they are all heroes." *It's a good one who says so,* Dugal scorned.

Less than ten minutes later they were already tearing along the flanks of the Col de Llosera. "That lucky dog had a narrow squeak," Dugal grumbled. "Not even a window-pane blown to smithereens."

"You daresay!" Meaningfully, they looked askance at each other. "Hey, after all, that bomb was meant for you ~ for us, Dukie."

"Bomb? Toy bombs. Hardly any more than a fistful of those Christmas crackers." However calm brave Catarí had kept after that 'assault', she was not to be soothed by such a sop now.

"Alright, my dauntless knight, I noticed how cold-headedly you observed that boyish brouhaha from the terrace. But next time it may be bingo." *Bang into the air, and we ourselves, or you, ripped to pieces,* lay on her glib tongue, but she held it back, as well as her impulse to give her Duke a good squeeze.

Instinctively he swallowed his bragging tirade about that gang of rabble who wanted to frighten them off by pulling out all stops. He put on the radio, for distraction. A few fading tones from Rodrigo's Para un Gentilhombre, marvellous to respire a bit. For a moment there was a publicity spot, for Colores del Mundo, Mediterranean-blue paint, and then suddenly, the whimper of some sissy was broken off for a special newsreel: " ...grande commoción en la ciudadela de Llosera ..."

With growing disbelief they both gazed at each other. This could not pass muster any more. Unaffectedly, that newscaster there was talking about the commotion that had arisen in Llosera after the outrage on the car of the Mikes couple. "Rumour has it that there is a lot of damage to the bodywork. Some eyewitnesses saw the actor running to his car, after preceding alarm tones and explosions. In the commotion that arose after the detonation of the explosives, Dugal Mikes's wife, who had dashed straight to the spot, is said to have carried him off. Probably with grave injuries. Our local reporter there ..."

"Reporter? Idiot? What gibberish is that bloke talking? As though they knew it in advance," Dugal raged. "And which eyewitnesses saw me being carried away, by you of all people? That half-baked constable surely. Now the whole comedy is getting a bit too daft."

Catarí's phlegm worked like a plaster on a wooden leg. "Don't get wound up about a storm in a teacup, as you always call it yourself. That's a put-up job, for sure."

"Right oh, a child could tell so. But that those jerks on the radio add to such a set-up! It's a downright shame."

And that you join in this game, she snarled, *as hot-tempered and snappy as in your best roles!* "The same again altogether," she whispered to herself. "What?" he said somehow distractedly, as usual when she reacted so laconically.

"Duke," she answered patiently, as if to a child, "you do realize, don't you, that that kind of vultures often are hand in glove?"

"Crafty or corrupted, what do you mean? Yes, yes, they make a deal with those vandals, for sheer sensation's sake, or through competition with the written press maybe, eh. Who knows there isn't even a mole on that channel that infiltrated so as to be in a much better position to blow up the whole affair. And then …, then that scene a minute ago would be just totally orchestrated."

"Or possibly not even so. It may also be partially manipulated. Look, love, in an operetta state like Marcaio …"

"Sorry, a zarzuela island, sweetie. O.K., I know what you're going to say. That the local potentates have their straw men everywhere over here. From the village brass bands to the media channels, everything is biased; everywhere they have a finger in the pie. Same as with us, across the big pond. So."

"So? You as a Yankee should realize they poke fun at that objectivity of the 'free press' all the time. Firstly. And secondly …"

Catarí had turned around her axis towards him, leaning on her elbow: the ultimate seduction. And thus, Dugal knew, the most sublime twisted thought could slip out of that smart little head of hers: "What about that other institute of spiritual freedom, Palmera's Alma Mater?"

"Roberto Marquez, again? No!" Dugal sat straight up in his seat, with the rock-solid positiveness of an enamoured fool who refuses to believe he has been cuckolded.

22

"Two miserable million dollars?" he banged with his fist on the table, right before Roberto's fleshy nose. "So ~ that's what those louts care about a unique historical document, fancy!"

And what about you? was the afterthought. *Haven't you any more say in all this either? Particularly you, señor Marquez, who wear your professorial integrity like a chastity belt ~ are you really that ponderous incarnation of unselfish objectivity? Or are you the slyboots with a double life Catarí takes you for: the sturdy baby-face that even femmes fatales like doña Francisquita get nuts on?*

Yet, the professor wisely skipped over that sore point of the bribe. Cautiously he kept rubbing his massive chin.

"I'm not sure if they are really that harmless, old buddy."

Roberto, an ace in the field of comparative literary studies as he was, had double the bid lying before him on his desk, but he was staring beyond it, far away at an indefinable dot in space. Dugal had tumbled in with the impetuosity of a battering ram. Pretty theatrically, typical of a star actor. Rather as if he, R. Marquez, were in league with those bomb layers. By the way, were those various incidents really such a sham, or had they been consciously half-miscarried, by way of warning? Which also went for their performers: clumsy mugs, according to Dugal, but who could assure they were all just isolated groupies working for their own account?

Anyhow, these redemption attempts were real. One came from the 'Central Service for the protection of the Cultural Values on the Bailares', and the second from a 'Viennese Faculty for historical document control'. Pretty obscure, both of these organizations. Prof. Marquez had got them checked and, as he expected, they proved to be totally unknown to the official instances.

"That 'C.S.' of our archipelago rather smacks of Blut-und-Boden nationalism," he thought, "but has little in common with the brawny lingo of some underground movements with republican strain, like the separatist ATE or Autochthonous Terrorists' Elite.

To Roberto the scanty million they offered, rather seemed a collection held by nostalgic small businessmen and some old-Marcaian families who shunned the new moneyed aristocracy like poison. An obscene gesture towards a stinkingly rich parvenu like this Yank, who cherished a much deeper affection for the Archidux, but could not help flaunting it like a fresh blood-curdling conquest. *That damned stardom, really,* he grunted.

But what about the second one? Apparently one with academic pretensions, but it had nothing to do with the Viennese varsity. Truly, the whole set-up pointed at a splinter group with swindler manners. What purposes could such a decent club harbour, Dugal was anxious to hear from him.

"Now we know at least what kind of hawkers they operate with, but the crux remains: who are the smart fellows behind this?" After the early-night visit of that Viennese slyboots at the Mikeses', the professor had not been idle.

"As to me, mí amigo, all that was quite a sham, indeed. We have of our channels a bit everywhere, you know, and …"

Dugal knew Roberto had a girl-friend who worked at the secret service, and instantly after that phone-call the Prof had pricked up his feelers everywhere among scholars and humanists. "And?"

"There is no Schnabel or Schnabbel, or however it may have sounded to your ears, rather unfamiliar with German, at the whole Viennese firmament."

From the all but accurate description by the Mikeses they had been able to frame up a robot photo after all, and what was the result? That there was a Mr Schwabe indeed who had once been employed at the manuscript department in Vienna. Dismissed, however, because of embezzlement and swindling with documents.

"So what?"

Prof. Marquez portentously bent forward. "That may mean that that little fellow - if your portrait matches him altogether - was working for himself. Unless …" Roberto's bear's claw pushed over to Dugal the data from the sample sheet they had been able to draw up about that customer:

for twelve years the archivist for the descendants of the Habiger clan; private secretary of the Imperial Landesrat (Country Council? well, well); former member of *the* lodge ~ *THE*, but on closer examination none of the contacted lodges wanted to have anything to do with a Herr Schwabe; co-founder of the Restauration Society, etc., etc …

"Mystic movements or Mafioso zealots, my learned friend?"

Anyhow, the Chest did seem to be pretty implacable this time. No matter how susceptible to humour he usually was, now he looked deadly serious. He did not want to frighten Dugal out of his seven senses, but if he asked him … Further publications? No, not for the time being at least.

"Why?! Just blow off the whole affair? So what? Those fellows would laugh up their sleeves, wouldn't they? And then go trumpeting about: 'What did I tell you, those ducal letters were a mere hoax.'"

No, honourable friend, 'recoiling' did not appear in Dugal's lexicon. Promptly he shoved another document under Roberto's professorial nose, which made the Prof look up in astonishment. And he enjoyed the effect of the surprise.

Roberto's reading spectacles, down on his nostrils, trembled with pure excitement.

"The next one," Dugal triumphed. "You are the first one to get to see one of the authentic letters with his very own eyes."

"Gracias," murmured Roberto, but Dugal noticed that the learned gorilla was too far away already to thank him for that honour. A bomb could explode next to him or Catarí Ionès sit down on his desk in bathers. When professor Marquez was absorbed in something like that, the tanned bundle of muscles became a pillar of imperturbability.

What does this letter-swallowing failed boxer care about such bashful, yet sometimes passionate outpourings of a nostalgic rover who did not find a fixed abode anywhere except for his 'roof gutter' of Marcaio? A bit like a tramp who is down and out, under a bridge across the Seine. And then got condemned to sit there, fettered to a chain with swollen elephant legs, in a chilly Bohemian castle, blowing a new breath of life into the girl-friend of his bosom. A sublime paranoia, that reincarnation wish, no? Dugal nodded. Copperfield's illusionist's tricks were nothing in comparison.

At the first reading Dugal too had devoured this epistle, just like the other ones, in one breath. In that little mezzanine where Catalí d'Omar had once served her own selection of wines. With the old mantle clock as his sole companion he had, at one blow, been sucked back in time, an infinite number of revolutions of the hour-hand. Swallowed up by that curly, dancing handwriting. In his quivering hands the letters, hardly faded yet, had come to life again. They had pulled his dilated eye-pupils from the trim vineyards of Maremira to the hilly woodlands around Brendais. Dugal's soul was floating along, his eyes dancing on the rhythm of the writing pen ~ jolting once in a while, then dipped into the ink feverishly fast again. He knew what was going to follow. Those words ~ how to squeeze them out of his tormented thoughts?~ he knew them already before he was reading them. Their minds had grown together. Dugal wás don Lois …

As Doña Dolores Francisquita turned her professor's cabinet door ajar, she found both gents in a strange kind of trance. "Hmm, professor Marquez," she cleared her throat, with the embarrassment of someone who catches two intimate friends in the act. Whether Roberto ~ eh, the professor still wanted that radio-recording?

"Dear child, you're coming just in time." Roberto leapt up from his turning- chair. He had just been telling his friend here that what he wanted to put down as a storm in a teacup, now threatened to become a tidal wave. "Yes, just turn on yesterday night's extra news for him, for then there was surely something else to do at the Mikeses' residence than listening to Radio Marcaio …"

The pretty assistant swayed her hips alongside Dugal's nose and was dawdling coquettishly near the recorder with Robert's cigar stub between her thumb and forefinger. A hint at the bizarre parlour customs in the fashion of George Sand or simply to assess the value of Roberto's phallus surrogate? *A born intriguer,* it flashed upon his mind, *cut out for a role as herself in the play he could make out of this, and the same goes for R.Marquez.*

"It appears they cast exactly the same flash on the telly. Namely during the break of the cup match Futból Marcaio – Sociedad Real. Strategically well-chosen, no?"

In an unusually vigorous tone a coarse voice, in contrast with doña Dolores' sensual introduction, was fulminating against the outrageous practices of a Dugal Mikes. "An unscrupulous, publicity-loving opportunist whose stunt about the so-called 'Secret letters to Catalí' ought to jack up

134

his waning Hollywood image. And notably by drawing on the status and reputation ~ horribile dictu ~ of his venerable predecessor at the old mansion of Ses Taca, which he appropriated in a dubious way …"

"Well I never!" Dugal grumbled. That rascal dared to call him all sorts of names, without turning a hair. Pretending that he wanted to drag the good name of the island and its figureheads through the mire, mala fide. "But then that star past his prime has reckoned without his host!" the unmistakable threat sounded. After which the crow's voice set out with quite a deal of imputations.

"What scoundrel may that be?" Dugal burst out, so that Roberto's cigar flew out of the señorita's hands. Without listening to the rest of it, he wanted to call the involved channels to order, sito presto.

"What did you think we've been doing, Dugal? Plus, we had that voice (deformed, of course) filtered by an expert. It's all a wasted effort."

Oh really? And at those studios they surely acted dumbfounded? Well, if that rabble played it so smart, he, Duke of Ses Taca, was going to give them tit for tat: calling in all the channels, if needs bringing up the heavy guns. "You know what I mean, Roberto ~ we know enough bigwigs here we can put under pressure. We 'll teach that gang manners."

"Dugal!" With an imposing stretch pose the Prof tried to rein in the tartar in front of him. "How, what, with what? Shooting wildly around you is sheer donquixotry, as senseless as the frontal hunt that American strategists apply on jackals in the Middle East."

Once more Dugal composed himself a bit, impressed by the gorilla airs of the academician. Although the latter regarded the Mikes couple as rather atypical specimens of Uncle Sam's lineage, he just had to vent his anti-imperialistic feelings a bit: "You Yanks still think you can exterminate a wasps' nest with an elephant leg. Yet, some weaker wretches often prove to be too clever for you, due to their guerrilla tactics: splitting up in innumerable nuclei, they attack you from where you expect them least of all. The approved razzia mentality …"

Salvation came from an unexpected corner: from doña Dolores' namely, who, with consideration for Duke's impatience about such professorial contemplations, also thought it would do now.

"Gentlemen, we are not getting any further, this way. I understand señor Mikes is fed up with the Philistinism of an invisible enemy. In this era of excessive hedonism and blurring of moral standards sweeping over our island, this must seem to him like ideas from the times of the old patriarchy ... Quite unthinkable, isn't it, that any fundamentalist would still care about the 'intimistic' traits of such an anachronistic document. Nonetheless ..."

Nevertheless, Dugal smirked, *I should not be taken for a ride by the mellifluous logics that would make you forget all sorrow and misery through the mouth of such a dazzling beauty.*

"Where I must agree with the professor ~ and add some nuances at the same time," she went on, "is that this doesn't seem to be just about some isolated actions of harmless homeland devotees." So, she too saw a clear connection between all those rackets and skirmishes the last few days. So far such tentative assaults probably had only the aim of a deterrent effect. But who could say ~ ...

"...that they'll leave it at that?" Roberto grabbed a chair nearby and sat down in front of Dugal with the renewed courage of a cross-examiner. "This is going crescendo, buddy: a real campaign to raise half the island against you. And one day those dilettantish little vandals will reveal themselves as ..."

Marcaian death squadrons that don't bother a straw about a stray graze or a fatal grain of shot? And whether a meddlesome prof and his amiable assistant can't save their skin at it.

"Or whether Mrs Mikes might be kidnapped." The apologizing smile and raised eyebrows of Roberto's right hand hit Dugal below the belt. All at once the gastric juice was playing up again which he had also felt a while before after a delayed SMS message from Cathy, before he had entered their room: *'Ferreted out some more: prof R.M., alias Gozilla, used to be praeses of the Bocambille (for the conservation of Marcaian culture) ánd a member of MP, a separatist movement of the Bailares. Do Mar idemditto.'*

He had assumed the latter referred to Dolores' membership of both 'small-size nationalist' associations, as Roberto himself used to scorn them. A courtesy affiliation probably on the señorita's part, by way of obligation to her 'boss'. *Ah, after all, what clubs didn't you join yourself, Dukie,* he thought, *in your student years: a communist groupie, Jesus, to please your lovey?* Or rather a green one, for she was a bit of an activist then. Or ...

136

was it just the reverse here, pretty Dolores being the brain and Roberto the executor?

"Professor Gozilla, what does MP mean? As far as I know, you are neither members of parliaments, nor army cops."

Seldom had Dugal's words produced such an effect. At least with Roberto. This bundle of muscles, otherwise so self-possessed, now showed a rather vexed mandrill behaviour. "What's the idea?" he went purple in the face. And, at Dolores's soothing sign: "MP? That's not what you think it is, amigo."

That's what all adulterous wretches say whose club membership card of Daddy's Hobby fell out of their wallet, Dugal congratulated himself for putting his scholarly buddy in check.

23

With the liberating euphory of an underdog who has just defeated the odds-on favourite for the one hundred yards, Dugal halted on the stairs of the Alma Mater. "Dugal, Dugal!" A prof running after you like a lover after a chick who has given him the boot: it doesn't happen to you every day. Doña Dolores's clattering heels behind him added to Roberto's plea. "I don't know where or how you were briefed, amigo. But that club has nothing in common with the Marcaio Popular."

"Our MP means 'Maddalena Panayia'," Dolores completed. "And now you can tap your same sources to find out what that means. A dios, señor."

Touching, the way she ushered the poor professor back in by his sleeve: a piece of comfort for the beaten athlete. *I could use such a perk myself, really* ~ Dugal was suddenly left with an empty feeling. *And what about that Bocambille, they did not make mention of it at all.* Actually he felt sorry for Roberto and of all things he would have liked most to close him in his heart like that: as the giant with feet of clay, with a yearning for the 'Weltgeist' ~ a cosmopolitan, wavering however between openness and his passion for that Marcaio of the draw-wells, the granjas overgrown by bougainvillea and cactus figs ... Any different from the unrelenting devotion to this little stretch of land that he, the down-to-earth Yank, had got affected with by now? Both of them loathed petty provincialism, didn't they? But they equally wished all unworthy rogues to the devil who wanted to can Marcaio in steel and concrete boxes. The building contractors, 'black' investors, say launderers, and other scoundrels who didn't give a damn for this gorgeous island.

Catarina noticed at once there was something on his mind. As Dugal picked her up at the Avenída Colón, the commercial artery of the town ~ armed with an ensaimada cake box and a hat box à la Ascott on top, in one hand, and three shoeboxes in the other ⸴, she missed his ironic "Oh, just three of them?".

Her "how puzzled you look!" worked like a laxative. "Ah, that couple of hair-splitters ..." he muttered. "What did I tell you, Dukie! Why have they helped you so well? To gain your confidence and thus diddle your little secret out of you. And when that did not just work out like that, those sneaks bamboozled you to some country bumpkins and cat-burglars."

Dugal's blank look told her she was not on the proper wavelength with him.

"MP is no nationalistic splinter group, baby." And he briefed her quickly about Roberto's Schwabe file and the scandalizing news flash that had been recorded by voluptuous Dolores. And ⸴ oh yes, that sharp-witted countermove by Mister Univ still echoing in his head: "Or whether Mrs Mikes might be abducted."

Dugal saw her swallow. On other occasions, though, his Cathy was nothing undaunted. And in this case one could expect from her a furious lash at 'that swipe in a lecturer's clothes'. Logical, for every woman saw a rival in any other smart one. Even if she was called la Ionès and knew that she, the wet dream of every movie-fan, was matchless. Or maybe that was just why?

"So they do after all, Cariño, admit implicitly they are involved themselves."

In a trembling voice she pulled at his sleeve, heading for the car. By harping on the fact that the whole witch hunt against them, the slanderous column in the local media and all those 'incidents' could be no isolated facts, the Prof and his skittish kitten betrayed their complicity.

"Cariña," he said, "I'm wetting my pants. You've acted in too many suspense movies." And, the shoeboxes on his arm, he was about to open the car door, when she clung to him, whispering: "Watch it!"

"You don't mean ...?" he said. The door clicked open, everything ok. Yet he had stepped back a few paces himself. "You see now, that's what those guys are intent on: that, at the least trouble, we should back down and eventually buckle under."

So those crackers in Llosera had also been a Santa Clause gift? Notwithstanding his soothing words, she got him to seek together with her. Everywhere, even on the backseat, to make sure. There, nowhere a suspect parcel whatsoever! And that made him think of it: it was time to put Miguel, that scaredy-cat of an editor, through the mill. *Now we're going to leave no stone unturned, baby. How did Pythagoras put it again? Give me a lever and I'll lift up the world.*

Catarí was tickled about his private jokes, as she saw him rummaging through the tapes, chortling: "Rodrigo, pop into my slot, I've got y' in my cot." Music to lean back behind the steering-wheel, look into the void and wits at zero: 'Junto al Generalife', an antidote for the desensitizing droning in those trashy cabriolets these days. Marvellous.

Suddenly it was interrupted by a screeching voice: "Señor and señora Mikès!"

Dugal, already half dozy, sprang up in a shock. That very same voice in a kind of double Dutch. *This can't be true ~ …*

"…I see both of you looking up strangely. So yes, after the message during yesterday's broadcastings we thought it necessary to approach you personally after all. In the end, after all the signals given to you hitherto, it appears you need more to be brought to your senses again. Nevertheless …"

How for heaven's sake …, Dugal grumbled, "Oh no, they won't …!"

His devilish brainwave had an infectious effect on Catarina and, quick as lightning, she started scrambling between their tapes in the little drawer. Out of the whole collection she grabbed a few of the most representative ones: La Francisquita ~ what a fortuity! ~ and Granados' Villanesca. Damned, it was all gone! All that they had given their old bands and braying up for, even her Cole and co., her last youth sentiment, had been erased. Substituted by that sinister prophecy of doom from the same bastard:

"…You particularly defy the awareness of old values among our population … we fear that you outsiders, entirely unfamiliar with the ethic sensitivities in Marcaio, might cause immense damage … a dog running across the skittles … we count on you sharing our concern, in admiration for his Honourable L.S.. Otherwise …"

Otherwise? I'll chuck you into the Hades, you little Pharisees, Dugal cursed. A few tapes were already flying through the window, narrowly past the ears of such a yuppie in a sports car, who landed in the hedge a little further. "Are you crazy?" Catarí shrieked.

"Rosicrucians, apostles of the holy Hierbas or the mob of the Marcaian imitation pearls, purveyor of holy images by appointment to His Majesty," he shouted back. "Fat lot I care who those clod-pates are. But now I want to know about their motives."

"But what if that's their intention, Duke?" she said, and at his dazed glance in the rear-view mirror: "That you should freak out, totally outraged, so you would do rash actions as they have exactly foreseen."

He was watching her with the empty look of a mediocre student whom you try to explain an axiom of Wittgenstein's. "I'm not out of my wits at all," he pressed the decibels strongly down. "But now I know what's to be done: walk up to those media-bosses here and if they don't turn up with names, it won't be their best day. Cause I ⁓ ..."

The phone saved him from further details. "Saved by the bell, darling," she said with mocking eyes. Both tallied to pick it up. It's not going to be ...? Until Dugal did, shouting: "Shove up my arse, you bunch of ... Oh, it's you, sorry." With the palm of his hand before the mike he said: "Mister Murdoch. Yes ...?"

That was his sobriquet for the editor-in-chief of the Diario: Miguel Mortado. "What ...? When ...? How ...? So you too ...?" The complete metamorphosis of her Duke, from a rock-hard sturdy hunk still a moment ago, into an interpellator of a infantile level, made Catarí burn with impatience. Finally, as he put the phone back, she was dying to get it out of him. "That sounded a bit like the question-time of the simpletons' union!"

"That one too," he mumbled, undisturbed. Cathy! She would not believe this. That poor soul's record stock too had been thoroughly botched up. But even much worse: they had turned his studio upside down, hacked the files of all his computers, mailed a lot of crap down the paper's sponsors' throat. And upon his arrival at his office, the façade was splotched all over with: *Mikes-Mortado, the kamikaze duo.* That poor Miguel was the dupe.

How long is that going to take, Catarí grinned sceptically, *until his compassion with the vexed little Murdoch will turn into spite, and then that shoddy editor of nought will have to atone for it.*

"What next?" she sounded him. Well, Miguel was thinking of an incubation period: withholding the publications at a timeout. So as to figure out a strategy how they could outsmart those blackmailers. In other

141

terms, that bunch of revisionists were to be lulled to sleep, till they believed they had hit the mark. And then …

"Are you going to beat the enemy at his own game, Macchiavelli?"

All well and good, but all the same, who said that in this olive republic of estate barons and tourist-suckers, that kind of potentates let themselves be taken in like that?

Ostensibly, Dugal got more and more absorbed in gloomy thoughts. What if Miguel's liege lords already aided and abetted that reactionary clan? Then the stocky newspaper king was bound to dance to their piping tune. That plucky hotshot, never averse from a bit of sensation, had gone far over the line this time. Bad enough, but that was no reason for a seasoned director of thrillers to back down at the least hazard. What about intimidating ~ who let himself be intimidated here?

Have they really turned that studio topsy-turvy, scared that little wretch out of his senses ~ or is that merely part of the whole sham game? Perhaps those blokes have caught the idea that Dugal Mikes does not simply buckle under because of some stunt acts and feints. Even though they did already prang his car once. Now that he was thinking it over: actually he had been nicely led up the garden path. Suppose they had brought in this Mortado to …

"If that scary Miguel has let himself been bribed by those sly dogs, this is not going to be his best day!" he grumbled. Under the ironic look of his wife, Dugal did not want to grant her the honour of being the first to hit upon that idea. Suddenly however, such a cunning change of tactics on the part of his pesterers became quite plausible.

He knew what he was to do. Catarí was going to rub her eyes. No vexed lion bursting out in frenzy, but a cold-headed fox with a diabolic scheme.

"What do you have in mind?" *It's working already,* he chuckled.

Hardly two days later it was hot front-page stuff for El Bailar. There it featured, in huge font: ACTOR MIKES DOUBLE-CROSSED BY THE DIARIO. His publication of the Secret Letters of the Archidux boycotted under pressure of Marcaian reactionaries.'

A lifelike jaguar on the loose along the esplanade in Pollenç would not have caught Catarí's eye any faster. There it was, after all. She paid for the newspaper, together with a fashion magazine that her sworn friend

Marcella was going to diddle out of her hands presently, at the same small round table of the bar where they used to date each other once a month. To 'catch up on the news'. For that's what this Marcella was better at than anybody else. Without giving you the feeling of degrading yourself to a gossip-monger, at 'ashtray level' as Dugal would sneer at that kind of chatterboxes. But then, he did not know Marcella, at least not thoroughly.

On the other hand, Catarí did not mind about that. Her bosom friend namely was quite a pretty piece of goods. On the whole earth globe one could not find her equal. Not that la Marcella made the men tumble from their bar stool with her dazzling looks. *As far as that is concerned, la Francisquita may be more competitive. But this femme fatale has more than one string to her bow,* Catarí smirked. After all, she had pushed a dozen men from their pedestal, in her former life, and not the least ones at that. The pick of managers, artists, politicians ~ philanderers each of them who had learnt a lesson from it for all their lifetime. She, la Ionès, had better become her apprentice in those matters. Until Marcella had run across her husband. No handsome strapper, not fabulously wealthy, but her 'cute bear' whom she steadily kept at her side. But at the bar in Pollenç he put her down willingly: "I lend you my sweetheart for a snug chat." As he did now again.

"Enviable. You've hit the jackpot, with such a cream of a fellow."

"So has he!" she chuckled. But truly, they were quite a remarkable pair. Masters in the art of living who had made la dolce far niente a full-time occupation. They worked for the local TV-station or the like of it. Simply with their daily comments on the local faits divers: nice pictures all the time, hot interviews, striking anecdotes which radiated one leitmotiv: their 'art de vivre'. To that end they scoured the whole island, in a constant holiday mood. Anywhere an illustrious contemporary had a mind to disembark incognito, the couple popped up too. As if by a fluke. There was not a native who could hatch an original idea, but they got at it like lightning. And that airiness of theirs, that's what did it. They were hot stuff on Marcaio, had been madly popular for years, with all layers of the viewers public. Owing to their easy-going application of Horatius' motto 'ridentem dicere verum': 'tell the truth laughingly', they dared to tell everyone some home truths, but in such a way that the assailed did not take it amiss. Consequently: they were in the picture about everything, and la Ionès was clever enough to take advantage of that.

From a distance Marcella had already twigged it. "What are you carrying under your arm?" Nothing escaped from her attention on this archipelago, she did not even need Catarí's El Bailar. "What, did you know about …?" Catarí could not believe her ears.

"The latest move of your own Dux? Even more than that, sweetie. In this edition you're not going to find the next of the Archi's intimate secrets. Here!" She was waving with a piece of paper. "Your better half has won, señor Mortado has already piped down. I don't want to break the confessional seal, but good old Miguel came to ask for our advice, and I had to make sure whether the game is worth the candle, didn't I? Just read!" With a grin Catarí took the text from her that the Diario was about to bring to light post-haste anyway. *Darned Duke, dratted Marcella!*

Querída Catalí,
Last night, one of the sleepless nights in a long row, I was
thinking of one of our many common secrets. For hours on
end I let that scene unreel in my mind. It happened during
our travel with the Nymph to Egypt and the Holy Land …

24

For quite a while editor Mortado was staring absent-mindedly away, over that one page of the Diario de Marcaio as it was going to sell across the counter early the next morning. And continually the same query was turning through his head: *why? How comes there is such a difference between the manuscript that mister Mikes has managed to fiddle out of don Lois's very own 'bastones', and the version prof. Marquez has turned up with?*

> *... during our travel to Egypt and the Holy Land ...*
>
> *'The most beautiful experience in my existence,' you called it. Another world seemed to unfold before you, Cariña, of which, in other conditions, you could only have dreamt. That is what often gave me the greatest satisfaction about my travels: letting others share in my discoveries - and the joy itself of discovering. Seeing those pyramids with your own eyes, so many things of a culture presumed lost.*
>
> *But also the facets of that country in our own era. The oriental atmosphere, the common people's way of living, ... their poverty. Particularly this penury left a deep impression on you.*
>
> *I noticed how it made you doubt about everything. Your belief, the traditions, the humble piety of your ancestors.*

That's how it sounded in the text published by Dugal. Whereas in the university version no mention was made of an Egyptian adventure. How was that possible? Yet, in the same authentic handwriting, the Archidux's namely, as to the Prof. So there was no reason to adapt his own copy of that letter - unless the man had turned half senile and wanted to correct his own memory. Miguel's granny came to his mind again, who had also constantly asked questions, as if to ask for self-affirmation about the past.

> *When I introduced you to my acquaintances in Alexandria, you presented some of those learned or high-placed gentlemen with an accomplished fact: why is so much knowledge needed, if it cannot help out the poor wretches and the homeless on this earth? And what justifies the harrowing inequality on God's vast pasture?*
>
> *You were not able to bother me with it. I enjoyed their annoyance, as they could not hark back either to reason, history or the Holy Writ to find any self-legitimation vis-à-vis a girl with a limited background!*
>
> *The atmosphere of that city ~ a melting pot of civilizations ~ infected you. Never before had you breathed such a cosmopolitan sphere yet. In those surroundings your concealed talents, which had not been able to come to the fore so far, welled up. The only thing that caused some discord between us, was your deep-rooted dislike of all that was unnatural. I shared that contempt with you, but I had learnt how to see it in a relative perspective. In the world of art and culture parasites and parvenus thrive abundantly. In that beau monde I found recognition for my work, my studies in the field of natural science ; you, on the other hand, thought that those people did not value me for what I was, but for what I represented. "They want to use you as a tool," you said, "to make you the pivot of a spiritual movement which runs counter to the disintegrating forces of this era …"*

In the other text there was no trace left of that whole passage about the Egyptian city. Omitted by the Dux himself, or spirited away by another hand ~ 'ausradiert'? Which movement did he mean? What did his Catalí foresee he was bound to be the key-figure of ~ a spiritual leader? On the one hand señor Miguel felt relieved he had shrunk back and, under pressure of Dugal's sneaking blackmail, had raked back the Letras Secretas. Not only had it cost him sweat and blood, but a pretty penny on top of that, to snatch that success column away from the 'Bailar'. Now however, he was left with a hangover. Okay, he had piled it on a bit, vis-à-vis that Yankee hotshot: about that havoc in his office and the studio, the tampering with his recordings and so on. And as for his computer files, one or another slippery customer had been snooping about there, indeed, but there was no proof of any hackers.

No, problem was his knees had started shaking, simply because of a few anonymous phone-calls, hazy allusions from a certain corner. But that way you can't rip off a Mikes. That's why he had put his fate into the hands of la Marcella, the sphinx of Marcaio, who was quite in the picture about the ins and outs in the under and upper world on this island. And she, the face of the local TV-station on the Bailares, had brought him round in her well-known crafty way: "But señor Mortado, you ought to take those harassments with a grain of salt, really." Yes, yes, cum grano salis, but in the mean time a lot of things could run out of hand. He knew those fellows, behind the curtains they managed everything at will, benevolently where they could and by violence if need be. In the case of paparazzi who did not let themselves be ordered about willingly, they did not shrink from applying the big means. "And in their eyes I have gone over the line far enough already, señora, by that unholy alliance with a blasphemer like Mister Mikes."

Marcella had had to put all her trump cards on the table. "Suppose I spread out the subject on the screen, you're not going to let yourself be prodded, are you?" That faced him with an accomplished fact: towards a coryphaeus who puts out her neck for you like that, you can't simply start back, can you? And certainly now he could not recoil, or else the Diario would suffer irreparable loss of face. The poor mope could not know anyway why Marcella exposed herself as a target, nor what compensations Catarína Ionès had promised her. A continuous contribution of the film diva would give a nice boost to the viewing ratings of Marcella's programme. La Ionès was quite aware of that: each lackey of the picture box was a vain peacock, and she, Marcella, was not the least one.

Disconsolately, Miguel thought of the crisis conference later that day, at his office. The mayor was going to be present, that toady; the regional minister of culture, that prig; the national chairman of the press union, a real windbag. On such occasions you could always expect Prof. Marquez as well, as a counterweight to the big boss, the main shareholder of Mediatec Bailar. Everything depended on the latter, a cool froggy.

He could either haul Miguel over the coals, calling him a nitwit and slob, or dryly congratulate him: 'a shrewd move, Mortado'. Precisely then you had to be on the qui vive. For by the same token he might give you the sack, one moment later: 'here, take this, old chap, you've deserved it'. And before you realized it, you found yourself on the pavement, with a golden handshake, it's true, and in joyful anticipation of a not so generous early retirement.

The annoying thing about the whole situation was that Miguel had no idea at all which of those fellows you could trust. For none of them he would stand bail whether they were involved in the plot or not. Even Roberto, the Chest, could play a double game. He, the devil's advocate in the matter of Marcaian culture, passed for the objectivity in person. Yet, the 'viceroy' of the Bailarean press had already been through a good many things and on further consideration many a big shot had ended up in the lowest drawer with him. All the same, Miguel was burning with curiosity how the Prof was going to interpret the big divergence in his handwritten copy of that letter.

> *During our travel to the Holy Land,* he read again the adapted (?) version, *I saw you blossoming out, Cariña. The confrontation with the historic sites, so much charged with events that belong to our past and have formed part of ourselves for ages, was a revelation to you. Compared to the Egyptian Antiquity, of which you had got a small impression on our way, Palestine filled you with deep satisfaction about your Jewish-Christian background. As if you got aware of a role lying ahead of us ...*

Feverishly he was looking for that passage again in Dugal's specimen, but there was no sign of it in there. Drat, this looked like pure self-censuring!

Knock, knock. "Yes," Miguel said absent-mindedly. He heard someone leaving the door ajar and clearing her throat. "Momentito," he repeated, absorbed in his reading matter. As he looked up, it proved not to be a clerk or cleaning woman, but a young lady who greeted him pertly: "Señor Mortado!"

Miguel seemed nailed to his seat. If there was something he melted for like for an ice-cream, it was ladies with style. Not that he was quite the type of womanizer or lady-killer, but they simply touched a tender string with him. His weak spot for female beauty was of a rather platonic nature and verged on an archetypical Madonna adoration. And this one was an absolute whopper. His meeting with la Marcella had shaken him up just a while ago, and señor Mortado was, from afar, a raving fan of señora Mikes. This specimen, however, was beyond any category. "Dolores Francisquita," she smiled and introduced herself as a lecturer and the first lieutenant of Prof. Marquez.

"Disculpe, señora, you are an hour early." Miguel exhausted himself to make doña Francisquita feel comfortable with a cup of cortado, an armchair without a stack of paperwork on it, and a few women's magazines.

"Oh, but I am not here on behalf of Prof. Marquez," she said, without moving a muscle. "I only wanted to warn you." The young lady was getting pretty straight to the point, thought Miguel, who used to feel a bit uncomfortable towards high-brow females anyway. And all the more so with this graceful apparition. She had got wind of the nasty mess he and Dugal Mikes had got themselves into.

Well, from a couple of phone-calls and ominous signs she had picked up in the environment of a colleague of hers, one could gather that some 'protocol-greedy bootlickers', as mister Mikes called them, were busy closing the ranks. That they made the famous actor their target, for being too cocksure, had become daily counter talk at the bars and bodegas. But also Mikes's 'cronies' were going to be

pecked at by those gents. And that they were not just going to leave it at that, with verbal violence, was beyond dispute. "You are quite aware yourself, señor," she added significantly, " what discourteous practices those gentlemen resorted to, in the recent past. Pierced car tyres, brakes that failed precisely in the descent … Not to mention disappearances that never got clarified, and mysterious abductions, cardiac arrests, inexplicable blazes during the absence of both spouses, etc …, etc …

Bull's eye, Dolores concluded from señor Mortado's distended eyes. *That beats all!* thought the factotum of the Diario. What this mascot of

Marcaio's varsity was doing to him, was about the same that he had tried to do to mister Mikes ~ in vain. Only too gladly would he believe she meant it seriously with him and did not aid and abet those shady groups she was scaring him stiff with. Yet, his sceptic nature induced him to circumspection. Ever since the Fall, man, falling victim to his own idolatry, had been hoaxed by the crafty ruses of one or other sex bomb. *Which is not going to happen to me,* he had sworn adamantly.

Point-blank he painted la Francisquita a picture of his failed genuflexion for Dugal Mikes. How he had implored him black and blue to give up his hubris, not to challenge the pettifogging 'gods' that ran the show here: some ultra-right powers behind the curtains whose only goal was to pull the strings tightly in these parts. Doña Dolores herself was also familiar, though from afar, with that kind of white-collar ruffians, wasn't she? Big shots, top managers and captains of industry included, from all spheres, as well as somewhat smaller shrimps. From shipyards to liquor distilleries, pearl and tile manufacturers, all who were a bit indebted to Marcaio's K.K.K. . "The local godfathers, you see. Even a lady like you they would not spare."

Doña Dolores nodded affirmatively. "In that respect Dugal is still rather naïve. He underrates the power of those crusaders to whom the emblem of the Marcaian Honour is sacred."

Miguel Mortado was sitting on the edge of his chair now. He and this stunning crumpet were entirely on the same wavelength. It was a delightful idea she had come straight to his office, without the professor's knowledge.

"In the mean while," she said jauntily, "I pushed such a drawn-out list as you are hinting at, under his very nose, at our office this morning ~ eh, he seemed pretty glum, you know, about some difference between the version he published and the one that rests at our premises."

"So he had got wind of that too?"

The señorita got lightly over that 'too' in Miguel's allusion. *That chick is quite a tough one; you can't get her off the track so easily,* it flashed upon his mind. Where she had got such a list from, then? Not quite the territory of an academician with such a beatific smile, was it? As far as Miguel knew, they had not even caught up with that at the faculty of criminology. And were green with envy at him, the news chaser.

"As you can fancy, producers/actors readily make up their own scenario (and for that matter, our 'Duke' may call himself a big fellow). But," she sighed, "just like politicians and academicians, they are walking on air."

"Pigheaded? Don't tell me! So, you didn't manage to make him change his mind either? Yeah, that's tilting at windmills."

"Well, not completely after all," she smiled knowingly. "Mister Mikes seems to be doubting at his fixed idea now: that if you just show those fellows you're not easily daunted and their deterrent manœuvres don't make you quiver like a wally, they will soon eat from your hand as tame pigeons do."

"Yes, fine! Buena imitación, señora, hmm … señorita. You really mimic him well," Miguel chuckled. Still, a bit intimidated again by her verve and fluency, he thought to himself: *beware of your own enchantment, old chico.* Somewhere there had to be a key to all that mysterious fuss about that old archduke and he felt it might be in the hands of this young lady after all. As a news serf, however, he had learnt to act relying on his intuition every now and then, yet without unconditionally trusting his feeling. *Suppose this lady has elaborated a scenario of her own and she tries to hitch you into her scheme, you'll get squeezed between the devil and the deep blue sea,* he thought as he asked her: "And you, señorita, as an expert ‑ what's your opinion about it? Those two versions, I mean, how is that possible?"

Again she produced that affable smile of hers. "How many versions of the New Testament are there, señor Mortado, besides the four declared sacrosanct by the Church ‑ or shall I say: 'purged' versions? And which of them tells the truth, nothing but the truth …?"

She got up with a mysterious elegance that, in Miguel's eyes, was not of this earth. "I must leave you, señor Mortado, for your guests will be arriving presently. May I count on you trying furthermore to restrain your occasional publisher a bit? Otherwise I am afraid some irreparable damage could be inflicted upon the spiritual inheritance of the Dux. You, hmm …" she winked, "haven't seen me this morning, have you?"

Miguel showed her out with the diffidence of a choir-boy who sees for the first time Botticelli's Aphrodite getting out of her oyster-shell. Too bashful to insist on her role in this whole affair. *I may as well put this into the corner of oblivion now,* he sighed, as he saw through the window doña Dolores vanishing under the arcades at the opposite side. None too soon, for there already the Chest got out of his pocket-size car.

25

Like a steamroller professor Marquez had invaded the office of the chief editor. With his dishevelled head of hair, flushed face, his tie pulled askew, there was something about him of a bulldog taking to his heels for a pack of street mongrels. "Nice visit you had here," he panted, out of breath. *Oh, now he drops out of his role,* thought Miguel, more cool-headedly than he had expected, *and he switches to the part of the cuckold who smells a rat and returns home prematurely.*

"Oh, you mean ~ ..." But the academician, his head turning as red as a turkey-cock's, did not let himself be brushed off: "I know that perfume, amigo."

"Do you?" Miguel retorted. "Then you must be on intimate terms with doña Marcella. You surprise me, professor."

"Marcella? Oh, our telly star. No, no, hmmm ... I was thinking, la Francisqui~ ..., well, my closest staff member, doña ..."

"Why! When even you at that college are getting on that well with our Beloved Marcaian Women ..." the editor giggled, hinting at the profuse application of 'BMW's'. "Unless the lady-assistants too assume such stars' airs."

Though quite out of his beat that day, the chief-editor fell back on his role of a rogue, as pleased as Punch that he could lead the professor up the garden-path. But once you have lied, you must go on lying, and that was no picnic if you had to cope with a Roberto Marquez, rather a brains athlete than an armchair scholar. Miguel had to go all lengths to make la Marcella's interest in the tandem Dux-Duke seem plausible. *And before long freshen up her own memory pronto pronto,* it flashed through his mind. Meanwhile he tried to take the Prof aside, to the settees, with a glass of amontillado and the question about that ambiguous last letter to Catalí.

There was already number two knocking at the door. Upon opening, he stepped back: la Marcella, radiant in the doorway. "Señora!" the editor hiccupped, and he tried to keep her outside. "Don't worry, Caro," and she slipped deftly under his arm. "I'm in the picture."

As soon as she saw prof. Marquez sitting there, she whispered, turning half around her axis, with a conspiratorial wink: "Dolores Francisquita, right? Women together. Smart arrangement, trust me."

Extending her hand she went up to the professor, a grand pose. While Miguel was holding his heart, he heard her making up a dodge, to explain her quick return. She had changed her mind, this meeting was not to be missed if you wanted to keep up with the scheming and plotting à la Marcaiaise …

The perfume! Miguel held his breath. Apparently, however, Roberto Marquez was too much stupefied by her dash to fall back on his olfaction.

That intermezzo gave Miguel Mortado a moment of respite to list all the points. Just what the Prof and the flashy presenter also had in mind, amiably chattering amongst themselves, so that Miguel, fiddling at the shelves, could use the sherry glasses as an alibi to peer at the strange couple.

By the time Messrs press tycoon, stock broker and petty political arrangers were dropping in, he felt strengthened, also by the sacrament of Marcaio's blessed liquid: the paló. That somewhat treacly concoction with a whiff of figs and carob beans, which not only made the tongues sticky and looser, but also the spirit. Particularly if you added a drop from the family medicine chest of Miguel's spouse.

A few hours later, now even more invigorated by the blessing of the same sacrament, the editor of the Diario got the impression that the lights of the boats were passing along the Avenido del Mar, dancing like fireflies in the twilight. Someone seeing señor Mortado's car zigzagging with little shocks now and then, wondered: has that chap's engine also got in a little more alcohol than fuel? *Don't sputter, amigo,* Miguel sniggered, without thinking twice there might be another reason for those little hitches.

You're a crack, Mortado, he smirked, as the scenes began to trickle back to his mind bit by bit. At every turn he was chortling to himself, because of all those grotesque faces. Yet, it had not been a cinch, fobbing off that bunch of heavy-weights. Especially the face of the Mediatec boss was spelling trouble. Any moment he had expected a torrent of carambas and hijo de puta's over his own head. Fortunately there had come some help from Roberto Marquez' corner, the latter starting to toast to the ponderous plutocrat and reciting an ode to that divine black nectar. The big man must have flushed a good deal of scotch or Quattro y Très beforehand ~ so fast it seemed to work. Then la Marcella took over, and she had managed to charm him out of his inborn recalcitrance. Apart from a few outbursts (about that 'kind of American desecrator' and 'those impudent vultures who did not show any respect for the local demureness'), the big boss had listened, reluctantly at first, but with growing willingness and more and more laughing wrinkles, to Miguel's propositions.

How he was aiming at a gentleman's agreement with Dugal Mikes. What had been published up to now, did not discredit the Archidux after all, did it? Every islander knew about his attachment to the pretty carpenter's daughter and this could only give a bucolic and more lyrical tinge to it. Quite nice though?

"As long as it remains platonic," the Mediatec man had flared up once more. "But from the moment this cockalorum turns up with spicy details ~ terminado!" He went on jabbering something about that hogwash they had tried to use more than once before to ruin Marcaio's reputation. That libertine messing around and lecherous cajoling with room-maids and country girls. Besides, he knew about that Mikes's reputation as a philanderer and ~ well yes, it had also come to his ears that the old Viennese, or Florentine, weirdo had been a maverick, never averse to one adventure more or less. But okay, they did have him anyway, and they had done their utmost to grant him a decent place in the schoolbooks. "And every scoundrel who tampers with it, to smudge our imago, we ... we shall air his dirty linen in public!"

But there, mister Mediatec's tongue, becoming heavier all the time, had started slurring. Marcella handed her overcoat to him: "At least one piece of myself." Whereupon he had burst out in spontaneous laughter and from then on the strain was broken.

"Now the point is to make it plain to mister Mikes that the Letras Secretas had better appear in book form. A truly bibliophile edition, in the end." With that sop Miguel had already tried to tempt his American friend once before. That would look nicer after all, let the document show to full advantage, and Miguel's publishing house could certainly cope with that ... At that very moment Dugal had been stung to the quick, but now there was a greater chance he would snap at it. Namely, readers who were swallowing don Lois's mellowy prose like sweetmeat, were likely to look forward to more of it. "And thus we can keep friend and foe at bay, see?"

That's precisely what Duke had imputed to him then. With a Marcella's support, however, it might succeed. "Why, that would make a nice modus vivendi for all parties," she sided with him, before the other gentlemen. Such a book was hard to stomach anyway for the general reading public, which, on the other hand, could not be kept dangling either and so they would be dished up some more filtered instalments.

Por supuesto! Of course, to every bottle fits a stopper, certainly on this island of arrangers, the editor giggled. That bit of an actor was going to come round, wasn't he, the Marcaian moral squad nodding self-complacently, Miguel's big boss getting between the sheets with his much younger mistress … Everyone content, Miguel content.

At a stone's throw from his house his car breathed its last altogether and it did not register with señor Mortado that his vehicle had just been filled up. *You just take a nap here,* he grinned and, staggering forward, he was looking for his latchkey. Keeping upright, that was the caper now, and that way he did not notice that the front-door opened by itself.

"You swindler!" That's how, the morning after, Catarí tumbled on her room-mate, sitting, a bit drowsy still, at the breakfast table.

"?" As he kept gazing at her straight-faced, she sneered: "Look at that, the injured innocence itself. And what about that cheque slipped into the copy for señor Mortado's latest issue? That was also done by mistake, I presume?"

"Cheque, what are you drivelling, Catarí?"

She smiled triumphantly, though, at his bewildered grimace. Yeah, yeah, that made him sit up, eh Dukie! What the heck did he think she had been up to all those days as bossie was whiling away his time with the private chares of a 160-plusser?

"Has that lousy Miguel himself been peaching to you?" he sniffed disdainfully.

"No, I've some more other sources, darling. You are warned and so, worth two men. It may come in handy against that gang."

Keep the flame burning." That brought Marcella's motto to her mind. *No worry, my flame will never die down, baby.* That had been Duke's personal experience during their previous night session. Custom is the mother of boredom, was one of his favourite aphorisms. Well, with la Ionès there was no shade of a chance to that, and least of all when there were rivals in the field, certainly of doña Dolores's calibre. "Or I'm going to devour you the way the female of the praying mantis does," she used to threaten.

Yet, these shady practices were not really to her liking either. A guy with business secrets is as unreliable as an adulterous spouse, was her judgement.

"Oh, that's an affair between men? Well I never, cheating me with a man! Look, Miguel or Dolores, all the same, it's a question of principles."

"Principles, principles! For those paltry five thousand europesas you needn't buy one dress less …"

"What, five thou- …" she yelled. "Have you given it a thought yet how many money grubbers have gone to the dogs due to the seduction of such bribery? Just suppose the phone started ringing here and an icy voice said: 'We have just heard a car fell into a ravine between … '. Yes?"

Gesticulating, Catarí was pacing up and down the room, exasperated about Dugal's pose of the meek choirboy ready to confess his juvenile sins.

"Cathy! If those rascals soon get onto it that we won't just eat out of their hands, they're going to change their tune." *Or put the thumbscrews on us altogether.*

That reflection was not fading yet and: Rrring! There it was. He saw Catarí stiffening. With that unrivalled little groove between her eyebrows that made her so irresistible when something bothered her. She swallowed, stretched her arm in slow motion, handing the receiver to him. "Hello, Mikes speaking."

"Hello?" Complete silence at the other side, as if the line had been cut off.

Stupido! Dugal could have given himself a wallop. *What duffer gives his own name first?* He was about to put down the receiver already. "You all go to hell!" Then, suddenly there was another grating voice coming through, as though from another galaxy: " …señor … Disculpe, señor Maïks …"

Your poor Miguel, he signalled to Catarina, relieved: no time bomb hidden in his suitcase, his wife (or mistress?) was not assaulted, nor his house set ablaze … So what?

"…my whole collection … señor, worth a million … to me …"

As the stammering editor of the Diario was gradually coming to his senses again, Dugal was not yet able to make head or tail of his story. "Tranquillo, amigo. Your collection? Okay, what collection, and what's wrong with it?"

"Larceny, amigo! Robado, Madre de Díos. Pinched, nabbed, sto- …"

Dugal kept the receiver an ell away from himself. *Going off like an alarmclock,* he grinned to Catarí. *Fat lot we care about that hardboiled hoarder with his collections that he has wheedled out of Tom, Dick and Harry, in exchange for the withdrawal of a not so flattering report. To hell with his golden ducats from Duke d'Alva's time or some antique amphoras from a clandestine diver.*

"That bloke is totally off his stroke," he sighed. Catarí's wit couldn't get a grasp on it either, but as Miguel's lament was spattering over him, a sudden idea came to his mind. *They have diddled him out of his Dux!* Where could you still find such a don Lois de Altdorf fetishist as this deuced typographer? All imaginable pen drawings of his Excellency, photos and manuscripts, plus a wealth of utensils ~ from binoculars, a chain watch, liquor flasks, worn-off feather pens, up to a brass sextant and a genuine inkpot in the shape of a globe. All that had slipped through the mazes of the museum classification ~ you name it, Miguel Mortado had got it. And now: vanished, embezzled by the grubby hands of a few culturally retarded minds, in charge of god knows which anonymous barbarian organization. "As if they have been pawing over your own wife or daughter, bah, fascistas!"

Catarí noticed Dugal's secret amusement about the pearls that señor Mortado was lacing up on a rosary of curses. *Translation undesirable,* Catarí sniggered. This was grist to Duke's mill: "Yes, Miguel. Those guys would do in their granny in the name of honesty and respect for a monument." Resolutely he threw the ball to the other side.

"What? Funeral mourners who shove underhand bribes under the counter of the local canning manufacturers, that's what they are! Just wait! I've got enough evidence against them, I'm telling you."

But what could he do? Dugal tempered him. Perhaps even that home-jacking was just the umpteenth macabre joke to scare them to death. For the same reason, though, they might be shadowed everywhere by their orderlies. "Want to bet this very talk is being tapped now?"

That was only adding fuel to the fire. The little typesetter, still so circumspect a moment ago, was now freaking out altogether. "Aren't we any better than a timid weasel that is startled by a scarecrow ~ same as a bigot is by an omen of the devil? No, Dugal, that's the limit, now we'll press on with it, even if we have to smoke the guardia civil out of its hole."

After letting him go on rattling like that for a while, Dugal put the receiver back down. "That hit home," he thought self-complacently. "From now onwards this Mortado is a time bomb under the buttocks of the revisionists here. At the end he was talking about a ~ hmmm …"

"Jordi Martell," Catarí said. "A graphologist. A manuscript expert who has some more forgeries on his record."

Dugal looked at her, flabbergasted as if snow were falling in their orange orchard at midsummer: "Well, I'll be! How did you know …?"

26

The quarter of the city where Jordi Martell lived, was totally in disproportion with his shabby appearance. The 'slob', some of the garrulous neighbour women called him. About his house, though, there was little to disapprove. No dingy curtains at all, or peeling door and window frames. Even the little front garden, though a bit more frugal than most of them, was not so overgrown with ivy and vinca minor as the brook was, a little further down.

Roberto Marquez liked passing here now and then, on one of his weekly jogging rounds. This quiet avenue, lined by plane trees and some mulberry trees, was still pervaded by the atmosphere of four decades ago, the building era in which small clerks and tradesmen sought refuge here from the increasing bustle in the centre of Palmera, then bursting out of its joints.

In his wild years the Chest had been a talented shot putter and a few times this crack had even represented the nation in hammer throwing as the country's champion happened to drop out. Now at this age, however, these jogtrots along the outskirts seemed conditionally more suitable to him than real power training supported by synthetic proteins and muscle intensifiers.

Anyone who had noticed how this sturdy figure (truly, without that boosted biomass from those days) had already looked around a couple of times, not at an imaginary opponent, but whether there were no snoopers close on his heels, could have observed an unusual wariness about him. Such as the lady in an inconspicuous car, about two-hundred yards behind him. A false blonde, squeezing her car in between two trees, at the moment when the sportive prof was about to walk up one of the garden paths along a fence.

She saw Roberto again peering around a bit awkwardly - *what a bungling intriguer,* she grinned. It took a while until Jordi Martell opened the door ajar. *A shrew mouse peeping over a spectacle-frame from the health insurance, anxious what eccentric may now be looking for its poor hole again.* The professor always got the feeling this marginal oddball could read his thoughts. As to him, Martell was a misunderstood genius. Too brilliant to mould away in the academic ambience or to render lackey services to police and justice. Covertly he envied the manuscript wizard for his phenomenal proficiency. Especially in the craft of the quasi perfect imitation of yellowing, age-old documents. That the 'Copier', as he was known in some dubious circles, also had a career as a jailbird on his record, made him all the more admirable.

"You know why I'm here." Roberto appeared to himself like a right-minded citizen wanting to ask a politician for a favour. Humiliating, no?

"Why should I?" Jordi Martell had this nasty idiosyncrasy of keeping his clients waiting in the doorway. That put their self-esteem to the test, some even started to find themselves sordid.

"Those two versions, come on, you know." The infamous graphologist kept feigning ignorance, until Roberto came down handsomely. *Hmm, slush money,* Jordi grimaced, and he showed the lecturer, sweating all over now, in after a lot of prodding.

About an hour later the false blonde, who had manoeuvred her small car a bit closer, saw Roberto Marquez coming out again. He looked radiant.

No sooner had the prof stepped down the threshold, however, than he contorted his face again. A lean, out-and-out southern type had jumped over the kerb and ran straight past him. "Hasta luego, don Marquez!"

Miguel Mortado, chuckled the lady in the car, *unbelievable, that fellow. It looks like keeping open house there, a hooker's booth with non-stop service.*

She hesitated for a moment. Was she going to leave the Chest, who, suddenly looking round suspiciously, beat a retreat, to his own reflections, and wait for the small, high-spirited editor? Her curiosity about the file in Roberto's hand got the upper hand. Even before he reached the corner of the street, she drove after him. Put on her sunglasses and, passing him as slowly as possible, without drawing attention, she was able to spy on him. Parked between the cars alongside, a bit farther, so that, peering in the rear-view mirror, she was able to watch his countenance again. Then she made a 360-degree turn and started the way back to Jordi Martell.

"This Martell seems to be one of the most colourful figures on Marcaio,"

Catarí explained with a pedantic air. "A bit like the local Champollion. Utterly non-academic, but unequalled when it comes to deciphering the apocryphal writings that his higher educated fellow-craftsmen could not make head or tail of. A few days ago he was on Canal Uno still, in a report of …"

"Of la Marcella?!" That could not be true, could it? That telly-babe was not going to poach on his domain, or else … "Do you mean that make-up pussy has managed to make that letter forger spill the beans ~ and don't tell me it was about those two different …?"

Dugal could hardly get it across his lips. What he had been putting his back into, would be snatched away by such a disreputable news chaser and her half-baked spouse, in alliance with a fraud. Actually he was pissed off with Catarí, because behind his back she had taken part in that scheming. *Women! They always want to get their way, to prove that this 'weaker' of their sex does not apply to their grey brain cells.*

"What is true about that 'expurgated' version and whether both are authentically from L.S.'s hand ~ an auto-correction by way of speaking? Something like that, yes. Yet, not only paper is tolerant, also on the small screen half-truth is the rule."

She did not need to say that to him, of all people! *The truth is an illusion and the illusion is the truth, and that goes for the peeping box more than anywhere else.*

"Oscar Wilde? Or Bernie Shaw?" she made a guess.

"Borrowed from a De Gourmont." He did not know a great deal about the French belles-lettres, but now he savvied where Cathy got her wisdom from.

"Don't tell me you and this Marcella …? You don't say so."

She gave him one of those most enigmatic smiles of hers: after making the takes about the Letras Secretas they had had a chat with that mister Manuscript. "Over a glass of wine," she said, her eyes half-closed. "And you know, 'in vino veritas'. And as Jordi Martell is an epicure …"

She did not need any more to convince her honey. That fluid between both of them ~ call it telepathy or a sixth sense ~ gave him the sensation that had befallen him upon finding the hidden walking canes. A nearly paranormal hallucination, he had thought in those days of his dilettantish tinkering with trowel and stucco, that something had survived at least of that branded couple. Something tangible, besides their gnawed-off bones, and somehow it had returned to this refuge, here at Ses Taca.

"Come." He did not need to insist, for Catarina had already gone before him.

"So, Dukie, you think you'll find the key to the L.S.-secret at that parchment worm's place?" Catarí sounded much more sceptical now than a while ago. They had been beside themselves and on their way she had reported on Marcella's interview of Jordi Martell.

How the snappy figurehead of Canal Uno dragged the dingy graphologist before the camera, with the witness value of a great-nephew of the prolific Franz Joseph popping up with a proof of the emperor's impotence. That clever Dick had stolen the show after all. Yes, he had explicit indications that the homesick don Lois had written such epistles at Brendais. Addressed to la Catalí, indeed. But whether he had rewritten some passages? Or had those letters ever been really delivered at the place of destination ~ tch, and what about that scenario of La Dama de Ses Taca's survival? There were some pertinent obituaries after all, or weren't there?

Señor Martell had turned and twisted everything, substantiated and yet dis-proved; he could blow up and put out a fire at the same time, and finally the viewers knew as much as before. "But what he keeps up his sleeve, can probably be found around here, don't you think so?"

They looked at each other as Bonnie and Clyde did before a hold-up. *Shall we?* One hand just on the door of the car, Dugal halted, half upright. Whom did they see there running out of the doorway, pursued by the devil, so it seemed? "La Marcella!" both shouted upset. At a gallop they dashed through the open door, almost certain what they were going to find inside there. Instead of an agitated Jordi Martell chasing the TV-star out of the house, in utter wrath and who knows even in the nuddy, the manuscript expert, however, was sitting quietly at his desk. Peacefully, but open-mouthed, staring over a letter into eternity.

Taken aback, they felt his pulse, touched his shoulders, his face. "As dead as a dodo," Dugal whispered. "And she was here, a minute ago." Catarí started back, her knees shaking. "Marcella?" she said, as he kept gazing at her hazily. "How terrified the poor girl must have been!"

"Cathy, just think a moment. What was that racy piece lounging about here, and what does that document here mean?"

Dugal picked it up and feverishly they started to ransack drawers, shelves and tables. "Hadn't we better warn the police?" she panicked all of a sudden and jumped towards the phone. "No, wait! Are you crazy, our fingerprints are everywhere around here." On impulse, Catarí wanted to wipe out all their traces ~ a hopeless task. Dugal was pulling at her sleeve to get off. "Let's clear out here, we mustn't act too rashly." First watch out calmly, whether there were not any neighbours lying on the look-out and then drive back to town unobtrusively.

Never before had they been so upset. Half an hour later they were sitting on a terrace at the Plaza de Rosas, recovering from their emotions. Dugal tried to look sturdy, but it did not come easy to him. "In the end it's a mercy he was such a loner. There's a great chance no one will care a straw about it."

How could you say anything like that, she wondered. Yet, she knew it was a mere pose with him. This was no movie, Duke, and besides, the poor fellow was a bit balmy perhaps, but they knew how every Tom, Dick and Harry trampled into his house for all chores and sundries. "Yes, even TV-celebs," he tried to banter. His black humour, however, glanced off on Catarina's deadly earnest.

"By the way, who says Marcella hasn't rung up the guardia civil for quite a while?" she said anxiously. *And a good thing too, for if we had done so ourselves, we were likely to be sitting at the police-station till now ...* Then the glass on Jordi's desk came to his mind again. Fortunately they had not touched it. Suddenly he recalled: the file he had hastily whisked away! Promptly he groped for the papers in the pocket of his jacket.

"Well, I never!" Dugal whistled between his teeth and showed the catch: a page from a diary, with on the present day an appointment with El Gorilla ~ who else could this be but the Chest?~ and La Bocca, the mouthpiece of Marcaio for sure, alias Marcella. The rest were fragments that the suddenly deceased had obviously been sorting out, and, yes, Dugal at once recognized that handwriting. They were the feuilles volantes, the notes the archduke made on his wandering tours hither and thither. Or had Jordi copied them?

"Look!" Catarí jumped up from her chair. A canary yellow cabriolet was tearing along the square and whooshed narrowly past their terrace. All in a mere whiz, yet enough to recognize the driver: "Professor Marquez!"

163

They could not trust their eyes. "Impossible, that dried cod in such a flashy thing, we haven't got a bout of a sunstroke, have we?" But it was not a phantom either. Nodding their head, they leant back in their seats and then … "Bang!"

With a terrible crash a number of cars parked nearby were smashed to smithereens. Metal pieces were flying around like shrapnel. "No, not …?"

Oh yes, this time it was a hit. Third time lucky! Dugal seemed rooted to the spot, glued to his chair. He appeared to himself like a spectator at his own funeral procession.

A few minutes later the Plaza de Rosas was teeming with wailing sirens. Before they realized it, they found themselves sitting in an ambulance. It was no use protesting. "Minute splinters," sounded the diagnosis at the emergency department.

"I thought we had been abducted," said Catarí with relief. At the exit, however, they were picked up from the street and taken to the police station straight away. "So *that* was the pretext!" Dugal was on the verge of exploding. *Please, say it isn't true,* Catarí sighed, for she knew him. *There's trouble in the air.*

"Sorry," the clerk silenced them at once, "all witnesses must be heard. My time is as precious as a tourist's is!"

A policewoman came up to him and whispered something in his ear, in the meantime glancing at the famous movie couple with a twinkle in her eyes. "Oh, señora y señor Maïks …"

Unbelievable what a metamorphosis that gruff chief constable with his bulldog face showed all at once. *Isn't it touching, how fame in no time can make you a persona grata,* Catarí grinned pitifully, while the arm of the law put himself out to find manifold apologies. "Disculpe por esta incomodidad," he excused himself for the inconvenience. Course, this was beyond his will, but they could not take any risks, with all those vandals and hotheads, etc., etc …

Oh, all right, but they were the butt of this action, and what was Mister Cop going to do about that? Keeping tabs on people, bragging and acting portentous, yes, but apart from that, everything was swept under the carpet!

Dukie just can't help blowing himself up again, sighed Catarí, and she pulled him along at his sleeve.

27

"*Por supuesto, tío.*" *I know, uncle,* the driver grumbled, as Dugal kept waving the street map before his nose on which he had marked the way to Prof. Marquez's villa. "But we've got to follow that deviation of the road."

"Deviation?!" Dugal began to rage at the driver: not a bit of it, he just wanted to lead them up the garden path and wheedle money out of them. The fellow turned round and said coolly: "Exactly, well guessed. You stay nicely here until I chuck you out at the place of destination."

A cold shiver running down her spine made Catarí stiffen. *What if that bloke takes us to a remote workshop or quay and within an hour we are squeezed in here: tinned in a taxi?*

All of a sudden Dugal seized the man by the throat from behind. He slapped back, but Dugal's strangling grip got stronger and the fellow had to stop alongside, where he was hanging over the steering-wheel, coughing and snorting, as Dugal and Catarí took to their heels. "That one's going to stay drowsy for a while," Dugal panted behind her, but Catarí kept running down the street as if any moment a shower of shot could fly around their ears.

At the next corner there was already another cab driving up slowly, canvassing for potential customers. "Pára!" This time Dugal overwhelmed him in advance with Roberto's visiting-card. "Ah, professor Marquez?" The driver's face brightened. "No detours, claro? To this address, and straight on, please! No larks as the previous bloke tried to make."

"Si, si, por supuesto, señor. We know him well, the professor."

This one looks decent, Catarí was examining him. A bit further the driver saw his colleague crawling out of his taxi. *That daft Lorenzo, blind drunk again,*" he chuckled. "That desperado?" Dugal hissed. "No way, that thug wanted to kidnap us and drop us somewhere for a bit of slush money from a Mafioso boss."

Noticing the surprise on the chauffeur's face, Catarí explained the situation. Upon which the good man burst out laughing. "Typical of Lorenzo. He a terrorist? No, he just wanted to pull your leg a bit, señora."

He turned into the Carretera Miró and chose a secondary road heading for Andairitx. "Hey listen, pal, are you hard of hearing or do you belong to the same kind as that other goofball?"

"Señor," the driver answered quietly, assuring them this was the way to the Calle de Pájaros; not its namesake, though, in that urbanization at the eastern outskirts of Palmera. The professor had lately moved out to the countryside: a dream of an old quinta, tipico Marcaín, a wonderful dwelling close to the modest hovel of the taximan's household.

"But for all that we might as well have been lynched or riddled with bullets," Dugal still insisted some minutes later, while running after Catarí, who was walking head upwards. Brusquely she turned round: "You've fixed this well again, Dukie," she said, swinging her arms round. Here they were, in the middle of nowhere. That damned wag with his 'dream' of a country-house! Bewildered, they gazed at the cloud of dust in which the taxi swept off as swiftly as an arrow.

Darn! Furious with himself, Dugal was spinning around. Hey, look here!"

Half hidden in a hedge of pittosporum tobira with its intoxicating fragrance there was a small plate above the mailbox: R.Marquez. Relieved, the couple followed the gravel path, more weeds than gravel, and there it was: a hacienda from the later years of Velasquez or Ribera, in its full ochre ornament as if the walls had just been dipped into the paint of the master himself. There was nothing to expect a Germanophile heart here that starts beating faster at anything blonde walking about, with blue eyes and a low-necked dirndl.

It was Mrs. Professor. Thoroughbred southern, not fitting in that Teutonic picture either, except for that décolletage, but quite in tune with the scenery. She recognized them at once, her heroes of the white screen: oh, señor Maïks and señora Ionès, here and there, qué honor!

But what about her husband? "Roberto, mi corazón, oh el pobre!" Her better half had been absent again all day long, the last few days he had been quite unmanageable. Seemed to be rather huffy, her cariño. Why, she did not know, he bottled up everything. But some people were edging him on, she was really scared …

By the time they started recovering from Mrs Marquez' avalanche of words, they were already dashing through the centre, straight to the Universidad de Palmera. "Yeah, yeah, the secretive prof," Dugal taunted, and she: "You can understand, if such a morsel of sensual intelligence falls on your lap at your workplace," scowling sarcastically/suspiciously at her Dukie.

They found a totally different Roberto in his usual den at the faculty: anything but hectic, plunged in his documents with Buddhist innocence. The Chest looked up perplexedly ~ or … he was putting on a fine act. Only, he gave a dazed impression. *Rather of an opium puffer; alright, literary shag is opium for highbrows.* With his clenched teeth Dugal was a truculent appearance; still, it was Catarí who chose for the frontal attack.

"I, milady, sweeping in a cabriolet along the Plaza de Rosas? No, my friends, do you see me as a kamikaze pilot …?"

His fit of fun about the scene as Catarina had evoked it, seemed too spontaneous to be feigned. "Who can play your alibi? Your harmless private assistant?" Dugal sneered nonetheless.

"I beg your pardon!" the professor squabbled in his turn, fed up with all those mean blows below the belt. His Maddalena was used to that sort of things, really. If you slip between the sheets of a letter-devouring weirdo like him, you know you've got to share him with his passion now and then. Rather than with a pretty rival, he added, pretty tickled. Suddenly he seemed to hit upon an idea.

"But wait a moment." His younger brother! A curtain of wrinkles drew up above the lecturer's eyebrows. *Si, tu hermano, ah si, profesór,* Dugal muttered sulkily. Yet, you could see Roberto was not making up a dodge: "I'm afraid he has got himself into a jam again. I could have thought so."

If Roberto's fearful suspicions were right, they had used their Benjamin as a bait. That had already occurred a few times before. A rather hazy organization blackmailed him sometimes, because he did not have quite a clean slate. Lately the police had passed on some signs to Roberto that something might happen to his family.

Oh, really? This could be no more coincidence, those 'shady' characters had called in a double: his own brother, to incriminate Prof. Marquez before them. Clever idea: that way you could drive a wedge between congenial allies. Unless … Unless the Chest was playing a double game, but then he managed to stage that double's act with an unequalled performing talent. Better than in any moving picture Dugal himself had been involved in for the casting.

"Bravo, con brío," he tested the cerebral bundle of muscles once more, but Roberto swore indignantly that it was true. He had warned his brother persistently, but why, you can't keep standing bail for your family, can you? "To put it in Kafka's words: 'Wer einmal dem Fehlläuten der Glocken gefolgt is … ' If once you have followed the false ringing of the bells … Ah, a translator is a betrayer.

"Traduttore tradittore," echoed Dugal, "I hope that doesn't go for you, hermano. Let's be frank: what are you withholding from us?"

"What are *you* holding back from *me*?!" the prof retorted exceptionally spitefully. "Let's put it like this: I have discovered some traces of the Dux that so far had been shrouded in veils. And which I suppose you are dying to see. But I know what you've got in your pocket there and so … the pleasure is mutual."

Shocked, the Miles looked at each other. Caught in the act, that's how they felt, for that was as plain as day: Roberto did know.

"From Jordí Martell?" But then the prof was also in the picture about their visit to the graphologist! And its fatal outcome. *He surely won't have …* Catarí swallowed. Panic, however, soon changed into a sense of power. *We know about his date this very morning and how that fake blonde rushed out of his house. Unless that bitch of a Marcella (plus Dolores maybe) had arranged it all with him and we were hoaxed all right.*

For the time being, though, Roberto acted as innocent as a lamb. "Precisely," he nodded. "He wanted you to get hold of it in the first place. He was honestly convinced that you would come up with it to me anyway."

Wanted. Was. The wildest suppositions flashed across their mind again. And snapped off at the apparent gap in prof. Marquez's memory. "Tomorrow Jordi is dropping in and we'll see if we can puzzle things together a bit more clearly. A reconciliation of paradoxes, rather." No mentioning of his assistant or a plot. *Is he so naïve or such a smart comedian?* Dugal began getting immensely annoyed.

"But professor," Catalí interrupted him, unable to control herself any longer. "A man's life is at stake and you are doing as if … ~"

She faltered in the middle of her outburst at the intrusive ringing of the phone. Annoyed, Roberto went to take it up in the adjacent room. "What?!" That was the only thing that passed his lips. When he came back, deathly pale, he walked to his radio-set, a fossil in an awful state, on which his coffee pot stood, as well as a pile of catalogues. "The seven o' clock news," he mumbled.

Buenas tardes, queridos auditores. The lady-speaker, rattling like a machine gun, came straight to the point: ' … señor Jordi Martell, un notorio grafólogo, ha sido hallado muerto en su casa.' It made their hair stand on end, while the lady was reeling off the main items of the news, before getting into detail. *Imposible,* Roberto murmured, utterly upset.

Yet the report sounded formal: ' … señor Martell was found dead in his house by a neighbourwoman, this late afternoon, after receiving a phone-call from an unknown person. Soon after the police arrived at the spot and rumour has it that a number of people are being searched urgently, amongst others prof. Marquez, his assistant Dolores d'Omar and the couple Mikes-Ionès …"

Like thunderstruck, they were gazing at each other. "Where did they get this from?" Dugal burst out, as soon as he had recovered his speech again. One question after the other bounced to and fro between both of them. "Who's put that into their mouth?" "Who tipped off the police then?", "La Marcella?", "Why us?"

All at once both their eyes focused on the professor, the way you look at a dog that has farted and then lies down at a safe distance from the locus delicti.

"How do you mean? I say, why are you watching me? This morning the good soul was still his usual self. But … wait a moment!" Now he in his turn was gazing at them suspiciously.

Yes, they confessed, equally indignantly, they too had been there, but by that time poor Martell was already having a nap ~ or had been done in. But hey, why

had lady Marcella dashed out of the door, had she put the cops on their …?

"Gibberish," Roberto said fretfully. La pobre Marcella was not going to expose herself to prosecution, was she? Warning that neighbour woman, okay, but …

"But what then was she lounging about there – or was she acting under your orders maybe?"

He did not say yes or no, but judging from his anxious countenance, they saw it seemed a riddle to himself. "Anyhow," the Prof concluded after weighing his words, "as far as that police interrogation is concerned, that's fiddlesticks. Otherwise those gents had been here already. That must have been some bluff poker again. By the way, such a plot theory about that manuscript wizard is also rubbish. Jordi had a delicate health. Swallowed analgesics galore."

"Together with amontillado and sanlucar?" Catarí struck upon an idea. She had seen the bottles in his study-room. But that could also be a cunning trick, right, played by fellows who did want to get under that unfortunate Jordi's skin – for the sake of some definite documents?

"A happy combination," prof. Marquez smacked. "But then Dolores showed up, at a rather inconvenient moment, and the illustrious unknown visitors beat it. *From the backside probably, altogether empty-handed.*"

"Which means the poor wretch may have kicked the bucket quite a while before, under pressure of those extorters," Dugal was brooding on, picking up the habit of the scenario writer again. "Right about the time those jerks were feverishly busy searching." *Whence that disorder, as we found out,* Catarí mused guiltily. *Why, however, didn't doña Dolores try to get into touch with us? For the same reason maybe as we didn't. Not to arouse unnecessary suspicions, namely.* And besides, what would she have done, all by herself, as a woman?

In the meantime prof. Marquez had got up to fetch a bottle. "I think we're in for some pep stuff, the three of us," he judged, "and let's now tackle those hot potatoes. It's no use crying over spilt milk anyway," he added, to drive away the dismay in the couple's eyes. Same as a priest tries to soothe the grief of those left behind with a plaster of belief.

Dugal tarried to get the creased documents out of his pocket. Then he chose one of them and began to read it, first with the stiff tongue of a stark drunk bar customer, but faster and faster and gradually more fascinated:

"Querída Miss-you-know-her-name *etc., etc* … His usual mellifluous tone … Here he tells himself: "…my previous letters must have seemed

170

full of despair to you ..., the twaddle of a senile, grouchy whiner." Pom pom pom ... Hey, listen to this:

> *Last week there happened a miracle, Cariña. I have been released. I escaped from my bird's cage! I thought it impossible, but I had contrived a scheme and at last I ventured to carry it out. At daybreak my bodyguard already came into the room. Officially to bring my breakfast, but actually to spy on me, like every morning, whether I did not meddle with any secret documents. As my watchdog, with his martial pace and as many scars as decorations, let his Argus eyes sweep across my writing desk and the other furniture, he scanned, according to custom: "Und, Eure Hoheit - how are we this morning?" This time, however, the words died on his lips. The huddled body on the bench beside the bed gave him the shock of his life. Hastily his trembling bony legs sprinted out of the room. "Unmöglich, unmö- ..."*
>
> *Fancy his bewilderment when a quarter of an hour later he turns up again, with a doctor and some funereal prayers, and ... the bird has flown!*

28

Dugal looked up, rolling his eyes, just as if he were seeking the vanished corpse in prof. Marquez's study himself. *Jesus, this is becoming a bit steep. A few hours before his ink pot dries up, that sort of repatriated emigrant is describing his own resurrection. Pure paranoia.*

"I'm sure that passage is not findable in my cañas." That meant one out of two questions: either the old ailing L.S. did not draft this letra secreta himself at all and so, this was all just a macabre farce, emanating from the brain of an insipid wag – the same copier who had already put them on the wrong track with those two different versions; or …

"Or that Lazarus story is right and it's getting clearer and clearer they've mixed up Luigi Salvatore's course of life badly enough, for obvious reasons. Almost the way they did with the real Jesus or other ingenious marginal types like that," Catarí reasoned.

"Controversial ones, please," said Roberto. "Go on reading, Dugal."

… Of course, I had prepared my escape. I knew where to go. Yet it was quite a distance to walk up to the family of our old coachman. He is one of ours, Catalí, his tongue is sealed for ever."

Dugal looked up at them, amazed: *One of ours …, what did he mean by that?* Once more, though, Roberto insisted impatiently: come on, hurry!

… Notwithstanding, to me it was a real ordeal. The day before my personal physician would have been lamenting: 'Unmöglich!' With that lingering disease, my elephantiasis legs, I seemed doomed to spend my last days in my living space there at Brendais. And truly, I had to exert myself just to get going with those limbs of an elephant that, after months of confinement, is no longer used to taking a step outside his cage. But what other choice had I? Up there, in that musty drawing room where countesses and old spinsters used to dwell, I was like a living mummy between the stuffed birds and boar heads. Even if they picked me up again on the road, one hour or a day later, I had nothing to lose any more.

About the welcoming that I got at the home of our stalwarts there (whose name I had rather not mention ~ one never can tell) I can be brief. It was short-lived, but touching. Brimming with concern about my health and how I was going to do throughout my journey, that whole family were in commotion to make the strange guest feel comfortable. Not only with food and drink, but even some extra care: from a herb-doctor namely who knew the noble art of applying the powers of nature to my ailments. He was to stay in my company for a part of the trip.

At our departure, I still remember, there was a late evening market, the beginning of the Advent. The air was pregnant with baked apples and the scent of cinnamon ~ with pleasure I would have liked to mingle with the people that crowded around the market vendors. But our coach did not progress but at a footpace and soon we might be halted by some soldiers or night watchmen. A pedlar swiftly reached a goblet of warm wine with cloves up to me, through the door of the coach. "May God protect you during your journey," he called after the carriage, as if the good man knew more about it.

How I outlived this ordeal, remains a mystery to me. Yet, the human spirit proves to be strong. Σωμα σημα, as an old Greek proverb goes: the body is a tomb. Even with a person who is near dying, like myself, the power of the soul can work wonders. An irrepressible urge finally drove me across the mountains, on the wings of hope that I could alight on my 'Wahlheimat' once more: my favourite homestead, to climb up the goats' paths, in between pine-trees and rock masses, right into the steely blue sky. Until you descry, beneath on your left, the red roof-tiles of the cartuja, and there, a bit further, the emerald bay of Maremira, the seigniory I wanted to mould after your likeness, Cariña, with in the middle of it the snow-white mansion in which you figured as the land agent of our vineyards.

Just to fly once more the swallow's flight and inhale the scents that swarmed around you as a child in the beatitude of your nesting place! I wanted to see the wild flowers around that low house near the medlar tree where you were imbued with that feeling of security that was so strange to me.

Without that dreamlike image I should have broken down in my place of exile for a long time. Without you it would have been one path of sorrow and *I myself a pathetic withering plant, deprived of the* soft mould in which it thrives. But the memory of that good time has strengthened me so as to bear the hardships of this last, and also my severest, travel. Even though I am doomed to rove like a thief at night, my companions can see the radiant light in my eyes: the reflection, that is, of your image which I carry in my heart, my dear. For you are my breath of life, Marcaio is my breeding soil. A stray seed, I landed by chance (?) at the right spot, to sprout there beside you. Just as I am yearning now to return to that stretch of coastline, near the mother plant, where we are, both of us, indigenous. For only there my spirit can, together with yours, take root and thrive till in eternity.

Catarina's hand on his shoulder brought Dugal back down to the prosaic reality. Her eyes dwelt far away - *deep ponds of melancholy,* he thought, but shrank from making her that poetic compliment, lest she should shake her head: *you, silly wretch!* "Only now do I realize what Ses Taca meant to them," she mumbled. "A binding agent. That vintry was to them the symbol of their pilloried love, a token of affection that he never managed to express before these secret letters.

"And a symbol of the Vine," added prof. Marquez. Like two falcons in view of a prey, Dugal and Catarí were staring at him. This was the first time they heard him make such a blatant allusion.

"You can't mean that, proffy." It seemed inconceivable to them that Roberto would adhere to the thesis of the Davidian branching. Of course, he had put some overzealous students on it, so they could give free reign to their diligence. Of late, especially Catarí had been taken in by such a genealogic study in which L.S. was linked up with the desposyni, supposed far relatives of Sions's scion and his family. *Jesus! Bed-time pep reading stuff,* she thought, like all those page-turners of the past few decades which aroused one's scandalitis instinct, because all kinds of historic figures were linked to the 'Sangreal'. Clandestine inheritors of that repudiated royal blood who, up to our days, had to keep that kinship a secret, for fear of implications. *And intimidations – who can tell?* Catarí would come up with a bed sermon, right at his doze-off point. If you looked at it a bit more closely: how much pressure, yes blackmail, hadn't the Roman-royalistic establishment exerted on some bigwigs from the 'other' camp, in Europe and beyond? While that 'holy' DNA might still be wandering about in the genes of those who denied it: some old aristocratic and royal families.

Well, what of it? Hogwash, and all so far-fetched, Dugal scorned, green with envy. He thought nothing of the way she was turned on by all those vendors of 'extirpation' theories within the Christian lobby, even as far as in the marital bed. Oh boy, women! But what peeved him excessively, was that the Chest himself did not discard such speculative conjectures about a Grail pedigree as rank nonsense.

"Well, I don't know," Roberto said. "First of all, you can hardly get around that contestable passage in the eighth letter. I've made some sleuths go after that too," he grinned, referring to his 'general staff', "and what appears?"

"That His Worship might as well mean some dissidents of all kinds as they knocked about in those days, Cis- and Transalpine? Without them having necessarily anything to do with Grail tales and freemasonry. The whole lot surrounding the Dux on his travels, were quite a bizarre sight for his days, weren't they? And wasn't the prodigal son from Vienna himself passed off as a bit of an anarchist now and then?"

"Yes, even as a veiled communist. Nota bene by his imperial cousin. Our research work, though, has not found any explanation for don Lois's hardly disguised allusions. Anywhere he is talking about 'like-minded' brothers, their 'carrying pigeons', children of Demeter, etc …, living sprigs of the Vine, the whole genealogy that she, Catalí, was familiar with – yeah, that whole symbolism points unmistakeably at an allegorical code. Besides, in the last fragment he also talks about that coachman as 'one of ours'.

Reluctantly, Dugal on his part had to admit that he himself had also dwelled on that line of thought for a while. Afterwards it seemed to him sheer nitpicking. Wishful thinking of academic zealots, possessed by one microbe: to make their thesis an issue.

"So many links, all pointing in the same direction – that can no longer be pure speculative interpretation," prof. Marquez reflected. "Suppose there was really no more behind it than a bit of playing hide and seek with the established values, on the part of an inveterate non-conformist. Weltschmerz, out of regret about lost chances, and the nagging urge to take the guardians of the old order for a ride. Would any obscure organization, now more than a century later, still take offence at that ? So much so that they are willing to prang your little car for it and throw smoke bombs hither and thither to scare all those involved out of their wits? Come now!"

What, come now! And what about the Messianic L.S. thesis then? What backward nitwit of what simplistic alliance would bother about something like that in this nano or quantum era? A question of honour and conscience of a (possible) key-figure in a hypothetic model of state-leadership, and that even according to an alternative old-Christian ethos. Salvator: the guardian angel of the harassed Occident, go and tell that to the marines!

"But Jordi Martell, what about him?" Catarí suddenly brought up. "You already seem to forget that today a poor copyist kicked the bucket and that … – that we have been declared hunted game."

Yes, Dugal challenged him. Where were the police now – or was a prof as inviolable to the guardia civil as the pope was?

Roberto shook his head pitifully. "Queridos amigos! Do you really believe it was authentic, that radio report? I had grasped it at once. That was a well- orchestrated move again, those fellows are playing cleverly, I must admit. Can spread such fake reports indirectly, so one of them must be pretty close to the source." He reached out for the phone and was about to dial the number of the police station: so, then they could hear the confirmation from their own mouth.

"Are you crazy?" Dugal put his hand on Roberto's, pushing the receiver back. Did he want them to come and run them in at once? Roberto was grinning again.

"If there really were a hitch somewhere, they would have come to pick me … us up long before. And besides ~ why should they?" He looked at them teasingly, as though to examine them if they had no murder on their conscience.

Yes, Dugal suddenly looked up audaciously, *who says they haven't found a natural cause of death after all, a heart attack, if only after seeing that disguised stunner Marcella? Or perhaps under pressure of one of their gang members who also paid the wily graphologist a visit in the meantime.*

"Moreover, I'm going to tell you something else," Roberto resumed his argumentation. "Jordi Martell was one of them ~ their brothers."

Dugal made Catarí a sign of empathy: *is he really getting crackers now?*

"Their brothers: barbarians?" she joined in the act, as if a raving prof is as scaring as a freaky terrorist.

"No … Their brethren," Roberto impatiently clicked his tongue. And as Dugal, straight-faced, looked even more baffled ~ Jordi a friar, or almost, well … he did not know that forger of documents was a celibatarian ~, the academician thought that would do. "You surely know what I'm hinting at." Dugal, who would have liked to feign innocence a bit longer, noticed that Roberto was not quite in the mood for slapstick now.

"Jordi Martell," he said, his eyes half closed, like someone going to unveil the greatest state secret of Marcaio, "was not only an unequalled expert, nay, a crack in the field of graphology. An underestimated genius, so it seemed, but he didn't care a damn about that himself. After all, he was also an eminent genealogist. In fact, that was his greatest passion."

"Was it? Well, the greatest dilettantes are sometimes the best of experts.

Catarina guessed what was going on in him. Her Duke was thinking of pa Mikes for a moment: a wrestler and trapeze artist, but raised to the starry Hollywood sky owing to his ambitious drive. 'Making your hobby your work' was a slogan for softies. Fanatical animation, plus stamina ~ that was the formula for professional skill, or call it obsession.

"Yet, how does that bring mister Martell to the crossing of our road?"

she wanted to know. The professor's pride lit up in Roberto's eyes: the ability to link up innumerable facts in a higher coherence.

"Well, as a member of a southern European lodge and connoisseur of the 'holy' kin, he was informed about the interactions between the European dynasties and the Priory of ..."

"There we go again!" Dugal jumped to his feet. All those armchair scholars with their irrepressible urge to dig secret corridors under modern towers of power, he was sick of it. "But wait a moment, let the professor finish his explanation," Catarí checked him, fascinated by the story.

"Well," Roberto went on spinning out his story, "Jordi was about to delve into the role of the Archidux within the European network of - ..."

This time his statement was brusquely interrupted by the whining of Catarí's mobile. Mozart's Kleine Nachtmusik in a gimrack performance of a tipsy James Last band. "Hello?" Catarí's forehead contracted like a drawn curtain, a foretaste of an oldie's frown. Then she got into action: grabbing for her handbag and jacket.

"Hurry on! Our house has been broken into."

29

· · · · · ·

"Important visitors."

They had seen it from a distance. Lighted all over, Ses Taca looked like a torch in a pine wood. *The gentlemen didn't even take pains to close the shutters.* "The things you're thinking of!" Catarí moaned, feeling shocked. On their way her thoughts had dwelled all the time with Colomá, the maid of the night shift. And the couple they had taken on just a few days ago. 'Our CIA brigade,' as Dugal scorned. Quite a robust couple, with the copper tan of that gipsy-like dancing group from Valle de Muša and a somewhat shady background. Shoe-shiners and pedlars from town, knife grinders, newspaper vendors and kettle menders, fandango dancers …, they reflected the motley scope of crafts from Palmera's colourful past. Plucky enough, though, Catarí had judged them, to safeguard the old wine-house from fumblers and other undesired guests. If someone bumps into those black peters at dusk, Dugal chuckled, he is sure to take to his heels.

Question was whether the home-jackers had just made their catch before the change of shifts. Colomá still had rung them up herself, but perhaps ~ and hopefully ~ the bronzed watchdogs had already taken up their stand by then. Comfortably around the swimming-pool, where she, that female, according to good custom, first had a few puffs on her pipe, and the man had a fresh dive, a matter of setting cheerfully to his duty. But absolutely reliable they were, to be sure. These people were not prone to corruption, for prying into their lives.

No sooner had their crunching tyres halted than Catarí dashed to the door, which was left ajar. "Wait, you never can tell," Dugal shouted after her, but she already slipped inside, smashing into José. The failed Moor was in an awful state: his shirt soiled, his arms scratched all over and in his greyish hair there were sprigs of rosemary. In spite of it all she could not restrain her laughter. "José, what happened to you?" Dugal wormed himself past her, impatient to see the chaos. The hall was in a mess already, but then, in the rooms: all drawers were pulled out, clothes lay flung all around, and papers everywhere.

"Just begin," Catarí sighed.

"Zey had begin alreddy." José's Maria had shown up and was posing strappingly in the doorway.

"Didn't you manage to catch any of them?" asked Dugal.

"Yesse … orr almost." José had run after one of the men, through the door-window, had all but got him by the short hairs, but then he slipped on a set of steps and landed in the rosemary shrub.

"But what about Colomá?" asked Catarí.

Maria led the way to the bedroom. There she was lying, the maid, stretched out in their conjugal bed, a huge lump above her right eye. Though still pretty off balance, Colomá made her circumstantial report. How, sensing danger, she had awaited the perpetrators behind the door, a pie-roll at the ready. Until the door had been smashed open and after that, she passed out altogether. So, nobody recognized? The three of them were looking sheepishly at Catarí. Then she realized Dugal was already further inside.

She found him in the mezzanine, of course, his Secret Chamber. "And?"

Nothing. Fortunately, the closet with the double wall was untouched, the collection of cañas intact. Back in the living-room, Dugal went straight to the fixed phone: "I'm going to ring up señor Miguel."

Why the editor and not prof. Marquez, who was certainly waiting, on tenterhooks? He did not know, but something told him he could use Mortado now. "They've paid such a visit to him too, right? Hello?"

Slowly Dugal put down the receiver again, with a disconcerted gaze. "Nada. No note of music. That means …"

That meant that this umpteenth incident, same as the previous ones, was not a mere warning, a sturdy show-off on the part of some ultra conservatives, incensed by the tarnishing of their old paragon. These blokes, whether hired or not, were not going to be content with verbal violence. The raid at Miguel Mortado's, the series of alleged 'assaults' on his (or their?) trivial person, the appalling death of Jordi Martell, the intimidating media campaign against him … These could no longer be single coincidences. Uninvited guests of that kind did not cut off your telephone line for fun. Okay, they were not born yesterday and they knew the masters of the house would presently run out to get their mobile phone from their car. But in the meantime the communication with the housekeepers had been disturbed for a while.

The desire to deliver a report on the event, was quite over now. As they were still staying outside for a while, to see their 'security staff' out, once more they were overcome by the sensation of walking in the footprints of another couple, somewhere in the starry night. Of inhaling, with the same intensity, the same stimulating scents of the blossoms. From all forms of life there seemed to issue a thrill that connected them with the spirit of their predecessors.

There was little chance of sleeping that night. Again and again the idea was spinning through their heads: *what will come next; is there a way back; shall we ever really face those activists; which of our co-workers can we still fully trust? Perhaps we'd better chuck it up, the game isn't worth the candle, least of all to put your beloved's life at stake.*

"No, thanks, Duke. It's a chivalrous gesture to sacrifice your plans for me. But now I'm getting mad about it myself."

He did not want to admit it but it was a load off his mind when before daybreak they were bumping up the gravel road to the Maremira manor. At that early hour the average villager was still under blankets. But in that hacienda, once so stately a manor where noble families had ruled the roost for such a long time, the four households or so that nestled in it now, got up together with the chickens. Only a dunghill failed on the farm yard to complete the picture, they thought.

What decadence, compared to the revival of Ses Taca! On seeing the garden stairs in the style of the Italian renaissance, Dugal's heart flinched. He assured himself that, when the time was ripe for it, he would make this his next priority. On the other hand, this step back in time gave it a special stamp. Catarí already fancied a Zurbaran or Ribera putting up his easel there. *They at least would bring this patio to life again. Immortalizing the crafts and chares of these peasant families, in that colour spectrum of the 17th century. Even a Velasquez would not have disparaged this background for a somewhat commoner model of his female types.*

"Rather something for Granados' Goyescas," Dugal mumbled, as they saw a jaunty farmer's daughter walking up to them. Her firm couple of airbags were extra emphasized by a low-necked straightjacket.

"Disculpe," said Dugal, producing his best Spanish. If they could infringe their early-morning tranquillity, for they had got an undesired visit and those crooks had cut off their phone connection.

"Ladrones, hè? Cortado il teléfono, hè?"

"Si si," Catarí now in her turn maintained. Those bastards had also pinched their mobile phones and now they urgently had to … Without much ceremony the gruff woman had already led the way to a small niche and now she left them alone with the apparatus in the hall, where maybe the Archidux himself had once sat on that very bench. Catarí had turned up her nose when seeing the rather stained receiver on the velvet, which had clearly seen better times too.

"A white lie," she said.

"How do you mean? They did steal our mobile phones after all."

Unfortunately, as Dugal had not noticed until they got up. *Just get those two dopes out of their bunk,* he had thought and wanted to ring up Roberto and Miguel from the car. No cell phone whatsoever in the glove box or anywhere else. Vanished, desaparecido, without any trace of burglary.

But it was not just that. His two cronies were the least of his concerns at this moment. If only he could get contact.

"And?" she signalled. Same here, Dugal shook his head. "You're cut off from the outer world here too," he said to the astonished woman, pushing a coin into her hand.

"So, really?" he said as they were on the road again. "They want double security." Or perhaps it was pure coincidence, Catarí put forward ~ a general breakdown in the whole zone. "You don't believe so yourself, do you?" No, this time their teasing spirits had demonstrated their skill.

In Deió they halted at the postmaster's, to make another trial. This man, a bit sleepy still, was a cross of all sorts of things: at the same time he was also an innkeeper, a grocer, an olive grower. He went on feeding his chickens, until they went to have a drink in his bar. "Verémos," he then said, drew them a cup from the jet-black concoction of the day before out of a vacuum flask and shuffled to the back. *What's he doing out there?* they thought, but then saw him in the street talking to a delivery van. After that the postmaster, scratching his head, returned with the news: the whole north-west sector was cut off.

Drat! Was his wifey right after all then? On this isle of the blessed everything was going smoothly, except for technical connections. Big-city folks were driven stark mad about the law of sluggishness prevailing here, the exponent of which was the decrepit little train from Palmera to Llosera. Gossipers pretended you could walk more quickly on foot to the creek coast than drive by bus to the south, where, simmering in your own gravy, you were belched out half a day later.

Meanwhile Catarí herself was veering round. Coincidence? Was it possible that all those facts just fell together: co-incidentia? "No Duke, there must be something behind this after all." Duke did not react to it any more, his steering-wheel had automatically turned into the direction of Palmera. *Extremist groups, revisionists, for my part anarchical anti-capitalists, I don't care a rap. I'm fed up with it, but now I want to know, I will know!*

"Is it going to be Miguel or …?" Catarí tried to guess.

A cool San Miguel would be fine, yeah, Dugal jested, but rather at Prof. Marquez's then. It was about time they were going to release that bit of a germanophile from his interrupted story ~ his 'Unvollendete'~ at last. Even if Roberto was not brimming with enthusiasm because a meddlesome Americano had come to cast the stark lyrical feats of one of the last Habiger heirs on their own market, like a pebble in a frog pond, yet he had taken them into his confidence now, hadn't he?

And I thought you didn't gush about that kind of Messianic conspiracy theories and the professorial deduction methods of señor Marquez, she smirked. One day before, Roberto's raving about Jordi Martell's research work would have been grating on Dugal's nerves. Particularly his flirting with hammer and callipers seemed to her a source of annoyance for her doubting Thomas. By the way, how often hadn't he been approached himself, on behalf of some lodge or other! But a Masonic cachet was wasted on him, as much as a Scientologist membership or a proposal for a political mandate. However, his inquisitiveness pushed him on as a mouse is lured to the trap by the smell of cheese.

It was not the voluptuous Dolores Francisquita who received them this time, but a Remedy Against Femininity, rather atypical of Roberto's badger's sett. "Where did he pick up that R.A.F.?" Dugal muttered while following the woman to the auditorium where the Prof was completing his last feat of the day: 'Literary fringe figures on Marcaian soil.' He soon saw them standing there at the side-door and he rattled off his speech hastily, for an academic quarter's break. *And, how did things turn out?* they could read from his eyes.

"Just say: welcome back in the land of the living. We've spent a day on another planet, completely secluded from the inhabited world. Heirs of a destitute squire and that in the era of the worldwide web too!"

That they should explain to him, the Prof shook his head ~ in god's name, how could they be so clumsy as to leave both their cell-phones on the backseat of their car? Knowing that such a gadget had an effect on Marcaian youngsters as a red cloth has on a bull.

"No, professor. We won't be fobbed off with fables of the stealing magpie again. Those louts knew what they were looking for. Besides, we won't put up with the image of a don Lois as a blend of Diogenes and John the Baptist either."

In the adjacent small lecturers' room Robert tried to pick up again the thread of his story. "I know," he said, "that you don't think much of wild assumptions, such as Martell's persistent attempts to link the Archidux up with an under-ground European movement. Notwithstanding, the good soul was honestly convinced the Dux's imago was purposely distorted altogether."

"Somehow like the Messiah's, yes, we know that by now."

"And perhaps his own death would fit in there, as an ultimate proof," Catarí in her turn interrupted Dugal's interference. How did she mean?

Well yes, if it should turn out that Jordi Martell had been ruled out, for fear of a leak that could give a twist to official history, it was obvious some ultra-conservative elements wanted to maintain that distorted image of the eccentric don Lois at any cost up to this very day. *See the picture?* Catarí flaunted her ingenious little nose.

Yes, yes, but then, the graphologist must have counted on insiders like Roberto who would never be disinclined to trumpet forth señor Martell's self-provoked death as a sacrifice.

But then they can regard us as his successors, Dugal continued her reasoning. *In the end, to those people I too seem such an unseemly louse in their fur now, same as all those navel staring applicant co-operators of Prof. Marquez's.* That martyrdom, however, he did not want to grant them.

"Oh come, things won't take that turn," Roberto soothed. "Meanwhile we've already got the result from the forensic investigator. The cause of death of our good friend Jordi would appear to be natural. He'd been taking too high a dose of beta-blockers against hypertension. With a sudden drop of the heartbeat as a side-effect. Wrong self-therapy, a daily fact."

While they were still munching a bit on that report, Roberto took them along back through the corridors of the university. Suddenly he seemed to be a bit less self-confident, rather inclined to consider don Lois's figure again in its complete, paradoxical complexity: a 'cask full of contradictions'. Half the night the prof had reviewed the accomplished research in his mind. Enough to go mad. And his conclusion was: the thesis of a mental malfunction did not exclude a hitherto concealed escape of the Archidux from Brendais. Catalí still being alive or not.

30

<hr>

Hotel Tesharon de Marcaio was basking in the beneficial late afternoon sun with the hedonistic complacency of a lizard: the green shutters closed, as if to protect its interior temperature from any disturbance. Anyone standing alongside in its shadow, however, could notice a hectic hustle and bustle. The personnel, in their flawless togs, were treating the guests on the terrace outside and in the lounge to a glass of bubbles and an appetizer. Dugal Mikes was standing under the blue-woolly cloud of a jacaranda tree, on the look-out: a strategic post chosen by the former owners from where they could watch any horseman, any carriage drawing up to them from the far-off Bahia de Palmera. In the meantime Catarina was taking the honours, surrounded by a host of gentlemen fagging and wriggling to please la Ionès. And trying to peep in her décolleté: "What an honour for us, señora", " …y para nuestra isla!"

Randy tomcats, Dugal snarled. But one could not blame them. Catarí was doing her utmost to divert their attention in every way. All the notabilities, the fine fleur of the bourgeoisie, the business world and the local intelligentsia had turned up there at the invitation of the Tigress Club. The chairwoman had hit on the idea to organize a series of lectures about 'Marcaio and its Great Spirits'. A long retrospective, as a matter of fact, with the ice-breaker: 'L.S., the uncrowned king of Marcaio'.

They've got a nerve, Catarí had mumbled when they got the invitation, just now that the Archidux was the centre of interest. Promptly they got a call from Roberto and Miguel Mortado. Those blokes of the club prided themselves on their pluck, the editor of the Diario assured: as long as it was 'hot stuff'. And that was the least one could say about don Lois. Besides, they were eager to involve the instigator of the hype, star actor Mikes, in it, by all means.

Dugal, who always had a ready tongue, was counting on the inspiration of the moment. Editor Miguel was to put in an introductory word; he himself was going to briefly shed light on his find, the Letras Secretas. But Prof. Marquez got the honour to go ahead first with the actual speeches.

Where could he be, for heaven's sake? At last he saw the Chest's unsightly little car coming up the winding serpentine, groaningly, leaving a plume of smoke behind, in full competition with the ferry down there in the bay. What inspired that scholarly bundle of muscles anyway, to react to the advances of a dubious society club? *What inspires the Tigress Club to invite a dubious ...* No, he grinned, he could not insert that into his little speech.

Upon driving up the front yard, the professor saw some paparazzi running up to his mini-car. Straight past the American celebrity. Still, there was no need to be jealous of Roberto. All cameras were focusing on the ladies crawling out of it: Dolores Francisquita and la Marcella, with full-fledged Hollywood manners. They looked radiant and Roberto revelled in Dugal's aggrieved face. *Phew, just like two babes getting out of a birthday-party cake*, he sneered. Roberto shrugged his shoulders. "There have even been pole-dancing performances here."

If only he didn't end up at a pole, Dugal said: the pillory. After all, what was the purpose of this burlesque? To lure their way-layers, the guardian angels of the L.S. icon, away from their lair? Clever idea perhaps, but then they themselves were likely to become the bait. And risked to be torn to pieces by the teased game. "Relax, darling," Catarí whispered, while Miguel Mortado was welcoming the motley company with a few apt allusions about the objectionable L.S. publications. The tenor had been set and there arose a hearty laughter in the hall. Dugal was looking around, shuffling on his chair. Nowhere any danger to be sensed.

But maybe that was the point. White collar villains could feign to be the nicest softies, Mafiosi these days no longer gathered in a shabby shed or the back kitchen of a bar. He would not be taken in by that again. Or maybe his wifey was right and this cultural circle could work like a charm offensive. For more than a week there had not happened anything suspect. *Those homeland ravers will come round in the end*, Catarí had reassured him.

"And now ... I call upon the professor to take over," the editor scanned. The difference between the two speakers was as big as between a pincher and a bulldog, Dugal thought. "Ludovico Rainer Maria Salvatore ...,"

Roberto started in a pleasant tone, "a dozen names for the last son from a nest of ten …". At once he got the laughers on his side, which was even enhanced by a well-nigh biblical opening: "The uncrowned King of Marcaio …", followed by a roguish dissonant: " …was no saint. No more than I am, obviously." An infectious laughter from the first row had an instigating effect: la Marcella's, they noticed. Clever move, Dugal had to recognize and Catarí nodded at him. Roberto's inspired humour was a practical test case. If they put up with that, he could cautiously build up his tarnishing viewpoints. Tearing down, step by step, the existing image of the matured, embalmed Archidux, to replace it by pieces of the unique, genuine "L.S. or don Lois, as he used to be called by the average Marcaian."

Five minutes had passed without any rotten tomatoes on the stage or Roberto's head being shelled with any projectile. Every face in expectation of the next laughing wrinkles. That was going smoothly, and in passing, the shrewd Prof managed to sketch a profile of the young, uprooted archduke as a potential intestate successor, in spiritual sense though, with some non-conformist (somehow anarchical?) traits even … Naturist, je m'en foutiste, nay, why not? Belletrist and at the same time (but thát Roberto did not say explicitly, he gave them to understand it between the rules) one could draw some Messianic parallels. Salvator, the Redeemer, bore an unspoken message within himself. Which the ego-tripper renounced, suppressed, but which was lastingly imposed on him from the outside. Precisely because of his passive, rebellious rejection, nihilistic pacifism almost, he attracted the spiritual elements of his era: a magnet encircled by great thinkers, social critics, freemasons, revolutionaries. In search of an alternative for the destructive powers, a Pan-European unity symbol of peace.

Dratted Roberto, Dugal whispered in Catarí's ear, he makes a whore a saint. Prof. Marquez subtly referred to the schizophrenic idiosyncrasies this aberrant noble scion was imbued with. "Not really paranoid ~ but ever since his youth, due to that escape from Palazzo Pitti and the rebels enclosing the grand duke's coach carrying his numerous offspring, young Luigi's mind was burdened in a deterministic/atavistic way."

He is rising in my esteem, also Cathy thought. The way he was able to bring an evocation of the aftermath of those days, that was something only a dab like the professor was up to. "The whole sphere of revolution, of spiritual destabilization in the Occident, the Umwertung aller Werte ... What an impact this must have had on an impressionable talent like L.S. !"

On top of that Roberto served a whiff of Viennese charm and sentiment, Horatian relativism, plus the eclectic eagerness for knowledge of that homo universalis. From that crossing of the Dux's background with a peculiar mixture of influences from different eras grew the portrait of an intricate personality. In itself a reconciliation of antitheses: high-born, but with a bias to simplicity; on equal foot with the scientists and thinkers of his time, but at home among humble craftsmen; with an aversion from display of power and sympathy for the plebs. "In brief: a piggy of Epicure's, but on a level with a Leonardo or Humboldt, and even a waft of Gandhi."

How is it possible, both of them thought, *that this decent company seems to appreciate this version of the Archidux?* Dugal could not help chuckling about the Prof's flair of interlarding his account with juicy examples. Exempt from any chronological order, totally to the taste of the easily amused nouveaux riches. He depicted Don Lois' bohemian-like airs by means of popular anecdotes, inter alia about his worn-off togs, his cuffs threaded together with tacking yarn, with which he by turns passed for a shepherd, a peasant, a sailor and even a cook.

"That way, he once got a tip from a farmer whose cart he had helped to pull out of a soggy field. My first pocket-money, he would tell later on. At Court they made fun of his one and only uniform, the seams of which burst one by and one in the course of time. Yet, that mocking at his creasy looks did not touch him at all: rather 'vielfältig', many-sided, than 'einfältig', simple-minded, was his opinion. And that was the picture Roberto wanted to make of him: a versatile figure, no halfwit, as they would depict his Bavarian nephew and namesake.

That was in total contradiction with the comments from the aristocratic angle, which the professor quoted on behalf of one count Crenneville on occasion of an incognito visit to Corfu. There His Highness was signalled in colourful female company, including a 'youthful apparition, the sex of which was not clearly definable'. To the aggravation of cousin-emperor, for whom that 'veiled communist' was a nail in his coffin.

Probably it was not by chance that his half-cousin, empress 'Lizzy', was equally enamoured with the same Corfu as her non-conformist cousin was. To the even greater annoyance of her imperial consort."

The arch twinkling in Prof. Marquez' eyes did not escape their attention as he was picturing Elisa's visit, by yacht, to Maremira, namely on the occasion of her 55th birthday. Which she liked to spend with her roguish, portly cousin, rather than with her ascetic spouse. "An absolute letdown for the imperial consort, who found it hard to stomach the congeniality between his spontaneous, ravenously popular Elisa and the hedonistic vagrant/scholar. Great consternation at Court," Roberto grinned, "after which the ascetic Franzl sent his wishes rather sourly, hoping that *'fatty Lois will attend to Your well-being'* ".

That gave the Chest, who was getting into his swing by now, the chance to dwell at large on L.S.'s lavish love life. "Grossly exaggerated!" he declared, thus anticipating all possible utterances of protest from the public. With a naughty wink at the "ribald, scabrous stories about the amorous kaleidoscope attributed to the archduke. You know ~ pub talk with which envious canters were eager to pile on his so-called escapades".

While Roberto was pleasantly drivelling on, Catarí and Dugal looked around. Quite at the back they noticed a few faces, contorted by a wry grimace. In particular due to the professor's light-hearted way of lampooning slanderers like those gossip-mongers in Palmera who had been spreading about that *'the Archidux used to shoot at all that moved, especially everything with a skirt on'*. "Mean chatterboxes," Roberto called those sources; to the great amusement of la Marcella in the front row. Obviously she grasped at once his allusion at the present smear campaign they were the butt of.

"And by the way, shooting? Fiddlesticks. In fact, don Lois never thought much of guns and arms. Hunting was not his dada. On his estate between Valle de Muša and Deió no tree was to be felled, no game to be killed. Maremira was a kind of pre-Biosphere and the Archidux a harbinger-ecologist. A thorn in the flesh of many true-blue Marcaians who held this to be an assault on the islanders' self-determination. Anti-progress thinking. But on the other hand …"

Here they felt Roberto's sympathy for L.S., the 'green fellow', rising. But one with a vision then. By the way, wasn't the chap's wine-growing scheme a classic example of rural development? On that stretch of costa the 'naval captain' managed to apply his know-how about Tuscan and Palatinate vines to the cultivation of Malvasía and other species. More than anyone else he was familiar with the Vine, hmm, hmm … Now Roberto was coughing a bit, over-looking the hall. "What a pity his recent epigones have much less notion of that." This was a dig at the new Duke's timid attempts at the yeast process with his own wine-must. Or did it point at his poor genealogical knowledge?

Hahaha, very funny, Dugal wanted to respond aloud, but Catarí managed to restrain him just in time. Right in that confusion they thought they heard a grousing from the rear. But imperturbably the professor was expatiating at large to put also the social engagement of that scion of nobility into the limelight. Visitors of his reserve were given shelter almost gratuitously in his inn or Hospedería. Which can hardly be said about our present-day tour operators. Gratis eco tourism, fancy! Whereas now the Dux's 'kinsmen' ~ *the* tourist cattle in particular ~ were stripped double as much, even in the hairdresser's salon. There was some annoyed grinning everywhere in the hall, after Roberto's allusion to the islanders' xenophobe, and especially non-germanophile, exorbitant price strategy.

"Also during his journey to California L.S. thus showed his philanthropic sense. By means of his book 'Eine Blume aus dem Goldenen Land', about Los Angeles, 'the flower in gold country' a hundred and thirty years ago, he wanted to open up the mild climate of that Spanish colony to asthma patients and suchlike, a bit similar to what Columbus secretly had in view with Hispaniola, for the sake of the Jews. But not in a sectarian way towards dissidents, freemasons or like-minded pacifists. On the contrary, even though don Lois felt the dark clouds contracting above Europe. It was he who, in Trieste, warned Ferdinand, the heir to the throne, about the imminent mischief, before his fatal departure to Sarajevo." In one breath, Prof. Marquez also mentioned the Dux's plea for allowing wheelchair patients at the world exhibitions. "Which in fact he used to scour, since, from his point of view, they contained a certain hope of peaceful development. A dualistic attitude? Maybe. Like everything with this nature lover, slaloming between technological progress thinking and his urge to conserve all that risked to yield to the demolition hammer of western civilization …"

There he comes, with his barrel full of paradoxes, thought Dugal. Contrary to the jetsetter's image that was sometimes spread about the Dux, the Prof postulated the viewpoint of the ascetic. The patient researcher who, particularly in his modest villa in Muggia, Istria, and even better on the 'Nymphe', devoted his life to science and writing. His 'arc of Noah', as they scornfully called the ship on which a loyal crew of monkeys, birds, cats and dogs, 'and other animals' accompanied don Lois on his discovery tours. So, quite unlike our plutocrats beating parties in luxurious villas and ditto yachts, he mapped out the flora and fauna, the population and culture of forgotten remote corners. "Do you see anybody doing that nowadays, unless some nerd from the non-profit sector?" Roberto concluded.

31

"My dear wifey had just whispered in my ear that this very learned highbrow here was allowed to mention us both by way of exception."

General grinning again. As usual, Dugal revelled in his success only as far as it helped him to impose on Catarí. As the laughter in the hall was gradually falling silent, he was considering how he could still float on a bit on Roberto's sarcasm. Perhaps with an episode that might serve them both as a pretext for strolling incognito on Marcaio's soil.

"I assure you that it's far from funny to go through life as a BMW (Beloved Marcaian World-Citizen). Everywhere you come, you raise the market values. In that respect, that dratted Archidux can inspire you with certain ideas, you know."

Promptly he produced a yellowed newspaper article from the pocket of his jacket. So he took them along to a Sicilian victuals market in Ragusa, anno 1896, where L.S. regularly moored at his berth. Or his hideout? From there they followed the archduke among his sailors, with heavy-laden baskets, and then, beside the coachman, on his way to Gravosa. An inquisitive harbour master who hoped to find a knight of the Golden Fleece on the 'Nymphe', got this reply from the captain: "We are all equals here."

Once more Prof. Marquez climbed the rostrum, next to Dugal, to confirm that story. Wherever the Archidux turned up to study the country, he did so in the local costume and preferably speaking the people's lingo.

"So, we've still much to learn, Professor," Dugal joked, thereby referring to don Lois's imperial half-cousin Elisa. He could not help implicating this 'Lizzy' in it once more, at the risk of badgering the public. She too, though of rather modest origin, say: impoverished nobility, showed the same bias to sobriety, informality, sympathy with the underdogs rather than the jeunesse dorée in those days. "But also to mono-diets of oranges," he sniggered, "which was just a bit too scanty for that piggy from Epicure's stable, as the gourmand L.S. sometimes called himself."

With Elisa, the public's darling long before the white screen discovered her, he had that 'condition de l' âme errante' in common. The mental agony of the heir of an old order that had failed its purpose, but was also to leave behind a black hole, never to be filled up again by the ideals of the new age. The feeling of standing somewhere on the turn of times, looking on powerlessly how a line of fracture was cutting up our civilization and definitively, irreversibly, disrupted the spiritual values. That *'Umwertung aller Werte'*, as the Prof had already called it. With the difference that she remained chained to the structures of that creaking machinery, whereas he, freebooter, tried to save some authentic morsels of a crumbling world from the flames.

Secretly amused, Dugal dwelled on the relation between the imperial cousin and Catalí d'Omar. Whether there were, after all, anything true about her being expected to drive a wedge between that carpenter's daughter and the prodigal son of the Habiger dynasty ? "Well, if that had been so, her venerable spouse could forget about it."

Dugal gloated over the annoyed expression on Roberto's face and the secret laughs in the hall. The professor could not help coming back to the mike again. "We have a pertinent answer to that," he declared, referring to some circumstantial studies. That there might have been something more than pure sympathy between Lizzy and L.S., was without any foundation whatsoever. Conversely, the cordiality with which the first lady treated the handsome Marcaian girl, was beyond question. La Dama de Ses Taca was an uncouth gem, and yet of a brittle tenderness, like that refractory piece of Cornisa along the northern coast to which the Dux had lost his heart. This Lizzy envied him because of his pertness, his pluck to prefer a commoner to the whole pick of nubile lassies from the ranks of the grandes. To take her along, even on his voyages of discovery, whenever he was in for a new whiff of air and he hoisted the sails, prompted by his insatiable love of travelling! Really, that was his safety valve: the study-addict in him could not be confined like a hermit, in the mists of his dreams.

"Fortunately, he had no lack of means or time. Even the most celebrated film-star can only dream of that these days," Dugal joked, fearing that his learned friend was prone to forget again his sense of time and space. The ice seemed to be really broken now. Dugal was on his favourite ground, with acute, unvarnished brainwaves, so as to enhance an impression of sharp-wittedness and win over even the most sceptic minds. He scowled at Catarína in the auditorium and he saw everything was OK. Phew, he needn't have worried at all. This chic society happening had turned out to be a cinch and he intended to round off the show as it suited a 'Dux' ~ with a touch of irony, verve and almost British phlegm.

"Señoras en señores ~ allow me this sexist rectification ~, I hope you enjoyed Prof. Marquez's lecture and, as far as my humble footnotes are concerned …"

As a seasoned actor Dugal let the ironic contrast hover above the heads, so as to parry the laughter with a vigorous move.

Yet, it did not get so far, for all of a sudden, he was seized by his collar, drawn backwards and led away from the rostrum by a few strong arms. Whilst spasmodically kicking about, he saw an incredible commotion in the lobby. Smoke, and a cluster of arms, trying to do the same with Roberto, the Chest, who was dealing out some sound smacks in passing, but still was lifted from the stage.

Dugal was near choking in his heroic resistance. The last thing he heard in the short corridor, was a hard drone, and the glass swing-door through which they had made their way out of the auditorium, was blown to smithereens. "Catarí!" he shouted, but his roar was drowned by the noise.

By the time he had come to his senses again, Dugal was sitting on the edge of the wall of the flower bed just opposite hotel Tesharon. Surrounded by some bodyguards that seemed to have jumped out of one of his thrillers. There's no cure for it, it flashed through his mind. One of those chicos had got a black eye and a good deal of scratches from Dugal's nails on his arm.

"Catarí!" he jumped back to his feet at once. "One moment, Mister Mikes," the leader of the group calmed him down. And brought it home to him what was going on. No question of abduction or seizing hostages. Just a mere bomb attack."

"Oh, a mere bomb attack, eh ?"

Yes, a smoke bomb, the stout boys tried to temper his choleric temperament. And what about his wife then, and the professor ?

"No reason for panic, Mister Mikes. Our service had got scent of an action, so we were ordered to balk any hazardous situation."

That takes the cake! Those blokes had almost dislocated his shoulder, tattooed his skin with bruises, and all that due to a false alarm! A smoke bomb that brought the whole congress hall into commotion.

In the meantime the hotel manager in person had run up to them across the lawn: "Sorry, señor Maïks, como va?" Inside, everything was under control. Señora Mikes, everybody by the way was unscathed, el profesór included. But the men of the security could not take any chances. The auditorium had been skilfully evacuated in no time, the guests were already treated to a glass of espumoso. By way of compensation for the emotional damage.

Once in the 'emergency hall', Dugal had to keep them all at arm's length. Catarí almost devoured him. "Eh, leave something for tonight, please," Roberto patted him on his back. They had been taken care of, indeed, but the trembling glass in his cariña's hand could not deceive him.

"So, Robertino, here's another vaudeville show after all ~ and once again, there's nothing wrong, eh ?"

Yeah, the latter mumbled, because of Dugal's cynical tone, but meanwhile all his notes were sent up in smoke; plus his documentation file. As if a deus ex machina had descended from heaven, and goodness knew who or what had come down here for this stunt. "Not exactly, Mister Maïks," a grating voice interrupted him. "We do have some suspicions. An informer had put us on the track of the ATE. Everything points to the fact that they were not really aiming at you personally, or at professor Marquez."

Roberto's way of nodding sardonically, showed Dugal what he thought of it. That 'association' of Iberian terrorists was a somewhat shadowy movement that provided some ambiance on the peninsula and the archipelagos with all kinds of escaramuchas: skirmishes like sham hijackings, fake bomb alarms and similar hoaxes. And with such a name: Atë, the goddess of mischief!

Pull the other one, Dugal smiled sulkily. So, this was the way Security explained things: a gang of nationalistic outlaws with Don Quixote airs liked goading the establishment every now and then, simply out of malicious pleasure. That things got out of hand once in a while ~ a little explosion here and there ~ did not matter that much. As long as there was not too much bloodshed, and even so … Those louts figured it out in such a way that the guardia civil was warned in time. Secretly a great part of the general public were laughing up their sleeve then how the police drove out headlong, like a vexed farmer searching for the next place where a molehill is likely to pop up.

"That way they always have a scapegoat at hand. That suits them well."

Roberto's pursed lips seemed to confirm his suspicion. At once, though, Catarí turned up from the crowd behind them, accompanied by two other illustrious beauties.

"Look here," said señorita Dolores, and la Marcella was waving triumphantly with a sheaf of papers in her raised hand: Prof. Marquez's file. How …? the latter was gazing perplexedly at the emerging find.

"Snatched away, in the confusion, from one of those rogues that had thrown themselves on the professor," the TV-presenter said phlegmatically.

Now it was Catarí's turn to give the bewildered gents a sample of female cold-bloodedness. She too had noticed how a couple of those Security blokes had detached themselves suspiciously fast from the group that were hastily piloting Roberto to the exit. Looking around, anxiously and skittishly, lest anyone should tumble to their way of behaving. Too swiftly however, for as Dolores ran into them, they were distracted in their hustle; they had not twigged that Marcella, with the map and all, was drifting along in the crowd.

"Infiltrants," Roberto mumbled, "even there."

Finally, sighed Catarí, *the male intelligence is working.* She had got it all taped for quite a while; it was astonishing how long it took the gentlemen until they dared to take the consequences of their suspicions. Even where jealousy came into play. With a lick and a chuck they could be soothed again, if one contrived it well.

"So what are we still loafing here ?" Dugal said. But the assessment of the facts was paralysing enough. Now they had the irrefutable evidence that everything on this damned island was sold out. Or ~ and that would beat all ~ the prof himself was up to his ears in this farce. But in that case he was playing a nice piece of comedy, the way he was browsing through his papers there.

"Well, professor, asked Dolores, his radiant assistant, "quite happy that your darlings have been spared ?"

"Some important fragments are missing," the Chest said sullenly. Looking so sincere that Dugal and Catarí's last suspicion disappeared.

Promptly they all started searching: in the corridor, the congress hall, on chairs, under benches, behind tables, everywhere … nada. *They are damned shrewd, for a moment they leave us the illusion that the household effects have been saved from the fire and in the mean time they are already gone for miles.*

It looked almost like a hunt for a yeti. Three cars rushing down the dusty winding road, and once below at the cross-road, they each chose another direction. In vain. Fifteen minutes later they were back at the same point, empty-handed. "Pero què, profesor ? What exactly is failing here?" la Marcella asked catlike, her eyes half-closed. Roberto, reading the suspicion in their look, took them in tow, down to one of the ventas along the coast. Where he could talk to them in confidence, without any eavesdroppers.

El patrón promptly dished up some olives, house wine and tapas to their heart's content, in a nook lavishly provided with azulejos tiles and a view across harbour and bay. "Here I can confide it to you, amigos, in all privacy, for I know: there surely is no mole here among us, no more than I am myself. Well, the documents that were snatched out of that file a while ago, were pretty confidential, concerning the private relations between the Dux and the Dama de Ses Taca. Those lads did know exactly what they were looking for. But …" A smug grin dispelled the wrinkles on his worried forehead. "I too knew what they were after. Those specimens were bogus, savvy? Both as for contents and shape." And he produced a package of crumpled copies from his inside pocket. *Copies from copies,* Roberto chuckled. "Here …"

With crammed mouth, he told about the anecdotes from second hand, from the part of a señor Ripoll, señor Heraderas, señor Marquès a.o. . Also about the 'petit harem' don Lois, that anticipatory feminist, surrounded himself with. And in which Catarí would only have excelled as prima inter pares. Adding to this, the envy of the provincial girl who, according to another version, was not apt to share her bosom friend with that abstract platonic ideal of beauty of his. The little fling with 'el capitan', the macho skipper of the Nymphe, with whom don Lois caught her in the middle of a hugging scene in his own cabin. Which, in another version again, was no more than some coquetry to force L.S. into action. Whereas in yet another zarzuela scenario her offended pride sprang from frustration about her little role as a sublimated model in his idealistic view of the woman.

One of those phoney biographers depicted his rambling tours as 'escapism', while a fairly objective source tried to find in the Dux's broad-mindedness, rather unusual for that time, a motive for mean gossip. Certainly in connection with Catarí's mysterious disease, probably contracted during their Egyptian cruise. Hepatitis or some lingering intestinal disorder? Quicksilver preparations, the kill or cure remedy of that era, could raise rumours about cervical cancer, cirrhosis, syphilis and the like.

However far-fetched, any explanation needed considering. Her premature return, straight from Venice, was rather to be seen in that context. After a romantic reconciliation in the doge's city (no relation whatsoever is flawless, either had to admit), it was nostalgia that drove her back to Marcaio, and him to the Ionian isles, for further research.

"About the latter I have irrefutable evidence," the professor concluded.

"So, a bit like all those scenes about Jesus depicted by non-eyewitnesses," Marcella mused. "Indeed," señorita Dolores confirmed. "Piled on, of course, and therefore I staged this whole show, in such a way that Roberto was able to decoy those document hunters."

32

From the lounge on the sixth floor of the Gran Centro Commercial de Marcaio, one had a great view of the harbour and the whole bay, down to the southern cape: Cabo Gato. Marcella Hortaz was all by herself in that conference hall, complete with a bar, projection screens and an oval glass table around which about thirty men could gather. In her black woman's suit, she was turning around on her desk chair, legs crossed, apparently staring in the void. She was thinking of what don Moragues, the big boss of Asuntos Bailares, might have on his mind whilst beholding this vista, across the Paseo Marítimo and its palm-lined ramblas, towards the cathedral and the mediaeval Moorish palace.

Here, from his financial headquarters, he was running his business empire, enjoying a feeling of power as did Charles V. By the way, that's what his nick-name was: Carlo Quinto, a peculiar likeness, for his real name was Carlo Moragues, the fifth in a row of a brokers lineage. They had started small-scale, with a couple of ships, a warehouse and the flair to forward any merchandise that was precious for the Isla de la Calma: olives, almonds, sardines, oil, wine … Now, a century later, Moragues & Hijos had become a notion in the world-wide business. The storehouse had turned out of use for quite a time, except as a museum; their home-based fleet, though, including an awful lot of giant cargo-ships and super tankers, was floating all over the oceans, from Buenos Aires as far as Hongkong.

What a supreme consciousness this must give you! La Marcella took a deep breath. This way it was possible to guess with what self-complacency this Carlo V could overlook the Gulf of Palmera, as if it were the epicentre of the world. A realm where the sun never sets. This building as well as the adjacent sister towers formed the fulcrum of a whole series of global activities. Behind the padded doors of Asuntos Bailares' business offices some deals were concluded that decided about many thousands of human lives. For that was what Marcella could almost smell here: at Moragues & Sons things no longer just pivoted on overseas trade. Petroleum, wine and olives - *the three pillars of modern civilization,* as don Carlos used to call them - they would always abide here, as basic products.

Sounded quite nice, this, but Marcella knew it was humbug. Something told her this signboard of the Asuntos was just a cover. The transactions this race of brokers were involved in, reached far beyond the borders of Mother Earth's primary produce. If you managed to rank up that far - among the top fifty of Big Business - you had more than one string to your bow. Then, you must be able to surf, with primeval commercial instinct, in between numerous trusts and concerns. It had not been up to Moragues Junior to start at that. If there was something this tycoon from Marcaian stock had inherited, it was that infallible nose for running affairs. *An atavistic idiosyncrasy everybody would like to be born with,* la Marcella thought with envy. But she assumed - and she was not the only one - that a great deal of assets of Asuntos Bailares had their origin in things that should not see daylight. Weapons, enriched uranium, cocaine and other hot items, who could tell? Nobody was able to prove anything, for their transactions seemed waterproof. Still, it was obvious there were few reasons for shareholders with a conscience to line up with señor Moragues as a form of ethic investing, that seemed beyond a doubt to her.

What in god's name am I doing here in the lion's den? she mumbled softly. *You must be nuts to cross swords with this magnate.* Precisely that challenge, however, secretly gave her a devilish pleasure. Carlos V was by no means a wally. "So? And am I a softy perhaps?" she had responded as Dolores Francisquita was warning her. With her she had devised this scheme, but a direct confrontation, no, that was no option, in her old bosom-friend's opinion. "He'll lure you into his web and crush you there." The sexy academician was in favour of the softer approach, in a roundabout way. In her success role as a newscaster and moderator, however, Marcella Hortaz chose for the frontal attack. But then with her disarming frankness, her seeming innocence (!), which in her victims' eyes often passed for naivety. A terribly smart naivety anyway, and that made them all walk into the trap, without any exception. Before they got aware of it, they gave way to her and la Marcella had them fully in her hand. Unlike any other interviewer she knew how to get people to expose their souls to her, to reveal their petty secrets.

Or ... was señor Moragues that exception? Would she have to acknowledge him as her equal, nay, her superior? Dolores had not pronounced it, but on her wrinkled forehead she could read the doubt. Same as with her better half. On principle, she did not take her hubby along on missions like this one: simply too hesitant. But now, for the first time, she felt forsaken. Nonsense, she pulled herself together. Señor Moragues was a great fan of hers. On the phone he had impressed it once more upon her: "Por supuesto! Course, you can interview me, you are number one on my hit list." It was a great honour for him, etc ...

At the same time, though, such an invitation at his headquarters contained a calculated risk. No one was able to enter the Gran Centro Commercial without being screened and scanned from top to toe. Señor Moragues did know what she came for, at least for 90 percent, and the rest of it was pure curiosity. Marcella's looks counted for a great part in this. Yet, with a man of his calibre, one could not rely on that. Pretty women were like diamonds and strings of pearls to him: show-window material, nice to admire but ~ as she had already heard him joke one time ~ a bad investment. And as a matter of fact, he knew her as a top-MP. At some celebration or other he had let slip something like: "I, the most reputable Marcaian Personality? I rather leave that honour to señora Hortaz."

No, the fact that he wanted to see her, pointed out she was an item on his secret agenda. The tycoon could surmise what she and Dolores still had in store after the incident at hotel Tesharon two days before. Those bogus secret agents belonging to the security unit both ladies happened to have locked horns with in that congress hall there, had been identified by a sleuth working in that department. The chap's memory even started working harder, when they invited him out on a dinner. The computer freak had traced those blokes as far as the basement of the Centro Commercial. They were set down as 'technicians' on the staff list which this boffin had managed to hack. *Strange techniques,* Dolores thought, so as to diddle the notes out of a prof and then vanish into smoke.

After la Marcella's phone call the big man of Asuntos surely had sniffed which two beauties had made his handy-men blunder. The couple of pages those two smooth chaps had at least grabbed away, possibly gave him an idea what meat he'd got in his pie. And how one could make a deal with them. After all, for a super-captain of industry of his class everything was for sale. On that level, acts of violence were barbarian tactics. By the way, with such juicy meat that would be a sin.

In that way señora Hortaz tried to weigh up the odds. Question was how far Carlos V wanted to go. And why should such a big shot indulge in that kind of futilities? By way of a 'Spielerei' maybe: the thrill of entering into a trial of strength with another celeb such as Mikes junior. 'Just for fun'.

Hogwash, Dolores Francisquita judged, and for that, Marcella's ex-school-mate had her reasons. *Am I also a genealogist, by the way, or aren't I?* At first Marcella had laughed at it ~ you never could tell, with Dolores. But this time she seemed to be serious: "Right, Marci, it's right." She had shown Marcella a reconstructed pedigree, and what did it prove? That the Moragueses, on a sideline, were akin to ... Carlos V, the real one then. Marcella's peals of laughter died on her lips as she saw Dolores's cold gaze. She meant it! According to those documents the Moragues clan originated from an illegitimate child of the last great absolutistic ruler. Slanderers pretended their name was actually a translation of Moorkens or Möhrchen or something like that. Which they denied tooth and nail as the greatest blasphemy.

One of the many flings they used to have in those days, covered with the imperial cloak of charity. Marcella and Dolores had turned silent over it. *Hence came that dubious fortune with which the great-great-granddad's dad had been able to start up that shipping and transport company.* So, that was no immaculate conception at all.

"And therefore," Marcella had started pacing up and down, "therefore our bastard Habiger is saddled up with an L.S. complex! Then, if you come to think of it, all that hullabaloo about Dugal's publications ..."

"...would not issue from a little club of outmoded homeland zealots? No question of soiling one's own nest and that sort of twaddle, but just old-fashioned self-interest."

Whatever that might imply. About that they were really groping in the dark, although ... Doña Dolores had an idea. Six generations, a good century ago ~ didn't that mean: the progenitor of Moragues & Sons, versus the 'Uncrowned King of Marcaio', legal kinsman of the imperial Habigers? Somehow, there must have been a rub there, but why?

Landed property, contrary business interests, prerogatives that an offspring from the unacknowledged branch was not entitled to ... Suddenly it had come into Marcella's mind and now she was thinking that possibility over again. It could be so that in the late days of the fin de siècle a hidden feud had arisen between the enterprising pioneer of the Moragues trade empire and the Dux, with his ambiguous attitude ~ progressive, also in a scientific-technical sense, but with viewpoints about nature preservation and green issues which at that time must have seemed incomprehensible. Marcella tried to project that scene of tension to the present day. Probably, in today's context of growing omnipotence of mega companies and refractory nuisances like Greenpeace, there would hardly have been any difference.

She herself had never had a face-to-face rendezvous with Carlos V. One could imagine him snorting, though, if *nowadays* don Loís had thwarted his megalomaniac plans. For that's what this money magnate did have, dead cert, also on Marcaio. The relatively undeveloped northern coast of the island, the L.S. side, was right up his alley. On the drawing tables of his project developers some urbanization plans had surely been outlined by now, the blueprint of which he had already got in his drawer. Underhand that had come to Marcella's ears, amongst others via Dolores Francisquita. How the academician had ferreted it out, did not matter, but it confirmed Marcella's idea. You should not try to find the resistance against an L.S. hype with a little group of nostalgic dreamers. On the contrary, it was the modernistic trendsetters, neo-capitalists craving to get the Isla de la Calma 'out of the middle ages' who did not get a kick out of a version of the *other* Archidux. As Dolores put it: *who had had the greatest benefit from the canonized Saviour ~ arch-conservative papists and church fathers, or wily potentates such as Constantine the Great?*

For over an hour Carlos Moragues had been overdue by now. The television star realized with what purpose. Big men like keeping the little ones waiting to make them extra feel the gap in market value. In this case, however, it was rather meant to mellow her up in advance. But there, he underrated la Marcella. She was trained to always keep a lead up her sleeve, and that something, that bit of superiority was what she now had in the offing. For that matter, the 'emperor' was powerless. He could not frisk her, abduct her or let her 'vanish'. The media were following in her footsteps, so he would have to come down with other means. At least he thought so. In fact, only Dolores knew what she was up to, but she was not going to tell him. The passage that she had with her in her handbag, contained the key that señor Moragues wanted to lay hold on at all expenses. A time bomb under his empire, of a megaton load. He had guessed well at that.

As she thought she already heard the echo of his heels, she called the words of the Archidux once more to her mind. The very sequel to Dugal Mikes's latest publication, to which the reading public of the Diario were badly looking forward. And would be gloating over, unless something came up in the meantime …

> … You will be surprised, querída Catalína,
>
> how I have survived all this, my peculiar escape and this whole journey, down to you here. I cannot grasp it myself. Whatever strong inner force spurred me on, beyond the Alps and the pain level: a mirage wherein your dark eyes merged with the mountains and deep valleys of your homestead … In my feverish mind, images from my childhood in the Boboli gardens, my studies in Vienna, my travels to far-off countries and my research work whirled together. Up to my separation from Marcaio and the 'exile' to Brendais, the dark Bohemian forests. In that way, this ordeal became an account of my whole life. It is as if I had been on a continuous passage ~ a restless nomad who sought refuge on the sea. My 'Nymhe' became my actual home, my substitute dwelling.
>
> I have always defended the human's longing to roam about the world as an innate impetus. Solely by the obligations of our civilization he has unlearnt that second disposition. A boat seemed to me a practical means to let us live again in line with our true nature, combining it with our artistic and scientific aspirations. Somehow a consolation between the nature lover and the inquisitive spirit within us. Thus the Nymphe satiated my travelling hunger for years, in that motley company of animals and

friends which, among critics, earned her the sobriquet of 'Noah's Ark'.

Now I realize that yearning was a mere illusion of an uprooted spirit on a quest for himself. An Ahasuerus, a Diogenes wandering around with his lantern searching for 'a Human'. As a matter of fact, my Nymphe was a surrogate of a self-chosen homeland. One time I believed I could find this in my villa in the Gulf of Muggia, near Trieste, another time in Maremira. That is what we, humans, are like. Never satisfied with the simple things that are thrown upon his lap, man gropes for the unattainable, without grasping the bliss of that happiness. Until it is too late and then, he desperately returns to that source.

In that state of mind I find myself now, Cariña. Scourged on by the hope to find the way back to you and, together with our kindred spirits, stem the insanity of this epoch, over there in our haven of refuge at Keppler's, where you gave them shelter yourself. I have taken off my old garbs for ever. For what else are we, terrestrial starvelings, but provisional beings, on an erratic ramble towards an unknown, elusive destination? If you start to ponder on that, there are no more fixed borderlines of space and time ...

In that vacuum I feel reborn, exempt from all limitations. My fetters have fallen off and so, Catalí, this little barge now is carrying me, on a silver path, towards you, my eternal sun..

33

For quite a while it had remained silent in the professorial chamber, where a penetrating coffee smell drove away the faint odours of old manuscripts and Roberto Marquez's cheap aftershave (*'my brand'*, with a jaunty flamenco lady dancer on it).

"Marvellous! How poetic, isn't it? And all the more so in such extreme circumstances."

"Hmm ... A bit mellow, maybe, but after all the old man seemed up to some-thing more than making pen drawings and mapping out some remote corners."

Dugal felt what a venomous look Catarína cast at him. Each time she was taken in when he acted 'the prosaic, utterly insensitive fathead'.

"Not any more or less than I had expected from this specimen," Roberto cut through their foreplay to a round of bickering.

"How do you mean?" Dugal heard himself say. His own voice sounded miles away, somewhere on a small boat, floating astray on the Tyrrhenian Sea. He too had been touched by that passage, more than he liked to admit.

"However, I don't really understand ... This piece is lacking in my collection from the Dux's bastónes, and you had no copy of it. How then has this 'De Profundis' got into the hands of that media maid? And what's she got in mind with it, over there in the lion's den?"

"From my assistant, doña Dolores," the professor said knowingly. He always enjoyed seeing others looking dumbfounded when he managed to put a missing link into a puzzle. *Professional deformation, so typical,* his friend grinned sulkily.

La Marcella had got this piece of harrowing self-confession from her crony-academician. But Roberto at once advocated the authenticity of that failing passage. That was something they, as actors, really should understand too: the fact that something was not there, did not prove it had *never* been there. And thus, hardly a couple of weeks ago, this precious gem had shown up in Palacio Vivot. You know how such things happen. While refurbishing the interior, the owner comes across a yellowed manuscript between the bookshelves. He was on friendly terms with the Do Mars and gave it to Dolores for a service in return. "Precisely the link we needed for your next instalment, isn't it?"

Catarí looked just as glum as her better half. *How can you still believe anything at last of those unrestrained Marcaians? Perhaps they are just half as bona fide as they look like?* After winking at her, Dugal told her what he had on the tip of his tongue: did they think they were dealing with mugs, or was there a hidden agenda, only for the initiated?

"Escuchame, amigos. That sudden disappearance of that forgotten document seems all too fortuitous to you. Suspiciously opportunistic even, okay." Roberto confessed his own mistrust, at the beginning. But hadn't exactly the same happened in the case of the miraculous finds of the last century? For ages the canonized gospels had remained sacrosanct. The apocryphal scripts, versions charged with heresy by the church fathers, seemed to have disappeared from the earth. Until a handful of zealotic bible scholars start poking about everywhere in the sandpits and crevasses of Asia Minor, and all at once they pop up, with clock-like regularity. Death Sea scrolls, parchments from Qumran, the stone jar from Nag Hammadi … As if they were put down there by sensation-loving treasure hunters themselves."

"By the way, your appearance here looks much like it, doesn't it? The new owner of SesTaca finds those darned walking sticks of Don Lois. At once those old copies in our drawers are getting an authenticity that was always called in question; dusty final papers are raked up again and a stray fragment gets an aha-effect in the hands of an aristocratic heir. God knows what spicy things will see daylight the next few weeks that otherwise would have been chucked into the dustbin!"

Hmmm, he might have a point there, the Mikes thought. *But that la Marcella needs had to besiege the Moragues borough with that find from Palacio Vivot! Without informing us!* Particularly Dugal felt poached on his domain and also for that the prof himself showed understanding.

"I agree. Dolores do Mar owes you something, but she intended to make it up soon. Believe me, this action is not what you think ~ an attempt to get things over to her side by means of some gutter journalism. But the fact is: with the implication of Carlos Quinto in this, his machinations behind the curtains and all those skirmishes of the last few weeks, this case is getting another dimension. And señora Hortaz knows what she's busy with."

"Quod est demonstrandum. Let's first see and then believe, señor pastor."

The way Roberto Marquez had unfolded Marcella's tactics to them ~ taking the big tycoon by surprise, waving the retrieved lyrical epistle about, and at the same time imposing on him with her perfect backing ("Each word that we say, is being listened in") … There was no guarantee whatsoever that the magnate would walk into that trap. The small gadget in her hand, he could as well denounce it as a toy. And as for the proposed deal? "You swallow your threats henceforth and we'll hush up adamantly about your urbanization plans for La Cornisa, with Maremira right in the middle of it. In return, you may figure with glamour in our docudrama 'The Uncrowned King of Marcaio'."

It seemed at least naïve to Dugal to think that a businessman of his calibre would be slavering for a guest role with such a media missy. And even if she tried to blackmail him with an old tribe feud between his great-great-grandfather and the Dux, so what? He would thank a bundle for the honour. And as far as the risk factor was concerned, why would señor Moragues harass a lady-journalist who wanted to get the blood from under his nails? She had no leg to stand on.

"Come on, Professor. That multi-millionaire is not going to moan about a few doggerel verses and some rumours, whether founded or not, about a witch hunt for underground lodge members and pacifists or whatever, orchestrated by the progenitor of the Moragues empire. Suppose don Carlos did have an eye on our stretch of northern coast, he would have made his wish known to me ~ sorry, to us, darling ~ for quite a while. Such a fellow doesn't lift a finger for a couple of millions."

"Millions? As if he doesn't know señor Mikes. After all, this Carlos V knows he would come away with a flea in his ears with you."

"Who tells you so?" Catarí said roguishly. What if they got a tenfold profit left from it?

But that was not the point at all, Dugal interfered. The question was that la Marcella's plot theory seemed too far-fetched. Why all at once wasn't it so obvious any longer that there was a bunch of ultra-conservatives behind all those actions? Why need it absolutely be …?

"That will do, gentlemen!" Catarí interrupted their arguing. Pressing her hands on her ears, she was sitting there and then switched to an elegiac scale: "The most remarkable declaration of love I've ever heard … As if it comes from the hereafter, so intimate. A voyage to the Light. La poésie pure. And here you are, the two of you spouting theories all the time about why and how, and who is behind it all. But all that quibble isn't getting us any further."

Suddenly the gentlemen absolutely agreed with her. Just to think that this Miss MP might be concluding a pact with the devil at this very moment. Merely to manage that whole L.S. hype at her will. *Damn it,* Dugal suppressed his annoyance. And the professor inserted a moment of reflection about the *other* possibilities. You could tell by his closed eyes and his Simon Stylites pose. After a few minutes he broke the subdued silence.

"At first, señora Mikes, I myself also started from the dementia theory. A sublimating escape into fantasy. A last 'acte de grandeur' of that decrepit seignior who, by lack of spiritual oxygen, gathers his last forces to take up his pen once more."

"And hmm … Let me guess," Dugal joined in with him. "Consumed by the old heartfelt longing, the languishing Dux returns to Maremira, his piece of La Cornisa, on the wings of the swallow … A fata morgana, a sublime piece of fantasy I want to sign up for. Hmm, hmm," he backed out, under Catarí's flashing eyes.

"And so … it was too nicely fitting into the romantic version of the official historiography. With Schliemann's doubt I started picking together the pieces of the puzzle … until *Dichtung* became *Wahrheit*: poetry coming true. I am sure, querídos amigos, the home-journey of our Ulysses did NOT appear out of the blue."

Full of tension, they were hanging on Prof. Marquez' lips. *Stop that twaddle, proffy, tell us at last the ins and outs of it. According to you.*

At the very moment when Roberto bent over to start off with tightly closed eyes: "Actually it's like this …", an uproar in the hall disturbed his report. Roberto's wifey blew in, frantically gabbling, followed by a desperately gesticulating registrar.

Catarí dragged him on to the street. "Let those lovebirds go on tussling." Dugal, who did not want to show he was peeved about the lost chance, walked straight on to the parking lot.

Catarí was about to catch up with him when suddenly she saw him spin round like a top and then shoot from one direction to the other. Like one of those wound-up toys they make turn round in a ton at the market.

"Gone," he said, deathly pale. "Gone!" In a squeaky voice that seemed to come out of a throttled larynx. And that precisely tickled her laughing-muscles. She too saw their car had vanished, but Dugal's reaction simply gave her the giggles ~ she could not help it, but then, it was such a ludicrous sight after all. And that's what made Dugal even more furious, of course.

"Thank god it's not your old Sovereign," she consoled him, also in a strangled voice now. That morning he had still hesitated whether he should or should not come in his old top model. Eventually they had taken that democratic little Seat, so as to be less eye-catching. Much as Dugal was devoted to his couple of old-timers, she knew the braggart in him was also superstitious, in such matters. You had better not defy Phoebus or Minerva with your fetishes, or they sent the Erynnees to you. *And then they say that women would sell their soul for a handful of jewels and a Jaguar under their butt.*

But this incident made him really freak out now. "While we're sitting in there, nicely waiting like … like nitwits for the result of the match Moragues-Marcella, they are just nicking your own car in the street.

Catarí had already picked her mobile phone out of her handbag to call the police, but no! They were not going to grant them that pleasure. After all, those fellows were surely watching them through their binoculars by now.

Quick as lightning Dugal gesticulated to a passing cab. As if per order. "Llosera, señor Mikes ? Disculpe, but I already have a call, in the city centre."

"No, well yes, exactly, take us along to the Plaza de España. Pronto!"

Jackass, doesn't he grasp it then? Catarí thought, but Dugal had already got in and winked, "Come Cathy! You look in the rear-view window in the front."

On one buttock he had already crept on the rear seat, to spy down the whole road surface behind them. As the taxi-driver was slaloming through the late afternoon bustle, he surveyed the situation: "No pursuers. I believe the coast is clear."

Of course, 'cause you have been hoaxed jolly well! Why do you think that cab happened to pass just at that moment, timed like in a trash thriller? Chè palurdo! But she could not say it just like that, for perhaps not only this bloke was overhearing them. Mini microphones surely connected them somehow with the headquarters of Carlos Moragues or such another maniac.

Cautiously Catarí coded her weird inklings in the cockney-like gibberish they used as their own secret lingo once in a while. "Th't riffraff pick'd you 'p naicely, taiking us to th' spot', maibi in th' naice c'mp'ny of ei M'rcella 'rself. Savvy, swit dolt o' mine?"

Dugal fell silent for the rest of the ride. When the chauffeur, however, put them down on the desired square, he gave the good man double the tariff and, taking Catarí by the shoulder, he pointed triumphantly at the outdated station beyond: "Ferrocarríles de Marcaio."

It made them almost forget the gravity of the swindle. All about this building ~ the pseudo-classic style which reminded them of the Gaudí church in Llosera, the plane and palm trees alongside, owing to which the entry and the platforms got the aspect of a lush patio; the old-time bar where all day long some regular customers seemed to bring to life some caricatures by Miró or Dali … and the coffee on top of it all: "I believe it also dates back to Gaudi's days," said Catarí laconically ~ everything here emanated the nostalgic bel époque ambience.

When the little train was drawing nearer, groaning and merrily hooting, they were still nipping at their second cup, but the lady at the counter put them at ease: "Tranquilo! That one first has to recover its breath, la vieja puta." Meanwhile she was chortling so hard that her boobs risked to roll out of her apron. Promptly she dished up a tiny glass of paló right under their nose: "To your health and success!" And she tossed one down herself, wiping her mouth clean with a cloth that looked suspiciously like a pair of knickers from her granny's days. "That old lassie," echoed a jaunty gent that was standing close to them at the bar, "needs coming to herself again. Greasing her rusted bones with olive oil, I guess. I'll give you a sign," he said. "I 'm riding with her myself."

The interval had been long enough for a treat at their expense, and also the little man stood one in his turn. After their stomaching three palòs within a good quarter of an hour, the rear of the station changed into a real Delvaux picture.

"Paula Dèvelou, eh, wasn't he a Dutchman?" Dugal wagered.

"Paul! Paul Dèlevow. Not at all ~ from Luxembourg," Cathy jabbered thickly. Which the little man affably adjusted: "Almost. From Bruselas, but that's quite near, isn't it? To American standards at least."

The old vehicle, in light oak varnish and with red lead upper panels, sighed as badly as they did themselves while getting in. *What does that little fellow want with us?"* Catarí mumbled. *In a little while he is even slipping into our bed between us.*

34

"El Rey, The king of Marcaio." Those were the first words he had spoken for half an hour. All that time he had been sitting there in front of her, motionless, without interrupting her in the least. And that's what surprised her most of all. She had imagined this man in quite a different way: haughty, power-loving, unassailable … Nothing of the sort. No condescending glances, no scornful contradiction, no verbal violence whatsoever. On the contrary. Fascinated by her story, he had got up from behind his massive, mahogany desk. Had taken a seat right opposite her, without turning his eyes away from her, in a baroque armchair, only nodding his head: just go on telling, please … His legs crossed, leaning his elbow on one knee and his fist under his equally massive chin ~ like petrified he kept staring at her. *A sculpture by Rodin, she thought: The Listener, with an R.M.Rilke-like verse underneath:*

> *'He hung at her lips,*
> *a leaden weight, and she felt*
> *the contents slipping down her hips,*
> *as his eyes rested on her belt …'*

Now and then she found it difficult to hold on the thread. There was something about that man. His wide-angle look, encompassing both her thighs and waist, mesmerized her in a strange way. Twenty years older and not married with a goody-goody sweetheart, she would have fallen for him at once, hic et nunc. L.S. or no L.S..

"Well, that's about all. Please, think it over."

"I have already done so. All the time. Nice story." Then it remained silent for a while, without him taking his eyes off her.

"El Rey. I, King of Marcaio," he then repeated, with raised eyebrows. Grinning for a moment, not at her, but at the idea. Whereupon he started shaking with laughter, and that changed into an increasing, irrepressible Homeric laughter. For minutes on end.

Now it was Marcella's turn to sit and wait there, motionless. Until his fit of laughter would pass by definitively.

"I'm sorry, Mrs. Hortaz. Or is it still Miss? I'm not laughing at you, you were fantastic. By the way, I've always admired you, you know. Honestly. A lady with class and pluck! Marcaio needs such characters ~ what with all those would-be announcers and bogus starlets these days, with a great lack of backbone …"

He watched her complacently, the way one admires a thoroughbred mare for her fine manes, slender loins and slim frame. From any other man Marcella would have declined this as sheer impudence. Under señor Moragues's connoisseur gaze, though, this came pretty natural: he had nothing to gain, had he?

"As I've said before: a prime story. And I don't regard your offer to figure in your program about the Dux as an indecent proposal. I would even like to do so. At the side of such a graceful figure that's an honour."

"But why then that burst of laughter?" asked Marcella, rather to cover up her sudden embarrassment.

A broad grimace contorted his face, but this time he remained serious: "Because it's far off the mark, Guapíssima. Whether there did exist any friction, or something like rivalry, between good old don Lois and our old lord here ~ the 'progenitor of our empire' as you happen to call him …? Perhaps. Although ~ I doubt if my great-great granddad, or his father, was already dreaming about the Costa Nort, let alone cherishing plans in that sense. But …"

"But you do, señor Moragues," she interrupted him wittily. "We are aware of your plans: urbanizations, developing projects in the tourist sector, with Ses Taca right in the middle of it. Maremira and the revival of L.S., plus Mister Mikes's publications and his devotion to that somewhat mouldy cult figure, must be a thorn in the eye of some advocates of progress."

"Really, you ought to go into politics, señora, with such a rhetorical gift. But once again, your little theory makes no sense. And why? Who is making up such wicked stories about me?"

Come on, she laughed, *she was not naïve. Neither was Professor ~ …*

"Professor?" The mocking light in his eyes betrayed his secret amusement because she had exposed herself. Humming, he walked up to the window. "Prof. Marquez … Hmmm, sympathetic fellow, sportive, nothing about that. But how those humanities scholars can indulge in fantasy, eh! " Smirking good-naturedly, he was looking outside, nodding: "Is he waiting there too, in a car? Eavesdropping every word we are saying, until I lose my patience and they have to rescue you, armed and all, ha-ha-ha." Grinningly he passed behind her, patting her on her shoulder, to sit down again opposite her for a pleasant chat.

What else should he have done? he winked. Grab in his drawer for his golden gun, foaming with rage? Or dive into a safe, grinding his teeth, to take a pile of hush money, but yeah … How much … half a million, a million europesas, that was a mere trifle for him, wasn't it? Or even steeper: snatch her, Marcella Hortaz, away from the regional broadcasting corporation, by means of a swell contract and a luxurious job. Well, that at least was more like it.

"You can't convince me, señor. Besides, your self-possession doesn't alter the fact that you cannot prove the contrary. Owing to an anxiety psychosis you could count on the Mikes being caught by the curse on Ses Taca, so they would leave the Archidux with his amourette and all his belongings in the lurch. Back to the States."

"Venga!" Don Carlos had got up. Curtly but decidedly he showed her out: ladies first! That was the end of the audience, she assumed. So, no concession whatsoever, no gentleman's agreement. At the end of the big reception room, however, he opened another door. From there she saw it at once, in an elegantly furnished room full of drawing tables: a giant scale-model and, on the wall above it, a relief panorama of Marcaio's northern coast. "La Cornísa, from west to east," he showed proudly, letting her enjoy for a moment the artfully elaborated draft of his villa complex. *So, it does exist after all and he is granting me an avant-première. Why?*

"I was sure you would like it. I give the preference to you if it comes to a presentation to the public." He seemed to mean it.

"It is quite a gem after all," she said, in candid admiration for the realistically designed miniature houses, in classical Moorish-Marcaian style, embedded in lush gardens, with a few water basins in the middle of them. Even the palm trees looked like real bonsais. "Where can I register?"

"This draft," he ignored her irony, "has nothing to do with the region of Valle de Muša or Deió. Here!" With a long stick he made a circle around two smaller settlements. "In Sant'Elmó and Cala Galera we see some possibilities for this pilot project. That is, at some distance from Maremira, one at the west side and one opposite Galileo. These holiday villages, both of them still pretty quiet, in nearly unspoiled nature, form an ideal frame for our tryout. Mind it … We don't want to give the building rage an extra impetus; there has been enough tinkering with concrete and iron in these parts."

"Which you yourself seemed to have a way with, after all, didn't you?"

"Oh, oh … I admit that we jumped on that fatal slide ourselves once. On this island I have, all-in-all, eight of those monstrosities on my conscience, indeed. But I badly mrepent that and by God, I swear I'll make up for that capital sin. Starting with those two places namely. There are already a handful of those soulless skeletons there, uncompleted witnesses of the human megalomania. For my penance I bought them up and I will rehabilitate those places."

Like a penitent he patted himself on his breast and went on with his plea against the era of bad taste. Not that he wanted all concrete in itself to be banned; already the Romans used it. It was just the application of it, a matter of style. And that's what he wanted to give back to HIS Marcaio, as a token of entity. An antidote against the boring sameness: characterless concrete boxes which all those paranoid designers devised to help this world go to hell.

"And in that sense, Guapíssima, I believe I've found an ally in señor Mikes."

"A pawn that you can stake for your game, you mean." She feigned not hearing that little compliment, the second in a row: 'Most Beautiful one'.

"No. I am grateful to him for rehabilitating Ses Taca. He opened my eyes with it. Before long I wanted to take up contact with him again, for I'm sure he has the best intentions with our island."

Her buzzing and whining mobile phone brought la Marcella back to reality. "Sorry, another message," she said.

Señor Moragues noticed her confusion as she was reading. "Any problem?"

It came from Dolores Francisquita. *We're on the wrong track. The Mikeses' car has been stolen in front of Roberto's office,* she mumbled.

"And where are they now?" don Carlos asked.

Harmlessly the TV presenter briefed him about what the academician had just transmitted. "In whose company were they in the train?"

"An unsightly little man, she writes, dressed in black. Looking like Manuel de Falla. She followed them as far as the platform."

Then he could think who it was, don Carlos said cautiously. "If that's the case, they are in for a few surprises, señora," he chuckled naughtily on seeing the perplexed expression on la Marcella's face.

The little train to Llosera, which was panting its way through the back-gardens of the city, was a real revelation. For those who, like the Mikes couple, had to do with a scanty historical memory concerning Europe, this unique specimen raked up some vague impressions of wild-west scenes and Dugal at once was tampering with the brass handles alongside. "This way," the slender gentleman helped them converting the back-to-back seat into a face-to-face position. "One century old, very soon, still built in the Cockerill workplaces," he said proudly, polishing with his sleeve the messing balls on the wooden armrests. "Belgian-made produce."

Quite smoothly the ramshackle thing changed from train to tramway rails and back, while street vendors were hurrying along, trying to sell some soft drink or melon to the passengers. "El Diario!" the little man shouted from the window, some change in his hand for a sprinting newspaper boy. Like toddlers Dugal and Catarí were sucking on a stone-hard carob pod …

"No!" she screamed, when a cyclist jumped from his bike and, in full swing, leapt on to the landing. They just saw the bike diving right under the skirt of a bending cleaning woman. So what!

"There's nothing like public transport, is there?'" the little fellow said from behind his newspaper. "Particularly when your own vehicle has broken down. Or has been stolen."

With a shock they looked at each other. *How could he know?!*

Promptly the man showed them the inside pages, with the local eye-catchers. *'Ladrones de coche. Car of movie couple Mikes stolen …'*

"But that has just happened! How can they already have …?"

Dugal got stuck in his outburst. Wide-eyed, they nodded at each other. There *it is, once again. Anticipated scenarios.*

"So, you were just coming from the professor?" their companion sounded them.

"You … know Professor Marquez?" Every second they got more and more stunned.

"Roberto Marquez, si si. Nice chap, but a bit unworldly, as most bookworms are. Clumsy. Doesn't it strike you? Anywhere he is around, something goes wrong. Yet the distracted professor himself keeps out of range."

The old fellow dished up a whole series of anecdotes, showing he had all his wits about him. He quoted from some books by the Archidux and seemed to have learnt particular parts of the published L.S. fragments by heart. Little by little an uncomfortable feeling came over them, until Catarí could no longer restrain her curiosity. "Who are you in fact?"

The man in the black suit, a cross between a mortuary chanter and an antiquarian, pulled a broad grin. "I once was a teacher of Roberto Marquez'. As a young lad he was already obsessed by that Habiger. So the tree, so the fruit, y' know. Oh, I 'm arriving at my destination." And he pointed at the little church of Banyulo, drawing nearer like a snail. "If I were you, I'd go and look beyond my nose. There is talk of some projects round about Galileo. Prof. Marquez has been spotted there regularly, in the neighbourhood of the church, and there's also a chapel in the nearby bay. Wouldn't there be any connection with the content in one of those last epistles? About that implantation of new vines, remember, and accommodating such specimens at the Keppelers' in the vicinity there. I wonder ~ …" But now it was high time to get out, for the guard had already whistled three times. "Your name?" Dugal called after him, through the window, but the sound got lost in the loud blows of the locomotive, which was preparing for the big climb across the Sierra Tramuntana, heading for Llosera.

Still a bit impressed by what had happened and the speculations of the mysterious little fellow, Catarí and Dugal were getting dragged along, in spite of themselves, between the passengers' bags and things: their booty from the city's shopping centres. This station at the foot of the mountains had something of its own, a surrealistic tinge. It might as well have been situated in Ecuador or Costa Rica. All their desire to go back home was gone by now. The station buffet, all at once bustling with activity, sprayed all kinds of odours and colours through each other, from garlic to cocas de verdura, anise, rum, coffee and lemons …

"Un momentito, darling." For a moment, Dugal had to add to this the extra fragrance of the loo. For that, one had to bend under a rope on which the station mistress's bras and briefs were dangling. No sooner was he standing there, his willy at ready, than a brutal lout pressed against his back, a gun between his ribs: "Tu dinero o tu vida!" Before Dugal was able to utter a sound, the little door burst open and the ticket collector positioned himself next to him. "Can you cope with it, boys?" he sneered. Dugal gave him a dirty look, but when he turned round, the thief had already vanished.

"Everything OK?" asked Catarí, seeing he looked a bit pale.

"Course. Except for an assailant who wanted to pinch my wallet and a train guard who now takes me for a daisy. What's it like again? *With public transport you always have a bit of fun.*"

35

At nightfall the silhouette of Ses Taca, from afar, stood out against the sea, at least for those who were able to descry it through the woods. About three times the taxi driver had asked the taciturn couple: "Esta muy lejos - still a long way to go?" It surprised them sometimes how badly they were recognized by the average native. *Nothing's so mortal as the ephemeral fame of the small screen.* Strange to say, neither of them felt inclined to return early after what had happened. So the snail's pace of the cab did not annoy them at all. Yet, as the fellow suddenly sped up to a devilish pace, closely grazing along a pumpkin cart, so the fruits rolled across the road, they suddenly seemed to get into a bloodcurdling thriller. "Estas loco? Hey, maniac, stop!"

The harder Dugal was yelling, the more the fellow was freaking out.

"Idiot! I'll teach you manners!" Dugal exploded, after the spinning car had eventually come to a standstill on the yard, in a cloud of dust.

"Out!" Without turning a hair, the driver pointed a gun at his nose.

Catarína was pulling madly at Dugal's sleeve, that he should restrain himself and commit no rash acts. "Mister Maïks," the fellow suddenly burst into laughter. "That's quite different from the movies, eh! Loco? No, we're no fools, but take care who you are dealing with, next time! And you, señora, do mind your business!"

And off screeched the speed merchant, in a cloud of dust, same as he had come.

Well I never, Dugal murmured, and Catarí, struck with dismay: "Who we are dealing with …?" And then: "Desperado, you scum, we choose the friends we like!" she screamed after that maniac. Dugal was staring at her, flabbergasted. He had not seen her driven over the edge like that ever since that con by which some adversaries of his tried to involve him in a love affair with a co-actress. Just to put her up against him, of course -

her, top of the bill in Hollyland at that moment, with the highest market value. A transparent game, but one that always works. Especially if you manage to bribe the dog at the skittles, in this case a competitor of hers. Which he had been able to make her realize, at the last moment: "That's precisely what those people want: to drive a wedge between us, Cathy. Out of pure jealousy."

He told her that again now, as she was standing there, trembling on her legs in an instinctive reaction. *What was that bloke dawdling about 'my case'?*

His arm about her shoulder, he led her round the back, but she was hard to soothe. "Don't you grasp it, Dugie? Those guys stick at nothing, and you see: that whole action today was a put-up job." *Forestalled by Roberto Marquez, who else?* Dugal's suspicion had never been so strong.

And then, just around the corner, towards the back porch, they got the shock of their lives. There she was, behind the old medlar tree: their green little scallywag, as if she had never been out of her shed. Unaware of any harm, like a cat who has gone a-courting and then, when you have given her up for quite a while, there she is suddenly back licking her bottom at her familiar place near the hearth.

No scratch, no note behind the screen wiper. A cold shiver ran down Dugal's spine. But what else could you do but keep plucky in front of you wifey like the sham hero in your own movie? The worst, though, was: they did not know what was awaiting them inside. And yet, recoiling was not possible any more.

Inside the hall the Viennese case-clock was ticking at the pace of the eighteenth century. And its little sister in the parlour, a Laterndl regulator that Catarí had got for a mere song at the market of Bonabini, chimed in with that indolent pendulum in its lighter mezzo-soprano. Enough to get the jitters.

The furniture, the paintings, the pen drawings and portraits of the Archidux … All seemed to hold their breath, waiting until the hands of the clock had turned back a century. As if at any moment don Lois in person was going to saunter in and then, exhausted, fall into Catalí d'Omar's arms.

Nada, nihil. This was impossible. Precisely that silence, that lack of any cryptic sign gave them an oppressing feeling.

Catarí withdrew in the kitchen. "Will you fill up the bath, Cariño?

I am feeling as dingy as one of those mangy mongrels in the streets of Palmera."

Meanwhile she would be providing for a cool gazpacho, with the inevitable garlic toasts. Delicious, to boost you up after that moral punch.

Course! Whistling an aria of the lyrical tenor in 'La Francisquita' (totally out of tune, but it was an approved trick, anyway, better than the best sedative, even if terror seized you at the throat), Dugal pulled himself up the stairs along the banisters.

Through the open door he heard a weak echo of his own serenade. But then, only as woman lips can do. *Kick it open,* was his first reaction. But, in spite of that impulse, he cautiously peered inside. And what did his squinting eye see there, on a stool, leaning aslant over the bathtub? A thoroughbred local chick in a maid's dress, white-capped and complete with the classical white apron on a very mini mini-skirt, her left leg dangling backwards in search of her equilibrium.

"Que pasa?"

In her shock reaction the poor thing made a kind of somersault, plop into Dugal's arms. For a moment light was fading before his eyes, and when Catarí, five ticks later, got to the spot, she found her better half lying there, half groggy, in a corner between bath and wall, his head against the edge. Left to the tender mercies of a far from unsavoury young crumpet, bending full-breasted over him.

High competition, she thought, *seen like that, from behind.* Some years before a similar sight would have set her aflame. Now, however, the ludicrous scene only made her get the giggles. Yet, she ran off without saying a word, knowing well what was to follow. Her felled hero running after her like blazes: "Cathy! This is not what you think. Damn it!" And the mysterious apparition tripping along on her stilts: "Señora Maïks, I can explain it all."

"You'd better!" That theatrical pose, applied in tens of film shots, came back to her like an automatism: the arms crossed, a steel look, sure to cut through every pseudo macho like a knife, and certainly through Dugal. Yet she looked straight at the girl behind him. "I had just begun to ... put up the curtain ... in the bathroom ... Then Mister Maïks came in and eh ..."

"...gently fell into your arms. Nice publicity, Dugie."

"Hey listen," he groaned, touching the lump on his head. But there was no stopping the girl any more: she had wanted to make herself useful all at once, after the lord of the house had given her a call saying she could replace the servants, because ...

"What?!" the Mikeses screamed both at the same time.

"Well yes, so they could go on a holiday. But when I arrived here, they didn't know anything about it yet, said this madam what's-her-name ..."

"Coloma?"

Precisely. Yet the couple were glad they could slip off for once. What a surprise, typically his lordship, they had said.

Dugal and Catarí looked at each other, as if they had seen a ghost. So that's how those fellows managed to penetrate into their privacy. Or ... bribe their personnel? But then, they could misuse their name for other purposes as well. *The way they can hack your PC these days, place orders and do banking trans-actions in your name ~ imagine such people would ...!*

"I've heard enough cock-and-bull stories about that, Duke. Alright, they can fleece you without your noticing anything, scoop you out and ~ ..."

"...undress you, sweetheart. Download photos, glue your photogenic head on someone else's body or vice versa. I mustn't think of it."

Thus they started grating on each other's nerves, until the new maid brought them back to their senses. "Disculpe, señores ..." The way she was standing there, harmlessly pretty, it was a shame sending the poor thing back home empty-handed. But ... who was she actually?

"Manuela, at your service." Promptly the girl produced her credentials from her apron pocket.

"What? Manuela ... do Mar!" Upon seeing that name, they startled altogether. Not related to ...?

"Dolores Francisquita, si si. D' you know her? Què coincidencia!"

Oh no, this couldn't be sheer coincidence. After leaving the nice niece up to her work again, the hypotheses sprang up. Who dare say now there was no cross-connection with professor Marquez in this case? Unless Dolores do Mar was falsely involved in this, intentionally ~ a tactical move to put them all up against one another. "Anyhow, this damsel doesn't look like a spy, bribed to watch all our comings and goings," Dugal thought.

"Tipico," Catarí sighed. "The men see a slender naked leg and all at once it's sunshine all around."

Maybe she was right. It could not all be that harmless after all. On entering the drawing-room already he had had the feeling of being peeped at. A shiver ran down his spine, but much as he wanted to, he was not able to look around. A stitch from his shoulder suddenly paralysed the whole upper part of his body. He only had the power to kick with his legs.

Catarí cried blue murder. Ragingly he tried to tear himself loose, yet, totally helpless to interfere, he had to watch a guy threatening her with a gun.

"Stop it! What has come over you?"

Wet with perspiration, he found himself sitting upright in bed, feeling his cheek on which Catarí had given him a clip. "What are you doing?"

"And you! You all but kicked me out of the bed."

Scrambling to his feet, Dugal dragged himself to the small cabinet concealing a fridge. Poured out a dram for each of them ~ an old vice from the sleepless nights when some pieces from his scenarios were flurrying through his head. How long was that ago? "Please, a sip from that local almond stuff," he sighed.

All of a sudden everything came clearly back to their mind. Whom had they found there in their parlour yesterday night, crouched in an arm-chair, a revolver in his hand, pointing straight at them? Señor Miguel!

"Oh, it's just you," he said with relief. *Just us, yes,* it came home to them like lightning. That sort of editor had jumped to his feet, promptly serving them up his story, with odds and ends, and seasoned with much southern verve.

After the raid and the theft of documents at his home, Miguel Mortado had set off playing kind of detective on his own account. Putting all pieces together, one could see there had to be a clear connection between the actions against *him* and his publishing house *and* those against the Mikes couple. Well, all traces were leading in one and the same direction.

"Roberto Marquez," Dugal said brusquely.

"Or Carlo Moragues? Maybe they're hand in glove," Miguel replied with a cryptic laugh.

"Señor Miguel!" Catarí shook her head. Now this was going a bit too far after all. Did the gentlemen pretend that in this banana republic there was an unholy alliance between two such extremes? A difference even bigger than between the deceased Franco and the present Numero Uno.

"Or between Faust and Mephistofeles. For money the most honest scholar sells his soul, señora."

So would he too then? she suggested. But the speculating publisher did not seem to hear that. Hadn't those duplicates of don Lois' secret letters set them to think yet? And why had they been 'frozen' all the time in Roberto's academic safes ~ food for sterile essays by thick-bespectacled students? By the way, how had they got in there? And what had Jordi Martell, that kind of corrupted copier, got to do with that?

Over his reading glasses he watched them with a significant glance that gave Dugal the shudders. What if his great find, the *letras secretas*, were not written by his Excellency L.S. at all, but were just, like everything, a farce, a macabre academic hoax? Bogus, fake, a mystification … But one clotted with money, blood money if necessary, like everything related to big projects on such an island.

"Man, I'm going to kill you, you're just fantasizing." *Besides, mutatis mutandis, he, petty publisher, could just as well have been sitting at that table of abundance, right?* With a squint Miguel Mortado took a list out of his pocket ~ a black list, he smirked, with the names of compromised personalities and renowned BMW's, including ~ watch it ~ la Marcella and Roberto's favourite assistant, sweet Dolores.

Once more the Mikeses watched each other with raised eyebrows. One short reflex however ~ automatism of the experienced actor ~ and they were in tune for a combined play. Looking at Miguel's list, with a doubtful countenance. Well, well, but eh … what was this supposed to prove? they acted sceptical, and then, feigning indifference: don Miguel had gathered interesting names, quite right, but how objective was his source? *Veiled imputations, dear friend, allegations, but nothing of hardcore evidence* ~ he had no leg to stand on …

36

It was already past nine when both were still scurrying a bit around in the kitchen, feeling unusually drowsy so late that morning. As if they had a load in the stomach after Dugal's nightmare and the exasperating conjectures from the night before. More than a few slices from a bruised mango was all they were up to for breakfast. Besides it did not give them much relish, as may happen to one's taste buds after a night out. She plopped down on the couch in her nightgown and he languidly turned on the telly. *'En directo desde Ses Taca'*, it was announced on Canal Uno.

Dugal and Catarí looked at each other in disbelief. This was really inconceivable. One of la Marcella's most topical commentaries, and from their own back-garden at that ‑ set in this very finca!

"…Ya es meravigliosa aqui, a unique scenery, isn't it, and it's here, queridos spectadores, that for some weeks an intrigue has been going on which seems to be poking up things that happened a good century ago, exactly at this place. Leading actors are: one of the most notorious professors of literature *and* his staff, and on the other hand, two celebs of the silver screen who, by this time, have grown into renowned BMW's ‑ Beloved Marcaian World citizens, that is. Namely, none other than the movie couple …"

Almost synchronously they dashed to the window. Nothing. They believed they had heard a noise outside, like the shoving of chairs; yet, except for their horny cat and a tomcat in charge there was nothing to see. Merely a broken jar.

Dart! That deuced Dolly do Mar must have cooked that up again. Marcaio's biggest tycoon on Marcella's lap! This is likely to outstrip Oprah and la Hunzicker. But what's that fellow going to blurt out there?

"Don't blow it up, Duke. Marcella surely knows what she's doing."

Of course. But what swagger she had! 'Right on the air', you must be bold enough to do that. They had certainly fixed this with an accomplice.

"Manuela?!"

"Oh, my dear." When Cathy looked at him with that ironic glance, he knew enough. "It has all been well staged. Hey, you know that."

"On our terrace at the backside, with our sea view? That speaks for itself. Only the time of the shooting isn't right."

"Dugal! You do know what those people can fix up, don't you? Mixing up pictures, you wouldn't trust your eyes. Soon they are gluing your head on a young bodybuilder's chest and this documentary film breaks all the records of viewing ratings. Gosh, you've been a producer yourself or haven't you?"

He was swallowing it down a bit. The way Marcella was handling this again, so jauntily ~ "Señor Moragues, or may I say Carlos Quinto?" … How had she managed to rope in that super magnate for her sake? "You certainly know more about what has been taking place behind the scenes, at the time of the Archidux and your hale and hearty great-great-grandfather …"

The way she let the old crocodile perform his act! In his amiable and self-possessed tone, he voiced his sympathy for Marcaio's uncrowned king. Lifted a tip of the veil about what that aristocratic underdog meant, could have meant, as a pacifistic key-figure. "He, with his amply spread circle of friends, among the intelligentsia and enlightened spirits of that epoch … A man of the world, truly, one of those cosmopolitans we don't see wandering about on this globe in such great numbers ~ regrettably!"

The laconic tic around his mouth made the looker-on throw a mental bridge to señor Moragues himself. After all, he had some more nicknames, this Carlos Quinto ~ from viceroy to the sheik of Marcaio. However, he rather wanted to damp that far too hard rushing gossip factory in the wake of the recent publications ~ with all respect for señor and particularly (he archly winked at Marcella) señora Mikes. Don Lois a failed Saviour? His umpteenth Christian name Salvator a predestining label to link him, non-conformist pig-head, up with a Messiah lineage? Next to, mind it, a Clovis, Arthur, Godfrey and some more of those parade horses of the Bloodline theory. Really, that was a scenario too far for señor Moragues. "Maybe food for movie script writers," the big man grinned. But he got up on his hind legs when la Marcella shrewdly took a byway back to Moragues the Old.

"No hostilities or frictions whatsoever. No more than there are between myself and señor Mikes. By the way, pretty soon you'll hear there is going to be a pact between me and the greatest movie star of our era: for the sake of Marcaio, our patrimony, our environment."

And the pretty presenter did not try to bridle Moragues. On the contrary, she even added fuel to his fire. The viceroy truly began to make a plea for eco-tourism on this island. *As if he wants to buy off a seat next to L.S. in Heaven,* Dugal scorned. But la Marcella did not wait either to do her share. These chitchats and odd peripeties of the last few days already shed light on what Dugal Mikes had in mind with the Archidux ... *And in the meantime she knows how to sell herself properly,* they both thought, with growing admiration.

The row of names was already sweeping across the screen and Catarí was about to switch off the telly, when Manuela, their new maidservant, appeared on the screen, ostentatiously swaying her hips in her far too short frock, down the stairs towards the swimming-pool. Click, there you saw Dugal, stretched out, peering over his sunglasses and newspaper; Catarí from behind, in monokini, diving into the pool; ánd Manuela, smoothly flaunting in between the two.

"What?! Me in monokini, never!"

"What rascal has fixed up that scene?" Dugal at once joined in with his outraged wife. The way a henpecked husband stands by his better half, unconditionally, when her repute is at stake. He also knew why he had to. Those pictures could turn against him as well; his covetous glances in fact pass for those of a randy faun slavering down the legs of a flighty young lass rather than his spouse's buttocks. *And you know how fast juicy stories begin to lead a life of their own,* he thought. Even just for that pungent end of the scene his opponents could strip his skin.

Now however, at this generous daybreak, everything returned to its usual Marcaian proportions. Leaning back in their lazy bamboo chairs on the terrace they were enjoying the language of the birds among the olive green and the stately cypresses. What the hell did drones and bees, or the sap current, care about the figments of the human brain?

"Du-uke!" Catarí shouted unexpectedly. Dugal leapt to his feet, as though the peak of the Orfe had shattered up. "What ~ how?!" he gasped as he arrived at the place where Cathy had just been watering the arums. *A miscarriage? A Ufo?* Following Catarí's widespread eyes, he saw the mischief. Swift as an arrow, he jumped over the banister, straight across the flower-bed, and in three ticks he was at the small sluice that regulated the overflow of the little torrent supplying the swimming-bath and the pond. Phew! That was a narrow escape.

By way of the ingenious system devised by the Archidux in his days, the crystal-clear water could be diverted so that it ensured the irrigation of the farming lands, via an 'estanque' ~ such an old Marcaian mix of a cistern and a fish-pond. Or to the small swimming-pool that Duke had built in addition since past autumn. But now someone had opened the lock completely, in the direction of the estanque, and jammed it with a solid boulder. One minute later the pond would have been flooded at full power. And that was not all. The partition was likely to have given way, dragging along everything in its fall: plants, furniture, putto statuettes. And all those things, with the inevitable sludge, would have got down into the brand-new swimming-pool, inexorably.

"Look there!"

While he was still standing there, panting after the intense effort and emotion, Catarí pointed at the yellow helicopter which, slantwise skimming over the trees, was searching for some camouflage behind the rocks beyond the coastal road.

"Those were no strangers," he roared. She rushed after him, into the car, and Dugal darted off like mad. "You won't see them again anyway," Catarí tried to calm him down.

"I wouldn't be so sure of that," he shouted above the howling engine. Two bends further his intuition was confirmed: "There, you see."

Sheltered under the foliage along the road, they could follow the escaping chopper, unnoticed. "Son Maraitx," said Dugal. As though by telepathic steering, the pilot swerved in above the manor, which stood out stately over the steep flanks. Soon after, though, the silhouette of Son Maraitx hid the machine from their sight. By the time Dugal had taken the loop of the road and parked the car at a strategic lookout, the chopper had already grounded. Just like that, on an artichoke field behind the manor, but no more trace of the crew. *Bad luck.*

"Notwithstanding," Dugal growled, once back in Ses Taca. "Now we know at least what we are up to."

The very storage-room of Don Lois' intellectual legacy ~ that somewhat dilapidated museum smelling of moth balls: bookcases stuffed with the products of the old chap's pen, some clothes, ceramics and so forth from the old-Marcaian domestic culture, down to a snuffbox and a goose-feather … And there of all places the mafia of his legacy managers had pitched up their tents.

"Without realizing it, we were in the lion's den," Catarí muttered. If they had been spied on like that, with that display of power, from a yacht maybe, by a team of frogmen, drones, hang-gliders or paratroopers, whatever … Hang-gliders? She had seen them flying regularly over their yard the last few days! Then ~ behind each tree, any rock there could be one of their men. "Or a camera," Dugal shouted.

Perhaps the whole wood teems with them; even our living-room can be bugged with eavesdropping devices. Catarí broke out in a cold sweat. Or was that closely thwarted inundation a natural coincidence, including that copter ~ too simple to be true, was it?

"Dugal, you know more about this! What are you keeping from me?" A hysteric urge to run away came over her and he had to keep her in his arms, shaking the fright out of her. "There hasn't happened anything yet, Cathy: the house hasn't burned down, nothing's been stolen. Look!"

While he was adjuring her adamantly that the world did not go under because of the yellowed expressions of love from a couple of skeletons that had been devoured by the worms for a long time, all at once it took Dugal badly himself. *Nothing stolen …?*

Never before had he dashed to the mezzanine like that: a whirlwind. Closed. What a relief! And the key of the closet was still on the ledge above the shelf with Marcaian cooking utensils. Tremblingly he fiddled at the lock; everything alright, the walking canes were still there, untouched.

As Catarí found him there like that, she realized what this meant to him. The way he was stroking those polished sticks and the elegant handles, visibly moved, it was enough to grow green with jealousy. No man had ever followed the sensual lines of her underframe with his eyes like that.

"Señor, are you looking for anything?"

"Ouch!" The heavy eagle's head he had just screwed off, to look into the interior of that cane, fell on Dugal's foot. Sure this was a murderous weapon! At first he thought that razor-sharp beak had pierced his toe.

"Manuela, what are you doing here?" both cried, full of surprise, rather at their stupid question than at her appearance. Instinctively they moved closer up to each other, in the vain hope that the re-conjured Cinderella had not noticed anything.

The girl blabbed something about Gabriela, the cleaning maid who used to come and flood their whole floor on Thursdays. "Enferma," she nodded, and from her explanation they understood that their habitual Miss Spic & Span had called off, some minutes ago. Due to some indisposition, an intestinal complaint.

That one too. A bit too coincidental, they thought. In itself you could, as a man, have no objections against such a replacement. In particular of a Remedy against Love, like Gabriela, by an incarnated Venus of Marcaio. And Catarí sensed that in Dugal the fatherly affection for that pretty thing had got the upper hand. Even after her metamorphosis by which she had exchanged the maid's frock for an equally tight pair of pants and a blouse with V-neck.

"D'acuerdo," Catarí resolved.

"Grácias. See you tomorrow then." Manuela made a bow, so a waterfall of hair curls was concealing the winsome view from them.

"Don't you find her a bit suspect?" By that Dugal wanted to anticipate any reservation with Catarí. But she already turned round again to the closet. "Duke!" *What's up again,* he thought, following her gaze. "There!"

She pointed at the right corner of the closet. Mesmerized by what they saw there, they felt each word sticking in their throat. A role of sheets, simply the same kind of those he had found, but which they had not noticed just before. *They ... those were not lying there at all,* Dugal wanted to say, yet he was not able to utter a word.

Like a lunatic, he began to open and watch each cane. It was all quite in order. "But that's inexplicable!" In a squeaky voice it finally came across his lips. "I did not put it there, and she ... Manuela can't have conjured it in there while we were standing next to her. Or are we getting totally crackers?" His bewildered eyes and ditto head of hair made her recoil. "You strike me with terror, Duke."

"I daresay," he mumbled, unfolding the paper role with quivering hands. And oh yes, there it was, in the same handwriting, only a bit more shaky, just like in all the previous letters to Catalí:

Querida Catalí … …

37

At last it has happened: yesterday I set foot on the shore of my beloved Marcaio once again. Feeling a bit like Ulysses, with the difference that I too would rather have roved the seas for years on end than secretly pine away in a chilly Bohemian castle.

You may call it a miracle that I am still able to experience all this, physically. To make this passage one more time with these racked limbs of mine … mon dernier voyage! No matter how long I had already travelled ahead with the swallows, I dared not hope I should see it … ~ see you, Cariña, ever again.

To me this was somehow like coming home in the House of the Father … That primaeval instinct, a collective urge imprinted in man's mind since times immemorial. From a rational point of view, though, that atavism ought to have drawn me to some more outlined destinations. Palazzo Pitti, Mount Zion in Jerusalem, the Ionic Archipelago … Not to mention Schloß Belvédère in Vienna. What, however, has linked my destiny to this emerald of the Bailares ~ to Maremira? The answer lies in your eyes, Cariña.

On the quay of Palmera my faithful companion left me to the cares of a Galilean. Just a pun, you know: one of our acquaintances from Keppler's circle. He was to take me to your refuge, but ~ much as I was yearning for our reunion, Cariña, yet the coachman made a detour along Ses Taca. Perhaps he apprehended something of my inner urge, for he already made a halt on the coastal road, at the place where the silhouette of our Saracen beauty stands out through the *foliage. Then he drove up the small lane leading to the manor. A pathetic meeting after all those years, I had imagined. Our former vintry, where once the air was buzzing with activity, and now: deserted. I did not get out, but in the carriage I recaptured the scenes from the past. The grape growers and seasonal workers who used to climb the path with full baskets; the wheels of the carts crunching on the yard; oak barrels were ready to be loaded … Some guests were sitting on a bench, waiting for the maestra, the dama de la casa, to come along with a wine jar. And now … Deadly silence, as if even the ortolan and the thrush had been stricken by numbness.*

Farther up the road I tried to shake off the old images. Still, the abandoned pockmarked contours of Ses Taca kept haunting me: the face of an old friend whom you see again after a few years, but who has changed so much that you get to feel a lump in your throat. And all of a sudden, that thought made me stiffen altogether. What if this also befell me myself? If the ravages of time had tarnished my appearance so badly that I had grown entirely unrecognizable for others? Even for you, Cariña. But that was reciprocal. An irrational fear seized me by the throat. Suppose neither I would. … After what had happened all those years. I saw you again on that bridge in Venice. How I let you get into the boat, helped you embark on that damned boat. Misled by the fatal course of events at that moment.

A deep pain penetrated my chest. Never, never should I have let you go. Two creatures, so connected, will break apart when fate separates them. And what remains, is but a shadow of their former selves. How can a man be so cowardly to let this happen? A pair of swans are inseparable, their faith links them beyond death. But only you, Cariña, knows it was no lack of understanding that drove us apart, or a shortage of affection. Even though they attempted everything to make it seem so. Sneakily, that is, rather by means of refined insinuations than base machinations, well aware that the

235

curiosity of gossipers is aroused by half secrecies. A small fire rapidly spreads in a small community like here in Marcaio.

It is no good retrieving bygone failures, yet I feel guilty. We should have fended off the slanderers, Cariña, and I ... I ought to have protected you against philistines and Pharisees. Have braved, head up, the whole lobby that wanted to decry our love and foil our secret alliance ... However, I was too much preoccupied with myself. Out of indolence, so I should not have to give up my hobbyhorses - my really dratted craving to safeguard endangered places on this earth from oblivion. Utter dedication to our spiritual brotherhood would have absorbed me far too much, and I shrank from a public collision with the bigwigs who wanted to crush our peace movement. The same enemies, Cariña, who were eager to nip our love in the bud.

The rest of it is quite familiar to you: the wildest stories about infidelity, my alleged libertine views and sodomy, your amourettes with el Capitán and secret admirers ... Easily fanned rumours, spicily seasoned and spread by so-called friends who passed themselves off as intimates. In times of spiritual disruption such tricks will always work. Petronius, Suetonius, Plautus already made mention of it in the prime of Roman tyranny and corruption.

Once more panic-stricken, I asked the driver to make a halt at the old tavern once again opposite the Mirador de Rocamar. The old landlord of the 'venta', well preserved himself, did not recognize me. Undisturbed, a 'tumbet' and a light local wine before me, I am writing the last words of this letter. Soon I shall ask the coachman to act as a courier and take this epistle to the village of Cappeler.

Here I shall wait for an answer, Cariña, resignedly, like a suddenly deceased husband abiding the coming of his beloved somewhere between heaven and earth, so as to join for their passage into eternity.

Dugal was watching the obsolete, rather thumbed document with the look of an obsessed nutcase. The more he attempted to seek something behind those words – a token maybe, a message to others besides Catalí; maybe to Mr Maïks himself, the chosen one, a good century later – the more the letters started dancing before his eyes. Leading another life.

"Dju-gal!" said Catarí, to bring him back to reality. "Don't read the letters off it. You've read it about twenty times by now; soon you'll know it by heart."

"That's a good one!" he grumbled. "Who didn't stop talking all night about the same matter?"

That was right. Even on the road, westwards, where that stagecoach must have left some track or other, his Cathy had spouted her theories. That posado (or whatever the Archidux called it – a 'venta' or so), there was something fishy about it. Their headquarters maybe or a veiled smugglers' haunt of those beachcombers. Something like the fulcrum for a secret society: *'to take me to your refuge'*, as don Lois' had written. What for god's sake was that peace movement the exhausted archduke was hinting at, and whose supposed key-figure he was, he, the 'uncrowned king' – just a kind of imaginary idealistic groupie, or what?

But the squabble was just getting really cranked up as the subject Manuela was tabled. Same as the night before. "A mole in our house," Catarí had burst out. Señorita do Mar could in fact be a pawn in their enemies' hands. Not necessarily a wolf in sheep's clothing, she had parried him with his first "Oh no, Catarí!" The pretty thing might as well have been hired, without her knowledge, to saddle Dugal with a so-called fling. A few snapshots taken from a distance, with him and that short-skirted crumpet on it, simply on the terrace, while she was serving up and Catarí was inside. Something like that: enough in itself to launch a real paparazzi campaign against him. Without the nice chick realizing it herself, she was like a toad in a basket.

"Catarí!" he had suddenly shouted. Look, there!"

Just before the road turned inland from the Cornisa, a signboard pointed to a tavern high up on a rocky plateau. 'Sa Roca Cappeler', the big letters straggled across the thatch-matted roof. They nodded meaningfully at each other.

One got a magnificent view of the valley sweeping down to Galileio, through the window at one side of the restaurant. "Almost surrealistic,"

Catarí mumbled. "Quite as antique as when the Dux alighted here," said Dugal, running his eye rather over the interior of the venta. "No. Or yes: antique, quite so, but on the whole it looks bright and fresh. There's something about it," his Cathy thought, just when the landlord entered the bar.

"Qué bebeis?" he came straight to the point. What they would like to drink? As he addressed the staggered guests with a friendly grin in German, English and French, they kept staring at him. At last he called for his Magdalen: "Die verstehen mich nicht."

"Doch," Dugal brought up his best German. Magdalen though spoke broad Marcaian as well as English and the rest: a charming Bavarian you could no more stick an age on than on a swan.

"Señor Mikes, Cappi, and this is señora Ionès! Catarí Ionès, the most famous actress of the last decade, Cariño." She looked indignant about her husband's ignorance. But he, señor 'Cappi', reminded you even more of a swan, with his medium long hair, tanned skin and the resilience of someone in his thirties. "Let's toast to this!"

Two bottles of house wine and a whole family saga later, Catarí and Dugal seemed more familiar with this tough, sympathetic couple than with their own relatives. She, a graphic artist, had, back in her thirties, given her heart to a late-developer in the matter of love, an ex-sports glory in his homeland, and her new boss in her sportswear company, already forty-five at the time. After some calculating work on his knuckles Dugal reached an incredible result: "Eighty-eight? But … that's impossible!"

The landlord nodded grinningly. So, he really was that old? They had been self-declared immigrants for twenty years by now. Only had got a K changed into a C on their passports. A bit later he appeared again, secretly amused, dressed in old Marcaian costume, a violin in his hand. This old tough customer had also led an ensemble once and had kept a series of recordings from that. So now he wanted to regale the honoured guests with a mini-concert, playing the first violin on the foreground himself. "Just say what you would like to hear. Paganini, De Sarasate …, or maybe some Slovenian folk tunes?" he left them ample choice.

"The piece they played here for the Archidux on his way to the protégés of señor Cappelèr," Dugal rattled quickly.

The innkeepers did not really stand there open-mouthed, but the garrulous prattler's words clearly produced some effect. Käppler or Keppler, or whatever his name had been, turned on the recorder and promptly started to join in with the orchestra. Virtuoso, molto vivace. At the end of his serenade he said without turning a hair: "Vivaldi. One of his less well-known concerti."

"Have we got any wiser now?" After a couple of tapas in that venta of the Cappelèrs they had still moved on to Galileio after all. A drowsy village or what you may call so: a handful of weathered ochre houses around a pockmarked church leaning one against the other on the hill-top. Quite as surrealistic as the view of the valley some hours ago. "There! That's it," Dugal had pointed ahead. "What, who?" "That chapel over there. That's what it must all have been about. That underground batch of guests. The brotherhood around señor Cappeler, whether or no he was an ancestor of those two old fogeys there. With such a biblical-sounding name at that: 'Magdalen'. "The inquisition would have found this to be quite a morsel to stomach."

Finally, Catarí too had become impressed by that vista ~ a sea of wild flowers and, high above it, the stacked-up hamlet. In the village inn, under the church tower, they had not found out much more either. As soon as you dropped a name ~ do Mar, don Lois, Cappelèr ... ~, it became even more silent at the counter than with their previous hosts.

Catarí on her part was twice as talkative, on their way back. With variations on the same motive from before: "I say, Manuela, that new flame of yours ..."

Oh yes, whether she didn't feel like adopting the poor thing, Dugal began to tease her all at once. Would make a gem of a daughter, wouldn't she? Putting another name on that illegitimate fruit of a branded relation would sound ~ ...

"How do you mean ...?" Catarí took a deep breath, before the last hairpin bend of the Col de Llosera. And then, the sun-drenched plain full of almond orchards in sight, the truth seemed so ..., so ~ ...

"Incredible? And yet so close. Today's quest has also put some ideas into your head, hasn't it? How many do Mars did you count on that churchyard?"

At least one out of five, she estimated, and the traits of their new housemaid had come clearly to her mind right there. Those curved lips, the sharply shaded eyebrows ... And then again Catalí's portrait – the resemblance was striking. But as for the name – how ...?

"Child's play. Particularly in the case of blue blood it used to be a gallant solution: use the mother's name. The 'culprit', so to say, was kept out of harm's way, and for some hush money some clerk or other was ready to arrange that. But here things were a bit different." *Course, the affair that was to be covered up there, was connected with persecution, with possible intimidations ... Herodes, the fear of child murder.*

Palestinian situations in the Dux's Marcaio?! But the most absurd of all was this frantic ride, on the search for a great-great-grandmother whose child was once baptized with her surname to conceal the consanguinity with the big Habiger House. *A side branch of the Habigers, Dugal guessed, reaching back to prince consort Carl. Such another shunted maverick like our Archidux: in the shadow of the Kaiserliche super matron M.T. Walburga Amalia Christina, yet secretly helmsman of the underground Christian contras. And look at me now, iconoclast of the silver screen, on my way to the only one who knows the answer. Even at the risk of finding a manor from the days of that very great-great-grandmother to be blown up.* Dugal's stomach turned at the idea, particularly of the stunningly pretty copy of the original doña de Ses Taca whom they had left behind over there.

38

One traffic fine and a hangover later ("That cop's face was what made me puke"; "Duke! How cynical of you!"), they whirred up along the Marquezes' dwelling. Deserted. They watched each other with raised eyebrows. *Could the lovebirds be ...* "gone off with the embezzled collection of señor Miguel?" Normally speaking the professor had a day off now.

"Sorry," Dugal apologized to the door, after wrenching it open with a crow-bar. "Roberto!" They both jumped out of their skin at the shocking sight in that living-room. It made Catarí forget at once her diffidence about this infringement of civil privacy. But their dismay at once turned into irrepressible laughter. It was a ludicrous sight anyway, to find that couple there entwined like that. Not tied up back to back, like after a common home-jacking, but breast to breast, chin on the other's shoulder. Even a pet name was not evident in that awkward love position.

It took some time until the couple was able to spew the wad out of their mouth. "Phew, bah," they tried to worm themselves out of that dire situation.

"Ah, and what do say to your rescuers from this spastic Kamasutra stance? Thank you, uncle Duke. Or was the professor in the middle of expounding the use of don Lois's sextant to his wifey?"

Roberto was not quite intent on jokes now. He was muttering something like Mik ... El ... Diablo, and at first Dugal thought he was aiming at him.

"Not at all. Miguel, that bloody publisher of yours! That rabble has played this trick on us." Catarí could not help bursting into laughter.

"What, Miguel?!" Neither knew any longer what to believe. So the aggrieved publisher had come to stupefy them in their own house ~ just so, with a sleeping drug in their own coffee ~ and then tie them up?

"And all that while señor Miguel pretended that yóu had ..."

"...diddled him out of his collection? Yeah, that's a good one. Just the other way round. If you ask me, that jackanapes and that mob of revisionists were hand in glove from the very beginning."

Don Miguel, secret pawn for a shady gang of clandestinos? All joking apart. But there was no stopping Prof. Marquez any more.

"My office, my office! Let's get into action, amigos, before that gentry's able to erase all traces, until no iota is left of the truth." Hastily the four of them jumped into the car. Dugal must have raced so hard past two cops that they had not even twigged it.

Roberto's vision of hacked cases and drawers vanished, though, upon tumbling into his own sanctuary: not a skerrick of disorder. *That takes the cake,* Roberto stammered. Whether it could all just be a blown-up hoax then? An unsavoury farce, anyway, the four of them thought. Perhaps those scaremongers were only eager to pit them against each other, ánd against the press.

Damn I care, thought Catarí, who wanted to clear out again as fast as possible. "Come on!" she commanded, meaning as much as: *hop it!* To Dugal that colonel's tone sounded familiar. In that case one had better follow her wisely like a lap dog. "You don't believe that yourself, do you?" she whispered, once they were out of hearing range. "What?" Dugal looked startled. "That comedy, Duke," she said with restrained impatience about so much naivety. "Really, that's a set-up show, to be sure, what those two performed. But just wait a moment!"

On impulse she took her mobile phone out of her handbag. "Hello, Manuela, is that you?" A good while it was like an alarm-clock running down at the other side. Catarí's only reaction being a series of repetitions: "Yes ... yeah yeah" and another yes. "What's up?" Dugal could not contain himself once again. "Burnt to the ground? Did a bulldozer drive through our lawn? A ... a bomb thrown into our pond?!"

"No, our new pin-up maid had the paella burnt on."

"Hadn't we better have taken the Marquezes back home first?" Dugal kept harping on the same string, while they were already strolling through the winding alleys behind Palmera's cathedral.

"Du-uke!" Catarí halted, straddling her legs, so a passer-by nearly stumbled against her. "I don't want to hear that name again the first twenty-four hours. No more than Dolores or Miguel or Moragues and the whole lot!"

Dugal at once assented to that, as her face spoke volumes: quite right, Cariña, it was about time they ridded themselves of those harassing pests. Or soon they would be seeing a waylayer behind every trunk, afraid to go to the loo by themselves.

Suiting the action to the word, he took her in tow through the labyrinth of the old town. Or rather: she was taking him along the tiny shops and pubs where there was still a whiff of bygone times floating in the air. "The spirit of don Lois and Catalína." Once again she stopped and again the passers-by were looking round. "That's what we're searching for here anyway. Or aren't we?"

So it has got hold of her too. As though our forerunners in Ses Taca have bewitched us. The forbidden love of a century ago, it's too crazy for words.

No matter how much Dugal put himself out, it was all in vain. The farther they strayed off in the back lanes behind the Almudaina, looking through the open gates, or through the lattices, to catch at least a glimpse of the plants and the wells on the patios of the palacios, the more she got lost in dreamy thoughts. *As if we're peeping into a scrupulously fenced-off seraglio,* thought Catarí, *in search of a veiled harem woman.*

What does a man of honour do in such times? The nostalgic tones of a fandango ensemble were blowing over from the side of the harbour and there were still some chattering families sauntering along the Marítimo, taking a breather in the blissful cool evening air. "Here, shall we?" Dugal managed to guide her adroitly to an empty table on a square behind the cathedral where some cry-baby or other was warbling a tearjerker. There, nobody would pay attention to them. Therefore the public were hanging too much on the young lad's lips, surrounded as he was by a pack of yeah-yeah girls. Of the flamenco-type, though, waving pleated skirts about to hide the lesser quality of the vocal art. *It always works, this ancient recipe of latino ingredients with a folkloristic tinge,* Dugal thought. Even his sweetheart, so sober otherwise, was melting away as the reminiscences of her own roots were flaring up.

The next morning Dugal was rubbing his eyes over the treasure of documents Roberto Marquez spread out before him. "Copies, all of them, for you see, if one of these days those loonies should happen to pass at your place too …" Henceforth the name Miguel was taboo.

In the small hall where Roberto had accommodated him this time, one could enjoy with pleasure the vast panorama over the sweltering tiled roofs of Palmera. Whilst his heartthrob was out on a spree in her favourite streets, hunting for nice must-haves, he could indulge wholeheartedly in Roberto's collection, with the heavenly feeling that pervades your limbs as you are plunging into the lukewarm creek beneath Valle de Muša … This time, however, Mikes Junior was not able to keep his mind on it. Again and again the scene from yesterday night returned to his mind.

"Poppycock, Dukie. Pure bosh and hogwash," Catarí had blabbed out in the middle of the performance. "To hell with all those hypocrites!" In vain he tried to soothe her. Some people sitting next to them were already hissing: "Shhht!"

"That prof just keeps you dangling; that bit of a publisher is a louse in the pelt, and those women? They are hand in glove. And Don Carlos is laughing up his sleeve, while they are taking you for a ride. By the way, that old Dux and his cracker form a mere alibi. And do you know why?"

Meanwhile Dugal was making signs with his hands: calm down, Cathy, quiet - but without too much hubbub, or else there would have been a total ruction.

"To get us out, Duke: Americans, go home!"

All of a sudden two arms of a woman were slung around him. "Venga, señor. Come!" In their private wrangle they had not seen the dancer coming down the stage, like every evening, to single out an unsuspecting victim. Before he realized it, she had towed him along to the dance-floor: the laughing stock of that night. That was a gross miscalculation, though. During the first round Dugal was hopping about like a dog on a skittle alley. Until he caught up on the cadence and from then onwards he tried to keep pace with them, unflinching. Stamping and bracing his breast like a peacock; and towards the end of the dance it was he who reaped the applause and he bowed with the airs of a full-fledged ballerina. Soaking wet and out of breath, but as proud as Lucifer he paved his way back between the tables.

Hey, how did you like my act? he wanted to say, relieved that no one had recognized him. Owing to that three-week-old beard and moustache maybe.

But ... no more sign of Catarí, at their table. Was she afraid of being recognized or was it only one of her whims?

In the back alley there was no living soul to be seen. Dugal was just on the point of running in the opposite direction, when he heard a clatter from a porch. "Cathy!" he shouted and kicked a swing door open. In the semi-darkness a stifled "Du-uke" resounded. And there he distinguished his brave girl, in a clinch with two louts, raising the devil. One foot clenched between the banister, and the other leg pulled up, she pushed off against the wall.

Dugal bumped into the first one, a strapping fellow. He lifted Dugal from the ground, as if he were a feather. All the adrenaline arising in his body a minute ago, shot through his legs again; all at once back in the rhythm of the dance, they were hacking up and down, with the power of a chopper. "Ouch!", the assaulter cursed and in addition, Dugal dealt him a backward bash in his crotch. Doubled up, the swearing fellow sank against the wall. Promptly the other bundle of muscles let go of Catarí and rushed up to Dugal, stumbling over his crony in the act.

In a kick-box imitation from one of his film scenarios Dugal aimed at the man's abdomen. *Bull's-eye*, he thought, but the grinning lump of flesh did not heave a sigh. As if he wore an iron chastity belt there. For a moment Dugal reeled backwards, groaning under some scorching sledgehammer blows. Almost ready to parry the next one, he suddenly saw the chap staggering a few steps back: Catarí had planted the full point of her beaked shoe right into his vital parts and her razor-sharp nails into the scruff of his neck. Whiningly the bruiser shook her off and grabbed for her arms. Just enough time for Dugal to snatch an earthenware jar from a corner and give him a vehement smack with it on the back of his head. Shattered to pieces.

"Holy ding-dong," sighed Catarí, "that one's carillon is going to keep chiming for quite a while still."

It made him chuckle, there in that secret nook of Prof. Marquez's temple of knowledge. Present in person, but still with that bizarre event of the night before on his mind. Head over heels they had rushed off. "Hurry!" He had dragged her along by the arm, for behind them you could already hear the buzz of a number of spectators who had got wind of the incident. Once around the corner she had flung her arms around his neck, with an intensity that he had not felt for years. Only then the fear really gushed out of her. "Thank you, Duke," was all she had been able to utter.

"Seen it yet, Dugal?"

"Eh?" He had seen Roberto enter the small hall, alright, but it did not penetrate to him. In passing, the learned Chest put the Diario de Marcaio on the corner of the table. But why should the bible of the local faits divers interest hím? After a while the prof came back from behind his pile of papers, strumming with one finger on a page of the unfolded newspaper. "There!"

Unbelievable! There you are! Today's leading article spread it out on the front page as if it were a piece of world news:

'INCIDENT IN DE CALLE DE LA LUNA': two men left for dead in the Barrio during singing and dancing night ... almost certainly famous acting couple Mikes involved in it ... not quite clear who molested whom ...'

How was this possible, they had been brooding over it all night, those darned paparazzi hitched on to the twaddle of some street crooks, already beaten to a jelly. Or some tough tugs, hired for this hoax. The crucial question was: by whom?

He had made up his mind not to make mention of it to Roberto, but now it was difficult not to. The tanned gorilla whistled between his teeth whilst curling one of his ear-flaps. It did not come to further speculations, for the prof got a phone-call. "Sorry, old boy: it's urgent."

Dugal stayed behind there, glued to his chair. Fretting about the identity of the possible gutter journalist who had made up that report. Miguel maybe? He at least might have something to do with it, as that article seemed already prepared. *Kind of anticipated!* Slowly his eyes returned to the documents on the table. And then they clung to a quire with Roberto's name on it. Obviously meant for publication, as it already opened with an abstract in three languages. Simply picked out of an anthology of some students' final papers. *Always comes in handy*, Dugal growled. A piece of cake, to do it that way. But as he was getting more and more engrossed in the text, he forgot about his scepticism and it sounded like Prof. Marquez's voice reading, from very far, a kind of fairy tale:

... However independent and wayward the Archidux' nature was, it turns out from our research that this craving for freedom in his acting and thinking was an atavistic feature. Inherited from his mother's side namely ...

39

That craving for independence, so to say, had been ladled on to the 'principe' with the breast milk. His mother, Antoinette, the sister of the Spanish queen, was keen on a 'natural' education, free from the etiquette. To the great despair sometimes of the ladies-in-waiting. If little Lois was not playing leapfrog with them in the Boboli gardens, he was often hanging in the giant trees, as deft as his bosom friend Baboo, the young monkey his parents had given him as a present.

One day, he wrote in a letter to Catarí, *I had talked over the lady-in-waiting who used to prepare my breakfast. She fastened the basket to a rope which I had lowered from a plane tree. But there was Baboo like a bird on it to nose about in the basket.. You should have seen that lady running off … But mummy was splitting her sides as she saw her perplexed face …*

… A terribly beautiful childhood that was: playing hide-and-seek with the other children in the halls of Palazzo Pitti, or romping in the fountains, roaming about in the park, looking down from a hill over the domes and roofs of the Tuscan capital. For hours on end I would dream such stories together. Not so much from the lives of the grandes or courtesans. I rather collected scenes from the chattering washing women at the Piazza della Signoría, or from the greengrocers or young maids who, paddling in the fountain, were spouting all kinds of anecdotes, without paying any more attention to the accessories of Giambologna's Neptune. By far more colourful anyway than the endless drivel of the guests

248

in our drawing-rooms, behind whose back Mummy used to
revel in their stiff ceremoniousness.

His father, a Maecenas and enlightened despot, was much esteemed for the public and social works he had committed himself to on behalf of his people. Yet, the days of the Risorgimento had come and those of the Duchy were numbered. The grand city of art got imprinted in the memory of the young archduke, symbolized in the timeless grace of Giambologna's Venus ~ to him the marble reflection of the Platonic ideal.

Which was to burden his unspoiled spirit for ever with an 'impotence pure d'esprit', Dugal chuckled and he tried to imagine what reply the prof was going to have to that. Look, there it was already:

... a bias to sublimation, which later on would safeguard him from the snares of his rank : 'marriages de raison', 'liaisons dangereuses' ... Besides, his nostalgia for the eternal volatility was interconnected with the Arno. Every day the young lad was observing the busy navigation on that river.

> *The spectacle of those ships sailing up and down the stream*
> *filled me with an irresistible urge for evasion ~ a mystic*
> *yearning for far-off coasts and hazy horizons. That 'Sehnsucht'*
> *from my days of youth, Cariña, was to put an indelible stamp*
> *on my soul ...*

And so, Dugal went on delving, *from that park with a view the little prince had built up his dream-world.* Or as the professor put it:

scenes from his childhood encumbered his normal growth into adulthood and formed an inexhaustible source of inspiration for his vagrant existence later ...

Imbued with that morbid escapism that will always impede the Byrons to get reconciled with Aphrodite, Dugal mumbled to himself, as his eyes, looking over the red roof-tiles and antennae, swerved to the masts and the chimneys of the sailing boats out there in the bay. But there was the reproving finger of Prof. Marquez: *oh, oh, one couldn't disentangle such a complicated case just like that, with Freudian forceps, reduce it to an arithmetical product of atavisms and education.* And yet the learned dab wrote it this way himself:

It is in the field of tension between those extreme influences that we can try to understand the disruption of the high guest's soul. In his case the uprooting experience of his dislodgement from his home-town when he was still a boy, was turned from Weltschmerz into a more balanced attitude to life, particularly owing to his close connection with simple country life, and to his love of nature. This also explains his affection for a girl of humble origin. In señorita d'Omar he found a strong anima, but instead of only sublimating it, he made it a point of honour to develop it and elevate it to his own level ...

Words, words, words. Nice theories, Dugal thought, looking peevishly at those pieces puzzled together with angelic patience, partially autobiographic. So, from such things an academician distilled his hypotheses! Was going to put his John Hancock under it very soon and Bob's your uncle. *Dash it, that's how they fix it. Putting everyone in for their goal, and they reap glory.*

He already heard Catarí scorn: "You don't believe such psychological twaddle yourself, Duke?" Course he didn't. Prof. Marquez was taking more and more the shrinks' line and Dugal had never thought much of that. But he felt the literary man coming on tiptoe. What was sly Roberto aiming at? Primo, that don Lois 'de Altdorf' had led his entourage up the garden path by creating an atmosphere of suffering and death around his beloved ~ quite a while after expelling her, for the world, from his harem of female bosom friends, out of offended pride, so to speak, on account of her alleged unfaithfulness. Therefore he had even staged a scene with the captain of his yacht, the Nymphe, and then leaked it. Pure rubbish, but the good man was bribed so as to take the disgrace on his account.

Secondly, that Sua Altezza, in order to substantiate that seeming split, would have sustained the hypothesis of his illness and hypochondria himself throughout all those years. Also his craving for sublimating things fitted in that picture, *and* the impotence of establishing a normal human relation, as a result of that idealized image of the woman, which had got a twist in his youth.

And all that just to isolate a woman coming from the hoi polloi and, beyond apparent death, abduct her to his horizon ... loin d'éternité. Even a romantic soul like his Cathy, he sniggered, was not up to such lofty ideas. How then was Roberto going to sell this to sober minds? That Catalí d'Omar, in hiding for years, would also have survived the exile of her protector. Or where and how the reviled couple were united again, and under what disguise, even a dab like Roberto could not make head or tail of it. No more than you could stage a meeting of Peter with Jesus near the Quo Vadis church.

The sun had used up most of the rays by now and the moon was displaying a clear sickle above the bay. It was thus that, a little later, Prof. Marquez found his friend absorbed in thought, on the lookout for an old well-known sail, somewhere on the horizon. Roberto pulled up the Venetian blinds. On turning round, he looked in the searching eyes of the famous man, who, in this short span of time, had become a kindred spirit. Partner in their obsession, for the sake of a long-deceased couple in whose wake they all risked to be dragged along.

Also Dugal recognized a sign of insanity in the mysterious haze of Roberto's gaze: "Cappeler," he said, and the other one nodded approvingly: "Galileio".

On their way back the Mikes looked like two birds from different continents. Catarí enraptured by Palmera's newly opened boutiques, taken up by her latest acquisitions: a pair of shoes (another one for her collection) and some trinkets from the handicraft shops ~ little must-haves for which her Duke also used to give way at other times. Not now though …

"Hey, has that old stunner from Ses Taca cast a spell on you again?"

The side of the road was sown with poppies, marigold and other wild flowers: moments from the Archidux' life that Dugal now tried to lay together piece by piece. Each words, each morsel from that strange story was bringing them closer to don Lois and his beloved one. In the rind of every carob tree here there could be a distinguishing mark, between the crowns of the plane and almond trees along the road there could stream some fluid, an old well-known scent that kept the secret of their love alive.

While he was driving, the words came back to his mind, as clearly as if Dugal had put them on paper himself, a good century ago:

> *One drizzly morning señor Ripoll had taken me on a trip inland. I was carried along on his exuberant mood, with the foreboding that this might be the beginning of a lifelong infatuation. And yet, the roads were one mortar sludge, the gloomy sky the opposite of Mediterranean beatitude.*

That scene recalled to my mind long-forgotten impressions from the corners of my memory: our retreat along the Tuscan roads, the snorting and gasping of the horses, the steamy windowpanes of the carriage ... I knew that tempered resounding of muddy hoofs, the start of a revolution in my deepest self.

Only señor Ripoll's good temper offered me a guarantee: "Marcaio is soon going to conquer your heart, Altezza."

How could the good chap surmise that he had hit the nail on the head!

The manor he wanted to show me, appeared with closed shutters. "Not too bad," I said. But while we were warming up a bit in the inn at Molí and I was gradually sinking back into sombre thoughts, all at once an illustrious stranger, a friend of señor Ripoll's, showed up. He knew the ideal bargain for me! "Maremira, a stately manor. A bit dilapidated, but exactly for that reason you can buy it for a mere trifle, señor."

A few hours later we were at the spot. On the yard of the old hacienda, the damp of the steaming horse bodies in our coats, I could still taste the wood smoke from the open fireplace in the tavern in my throat. "Maremira! What a grand vista, isn't it?" With his arms Ripoll drew a semi-circle around the summit of the Montemayor. He was standing there a bit awkward, though: a meagre compensation for this ramshackle place, he must have thought himself.

Dugal was quite able to imagine that scene: don Lois, breathing deeply as he was looking around, swallows' nests under the rafters, cobwebs on the window frames and sills ... "I shall buy it," he said. To señor Ripoll's great astonishment.

That zest for life that suddenly must have risen in the strange guest's heart ⁓ Cathy and he both knew it, from the moment they had set eyes on Ses Taca themselves, face to face with their love nest. They too namely had had their private jokes at the dismayed face of the chap who was then showing them about.

*How could I bring it home to my astonished host that at last
the sun had entered my heart – merely by the sight of a plain
girl along the road? A momentary impression, in the fashion
of Monet or Renoir. Like a flashing ray of light through a
gloomy landscape. It was also literally so: after days of rainfall
and all that señor Ripoll had undertaken to break my spleen.
How the poor fellow had done his utmost for me! Just so that
I should get something decent between my teeth from the
simple local kitchen; and look forward to a tête-à-tête with all
possible beaux and belles from the well-to-do circles. Nothing,
however, could have cheered me up, and least of all that star
parade of dolled-up gentry lassies. Ripoll must have felt like
a merchant looking for the highest bidder for a thoroughbred
horse. And I? A valuable asset in a curiosity shop.*

So did we, Dugal smirked, and in don Lois' description of how the
formalities with a notary and enterpriser had been settled in a jiffy, he
recognized once more their own vicissitudes. "You must have an absolute
crush on it, really," their contractor had said, as they were standing vis-à-vis
Ses Taca. "To fancy an old maid like that!"

Now, however, Catarí brought the subject back to Roberto Marquez's
study about the Dux. They wondered what don Lois himself would have
thought of the way the Chest represented him: driven by a strong inner
force,

… the 'anima mundi', as the Prof put it, the 'Seelesgröße' which the
Archidux had received with the breast milk. A blending of the strong
urge for independence from his mother's side and the liberal spirit of his
father, the last heir of the great Tuscan patrons and enlightened despots. In
Maremira, far away from Florence, Vienna and Prague, his boyish dreams
crystallized into a second homeland.

It was easy to call the picture to your mind, in Roberto's evocation:
crowds of workers bustling about, Ses Taca not only converted into one
building site, but that whole tract of the Cornisa … reshaped by a conjurer
into hanging gardens and vineyards, traversed by paths and belvederes.
Babylonian terraces in a Bailarian fashion?

When they halted on the verge of the road above their Moorish dream,

Catarí said without looking at him: "That? You want to restore that, Duke? Retrieve this old boy's dream?"

How could she possibly guess his thoughts? She turned her face to him, with that roguish smile of hers, those mocking lights in her eyes which would have made him creep on his knees up the Calvario of Poyença.

"Changing water into wine. Ses Taca into Ses Cañas. After all, I'm called Catarí for some reason, aren't I?"

40

It took a while until Dugal's penny dropped. Ses Cañas! Dugal looked at her disbelievingly. Finally he had hit upon it: the popular nickname for that area where once don Lois'sss vines were thriving, was … Ses Cañas. But no, that likeness was too far-fetched, wasn't it? And the same went for: Catarí and Catalí. By the way, that fabrication about water and wine in Canaän, a metaphor for rearranging the tables and beverages for high guests at the wedding of 'the son of David' himself … Might L.S. in this have seen a parallel with his relation with his landlady of the wine tavern?

Oh dear, stories from the slack season, Dugal smiled sullenly, *and with that sort of trifles such an erudite nerd fritters away his time?* Roberto even dared to make mention of a 'mystic matrimony', but then he connected a mating of southern warmth and northern fertility to it, on the co-ordinates of Maremira. And in the middle of it: Ses Taca, a Saracen fairy tale in immaculate meerschaum, in honour of a dreamlike vision of a girl along the road he had not even addressed. *What an ethereal declaration of love! One would almost think that the Chest has been sublimating his own day dreams,* Dugal grinned. Besides, didn't that also count a bit for his quotes about the Archidux himself?

> *You should have seen the surprise on Ripoll's face! It could not have been greater, if I had set my mind on a lady of dubious reputation: a destitute bride whose debts you take into the bargain. However, when he, standing next to me, followed my eyes watching the vast coastal area, the good man seemed to understand. Maremira had already become part of myself, same as Catarí d'Omar was part of my soul.*

Whether that really came from one of don Lois's stray letters ~ or from Roberto Marquez's wild fantasy, Catarí was eager to know. "I've seen it myself," Dugal fibbed. Yet, in a way he did not, for in his pensive reflections, over there in that academic side room, he had gone through all that had ever been said between the maligned couple. As if, beyond death, whispers from another dimension had come down upon him.

But that was difficult for him to tell her, or she would certify him insane. To his Cathy, love was something unconditional; such an airy relation as there had existed between their honourable predecessors, was wasted on her. That he had experienced to his shame ‑ truly, no sinecure in a profession like his, where the lady bounty hunters were hanging around you in droves.

Or was there any higher vibration that had passed on to her too? Also to Catarí there seemed to be a haze of alienation hovering over this place. As if there were something around the things that did not belong to themselves, but was living more profoundly …

A bit ashamed of that sensation of budding wonder, they continued driving at a walking pace, with a feeling that this veil over the banal images which otherwise you pass by a hundred times, was bringing them closer together.

The child is father to the man, Catarí said under her breath. "Pardon?" Dugal asked. "Wordsworth," she mumbled, as though this struck another dimension, far beyond his reach. That fresh look of an impressionist that lets you guess the vibration of life's mystery behind each tree, each dragonfly or orchid ‑ how could such an incurable macho who is always chasing his tail, grasp that there is something more in life than performing and acquiring? But his reaction came as a pleasant surprise to her: "Our adult consciousness has got stuck in rigid categories, in fixed patterns … Yes, there's something about that. Perhaps we ought to regain the naïve view of a toddler, so as to understand something about nature. May that have been L.S.'s secret?"

All this brought Catarí into an even more philosophical mood. *Wonder begins when you look at things not just with the freshness of the first sight, but also as if it may be the last time …*

In that tense frame of mind they had reached home. Watching the surroundings with double intensity. He remembered Cathy's lecture from the previous time, about the Platonic world of ideas and our objects being sheer projections of it. One of her impulses to fill the gaps in his education. How fast this earthly house of cards could be smashed to smithereens, by a whim of Jupiter's or an anarchist's!

Once on their drive, the engine turned off, they hardly dared to open their eyes, lest an evil fairy should have changed their old love nest by a magic wand.

"No traces of bulldozers or bazookas?" Dugal ascertained, before they set foot again on the apparently peaceful ground of Ses Taca. *One only realizes what happiness is, if everything has remained the way it was yesterday.* And this very spot seemed to have kept unscathed in time, as if Catalí had just been walking around here a week ago … Or was that deceptive quiet only a lull before the storm? *Take care, turtledoves,* the palm trees whispered, *or the same may befall you as what happened to your predecessors here.*

"Who's kidnapped Sleeping Beauty?" Catarí suddenly thought.

What? Who? All at once sober again, Dugal got the same idea: Manuela! What hag had flashed away that dazzling appearance?

"Señor!" As if summoned by magic ~ who was standing there, downstairs, under the window, practising her falsetto voice? Dugal had to rub his eyes. Oh no! Cinderella, conjured back as an R.A.F.: Colomá, Remedy-against-Femininity.

"Colomá! What are you doing here?" The old maidservant made her comeback with the furore of a diva who has run away from the set, but returns through a backdoor, aware of the fact that without her the play will fall to pieces.

How and where Dolores's cute niece could be then? Dugal was taking great pains not to show his disappointment. Now, however, it was Coloma's turn to be completely taken aback. What! She and her husband on a holiday ~ were they joking? By the way, they had not seen a Manuela at all. But there had been a tall gentleman telling them that he had been appointed by the Mikes as a bailiff and had to choose a new staff.

Dugal and Catarí were gaping at each other, open-mouthed. The letters! In two ticks Dugal had been there and back, once more: everything untouched, the walking sticks were hanging there just like a century ago, as he had seen at a single glance. Thank God!

"You sure?" Cathy's suspicious glance made him hesitate. "Why not?"

She did not mean that …? "Yeah, what did you expect? Never heard of tiny cameras and microchips, Dukie?" He shook his head, like a petty desk-worker in Singapore who believes seeing la Ionès in person in the street.

Of course, he knew those practices, from the world of crime movies and industrial espionage. But it would never occur to him that … Manuela ~ come on, not that girl, such a … an ~

"Angelic apparition?" Whenever his Cathy produced such narrowed, catlike slit-eyes, Dugal's brain cells started working twice as fast. Oh, simple-minded dove, bells start ringing, yes?

Manuela and Dolores Francisquita … Whether Roberto's academic play-doll can be behind all this? She did not need to pronounce the name of 'auntie Dolores' again, her silent nodding made him grow giddy. How foolish he was! That gorgeous clone of the Dux's beloved had been eavesdropping on them after all, as he and Catarí had been standing there before the open closet: caught in the act, the artefacts in his hand. Manuela's innocent eyes had dazzled him. But what if even such a sham housemaid was able to take them in? Then they had been lured into it, enwrapped by a network of plotters. Maybe also encased by a media giant who could make them eat out of his hand.

"Señorita do Mar," he whispered. "After all, you don't believe …?"

The next morning, however, the sea appeared more unruffled than ever: a reassuring sign? *The soup is never eaten as hot as it is served,* the local saying went. Only, they both had to suppress their disappointment about the unclarified disappearance of their interim-girl. "You notice the difference," Catarí also remarked laconically, as she was now already missing Manuela's sunny radiance. And had to arrange the breakfast table herself. With Colomá you knew, of course, what you were up to. *Yeah, her sergeant's tone in the first place as she throws the early morning paper on the table,* Dugal grumped sulkily. *And the inevitable rolls or toasties with manchego or serrano, instead of the fruit bowl the young missy had served them the other day, brimming with succulent pears and peaches, kumquats, pomegranate seeds, cherry halves on a bed of coconut.* The most addicted buttock pincher would shrink for that warden's gruffness.

From his chair he angled, with a sigh, the Diario up to his lazy self. Too late, for Catarí snatched the paper away under his very nose, only leaving the interior quire: the local world news, look at that! The first alderman who handed over the cup to Miss Palmera, thereby almost plunging his nose into her décolletage. *What a banana republic!* Morosely Dugal turned the front page. The photo was still having a bit of an after effect on his retina, so he had almost overlooked it. And then he choked on it. Had to rub his eyes three times on seeing that incredible picture on the second page.

Catarí grabbed the page from under his blank stare and read dryly: 'Celebrated actor once more in a courting act.' In her turn she lowered the paper and Dugal was faced with the harsh reality. There he was in person, in an unmistakeably far too familiar pose with what was showing off, in huge letters, above his head: 'Señor Mikes's latest conquest'.

"But ~ ... impossible! That's pure balderdash. How ludricous!"

Of course it was impossible, but obviously, the press shrank from nothing, nowadays. Fake pictures, Catarí knew that as well as he did. They could join all things together. But all the same, there they were, both he and Manuela, almost glued to each other, and Catarí cut out of it.

Look, such things would drive him wild. What made it even worse, was Catarí's icy air on such occasions. As if it were his fault that those vile rogues would turn a decent child into a flighty chick. "And you into an old lecher."

I'll get them by the short hairs!

Like a teased jaguar he raced across the mountains. In their little Seat, it's true, but it enabled you to slip through between all those bulky cars. That's why the cop spinning round at the first crossing in town misjudged his number-plate.

"Señor Miguel? He is not at the editorial office, Sir," he was told.

What the hell did he care about half the press pack following him with bewildered eyes! From this they could at least draw some subject matter again for tomorrow's edition: 'fuss caused by freaking actor'.

Notwithstanding several attempts to catch that sneaky Miguel by the scruff of his neck, Dugal had to compose himself. Nowhere ~ neither at his office, nor in the bar or the printing office? Everyone tried to let that mean typesetter vanish in smoke, okay. But a Mikes cannot be fobbed off with a mere sop.

Determined to find the culprit who had hit him below the belt like that, he was already tearing across the same mountain pass, a few minutes after. Not, however, without a phone message to his dearest: " …I'll pay him out for that, what does he expect?"

The old hacienda was lying there pretty desolate this time. There was nothing to arouse the suspicion that this estate, promoted to a museum now, was a cover. *Odd*, Dugal thought, keeping an eye on the sleeping mongrel of a terrier near the porch, *here is the figurehead of the psycho-thriller walking straight into the lion's den of extreme right-wing Marcaio.*

The dozing custodian stifled a yawn. "Please, look around," and he already tore off a 5-europeso ticket. On seeing the gun under his nose, the poor soul jumped a yard back. Dugal all but burst into a fit of laughter. Ay, what an effect, just for an amateur's specimen that had been lying in his glove compartment for years. "No pranks, amigo!" That Hollywood grin caught on, evidently, for the old fellow promptly walked up the staircase ahead of him as a human shield. "Well-kn … known g-guest!" he acted Simple Simon, by Dugal's order. "You me-mean this gentleman? Señor M-Marquez!"

Perplexedly, Dugal dropped the small revolver. From the shot ~ or with bewilderment ~ he was dancing around, foot in hand. Accidentally the butt of the gun had come down on his big toe, and the toy bullet had grazed the professor's earlobe, straight on to a bust of the Dux. Fortunately, the projectile had already lowered by a millimetre in its trajectory, just enough to scorch the underside of the bust's nose.

"You, Roberto?!"

"What did you expect," the perturbed scholar grimaced, "a reincarnated Al Capone?"

In the small hall where Prof. Marquez had installed himself, at a table piled up with don Lois's bulky tomes, and behind a collection of the most eccentric objects and pieces of traditional costumes, Dugal took up his position close to a window looking out on the gardens of Son Maraitx. Outside there was no soul to be seen, except a raking gardener; nowhere a sign of the chopper that had led them to this manor some time before.

Unapprehensive, he looked in the Prof's ironic eyes. "You haven't the foggiest notion what it's all about, eh, amigo?" grinned the grey-haired gorilla. What was there in the drawer right in front of him: a dagger or paper-knife or paper-weight ~ any object whatsoever that in the hands of the learned athlete could turn into a murderous projectile? Dugal clenched the toy revolver in the pocket of his trousers. "There're a lot of things I start to connect. And in the end nothing can surprise you any longer."

"Even if a bookworm of my calibre lets himself be brought round for a few quid, eh?" Roberto laughed. "Querído amigo, I can readily understand your confusion. In your fury you're racing our countryside, as you hold the world to be one cobweb, and Son Maraitx here a devil's nest. The provoked prey going on the offensive. Bravo! Rather a dead Duke than a cowardly Duke."

Oh, oh, Dugal challenged him now in his turn: "Mister Scribe believes he has all cinema-heroes in his pocket. But I won't be trifled with."

"Querído amigo," Roberto shook his head pitifully. "Sit down and listen for one minute to this dry Marcaian stockfish." And patiently he explained what a willing victim Dugal actually had become, from the moment when he had gone off so hard with the publication of the letras secretas. Too hard, indeed. At least according to some patriarchs with blue blood who had invested a lot in the accommodation of the tourist cattle, but were not so keen at all on a rioter who was going to disturb the whole respectability of their clan. "Naïve, isn't it? Too naïve, amigo ..."

41

———◆➤◆✕◆◀◆———

"Naïve ~ on whose part then?" Dugal lashed out at Roberto's ironic gaze.

"On both parts. You could have known that those fellows' strength relies on a crowd of simpletons. But such a pig-head ~ sorry, my friend ~ who puts himself in the shoes of his predecessor (just as much a stubborn mule himself ~ sorry again), no ... that doesn't suit their purpose."

So, what with your actor's dough, you still belong to the plebs, Dugal chortled, *the docile 'tourist cattle' that guzzles crustacea and wallows in sun lotion, and is so easy to milk.* And he had broken that code of behaviour, which had stirred up bad blood among the local establishment. Yeah, had brought the Iberian blood of those old-style potentates to the boil, and even far beyond its boiling point. There the Prof made a point: in their place you would also take the press and co. hostages and throw in some saboteurs.

"You would do so for less, if they come and desecrate your canonized icon," Roberto agreed with him. "And so," (here the Chest drew an imaginary dash in the air) "according to that pattern of thought we were considering at first a network leading us as far as Vienna. Alas, it got no further than local intimidation."

"Intimidation, eh?" Dugal snorted, as he produced the rebuked article from his pocket. "And what about this?" From Roberto's raised eyebrows one could conclude that following up the Diario de Marcaio was none of his cares.

"That? Sorry, amigo, that's beyond the reach of our planning."

"Planning!" Dugal looked like the Etna on the point of exploding. They had taken him in pretty well, the Miguels and Robertos, with their tilting-games and combines.

"Listen, Dugal," Roberto cut him short, "don't feel so strongly about it."

"Not feel strongly about it?! That's a good one!" Dugal taunted. And he confronted his friend-academician with the nice prospects. Tomorrow those jolly good fellows were sure to come along with the wildest speculations about 'matrimonial troubles as a result of … '; the day after tomorrow probably: 'gale force at the Mikeses'; then: 'divorce imminent at Ses Taca'. Thus it would go crescendo, according to the approved home recipe of the yellow press. And that those hyenas were going to pull out all the stops, was as sure as death.

"Oh boy," Prof. Marquez had another critical look at the photo, "with such a super babe at your side I know that someone of our hmm … age hasn't the ghost of a chance, but that's not how the ladies think about it, alas. But all the same …" ~ he was tapping on the writing pad with his knuckles ~ "I think I can put a stop to that."

He?! What could a hardboiled word-splitter do against a scandal epidemic? What's more, he did not know the slumbering volcano Catarína yet: she was worth two Etnas. No, dear friend: this whole thing was bound to miscarry after all.

Soothingly Roberto bent over the desk. Look, from the very first letter Dugal had published, this had not only aroused protest, but even more so, an interest from various sides. Roberto himself, regarded as an L.S. authority after all (he coughed with the false modesty of the vainglorious), had seen some enriching material in it for a study he happened to be busy with.

So, all the more reasons to stir Dugal up a bit. Now, that precisely was grist to the mill of the 'Fomento de Marcaio', say the local propaganda machine, for those fellows of the tourist sector were badly in for a bit of a fillip. Just let the press jump on it and whisk up the whole affair! Even negative publicity was always welcome in times of sharp competition.

It's true, Marcaio's star was waning bye and bye due to the unfair rivalry with some exotic paradises. And a pepped-up soap opera in pure fin-de-siècle sphere could only bring about a favourable sea-change. Certainly now that Mr Average was ladled up the caprices and flings of the glamour stars ad nauseam. That's what the island was again in need of: a taboo romance as that French drawing-room writer had had with her Polish piano strummer at the time. Such a dead legend who cannot give any more comment anyway ~ that was meat and drink to the general public, as long as there could be made a link with present-day celebs. Even if, like señor and señora Mikes, they had got settled and ... sorry (here the Prof was coughing once again) a bit over the hill of sensation.

"And Mortado the Vulture was there like a flash to ..."

"Señor Miguel? Willy-nilly he had to play a double game. Mind it, personally I even doubted sometimes whether that sly fox wasn't double-crossing us too by paying lip service to some obscure lodge or so. Particularly after that poker game with my documents ~ making it look like me being after his collection! That was also just a bit over the edge, I thought. Miguel was too much wrapped up in his role. Soon it appeared that such an anonymous club was totally fictitious. As for the offspring of this Habiger branch ..."

Prof. Marquez smirked when he noticed how Dugal was fidgeting on the edge of his chair. *So, a dry arm-chair scholar can really compete with a thoroughbred actor,* he thought proudly. "I have been ferreting out those ... hmm ... surviving members and approached them with the necessary discretion. And what turns out? That they were not terrified at all of a scandalum magnatum of their illustrious forefather.

The only thing they feared, was that this hype would turn the floodlight too much on them personally. And that, by stirring up the case, one could awake other sleeping dogs. Right: those ultra reactionaries who had been keeping up the lies all those years, as they benefited from the image of a somewhat eccentric but altogether harmless Rainer Maria L.S. . The same people, in fact, who, with mixed feelings, saw the Mikes couple alighting at Ses Taca and grudgingly had to bear the idea of such a sort of actor with, well ... a certain repute, snooping in the past.

Dugal was getting more and more peeved about the paternalistic overtone in which the Chest displayed his superior research work to him. But even more so perhaps because he himself, though a born sceptic and suspicion in person, had indulged in being manipulated in that tricky game.

"Because you see," Roberto was harping on, "those ... desposyni, far relatives, so to say, who always shunned publicity, needed every new sign of attention like a hole in the head as it threatened to put them into the focus of the notorious Marcaian crusaders of Virtue."

"And that 'holy family' ~ if they really exist ~ were jeopardized along with you ~ phew! And I thought the scholarly Messrs. Humanities were unselfish and neutral. What if even such noble minds sacrifice all their erudition to the private interests of the island economy?"

"Oh, but I'm sure you didn't doubt at any moment about my unimpeachable integrity," Roberto grimaced.

Well… Dugal readily admitted having taken the professor for a plotter now and then. But that could not get Roberto off-balance.

"Justly and reasonably, amigo!" He had been obliged too long to join in that comedy, and frankly, now he felt a bit accessory to the matrimonial defamation at their expense. But this ~ he snorted, with a look at the objectionable article ~, this was way too far. It was not Miguel's style either, really, there was another pirate on the lurk who had outrun Mortado.

Then, Dugal concluded with a button-mouth, it was up to the responsible publisher to rectify that gross error. A bend of one hundred-and-eighty grades, exit!

With a pick-me-up hierbas bobbing up and down in his stomach, on top of a few tapas and a cup of Arabian coffee, Dugal was floating in between euphoria and a heavy feeling in his legs. That, he reassured himself, would be caused less by the alcohol than by the hectic hustle of the last few days. On his way to the Plaza Mayor, close to the parking lot, he could not resist the temptation. There, his legs stretched from a rattan chair, he tried to recall a Horatian verse. Autogenous training of one's imagination: *Nothing as lovely as dipping your feet in a lapping brooklet. Isn't that the highest worldly wisdom?*

He shifted his chair a bit aside for the bulky gent that pulled up next to him to read his evening paper. Promptly the elderly man lit the Havanna in his big face. The thick smoke made Dugal start coughing so that the tears sprang to his eyes. When he was able again to look through the haze before him, he got the shock of his life.

SES TACA BURNING. It was written there in huge letters, and underneath his very own portrait. The picture blew like a blaze into his face. He blinked a few times, but there he was, unmistakably, gracing the front-page: *'actor Dugal Mikes out courting descendant of the Archidux'.*

The photo was explicit enough to get a heart stroke; the previous edition, compromising though it had been, was but a trifle in comparison. Its effect could not be less than that of a swarm of wasps on the scruff of his neck.

A vexed lion, that's how he felt while racing through the outskirts. And then, he had not even read the commentary of that nest soiler. *If I ever get my hands on that dirty bastard, whoever he is, he is a dead man. Adamantly, as dead as a doornail!* His blood was boiling in his veins. And poor Catarí ~ he didn't dare to think what state she was in.

A bit more than halfway a thunderstorm began brewing. At the first hairpin bend the floodgates of heaven opened, but he did not care. Sight or no sight, he did not drive a mile more slowly for it. Towards the end of the descent, streams of mud and stones were pouring over the road surface. Above the area in the direction of Maremira, though, the setting sun drove a wedge between the stacks of clouds which were breaking up, standing out imminently against the ethereal blue behind it. *Hallucinating.*

Once past the last bend near Son Maraitx, however, his heart chilled. A thick smoke drew nearer to him (*like from a battalion of Havanna puffers,* it occurred to him) and a bit further it obstructed the view altogether. At a footpace, his head leaning out of the window, he kept driving on. Before long it began thickening and choking him. Coughing and snorting he glided further down in the valley, and all of a sudden he had got through the intoxicating smokescreen, as surprisingly as it had started. It was almost a wonder he had not tumbled down in a ravine.

What happened after that, was even more terrifying. A singeing heat came along from the wood, and there it struck his eyes: half charred trees glowing like extinguishing torches; ferns and shrubbery just like crispy parsley fried in oil. *Horribile vistu!* Half petrified himself with the shock and confounded by the heat, he seemed to be sinking into limbo. His glowing brain seemed to stand still, paralysed as it were by the fear of the worst …, which was still to come.

And there ~ a few hundreds of yards further down, dancing in the last waves of the heat that was heaving away, it stood out: a white, wiggling mirage, baked hot in the ecstasy of a harem dancer. But *still a white mirage, thank god,* it crossed his mind. The fire had moved up as far as the belvedere on the cliff above Ses Taca. The high tussocks were still smouldering on, sizzling in the duel between the extinguishing rain and the fire. Hardly a better fire brigade than Chaca, but that was the Maya rain god ~ what was he called here?

His next thought wa*s: Catarí!* At once he felt no more exhaustion, thirst or heat. The few minutes up to the lane leading to Ses Taca looked like eternity. How stupid he had been ~ of course! *SES TACA BURNING*, the letters from that man's newspaper in town were dancing before his eyes.

In his hurry he remembered one of the threats he had jeered off. If need be, those guys would smoke them, unjust owners of the old venta, out! And this now was just like it: scorched earth tactics. Need your name be Mikes to see the picture? The insatiable urge for power of the Marcaian land speculators and estate agents ~ it was so self-evident. And you could bet your life on it that emperor Charles was behind this! Yes, yes, señor Moragues, he always managed to give things a twist: that he had no concern in it and least of all in Maremira, a pick of Marcaio's heritage. Carlo V, supporter of the eco-cult ~ the new trump of this island? *My foot!* Super magnate or not, in a wide net of aiding and abetting no human soul will hear about his part in it. *What an actor!* Pa Mikes had taught him: big businessmen are always a bit devious.

Smoke us out! Darn, what agony Catarí must have gone through. Deathly pale, he burst into the house.

To his astonishment, Catarí was there, packing her suitcases with icy calmness. The torrent of words he had wanted to pour out, got stuck in his throat, his tongue felt kind of lamed like a lava skeleton's in Pompey. "What … ~ How, Cathy …?" And Cathy went on packing.

"You're not ~ we're not running off for those terrorists? Cathy, don't you see: then we surrender. That's just what they want: to get us out and put this whole stretch of the Cornisa on sale for a mere song. And for whose sake?"

At last she looked up at him, with that unmoved sphinx look he knew only too well. "I don't give a damn, Dugal!"

That one hit home. And so he knew what the odds were. With ardour and passion no one could get an agitated Catarí out, but … So she knew about it, but how? The evening edition of the Diario! Yet no, Mercury had not brought it down here through the clouds of smoke. Impossibly, unless … Radio, Internet, TV, of course, they had probably spread the news like wildfire. *Who do you think, Dukie?* her eyes seemed to say. *The same henchman who put fire to this powder.*

"The latest feat of those meddling fusspots, so you've been informed, Cathy. Some more of those distasteful samples of gutter journalism. I've seen them myself: a collage of various pictures, all faked. Whatever suits those publicity makers' purpose to keep Marcaio topical."

He wanted to hold her by the hand to stop her, but she pulled the suitcase away. "No need of a lift, the cab's arriving."

And at the first grinding of the tyres on the gravel, she was already carrying the suitcase outside.

42

The end of an affair, it flashed across his mind, as a possible title for an autobiographic movie - far too cynical, and the alternative was even worse: *Beyond shame,* for he had already experienced that himself, at the time when pa Mikes had managed to pick up the pieces again. Then, however, there had only been some rumours; now it was a matter of 'photographic evidence'.

"It's all fake, Cathy, bogus! You know that," he shouted, and he wished for all the world it had been the other way round. *He* would have walked through fire (quite applicable now) to prove *her* innocence. Strange enough, that had never occurred. La Ionès, yet the diva with the highest vamp potential, seemed to give the machos a prompt letdown. How did you explain?

And the most appalling thing was: she knew what was behind it all. So why then was she so stung to the quick? Catarí already stretched one - long and matchless - leg into the taxi, when another, Nile green Jaguar turned onto their front yard. *The car of the upstarts, but let's admit, of an equally unapproachable beauty.*

Nouveaux riches. Dugal swallowed his words just in time upon seeing the spry girl that jumped out of the car in a hostess outfit to open the door jauntily. Then, a cap under the arm, she took her position beside the door, turning in his direction.

"Manuela!" The couple that were walking up to him, nicely brushed up, sensed his apparent amazement. "Señor y señora Maïks, encantado! May we introduce ourselves? Rosanna and Raniero, and … our granddaughter Manuela, or Manolita, as you like."

"Do Mar?" Again his voice seemed to stick in his throat. *Just like Peter's as he ran into Jesus near the venue of Quo Vadis church.*

"Exactly. But perhaps we'd better explain that inside?" proposed a third lady, appearing out of nothingness. La Dolores! So even she, Roberto Marquez's elusive, mysterious right hand!

Also Catarí, all at once back at his side, stood speechless with surprise. They looked at each other and then at the foursome again, pinching each other's arm. Where have we seen them before, in a dream or in a former life?

The somewhat aged couple (he with a strange silver haze over his hair; she with already some wrinkles around her eyes) nestled on the couch quite comfortably. "We are quite familiar with this house," said the man, without a shade of arrogance. And his spouse: "How relative time is, eh! Just as if we had a glass of wine here, together, only yesterday."

Manuela, or Manolita for a change, had guessed their thoughts and was already setting the parlour table in front of them with six wine rummers. "Make yourself at home," said Dolores Francisquita, and that did not even sound sarcastic. She sat down astride next to the amiable lady, with a significant nod at Catarí and Dugal, while both the elderly ones were complacently looking around. As though each painting, each artefact wanted to tell them some episode from the past, hidden somewhere in the darkroom of their memory, but which had never been really erased.

"You have brought your bodyguard with you," Dugal remarked, rather to come out pungent towards Catarí than to shock Dolores.

"Oh, our dear niece, you mean?" the slender gentleman laughed, and that sounded reassuring: *you know, an old acquaintance of yours.*

"Well," Catarí started to pour out, with ice-breaking coolness, "it's no use crying over spilt milk and apologies are like sticking-plasters on a wooden leg, but all the same, señor eh ... do Mar ~"

"...von Habigsburg, as a matter of fact. At your service," he smiled, "but please, just say Raniero, as my wife does."

"Von Habicksburck ..." Dugal parroted their guest and stood up, flabbergasted, gaping at them, one after the other. "And we thought that ..."

"...we were all named do Mar? In a sense, you are right. Our granddaughter will call herself so, deliberately. Sounds quite a bit ... simpler already, doesn't it? But to repeat Mrs Mikes: apologies are somewhat out of place here. We do not expect them from your side either. In fact, we are here for a statement from our granddaughter Manolita. It's about time we should dispel some misunderstandings."

"Misunderstandings!" Dugal muttered, but Catari exhorted him to keep calm. Her female intuition told her that this young woman possessed the key, not only to their own home peace, or the trespass of it, but to the secret of Ses Taca altogether.

"Mister ~ Mrs Mikes, allow me to reveal to you that we were as surprised as you when we … heard the news. We were able to imagine at once how you would react to it. In your place, as the wife of a world-famous actor, I should have thought the same. Therefore we hastened to this place head over heels. To testify in favour of your husband."

The girl with the enchanting waterfall of hair waited a bit, to give Catarí or one of the others a chance of making some comment. Her whole attitude, however, seemed to instil confidence into Catarí. Just go on, she signalled.

"I think it's a pity, and more than embarrassing to you, Mister Mikes, the way it all happened. The reporter who put together those pictures of us, must be quite skilful. This seems real. Anyhow, I'm the only culprit. If I hadn't turned up here, there wouldn't have been any cunning photographer to compose any aggravating evidence of that kind. Mea maxima culpa."

"But why, Manuela ~ why did you pop up here, as a substitute for Colomá? We doubted that dodge at once about their hmm … holiday. We were not so naïve to be hoaxed by that."

"Colomá wasn't either. Yet it seemed nice to her to … be off just for a while."

"And so …?" Catarí had come to stand upright next to Dugal, with raised eyebrows.

"So I cheated …, well, hoodwinked you a bit. But I'll confess why. In fact, my task was to find out where those alleged letters to Catalí came from."

"Well, that takes the cake," thought Catarí, and Dugal took the words out of her mouth: "To rob us, if possible, in our own house, that's a good one!"

"Sorry for interfering," Manuela's grandfather interrupted. He quite understood that the couple wanted to vent their spleen a bit, but there was no question here of stealing. "And least of all in your own house."

"Oh no, and what would you call that then?" said Dugal, not allowing señor Raniero any time for subtle nuances.

Well, simply," Manuela took up the thread again, with a disarming smile; and patiently, as if she were dealing with children, "because this could never be anybody else's due, you see. I mean: belong to strangers."

"Strangers?!" Dugal flared up. "Who nota bene forked out a tidy twenty millions to the previous owner."

"An unlawful owner, señor Mikes," Mrs. do Mar smiled in her most affable way.

"That's exactly the point," Dolores Francisquita now came out for the first time. "That man was a swindler who had misappropriated Ses Taca underhand."

And, like her echo, the grey-haired man added to this: "Through corrupt political channels, my dear niece means."

It could not have mattered that much, though, to the lineal heirs, Catarí brought up, if you saw in what condition they had left the old wine inn behind.

"That," said Manuela's grandfather with raised hand, ignoring her offensive undertone, "is another story. It would lead us too far if we tried to elucidate how we were deprived of this gem at the time. Anyhow, Ses Taca was badly in need of restoration just when our family was tricked out of it by a really crafty sneak. Truly, it was an absolute relief to us when *you* wanted to restore the dilapidated mansion in its old style."

Why then that whole spying affair? both wondered. If this composed elderly gentleman with his female fan trio was the brain behind all the browbeating attempts of the last few days! They did not look that backstairs after all, that they would have been able to harness a Prof and a chief editor, get the whole media merry-go-round after them and perform a game with paratroopers and choppers. Let alone that inferno today: setting afire Marcaio's greenest oasis just as unscrupulous barbarians (or land speculators?) would do.

The pater familias seemed to be reading their thoughts: "Manuela has made this bold venture because we saw what was happening. Your publications in instalments, señor … All that fuss in the press and the apparent action against your person from a higher instance. We were wondering ourselves, as much as you were, who and where all that originated from."

Dugal brought up that they even had had some suspicions about some shady lodge, embedded in the Viennese chancellery, whose main reason of existence was to cover up the old secrets and scandals.

"No no," the old couple smiled. "Then we should have known all about it. For you see ~ that apocryphal society you allude to, does exist after all. The director of that office happens to be a relative of ours. Its principal goal, however, is only to treat the memory of the kin as discreetly as can be. So, certainly not to f …"

"…ferret out a case like this?" Dugal completed sarcastically. "Gee, isn't that reassuring for us! But … then, you yourselves are …"

"…lineal descendants of …?" It was now Catarí's turn to take the words out of his mouth. But she faltered, same as he did, at the thought that, all of a sudden, their suspicions now seemed to be superseded by the living truth. They were standing there, speechless, comparing the facial features of each of the four guests.

"You've guessed it," doña Dolores finally clapped her hands, but then she looked aside, to leave the honour to her honourable relatives.

"My husband is a great-grandson of ~ well, no, not of don Lois, but one of his sisters. You must know, the Archidux stemmed from a family consisting of …"

Yes, yes, Dugal could not help interrupting their explanation, out of pure nail-biting curiosity: that nest of ten, they knew them all by name. A real scion, so to say, Manuela's granddad, from that ramified Habigers' clan: the so-called Vine. They had bred jolly well and lavishly out there, down to Palazzo Pitti. *In that respect they did not fail in keeping up with the common starvelings,* Dugal thought, without any cynicism this time. Therefore the physiognomic likenesses were too conspicuous. He sensed that Catarí too was trembling on her legs, and that was not only because this Raniero, slightly made up, could step into the Dux's shoes just like that, in the film script that he was already bearing in mind.

"And my spouse," said the elderly man with ironic courtesy, "is even a bit more closely related. Namely, Rosanna is a genuine great-granddaughter."

Genuine? That meant the equivalent of a real Do Mar, so … d'Omar, instead of that patriarchal von Habig hallmark?

With a discreet nod the couple took them into further confidence. "In the tradition of the best of matriarchal communities," señor Raniero seemed to be reading their thoughts. "The way our very own granddaughter Manolita prefers it. For you see, what has repeated itself in us ~ and has come to a propitiatory synthesis in our Manuela ~, that's the marriage, never officially consecrated, of our renowned ancestral couple."

"And that presupposes," Dugal could no longer be restrained, "that don Lois's beloved Catarí d'Omar ..."

"Her daughter was my great-great-grandmother," Manuela suddenly blurted out, with the uninhibited pride of the youth that is tired of standing in the shadow. She could as well have told them she was a child born out of wedlock, procreated by the pope ~ so what?

Charity begins at home, but that consideration did not make Dugal and Catarí more disrespectfully disposed than a disbeliever gloating over the treasures of art in the Vatican museum. In the short silence that followed, both felt ill at ease towards this truth that had never seen daylight, yet seemed much simpler than the web of assumptions they had been caught in.

"It's as clear as daylight." As doña Rosanna broke the silence, it sounded like a fairy-tale from your childhood: long forgotten, yet it was always slumbering there, in a mezzanine in your memory. "You can already guess. Catarí's enigmatic seclusion at Ses Taca was sheer fiction. A smoke screen, a misleading manoeuvre that had nothing to do with psychic torturing ~ a 'jealousy drama'. In fact, she did stay there for a while, to repose herself, to recover from a traveller's microbe. A literal one, in fact. Such was the impression some caterers then brought back from the mansion to the village. Still, it had neither anything in common with poisoning, or slow self-poisoning through excessive alcohol consumption, from pangs of love, nor with similar stories that were scattered around. And least of all with any malignant disorder (or even: venereal disease!) she would have contracted on the Nile or so. Village gossip, you see."

Dugal and Catarí's polite cough and askance squint confirmed their account. If there was one couple who had experienced personally what mischief could be inflicted on a relation by bad rumours, it was undoubtedly them. No more than a quarter ago their own 'fairy tale marriage' seemed to be wavering again as much as the Roman empire had been under the feet of Marc Anthony and Cleopatra. Was there a curse on this house, then, that they too, just like their predecessors here, were tried in their most tender emotions?

"An evil ghost haunting Maremira and Ses Taca, that's how it must have appeared to the local villagers," Dolores now went on in a didactic tone. "Step by step there grew a kind of spiritual barrier around the estate. And a couple of Oberländer sheepdogs even enhanced the effect of that seclusion. Nobody was eager yet to enter the domain, let alone to work there. Mysterious illnesses, you see … You know how countrymen are."

Dugal was about to ask her straightforward whether all those facts were also material for academic publication, but there doña Rosanna again filled in for her: "That was one thing. But in addition …"

"…the mysterious female double came into play," Dugal mumbled absent-mindedly.

"How do you mean?" asked the four visitors in chorus, open-mouthed with astonishment.

43

"How did you ~ could you know?" Manuela tackled him, but then she bit her tongue. Señor Raniero put his hand on her shoulder, in a fatherly way, as one does with a loose-lipped child that has spilt the beans.

"What did you mean: her double?" Catarí asked without batting an eyelid. It vexed her immensely when Dugal knew something he had not told her first.

"She was … The person concerned …" ~ la Dolores looked around sphinx-like, weighing her words, as if to retrieve the magic of the surprise at least a bit ~ " …was no more than a cousin of hers, but made up with the necessary finery, she and Catalí d'Omar were as like as two peas in a pod."

Roberto Marquez's right hand was revelling in the confusion that visibly overwhelmed the famous couple. Particularly the way Catarí was gazing at her, showed that she wanted to take the words out of her mouth. As befits a good-looking assistant and aspiring professor to keep the enthralled public hanging on her lips ~ and not at the least the male students ~, Dolores began to lift a tip of the veil bit by bit. That 'mysterious' cousin of the carpenter's daughter had been living in Cordoba for some time, where fortune had treated her rather adversely (the details of which la Dolores diplomatically left to one side). So much so that ~ adding a bit of good luck to misfortune ~ the archduke managed to fish her out at an appropriate moment, in order to … To cut it short, the stray sheep enabled Catalí to vanish, as it were, into smoke.

The Galileio connection, Dugal and Catarí looked at each other once again, baffled as they seemed to exchange thoughts perfectly, like two communicating vessels. But also the do Mar kin (or were they entitled to say now: the four Habigers ~ what's in a name?) obviously saw what was going on in their minds. The three ladies left it to don Raniero this time to reveal what the image of that 'smoke' stood for.

"That hmm, hmm, substitution ~ by a presumably far-off cousin namely ~ meant an ideal mode of escaping. For owing to that vanishing trick Catalí also got a chance to frequent the Dux's favourite haunts ~ Ragusa, the Gulf of Muggia, Kerkyra and so many Mediterranean pearls he had rediscovered. However …"

He smirked at the unbelieving look in the couple's eyes. "Apparently you can guess some more already. The new refuge where Catalí went into hiding, amidst a discreet host of intimate friends, as you probably know, formed the perfect operational base for an excursion to the opposite side … 'le Midi'."

Dugal was only listening with half an ear to the honourable grande's further account. His little computer was crackling as a result of the frantic interaction in the corridors of his memory depot. *Le Pays d'Oc, Septimania, Aix* … And all at once it struck his mind again: *Aix? Del Acqs* ~ do Mar. It was no sheer visionary hocus-pocus, he had got it from one of the essays at Roberto's study office. Maybe from the hand of Dolores Francisquita herself. There was that rather hazy thesis linking Catalí's family ties to the desposyni: the holy descent, interwoven with the clandestine Magdalen adoration and the stories about the legendary disembarkation of the three Marys on the French south coast. All that in the best tradition of the sea-goddess, the Madonna nera and that whole rumpus about a presumably lost 'vine'.

Dugal had never thought much of such raving claims to a higher origin and now again he was getting more and more peeved as the languid murmur of don Raniero's story was stealthily alluding to 'the missionary role' of 'il Salvatore'. *The Saviour, the Redeemer*, Dugal grinned. That ornate epithet so detested by the Dux himself, was passed on to him by a higher destiny. *A nasty bit of an appendix, yes, that had suited His Highness pretty sourly in the end,* Dugal mumbled. *Saver, phew, of what ~ the Occident? The first Mister Europe, doomed to fail in his spiritual assignment!* Dugal thought he knew his predecessor at Ses Taca fairly well enough by now: as a sceptic, as a non-conformist ~ how could don Lois ever have believed in such a mission impossible?

Don Raniero did not seem to have heard it at all. In passing he even drew some parallels with other unsuccessful missions, such as Friedrich the Winter King's, Richard the Lion Heart's, or Godfrey's kingdom of Geruzalén ... Not to mention the Nazarene, or rather: Nasrene, in person, who basically had been an anarchist, hadn't he? By the way, also Catalí's feigned funeral called up certain similarities with the staging of His 'sacrificial death'. And the same went for their hushed-up offspring.

Dugal wondered morosely how his Cathy, brought up still in a half-church-going fashion, would put up with the man's blasphemies. Yet, in his complacent tone don Raniero continued: "But you did already suspect most of it, didn't you? So the rest of it will not surprise you either: the birth of their child ~ though not in a manger or a stable, but anyhow, in total secrecy."

No, they did not need to hold each other upright, not to keel over. The last few days they had learnt to ward off some more blows of that kind. However, they wondered, Catarí suddenly said out of the blue, why that forbidden fruit of that ... 'posthumous' marriage had never been 'detected'. Particularly in this small world of Marcaio and with the intelligence service the Viennese court had the disposal of in those days.

"Primo," señor Raniero smiled, "life kept going at a snail's pace here at the time. Even a top gangster or terrorist could have gone into hiding here, undisturbed. And secondly ..."

Now he passed the torch on to doña Dolores again: "A second factor was that the star of the Habiger dynasty had been waning for a long time, in Europe. You must know," said la Francisquita with an amiable smile that showed total understanding for the lack of historic perspective with cosmopolitans coming from across the Ocean: "the Viennese chancellery could expect no good from any further 'expansion' of the Gotha lineage, and even less from such 'flings' of discredited family members leaking out.

Centuries of suffering under the burden of power had worn out this race. Eroded their very nature. No one had felt this better than don Lois. With deliberate abstinence he stood down, by way of expiatory sacrifice ~ the terminal point of an irreversible evolution."

"Despite the pressure of the big Brotherhood which wanted to launch him as the spiritual leader of the Old World? An uncrowned king of peace of the new age ..." Dugal's considerate remark was received with general silence. *Agreement, in fact*, he concluded for himself.

"And we," señora Rosanna once more took the floor in her indolent way, "we, who still carry the name of that odd couple, are anxious to maintain the spirit of that abstinence."

The way the elderly couple were sitting there before them, so peaceably, it was not hard to believe. Whether they too, however, had refrained from any material activities? Anyway, they did not look destitute at all.

Anticipating Dugal's question, as though he was able to conjecture their train of thought, don Raniero confided to them that they had set up a small sails business of their own in Palmera, without any help of their old title: quite flourishing, in fact.

That ran in the family then, Catarí grimaced. A remark that was received with a hearty laughter by the four of them. In the mean time there had grown a totally distracted atmosphere. Even Catarí was loosening up by and by. Dugal was also exerting himself to provide each of them with a snack and a drink. Twice as carefully though towards the daughter and the niece. *A pissed tomcat, containing himself because his mistress is watching,* she thought still on her guard.

"A genuine Habiger," Dugal joked crudely, toasting on Manolita's choice: a rummer of cooled Riesling. But as doña Rosanna parried in a glossing tone: a d'Omar with Viennese blood in his veins ought to show himself in his true colours!

Whilst they were clinking glasses to the common spirit, the common goal: 'the honour and the inner peace of the sorely tried couple', the Mikeses could sense that their guests were gradually getting closer to the motive of their visit. No single diplomat could have tied himself in knots as don Raniero was doing, to get Dugal where he wanted to have him: " ...and therefore, señor Mikes, if the memory of our ancestors means anything to you, please leave their spirit in peace. We ask you, we beg you."

Dugal thought he was going to faint, but the old man went on with verve: however captivating Dugal's initiative seemed to them, whatever deep and moving feelings this idyll had stirred up among the big reading public, a shady but also dangerous group, lurking behind the scenes, was eager to take advantage of this polemic. "And that manipulation of the L.S. case, and both yours, señor Mikes, would mean the finishing stroke to our family."

The two experienced actors were gazing at each other, utterly baffled by that strong piece of theatre. Hardly a quarter of an hour ago, this honourable quartet had seemed rather suspect themselves ~ possibly even the main instigators of the whole plot ~, and what appeared now? That they came in person to make a demarche, imploring them to be their allies and offer them protection against a secret society which had already harassed don Lois and his beloved.

Cathy, one minute ago still irate because of his alleged unfaithfulness, now fell like a log for that sympathetic party and threw in her lot with them as a fifth claimant opposite him.

"You're making things extra difficult to me," he sighed. Just before, he had sworn he would persevere against all common sense, but now all of them were closing ranks against him by working on his conscience. *Forget it, Duke, let's sweep it under the carpet, Duke, for the sake of our peace of mind and the serenity of the illustrious deceased couple.* But Catarí knew her pig-head: if Dugal Mikes had something in mind …

"I've left no stone unturned to get their love out of the ban of oblivion at last, and now you come here to tell that Sua Altezza, here maligned and there raised again as coryphaeus of the tourist industry, should creep back in his dusty manuscripts?"

The longer he tried to repress his spite by reason, on behalf of these far descendants and their rational motives, the more he was feeling peeved. After all, he had put his back into it and, as it was his nature to arouse some controversies, he had set a number of people up against himself. *Hypocrites, ultraconservatives,* he had thought. Erroneously, in the end, for this whole charade had been set up by a number of clever fellows who had left him to his fallacy. Yes, even forced him into a sham fight with imaginary Mafiosi. And why? Right ~ to create a scandalous atmosphere around both the Dux and his own person.

"In other words, I've been tricked into it?!" he chanted. "The press, the Marcaian dream manufacturers, including the Mortados and Marcellas. And all that with the sole purpose to give the faltering economy on the island a leg-up, to boost up the slackening hotel bookings."

"And that's something you won't lump," the slender gentleman smiled. "You are used to picking up the gauntlet and dragging such dabblers to court. We understand."

"But have you calculated yet," Dolores Francisquita began to speak again, "that this is precisely the trap they set for you? However, *not* the people you have just mentioned. They wouldn't apply scorched earth tactics, would they? In the end, that would only harm our island."

After a short exchange of looks Catarí said hesitatingly: "That's right. A conspiracy then, ever since don Lois's days? Hmmm … Probably we've got to look for that from another corner. At … Asuntos Bailares, maybe ~ Moragues & Granddads?"

"A good try," don Raniero nodded, while Dugal was envying Catarí for her acumen. "Yet … no. Although the great-great-grandfather of don Moragues (or Carlos Quinto, as his popular nickname goes) vied with don Lois for the prevalence here, they were in fact allies. Alright, one was an enterpriser in heart and soul and the other a naturalist, genuine nature lover, the harbinger of the 'greens'. On that issue they often were at loggerheads, but as pacifists they joined hands."

"Professor Marquez," Dugal suddenly mumbled with bewilderment, that he had let himself be taken in like that. "Not him ~ Roberto, a mole!" *Or your errand-boy,* he thought grumpily.

"Señor Maïks! Professore Marquez, your best friend, a telltale? Good gracious, no, he got the lion's share of his information from us. Truly, he is the integrity in person," said don Raniero. But Dugal could not help saying: "Of course. With a doña Dolores as his mainstay."

"You can take it from me," Dolores retorted candidly. "Roberto is altogether neutral. As objective as an academician may be expected to be. Still, we suspect him of watching the development of your conflict with the media with an ironic eye."

The academic stunner was secretly amused about the way Dugal was overwhelmed by surprise. "When you pressed your plan forward (quite to the liking of our opponents), the professor realized there were no bridles to rein you in. Besides, it suited his purpose ~ with a view to his studies about the Dux, in particular ~ as also the lyrical side of that royal romance was now getting widespread among the public. To do history justice, you see. The eternal sentimental weakness of a historian."

The longer the conversation was lasting and the degree of confidence growing, the more he began to feel uneasy, and he noticed how Catarí too was fidgeting on her chair. Why hadn't this bizarre quartet come any earlier to them with their strange story? And how vague and fuzzy they kept it all, with that naïve entreaty to join in their cover-up operation. By the way, how certain could they be that these guests were really genuine relatives? Let alone descendants of the Archidux and his Marcaian flame.

"We'd like to believe you, guys," Dugal sighed.

"And maybe belief is the highest virtue," Catarí added wholeheartedly. Thus she was at her best, with that sugary lineament around her sensual mouth. And dangerous. Dugal knew then that his great sweetie was keeping something up her sleeve, one of her knacks. "But how can we be sure you are really the butt? And what about that big, terrible secret then? Or … aren't you yourselves involved in the combine and you had no other choice than appeasing us, now that it turns out my pigheaded beloved here will never back down, in spite of all this water and fire?"

Yeah, Dugal in his turn at once threw the gauntlet down: wasn't that maybe the shady plot some petty professors, publishers and their henchmen too were mixed up in?

While the four of them were exchanging resigned glances, don Raniero said with a deep sigh: "No, my friends, they are not. But Jordi Martell is."

44

For a few moments they had kept sitting there as quiet as a mouse. The old standard clock kept on ticking unflaggingly, at the pace of their heartbeat, as if it wanted to pass that from L.S.'s days on to them. The quartet was looking a bit stunned, feeling half-guilty, like one of those backbiting vixens who did not intend to blab at all, yet spilled the beans again.

"Jordi," Dugal was eventually able to utter, and then there was no more stopping Catarí. "Pobre Jordi Martell! Then that poor copier failed to save his skin after all in this affair. Victim of his own curiosity and meddlesome character."

"Well, you see," said don Raniero de Habigsburg, clearing his throat. It was too late to back out anyway and in the end, the Mikes couple had a right to the truth, he thought, after all the ordeals these last few days …

The hale and hearty old man was about to go ahead with his story, when a ramshackle old-timer was driving up the yard. Catarí and Dugal leapt to their feet at once, prepared for a new assault. But the 'sagrada', this 'holy' family, seemed to be expecting this. "That must be him," Manuela cheered, "señor Marquez!"

Dugal and Catarí now looked like thunderstruck. "The professor," she whispered. This could be no coincidence. Even more unwieldy than ever, the Chest was creeping out of his decrepit gem from a prehistoric building year.

"I never thought I would get out of it once more," he already said when coming to the outer terrace and wiping off the drops of sweat on his forehead.

Fortunately it was not her little Triumph, la Dolores sighed.

"No, Marcella's," the Prof said and without much ceremony he flopped down in the settee, so the frail doña Rosanna bounced up about a hand's span.

"You are quite a bunch of sycophants, really!" Dugal suddenly lashed out.

"Leading a man up the garden path and then taking him hostage in his own house!" There was no stopping his torrent of words this time; even his Cathy had rarely seen him so vicious ~ turning as red as a lobster. The worst of his suspicions had come true in the end: that Roberto, who had not imbued him with a whit of trust from the very beginning, had sneakily tried to hitch him into his plan, yes, had deliberately hoodwinked him, and all that for the sake of this nice lot of pretending inheritors of L.S.. Besides, who assured him it was all true, about that lineage?

"No, Mister actor," Prof. Marquez retorted, quite calmly, but decidedly. "You're wide from the mark, Dugal. Look, do you see that little car over there? I should be glad after all it has not been riddled, just like myself by the way."

How he had got to that little vehicle of Marcella's then? asked Dolores, no longer able to restrain her suspense. What Roberto began to disclose thereafter, was to make the new owners of Ses Taca go out of their mind altogether. And he did prepare them for that too: "Querídos amigos, brace yourselves for a moment!"

A few hours before, the professor had left his office with a folder in his hands ~ "you know which one," he said to Dugal's guests, but he would come back to that later on. And there, on the stairs of the Alma Mater, two guys unexpectedly had popped up at his side, pressing a metal object against his ribcage. What they wanted to get out of him? That's what they were going to make clear to him presently, in a van that was waiting nearby. Roberto could do nothing but consent under that threat (for else, he showed his big palms, he would have taught those louts a lesson). Inside there was the Leader ~ "you know which one," he nodded again aside ~ and that one came straight to the point: "The list, señor Marquez!" He wanted to lay hold on the 'list', but the Prof had suspected that for a long time. Yet he was playing the innocent bystander, but that boss with his huge sunglasses hadn't got much time. "Open that briefcase, you blockhead!"

That too seemed obvious to Roberto: that this was bound to happen one day. "Because," and he addressed himself again explicitly to Dugal, "you personally weren't … eh, neither of you was the target all that time.

I was. Those harassments at your expense were sheer feints. Distraction, to draw me out."

What's he babbling now? That damage at our water-furrow outside ~ the sabotaged estanca, that 'little arson' just a while ago, not to mention all stalking acts and persecutions ... They were all meant to strike him with terror, him, mister academician? I daresay!

Roberto was grinning impatiently now at L.S.'s family, but he took up the thread of his report again. "Mira, amigo. What I ought to have in this briefcase here ~ was supposed to have ~ was a list of names." Here Roberto dawdled a bit, but don Raniero nodded encouragingly: *go on, tell us.*

"Those gentlemen who were so eager for my briefcase, absolutely wanted to get that coping-stone from don Lois' intimate correspondence. A passage that failed in your copies. Or: no longer occurred there. And those fellows were in the know ~ as we already feared."

Who those ' we' were, Catarí was anxious to know at once. This time, however, Roberto ignored it. His kidnappers ~ he explained, pulling his knees up high, there on that settee, like an animator on a reclining chair at the beach ~ had then grabbed the briefcase from his hands. Greedily searching for their prey, they threw all other papers around ... Nada, nothing at all, patrón!" The fatty in the front of the car, swerved his head round, turning as red as a beetroot. Roberto, preparing for the next step, had to let the man insist (at the risk of him exploding); otherwise it would have seemed suspect.

Really, were those idiotic letter-worshippers totally nuts after all ~ or backward? "THÉ list. From Galileio. Of the bigwigs gone into hiding there, who had been given asylum by the Dux." The professor had to keep feigning as if he had not caught up yet, until his opponent was near choking. "Oh, *that* list! I was thinking of the other one."

"Which other one?" the sunglass man flew up. To which Roberto reacted sheepishly: ah, those of the other camp ~ the bantams who at the time took profit from an armed conflict and did not bother about the canon fodder, a few millions of victims more or less. About the same kind we find there today: arms manufacturers, bomb manu- ...

The threatening dig, on both sides, from a strange object between his ribs, told him it was about time for him. "The latter, hmm ... I haven't got it with me either. If I had known you would pay me a visit ... Well, a copy of it is kept in a safe ~ at a bank in Vienna. But the original, señor Moragues can deliver it to you. By the way, he is also in the possession of the other one, the L.S.-list, you see ... About the pacifists, the historic simplistic ones, if you like."

"Where?!" Roberto had been afraid his nose was bitten off this time, he said.

"You said so yourself: in Galileio, really. Where else?"

It had been an unequalled wager. Not 'on the spur of the moment', as Dugal called it, but by considered inspiration, long beforehand. What those scoundrels were not aware of, was namely that the professor had already pressed on a beeper a while ago, well hidden under his jacket. Hoping now that that little device would do its job: set off a chain reaction of SOS messages. Despite his self-possession Roberto had certainly pressed tens of times on it with the inside of his arm, to make sure. If all went according to plan, a small army of security agents would be pulling together towards the appointed place by then, ready to carry out operation Salvator. If ... these mercenaries did not smell a rat and were not going to dump him, smart little professor, along the road. In a ditch, that was, riddled with bullets maybe or his ribcage stabbed with a dagger.

"Fortunately, they fell for it," sighed Roberto, putting himself an imaginary medal on his collar with a wet thumb. He had piloted them exactly in the direction he and Carlos Quinto had fixed up with his general staff.

"There." The fellows had gaped at each other and then stared down again, deep in the valley, where at other times no living soul came. Even on them the breathtaking panorama seemed to make a deep impression. At the spot Roberto pointed at with his finger, stood an old quinta: the refuge where Catarí d'Omar at the time had escaped from history. "Only an old janitor," the prof panted with fear, so to speak, as the bespectacled leader pushed a gun under his nose. He begged him not to leak anything about his role, for if señor Moragues got wind of this ... And he made the fatal sign with his thumb-nail across his throat. As if he did not realize what was going to happen to him, once they had got what they were looking for.

"Still, I wasn't quite assured about it," he grinned, again enthralled by the experience of that ultimate crazy piece of ride over the dusty country road to that house below. Now a country dwelling of señor Moragues', completely outfitted with hidden cameras, secured fences and all possible sophisticated ICT gadgets. And at present occupied by his private militia, armed to the teeth. Like rats driven by hunger, the kidnappers were driving into the trap.

"And yet, it was a near miss," Roberto sighed. At the very last moment even the best timed commando action can end in a disaster. Right in front of the slip road to Moragues' weekend pied-à-terre a hay cart was smugly trudging across the path. Their driver had to jam on the brakes, yet could no more prevent a rough clash with the mediaeval vehicle: wham, head-on into the rear of the cart! Nicely in tune with the scenario of don Carlos's bodyguards. At least he thought so. His unsuspecting guards next to him were reeling to and fro in their seat-belts, like sparring-partners beaten to a jelly between the ropes. It was child's play for the Chest to bang the two blokes' heads against each other an extra time, worming himself through the ripped door and dashing like lightning into the arms of don Moragues' private security team.

That's what he thought. Ten steps further though he knew things were going at sixes and sevens. For once behind the hay cart he was grabbed by a rantipole farmer by his fluttering shirt. "Palurdos! Who do you think you are?!"

The good man had turned up from behind the bushes, out of the void, while Carlos's men had taken position about a hundred yards away, behind the fence. Roberto shook off the hay farmer and took to his heels. None too soon, for the bullets were already flying around his head. "And one on this heel," he showed, shoe in hand.

"And what about Moragues's private riflemen?" Seeing the worried frown on Dolores' forehead, one could notice Roberto's right hand had been put in the picture, as far as the preliminary strategy was concerned.

They had got into action straight away, the professor grimaced, still sweating with dismay. Obviously those boys were trained in keeping the wolves sated and the sheep unscathed, but now the fat was in the fire. A barrage from machine guns, whizzing right past his head. "I thought all hell had broken loose over me." Roberto had just heard the slamming of a door of the gangsters' car and how they tried to turn the vehicle. Then the tyres were skilfully shot to tatters, there was a crash against a tree, and before Roberto's abductors had come back to senses, they were lying fettered at their feet. The hay farmer, rooted to the spot, standing there as a silent witness.

After Roberto's story Dugal and Catarí had become quite as silent now, as an audience. *Why should such a bunch of bandidos be interested in that kind of documents? Name lists from a century ago, come on! Even if there are any ideological inheritors in both camps, times have changed that much!*

"And what we fail to see," said Catarí to the do Mar kin, "is why you have come and begged us to banish everything to the realm of discretion? While it would at least be useful to the outer world to be aware of what kind of rogues orchestrated this whole witch hunt."

"Mira, señora Maïks," don Raniero crossed his arms. A sign of angelic patience with regard to those cultureless plebeians from over the Big Pond, so it appeared to them. But as for that, they could forgive this spiritual aristocrat, for whom their admiration was growing every minute. "If you start stirring up a cesspit …"

"…the whole of Marcaio will soon be reeking of the odours of that vermin." They all could not help laughing, the way Dugal came out with another blunt remark. However, the problem was, don Raniero resumed, that their 'aficionados' (the fans of L.S. and his pan-European bearing) were still as peace-loving as they used to be in yonder days. That is, averse to the aggressive methods, so peculiar to the rival party, who did not shun any means to force them into a corner ~ to put it mildly. *Or help them kick the bucket*, Catarí shuddered, with a shivery look at the professor, for the latter's tall story was a match for the 'foretastes' they had personally experienced. Then she noticed the look on Dugal's face. And knew at once where they were standing ~ her pig-head was not going to let the matter rest. From the sullen expression on his mouth she could guess what he was thinking: *dear me, what a funny situation! You, slick customers, have kept me dangling all the time ~ me, a harmless angler who is meekly gazing there, fascinated by that same float. And just at the moment when the big catch seems to be within reach … plop, a sadistic bait-layer catches the delicious fish away under your very nose. So, good old Archidux and his Marcaian honey are in for the mothball chest. And what about those apocryphal love letters of his? Thrown into the wastebasket! All of a sudden he may play the old-fangled dolt again, hopping across the poppy-fields with his butterfly net, in pursuit of rare herbs and insects.*

"And he did his share in this, that fine gentleman," said Dugal with a poker-face grin. "Yes yes, your nice Charles V! You can't teach an old monkey like me any more tricks. He hitched me and Miguel to his wagon, extolled you and Marcella for your beautiful eyes, and thus he scored a double gain. Now he knows both those belligerent comrades in arms and your simplistic alliance of Peace Doves. Can play you off against each other and meanwhile he can extend Marcaio as a free port of his neutral empire."

Prof. Marquez and his assistant were clapping their hands simultaneously. Contrived that yourself, señor Mikes? They left the counterarguments, however, to his grey eminence: "Then you have a totally wrong view of señor Moragues. By the way, it's about time you really made acquaintance with him."

As quickly as a jack-knife, young Manolita whipped to their TV-set. "May I?" *Please, go ahead*, Dugal and Catarí nodded, dumbfounded. *Make yourself at home.*

Daughter do Mar (or should they say: señorita Habiger?) turned on Antenna Bailar. They saw an unusually slovenly lady speaker who was talking a bit out of the back of her neck. *Hmm, one of those Remedies-Against-Infatuation cases again*, Dugal growled, as he used to brand that kind of female intellectuals. Suddenly, however, he sat down on the edge of his chair, for the complacent woman interrupted herself for 'a statement of public interest'.

"And now … Mister Carlos Moragues speaking, para Ustedes, señores."

45

Their consternation could not have been more complete. There, on the screen in their own drawing-room, appeared a beaming figure in a dark striped suit, without a tie but wearing a sportive little scarf tucked into his white shirt collar. *Typical,* Dugal groused; with envy, he admitted to himself. For there was something about that chap. Living publicity for Armani and Colgate, the way he smiled, exhibiting his immaculate set of teeth. *Spanish gigolo,* but then a stinkingly rich one - what lady would not fall for that, despite his age?

"Buenos días, everybody, and in particular I am going to address myself today to … señora Catarí Ionès and her husband, Mister Mikes."

Both were shoving on their chair, looking in a flash at their five uninvited guests. *How did you pull this off?*

"Like every Marcaian I have a very deep admiration for this graceful and equally smart actress, and - without my being sexist - her husband, just as celebrated as she is, and her professional equal, who do honour to our island by dwelling among us …"

Hmm, idolaters, blandishers, Dugal scorned. Had they forgotten maybe that he had helped her to find her way up in this metier? Oh yeah, the transitoriness of glory …

"I hope that they, by now the most famous of our BMW's …" (with a wink don Carlos explained the allusion), "are listening to us at this very moment. If it's all well-timed - but my friends will have taken care of that …"

With a matchless charisma, they had to admit, the old charmer addressed himself to them both, but in such a way that every islander as well kept sitting, glued to his chair. "The last few days - that can't have escaped your attention - our archipelago has been living again under the spell of our Archiduque, L.S. or don Lois, as we like to call him. All that owing to Sir Mikes and the secret letters that he published in our Diario several times a week. Sent by the Dux himself to his beloved Catalì. Every day again people were queuing up to the news-stand. Mister Mikes, it's greatly to your credit that this most human trait of our Dux has come out in the limelight!"

At once the pitch had been given for a personal gesture. With some apt strokes the adroit businessman depicted don Lois as the Uncrowned King of Marcaio. A comparison with himself was not far-off. He wanted to step into L.S.'s footprints and safeguard the island from foolish interventions. Together with Dugal Mikes. Similar to what the Dux and his own great-great-grandfather had done a good century ago. Señor Moragues did not beat about the bush: the founder of the Moragues dynasty had been portrayed more than once as L.S.'s antipole, he was aware of that. And yet, they had been congenial spirits who grew closer to each other, beyond the differences. Perhaps don Lois was a premature ecologist, agreed, but he was also a progressive mind with an excellent knowledge of sciences and a great interest in technology. Much more than the petty, conservative enterprisers in those days.

"By the way, has anything changed at all? Which of our present-day captains of industry is ready to invest in the welfare of our planet?" Don Carlos spread the palms of his hands, as if to challenge his colleagues-plutocrats. "If the Archidux had lived now, he would have done exactly the same, mutatis mutandis, of course. As a champion of green energy, for instance. Or as a protector of endangered species and biotopes, as he already used to be at his time, operating from his yacht 'The Nymphe': his Noah's Ark. In our era, that's for sure, he would have made Marcaio an oasis. No private clubs for VIPs, as today's jetsetters are prone to do ～ hmm, except for some exceptions like you, señor and señora Mikes …"

Dugal saw Catarí moving to and fro on her chair, as uncomfortably as himself. Carlos Quinto revealed himself as an inspired actor, not deprived of some melodramatic tricks. *He should have gone into politics*, he chuckled. Moragues knew how to captivate the attention of friend and enemy, until, like a seasoned pulpit preacher (or a boxer, thought Dugal), he made his strike precisely there where he wanted to: "And no playground for woollen sweater world reformers either, for that's what certain reactionary elements wanted to put our Dux down to: an unworldly dilettante, a dreamer.."

291

Bull's-eye! Dugal almost jumped to his feet, with the uncontrolled enrapture of fans near the boxing-ring. Full of growing admiration, he could foresee how don Carlos was leading his audience to his goal. "But that's not what L.S was like," Carlos went on arguing with verve, "and my adversaries know ~ our adversaries, Mister Mikes. Indeed, what benefit do they get from that picture of a somewhat 'special', yet rather innocent, so to them innocuous, aristocrat whom they can shove into the drawer of the Ancien Régime? Every bit of a benefit! Because our Archidux, with his deep yearning for freedom, transferred to us also another desire: that namely for a world exempt from arms, for development without oppression."

That man has missed his clerical vocation, now mumbled Catarí in her turn. *But no, Carlos V has deserved his name*, Dugal thought, for this was no more or less than a declaration of war. But one to a really dangerous lobby in this case. That's why the old crocodile precisely had to be a hundred percent sure of his ground. And that, he was going to tell them straight away. Dugal was now dead certain this man was not going to swim with the tide again.

It was as if don Moragues had guessed his thoughts, by some mysterious screen telepathy. "So the great moment has come to lay our cards on the table, and I hope ~ I'm sure ~ that my kindred spirits, such as the Mikes couple, will line up with me in this matter. Look, believe me or not …" With disarming open-heartedness don Carlos unfolded his plans with the Cornisa, a big bite from Marcaio's north coast. A plan to the liking of his predecessor, the Archidux, a rehabilitation of his 'green' development idea. Quite different from the relentless urbanization mania of what he called 'those short-sighted shareholders in bad taste and vulgar profit-mongering', Maremira II would offer the old-Marcaian arts and crafts a revival. Framed in a green decorum, stylised in L.S.'s fashion: with vineyards and belvederes, footpaths through protected wooded area … In brief, eco-tourism to man's measure, and yet beneficial to the inhabitants' purse. Though a bit less, he grinned, for the pockets of impudent project developers who reduced Marcaio to one construction site. "In other words, let's call a halt to steel and concrete!"

Don Moragues went on fulminating against the unrestrained tourism-terrorism. But how was he going to relate that to the bandidos don Raniero and his own sort had locked horns with? It was remarkable how this passionate enterpriser, in the thick of his argument, was carried away by the animation of the moment. *Before long he is even getting lyrical about don Lois' philanthropic devotion,* Dugal mumbled, while he heard the guest speaker talking about 'democratic prices for like-minded people'. "That way Ses Taca may get some rivals after all, señor Mikes," Moragues winked.

All at once however the unsurpassed viceroy of Marcaio made a bend of a hundred and eighty degrees. "But what I actually wanted to discuss with you …" Don Carlos cleared his throat. Not out of annoyance, as he was losing the thread of his argument, but to raise his glass to the island and its future … "with our unmatched panacea," he toasted facing the camera, so the scent of the hierbas was almost rising up to the spectator.

"In the course of the publications of the Letras Secretas one thing was getting clearer and clearer," the big man bent forward, confidentially. *Victoriously,* thought Dugal ~ *if only we had such a president, one of that poise!* Without batting an eyelash, señor Moragues elicited how the adversaries of L.S. had first made it piping hot for Mister Mikes and co. Particularly to goad him into persevering. For they knew Dugal's proverbial stubborn~ …, hmm, petulance. What those fellows stealthily hoped for, was that an old secret would thus come to surface. Not so much the very nature of the bond between Catalí and her L.S. ~ "el encanto del amór", he smiled with a grand gesture ~ as the question which other, much older lineage they passed on: that of a peace realm which L.S. never got a chance to achieve, but which the war lobby still is stiff scared of up to these very days."

Don Carlos was now leaning back, sniffing. *The picador who withdraws for the matador to get in,* thought Dugal, but that was a scarcely peaceable comparison. "Until it came home to those gentlemen" (now Carlos laid heavy emphasis on that word) "that in this way that mystic society of pacifists within the young European union ~ say: the Dux's inheritors ~ would not emerge in daylight. The óther party, however, the hawks, whose names I now have in my pocket, they would."

The old macho is gambling, Dugal grumbled, but on the faces of Roberto and the others he saw confidence in don Carlos's approach.

"Probably Mister and Mrs Mikes now wonder why I am not getting the wind up because of those louts." His broad smile was also meant for 'those', that was for sure. Carlos seemed to be speaking rather to them than to the Mikes now.

"The answer is obvious: they know that a living Moragues is less harmful to them than a dead one. It is similar to a test-tube in a lab: break it and the lethal bacilli will be scattered."

Promptly he picked a large key out of his pocket: "a symbolic one," he said grinningly. The key to the L.S. secret ~ that's what their opponents liked to have more than anything else. "But if I throw it into the water ..." With half a turn and a casual gesture he did so. You could see the glittering thing fall into the water of the harbour. "That's that," he laughed, "it's gone. Yet, does this mean the key is no longer there? Course not. Even if they dive for it without finding it, still it's lying somewhere on the bottom of the sea. And what's more ~ there are many copies of it. So, my dear friends ... and enemies," he blinked archly, "the same goes for our secret."

Just as if he is going to take it with him into his grave, Dugal mumbled. The big shot was about to get out of the picture, changed his mind and, as if he had heard Dugal's reflection, he fetched a lady from behind the curtains, returning on his steps with her. "La Marcella," Catarí stifled a scream.

Can you be somewhat less cryptic, señor," Marcella smiled, "our public deserves it." And without any transition don Carlos said: "Oh, why not, after all? Don Lois's ultimate dream was not merely to make Marcaio a free port for kindred spirits, but also and especially ... an arms-free haven! A pious wish, in his days, a neutral zone from which his idea of peace would be able to spread. And today? As good as reality. The mooring of warcraft I can ~ we can" he rectified with false modesty, "hardly inhibit. We don't really object to that either, as long as they help to maintain the balance on the international scene. But arms trade and similar trafficking? Jamás, never again, over our dead body! Now, that's precisely hard to accept for those gents, and yet it's an accomplished fact. Eventually we do realize it now. Attacking us works like a boomerang on them, the way a nuclear conflict leads to self-destruction. That, amigos, is our best life insurance ~ no threats whatsoever can change anything about that. For they realize: by blackmailing us, they expose themselves."

That sounded like music in Dugal's and Catarí's ears. Such a presidential speech, their citizen number one could only dream of it. All amiability, Carlos V showed himself all at once from his propitiatory side: he wanted to spare everybody the details about how they had managed with that canny stroke, but at any rate, without the Mikes couple they would never have pulled that off. And therefore ~ he concluded ~ the ultimate, most intimate letter of the Archidux was their due. "A specimen that unfortunately fails in your collection of the Letras Secretas, señor Mikes. You and your lady will be able to read it in all serenity and then decide what seems best to you. Either let the famous couple rest in peace or make their romance exactly revive in its true dimension? You won't surely be at a loss for a scenario. An unrivalled one, to be sure! Featuring yourself, in the wake of the beloved pair, we can fancy. While the peace of mind of the genuine heirs remains unmarred …"

Both Catarí and Dugal addressed themselves to the Habiger clan with crossed arms and a significant "Yes-yes-yes …" *We may stick out our necks and the desposyni keep out of harm's way. Privacy ensured.* But it was Dolores who took their breath completely away: "They are onto it, cousin," she said, taking Prof. Marquez teasingly by his arm.

Roberto … 'cousin'? Now they went from one surprise to the other. '*Marquez!*' *But of course, that's a name one can use for all purposes; they walk about in swarms over here, same as there are thousands of Williamses or Schmidts or Duponts. Now I see why …*

There was not much time left to elaborate on that reflection, though, as Carlos the rhetorician had fully captivated them again by his performance:

"One thing is beyond question, querídos amigos: for us, Marcaians, this whole affair didn't show any snag at all, on the contrary. I even call it positive publicity and hopefully it will help us separate the wheat from the chaff. Owing to this attention ~ auspicious media attention for this once ~ our island will also get a bit safer at that. Besides, children of the Vine, peace sowers, you can sleep the sleep of the just: the L.S. stock will go on thriving here, whatever the señores Mikes decide to do."

Damn! Don Carlos had already turned his back on them in a theatrical stance, when he made another rotation on his heels, towards them. As if Dugal's thoughts were working upon him through the screen, he produced a scroll and, with a broad smile, he waved the yellowed document about in his hand. "Oh yes, before I forget: our deal, señor Mikes: the spiritual testament of His Highness L.S., as arranged. And may it not be a poisoned gift this time!"

Señor Moragues stretched his arm ostentatiously towards the camera, thereby covering almost the whole screen. Just as if he wanted to hand it over to Dugal in that way, and with an automatic reflex the latter too stretched himself towards the screen. "Got it, Mikes?" said Catarí laconically. They were all laughing, in spite of themselves. Including la Marcella at the other side, who concluded the broadcast with a quip: "So you see: the past can reunite us in a fraternal manner. We wish Mister Mikes ~ and his lady ~ much success and ... hmm, we hope our recent report about the Dux can bring him some more inspiration."

46

"And? Can señora Ionès inspire mister film director? Or maybe there's some other, indigenous game roaming on the cliffs …"

Her arms put around him from behind the couch and subsequently one leg stretched over its back, with a very scanty piece of textile leaving little to the imagination. A superbly rested, and spry, Catarí ~ even the most powerful man in the world was not equal to that. And least of all Dugal, after a well-nigh sleepless night.

"I'm telling you one more time, baby," he sighed, "even ten stark naked Marcellas would leave me cold. And little niece Dolores Francisquita is no match for you either. Besides, she's Roberto's bonita, as you may know by now."

The only thing that annoyed him excessively, was that his legal spouse had sawed through ten oaks, in all tranquillity and despite his latest two Quies earplugs. While he had been tossing from one side to the other. *And all that just for a scrap of paper, some literary trimmings that would not change the world a bit, let alone make it any better.* All the time he had tried to inculcate that on himself, but it was all useless. Even a few glasses of sherry were. Those had only stirred up his brain, but sleeping was out of the question. And least of all after he had poured down another Paló and on top of that an extra rummer of TeKillA, a horrible home-made concoction that would have knocked over even the worst of bar-clinging customers. Still, not him, son of the sturdy Spartan, he had decorated himself with a wet thumb.

Just when Dugal wanted to give himself up to the blessed horizontal position at the side of his sleeping beauty, the prettiest on earth, the room had begun to spin around, even in the darkness. Two minutes and an emptied stomach later a leaden weight came down over him, as he was still sitting on his knees, leaning over the toilet bowl. Half groggy, knock-out, the hangover of his life.

A deafening noise had made him jump to his feet and run head over heels through the door of the living-room, which seemed to be ablaze. The shock of his life! Out of his senses, he stumbled to the window, chased by Catarí, who came dashing down the stairs in her nightgown.

What they then saw there, gave them almost a cardiac arrest: a chopper getting down on their fully lighted lawn. Dugal had already run to his bureau and back, to fetch the old sten gun Cathy did not even know of, when she shouted: "Duke, come and see that!" "What?"

There they were, rooted to the spot, standing barefoot on the chilly floor. The team of night revellers who were fussily crossing the grass, seemed to regard this kind of stalking in the twilight as the commonest thing on earth.

"Mister and Mrs Mikes! Excuse us for the early visit."

"Visit?! Hey boys, d' you know what time this is ~ have you gone mad?"

"Five o'clock. Still, not raving mad for hardworking people like you, actors. Those are usually early birds, aren't they?"

From between those fellows, shouldering cameras and muffled sound equipment, a lady with a head scarf on appeared out of the spotlight. "Marcella, you!" Catarí shouted. "And we who thought it was that terror gang again."

It was going to cost the illustrious Miss Reporter sweat and blood to win an enraged Dugal over for her stunt. "Please, do it for our common pact, Dugal. With señor Moragues and against the anti-rationalistic powers over here!"

She had to beg him three times until Dugal cooled his heels. Finally they burst out laughing, though, seeing how they were standing there: in their half negligee, least of all looking like the glamorous couple the film fans would swoon for.

At the break of day they found themselves all right at last at a working breakfast on the terrace, Dugal and Catarí, a bit made up, relaxing in the broad rattan chair. 'On Marcella's talking couch', as the early morning programme was called ~ she herself aslant opposite them, transformed as if by magic from the working silly-in-jeans into the real show beast.

After a few questions Dugal was completely back in the picture. Not like a sheer ephemeral success actor talking a bit out of the back of his neck, but the captivating conversationalist people had always taken him for. Apt and witty. What he thought of señor Moragues' oration? A real pearl for anthologies. Cicero could not have outdone it. What about don Carlos's idea of Maremira II and a Marcaian renaissance? Simply sublime and, as for their part, a pilot project for the whole mankind ‑ which was urgently in need of authenticity and character. Dugal thought the businessman had made a smart move by linking his proposition to a call for cosmopolitan co-operation and more peace industry, while maintaining the regional entity. An ingenious trick, by the way, merging that post-modernistic idea of progress with the L.S.-revival: the figure of the Archidux as a draught horse, an exponent of a new élan. No bad idea, at a time when the youngsters were getting their mikes-swallowing idols from cacophonic mega dancings.

How and if he thought he could make it, after all those tribulations about the Letras Secretas, Marcella had put him on the right track. "Jolly well," Dugal laughed. But it would be quite a chore to get don Lois from under his dusty manuscripts. Far too long some hair-splitters had anxiously kept him there, lest his figure should appear in its true dimensions. They hardly cared about the nice dilettante/ naturalist and ditto scholar. Another time he was depicted as the louse in the fur of the Viennese bear, the dissident/ nihilist, or the decadent parasite or playboy ‑ as it suited their purpose. But always for the same reason: for fear of recognition if the real ins and outs of the matter came to light.

It sounded fine to Dugal, with a little sarcasm and still a threatening overtone: *beware, boys, or I'll come up with that spare key of don Carlos! And if you dare to lift a hand at us, we shall air your dirty linen*!

Obviously Marcella was as pleased as Punch with that recording and in Catarí's eyes he thought he saw admiring approval. Thought ‑ for when they were gone at last, she did not hide her displeasure any longer. But that, he rather imputed to the presence of Marcaio's show lady n° one. In the same way as he had felt a great deal of spite on the part of his honey-bunny after the do Mar family, including Dolores Francisquita, had taken leave the evening before. In la Ionès's realm there was no place for female rivals.

But actually ‑ that ought to tickle his vanity, no? Worse was that he himself had fallen into a black hole at once. That had also been the reason of his sleepless night. *As a matter of fact, what motive had brought them down here?* it kept running through his head. The holy Trinity, plus their niece as the black Madonna, afterwards even reinforced with Robert the Wise ~ it all looked a bit like a parable, Luigi Salvatore and his Catalí forming the stakes: the taboo marriage of the canonized couple. And in the end, what had they intended to beseech from them: discretion about their identity, participation in their esoteric pact! While a bit later his Lordship the Viceroy of Marcaio came to notify to the world that a Dugal Mikes got a licence to spit out the unvarnished truth publicly. However, with the contested 'couple' as icons on a pedestal.

The more he was brooding over it, the more it was beyond his comprehension. Particularly after the whole performance of la Marcella a deep sluggishness befell him. Just like after a night's outing at Golgotha. And all of a sudden he had overwhelmed his Cathy with a heartrending impulse. "I give up, Cathy. For my part that whole funfair can go to hell. I don't want our marria- …, you to become the victim of all that fuss about some old thumb-marked scrolls of paper. You believe me?" She nodded yes, but her eyes were saying something different. Her pitying smile was a sign to him of her disbelief about his conversion. His will to become 'a different person': an unconditional lover who was going to take her by the hand, hopping carelessly and free of complexes across the island with her, his soul-mate. She was following him with her eyes while she was rummaging a bit around in the kitchen.

He was pottering a bit in the garden, poking about to find something to do, but evidently he was not on the qui vive. Like a dog sniffing everywhere for his master. And one moment later, when she had not been watching him, he was gone. Through the window she just saw the door of the side room ~ the L.S. cabinet ~ click shut. *There he goes, my detoxer. Back to his chambre séparée.*

A few ticks later Dugal staggered outside, looking pretty stunned. *What's up now? Makes you think of Carter stupefied by the curse of the pharaoh, after the cracking of Tutanchamon's tomb.* Just then it struck Catarí what he was waving in his right hand.

"I've got it, got it!" *Moragues' letter,* he signalled, right before her perplexed face. His hands and voice were trembling as he began to read out aloud, without wondering how that thing had got in there all at once.

In another walking stick by the way, as if the holy ghost of the Dux had descended upon him. On unfolding the roll he saw that on the left side quite a big bite had been burnt out of it.

rída Catalí,
Probably it sounds somewhat unbelievable
 … ut by the time we have sailed from here, we may have
 … fficially been interred in the Viennese crypt, or otherwi-
 … n all silence have got a symbolic grave, somewhere at the
 … skirts of the Bohemian Forest.
 … haps nobody will ever find out the truth and if anyone does,
 ..derstand it. Even for us, now that we have found our peace of mind, it all seems very astounding. We have been yearning for this reunion so long, Cariña, and ultimately it has come true. The question whether we have attained our objectives, seems to be entirely fading. The fact that we have secured some specimens of the Vine for posterity, and a seedling for ourselves, can be a consolation to us.

 We always regarded Maremira as a kind of natural reserve, an oasis where the best of mankind can survive, so as to reproduce itself later on, in better times. Just like on the Nymphe, remember, which some scoffers thought reminded a bit of Noah's Ark.

 In the mean time, however, the world has grown different, our ideal outdated. While part of the world is falling to smithereens, no one cares a pin any more about our dream of spiritual emancipation and peaceful unification. Those who had attributed a certain role to me in that matter, were sidetracked themselves. Or ruled out. Resignedly we had to watch the Old Regime crumbling down with geriatric complaints, same as the last emperor was suffering from rickets. Thereby leaving a gap, however, which our civilization was unable to fill. In its downfall it has dragged along a hotchpotch of nations, peoples who are now at loggerheads to snatch away a morsel of the old heritage. Yet, it had already been nibbled on pretty much. A few big neighbours are eager to appropriate a substantial part of it, and for some time it would appear that the vacuum of power on the spine of our dilapidated continent is filled up again by the old antagonists. Hyenas who have been on the lookout for a long time to get in their share of the booty.

The eternal wheel of History, you know, repeats itself herewith in the ancient inheritors of the Carolingian realm. As a matter of fact, that last European empire perished due to its own nepotism. And what can the 'victors' oppose to that? Not so much, according to the Hegelian dialectics. Some dilettantish finger exercises and reforms that lead to confusion and will plunge the Ancient World into utter chaos. I fear there are big social troubles at hand, so the new Turks risk to forfeit their grip on the economy of the nations. As usual, after the collapse of an overdue, expiring empire, demagogues can abuse the disruption to mislead the people.

A few decades further on I see once more a bunch of iconoclasts raging over Europe, false prophets hawking about with false ideals to which the people, craving for stability and new values, will surrender unsuspectingly. And such wily agitators always happen to find whole nations inclined to be placated with empty promises. The time is almost ripe for pathetic, hollow lies about salvation and redemption, and once again the amorphous hoi polloi, feeling adrift, are apt to clutch at a straw. This time, however, there is a risk that, with all the new weapons and means of power, that kind of instigators are going to mould a self-declared Messiah who, by means of the most vulgar sallies and platitudes, exceeds the boldest of their dreams. Unlike all the other Caesars, Alexanders and Napoleons, though, such a marionette can start leading a life of his own, similar to a Frankenstein who grows apart from his inventor and proves to be capable of pitting the peoples against each other. The vile war that is now being battled out in a remote corner out there in the west of the continent, might just seem puny compared to the big fire which can scorch Europe, and other continents likewise.

But perhaps I am taking too gloomy a view of things, Cariña, and I hope our offspring will be spared a lot of misery. Yet I hardly cherish any expectations from the new order which is to arise from the ashes of our cremated Occident. The reallocation of Europe is likely to come about on old foundations; the social paradises being rooted in illusions: old wine in new bottles. Want to bet that, within less than a century, the architects of the new laws will be stuffing themselves on the people's backs, as did those marionettes in the days of the Dancing Congress in Vienna?

Yes, maybe it would be fine if our own dream of a union of the European nations came true. But whether it could bring the people closer together, to fulfil our hope for a more humane and righteous world? I have never seen a codex which is capable of imposing restraints on man's avarice and self-interest. I know, Cariña, this sounds like betrayal of our own ideal. Throughout the years I have grown more and more sceptical. Sceptical, indeed, but not cynical. Sometimes I regret not putting my back enough into the spiritual movement in which my congenial spirits attributed to me a place as a leading actor. You will say: do not blame yourself too much, even David's son was unable to carry the burden of the world, the way Atlas showed us. Thanks for that, for only you know me as I really am. I was simply unequal to such a task, my belief in mankind too weak. The Enlightened Despot of the future needs the ardour of the naïve charismatic proselyte who can reconcile the extremes with his message.

Alas, the materialistic Western world does not spend sleepless nights because of an idealistic view of society, even if this comprizes the only balanced solution. Our secret peace movement seems to be condemned in advance to founder on the lower mainsprings of humanity. In fact, the rising state policies readily confuse democracy and welfare with *unbridled freedom, as the new money-based nobility can use that to disguise its own gain of profit. With that motive they manage to rope in and soothe the common people. To subjugate them without giving them the feeling that they are little slaves, grovelling for the snacks the usurer offers them. Which world reformer can vie with that, Cariña?*

And still, I hear you saying: is that what we have lived for, is there no spark of hope on the horizon? Well, that too, Catalí, is a human peculiarity: diverting, against our better judgement, our yearning for peace and forgiveness to the future, in kindred souls. Even the satirist Petronius mixed the blood from his wrist with that of his beloved female slave. And likewise you and I exchanged a sign of ultimate congeniality before the step into eternity. I recall your words: "What we were unable to achieve, may, within a few generations, be realized by another couple." So, to them, to us, querída: Duc in altum!

47

"Duke! Hey, Dugal, please, stop it, wake up!"

Vaguely he had heard her crying and begging all the time, from very far, like in a light coma, as one can hear all right what the bystanders are saying, yet no single word passes from one's own lips. He even felt her going on with fresh hankies and lavishly sprinkling scent on his temples.

"No, not ... not a bit of it," he was finally able to utter. "A doctor, are you going out of your mind, Cathy?" She was already standing there, phone in hand, and the voice at the other side asked if her husband had drunk anything. Hello? A household product or so that she had poured into an ordinary bottle, of mineral water, lemonade or so.

"You were acting queer, really, darling," she said, deathly pale. Whether he wasn't always acting that way, he tried to bring her back to her senses. Presently he would have to call for an ambulance for her. But to Catarí this was no laughing matter.

"You looked like petrified," she said, trembling and still holding the receiver. That letter, of course, it was quite touching, it had seized her too by the throat. But so badly ...? In the end it was normal that the worst came to your mind first ~ a blood congestion, a constriction of the heart or whatever you called it. Most of all for him, who had staged so many blood-curdling scenarios! So, in comparison, this piece of belles-lettres should just be ranked with the category melodrama and similar columns.

Ducinaltum. How can I imprint that into that pretty head of hers what the implication of our little persons as successors, as 'spiritual heirs' of the L.S. plan, comprises? In fits and starts Dugal began to clarify the absurdity of don Lois's projection to her. And of that queer motto.

Now the conversation he had had about that with Prof. Marquez, came back to his mind in full clarity. That was precisely what had paralysed him so much now. That trivial Latin twist that had struck him from the very

305

beginning. A neo-platonic catchphrase, purely idealistic, that the Chest had mentioned in passing. *Duc in altum* - there were many such biblical sayings in the way of: *Lead us Up High* ... Neo-platonic? My eye, this could not just be a little piece of worldly wisdom, a perk for college boys, but rather an esoteric sign of recognition, a latchkey for the initiated! In synergy with 'L.S.' it must have meant a kind of code to them, the entrance to the safe of their spiritual brotherhood - symbolically speaking though.

All of a sudden, it came home to him, as plain as a pikestaff. Dart, why hadn't he seen it before! He struck his forehead with the palm of his hand. Catari's archly drawn-up corner of her mouth betrayed her having her doubts about his reaction. She could not grasp it for all that, as this went back to his own youth.

"L.S. and your youth, Dugal - how ...?"

"I haven't told you, dear, but when Roberto broached the subject, I started ferreting it out."

L.S.: Lux et Spiritus. One of the PhD theses on Prof. Marquez's desk! He saw it again, lying there before his eyes, and the articles about the same subject the latter himself had ventured upon. Then it had been a sheer academic item like any other. Yet the connotation had kept hanging somewhere in the back of his head, and now he knew why. *The Spirit and the Light*, in that reverse order: it had been the leitmotif of his father as well. Not only in his vitalistic view of life, but also in the scarce non-fiction that his dad read, those notions kept showing up as a constant factor. In Mikes Sr.'s little cabinet that reading matter, rather bizarre for such a man of action anyway, was a main thread throughout the shelves. Dugal had always held it to be some silly idiosyncrasy of Old Sparto's, rather something for a softie, and mum Mikes disparaged it as a compensation for his extravert nature.

Yet, was it possible that senior had sunk his teeth in that kind of intellectual legacy, let alone on the same level as the concealed Archidux clan? "Well, what of it?" said Dugal. "Some pseudo philosophising, after a mental care impulse, okay - you know what that's like, in the States." But on the other hand, the longer he was dwelling on it ... Those strange personalities who had been dropping in at the Mikeses', during Dugal's last adolescent years ... They did not look exactly like Mr Moon, nor like any woolly activists. Fine people, but not quite eager to lead the New World order in the end. Or were they? In fact, were those architects of the global state really the famous bigwigs themselves from the highest banking and industrial circles? Who assured him that his dad at the time was not an abettor or maybe even a figurehead of that upper lodge behind the scenes? *But rather one with an anti-imperialist stamp,* he thought, *for he has never thought much of the idea of a nationalist super state. Hubris*, that was another of dad's classical key-words that came to his mind: old Greek for high-mindedness as the greatest human vice.

Yet no, this was more than intuition. Dugal knew for sure old Mikes was not to be bribed with obscurantism and diabolic plots. Truly, he did harbour some rather rum habits and mottoes like … Like the 'ducinaltum', damn it! Vaguely but surely it all began to resurface. Also his games with figures, which Dugal had always pityingly taken for infantile behaviour ~ numerology and that kind of stuff. Which was it again, his favourite number that junior had seen here and there at his office? 12, or was it 21? Or was he seeing connections everywhere now?

The old Spartan a furtive anti-globalist! A plotter behind the scenes, opposing the great cannons of a power elite ~ if that really does exist?" Dugal watched her, examining if those mocking lights weren't appearing in her eyes again. This time however she kept thinking aloud, button-mouthed. *Daddy-in-law really was a special one after all. And besides, the States never became his real homeland, did they?*

"How do you mean?" Even before he had pronounced that rhetorical question, Catarí turned round, with a hazy stare that went right through him. *His true origin, Duke. That was on this side, his future on yonder side of the big pond. Like an irrepressible comet, that's how Mikes Sr. had emerged from the void. The prototype of the swaggering upstart: New England made me. But as for his roots …*

Without her moving her lips, Dugal knew what she was up to. The old Axis … the Austrian-Magyar empire, ~ oh yes, family bonds with the old lung of Europe were undeniably there. But that could hardly point at a fortuitous link with the L.S. case. Or did she think his dear father …?

"I don't think anything, Duke. But what explains his sporadic travels to the old centre, without any definite destination? AND his favourite holiday haunt, Alexandria. His favourite author: Lawrence Durrell."

How did you know …, he wanted to say, but this time he kept standing

307

in front of her, stiffening like Orpheus. He knew Catarí's weakness for his old dad; at times he had been jealous because secretly she showed more admiration for Senior's acting performances and record of achievements than for his. But would he have taken her in confidence rather than his own brood?

"Sometimes you cling too much to serendipities, Dugal, and you don't take enough account of causal links. Why then shouldn't your father have had any connections of a different kind? Not such an unusual thing for movie celebs at all. One converts himself to Buddhism, another becomes a member of the Sciolistic Church. It's a pity for you there isn't such a thing like the sect of Scepticism, or you too would now have a pseudo belief."

Before she could turn away from him with that empathetic glance of hers, he seized her by the arm. "Are you saying now that …, that this whole performance seems no humbug to you? Cathy, what do you know more than I do?"

Not without a triumphant smile she confessed what she had been ferreting out herself, whilst her hubby had been browsing in the city library and Roberto's faculty. Via the web you could look up some other things than film and fan sites and YouTubes, you know. The www.ducinaltum. Alex e.g.. And what Duke's daddy had been able to go and seek out at the Bibliotheca Alexandrina. Or what an innocent woman's voice managed to find out by means of the number 12 21 12 e.g.. After the obligatory district number of course. Of Palmera, for instance.

"For instance?" he echoed, perplexedly.

Therefore he had better put it to the test himself, Catarí said slyly. That way he would find out, amongst other things, why he himself was called Dugal. So, Duke, and not Michael or George or such another plebeian name.

Oh, come on, she knows quite well I don't think much of the predestination theory and the like. You can't take me for a ride with that, dear Catherine, he laughed at first. Her unusually serious gaze, though, made him waver. "How then?"

It would be a proper thing for him at last to assess the realistic value of that last epistle by don Lois, she insisted. "Really, I think it may be a bracer for us, Duke. Or shall I say … Duc or Dux?"

Oh, oh, oh, now she was putting it on altogether; that would do, or by and by he would be going for that epithet of 'duke' after all ~ purchased title,' course. But even that banter did not leave Catarína totally unmoved.

"Let me test your memory, to see if it's still intact, darling, after all those shocking events of the last few weeks," she said, still deadly earnest. And she made him return in his thoughts to Prof. Marquez's office. Whether he could recall a certain proverb maybe, at the top of a wall or so. For a few moments Dugal was racking his brain, but then he had to give way. Only those two Greek words above Roberto's door, nothing more came to his mind.

"Precisely, Dukie boy! And what do they mean?" But okay, you couldn't expect a Hollywood star to carry that much culture in his luggage, could you?

"Hey, mind you!" he responded indignantly. Even Roberto need not have spelled out that Socratic imperative to him. Γνῶθι σεαυτόν, *gnothi seauton*, yeah, yeah, Cathy, even a classical illiterate was familiar with that magic formula of the Gnostics. Their 'know thyself' worked like a Sesame in the query for heaven: how can you grope for the gods, if you aren't even able to look into your own soul?

"Wrong, little brother, wrong! Or at least partially," she said, seemingly patronizingly. Actually it was not *seauton* that was incised there, but *seautous*.

So what? In the plural form, maybe ~ a difference of two letters, what did it matter?

"A world of difference! *Know thine, your own folk*, that's the meaning of it."

No, his empty look proved to Catarí he did not catch it. Look, this was not a mere Gnostic imperative, but an aphorism for initiates. Or in other words: know who your allies are and who the betrayers of your case … Infiltrators.

Dugal was staring at her with narrowed eyes, the way a scientist does when a quibbling lady-assistant dares to point out the gaps in his discovery.

And did he know where that very variant of that motto was also put up? She saw it started dawning on him. "Not in …?" Now he vaguely remembered, but was it precisely that 'Gnothi se- … '?

Oh yes, Catarí nodded significantly. Also in his father's little office. "And ending in –ous, truly: the plural form, as you say. "Saftous', in modern Hellenic," she said, with an air as though she knew her self-tuition manual 'Greek without effort' from alpha to omega and vice versa.

Dugal, however, was already far beyond that, mentally, to get annoyed about any such priggishness. Suppose …! *Supposing all this is right and that twisted neo-platonic aphorism warns against intrinsic spies within the L.S. movement, then how clairvoyant must don Lois have been?* Were his long-distance travels, including that voyage of his around the world, in Magelhaes' wake, more than sheer escapism or an exploratory urge, indeed? Did his contacts reach any further than 'Austausch' ~ a spiritual exchange of knowledge and ideas with scientists and thinkers, the pick of his era? If they did, then that shunted peer had created a lot of appearances. Even his dedication to the world exhibitions would prove to be no more than a pretext, camouflage for their hidden agenda. Fancy him wandering about all over the globe, in his yacht, the 'Nymphe', as far as remote California, appealing for support and resources for 'Lux et Spiritus'. Almost too absurd to be true, wasn't it?

"Yet, it could e.g. explain why our goody-goody Maremira dreamer was in the position to warn archduke Ferdinand before his fatal journey to Sarajewo."

"Exactly. Because he knew that dirty war had been delineated. And how and why," Catarí completed his line of thought.

"And by whom!" Dugal mumbled. *The Dux was familiar with the Rockers and fellows and their unscrupulous schemes for financing armed conflicts. So as to manipulate the industrial complexes at their will. Manifest 21 was already in the making: divide and rule, and tailor the world to your size!*

"But so … That would presuppose he had found out the peace movement had been betrayed from within. Already back then."

Catarí was sitting there, just gazing at the receiver. As if that contained the answer to all questions.

12 21 12, she had said. Who had thought up that number ~ the universal 12 as the opposite of the magic 21? Where would they be connected then? Certainly not to a bureau of the U.N.. What preoccupied both of them, though, was the question how they themselves fitted in this whole scenario? What had led them to Ses Taca, them of all people, instead of some more autochthonous tandem ~ such as Tonio Brasandes

and his missus e.g.. You weren't going to tell them there was a higher power involved, and even via father Sparto at that.

"Imagine ~ Mikes senior, a pawn in the tradition of the sanctified spirit!" In their family, nota bene, moulded in only one belief: in Fortuity, as absurd as the astrophysical laws. But he was thinking of the ambiguity of don Lois's portrait. A bon vivant with a certain devotion to the holy Mary, albeit for M. Magdalen probably. All of a sudden he seized the receiver.

With ice-calm fingers he dialled number 12 21 12, suggested by Catarí, behind the Palmera area code. After a few ticks without any reaction he already wanted to put down the phone, when all at once a female voice came through. "Voice-mail probably," Catarí thought.

"Gnothi …?" a voice said and then halted a moment. Once more he was about to lay down, but changed his mind. " …seau …, seautóus," he went on, with the sudden consideration it might be a code connection. Promptly there was a response from the other side: "L.S.?"

"Lux et Spiritus. Light and the Spirit," he said vigourously.

"Alex?" the voice sounded again. *No Alex at all, baby*, he grinned, but he just kept himself from mentioning his name. They were looking at each other in despair. "Maybe they mean the Duc~ …" Catarí made a guess, and "The Ducinaltum?" he said quickly, short of breath like a first-year student, afraid of spoiling his last chance.

It remained silent for a while. Were they way off the mark and did this work like a one-time chance for logging-on? "Alexandria? Bibliotheca Alexandrina," he rattled, in an ultimate attempt. "We're putting you through presently, hold on," a voice said. Followed by an intimate passage from De Falla's Jardines de España.

"I know that voice from somewhere," Dugal murmured. "Marcella," said Catarí apodictically. You're kidding, he repelled the idea, and as there came no other reaction, for some minutes even, he himself began to believe it was an insipid joke. "Lay down," even Catarí agreed. At that very moment, however, there was a click on the other side and another pre-programmed voice sounded: "Bienvenido, señor Dux. We have been expecting you for a while. Finally you have managed to slip through the different security locks of our secret connection. This 'Bienvenido, señor Dux' proves that you are THE person to lead and support our operations … You will be given further instructions on another number," the speaker concluded after a few moments in a humoristic overtone.

Don Carlos, Dugal mumbled to himself. *I could have thought so.*

With an automatic reflex his arm reached out for the receiver again. Perplexedly Catarí watched him, clicking the numbers as if some spirit from above whispered them in his ear: … 21 12 21, in the reverse order. After that he nodded at her, sure of himself, that he could efface the question mark between her eyebrows. *Señor Moragues, you'll see. Who else?*

Another female voice picked up. "Dolores!" said Catarí straight away. Now it was his turn to look baffled. *So typical of women, that primeval instinct that enables them to smell their rivals from afar.*

Exactly the same keywords, the identical way of putting you through. Would that connection too be programmed, or live? Now it really looked like eternity, while the questions were rushing through their heads, the tension all but strangling them. If it came to a conversation … ~ íf, then it would cross his lips right away: *Has Lux et Spiritus been completely hauled in once again also this time? Infiltrated and scooped out by the financiers of 21?* They did not dare to look at each other any longer, but never had they been so closely united in spirit, so intertwined. And in case they were not going to be shattered, swallowed by an anonymous Mogul, how then in God's name could they, the chosen ones, stand up against the financiers of the eternal hatred, ingrained in mankind?

"Bienvenidos, señor y señora Mikes. Time has come for our action."

Speechless the couple were sitting there, their hands clasped together.

"Hello, are you still there, señor Dux?" Yet it took Dugal some more seconds until he could clear his throat and ask in a hoarse voice:

"You, Roberto …, why you?"

48

At once Dugal had jumped into his little Séat. Spurred on, like a lunatic who had swallowed a cocktail of LSD, extasy and coke. And without thinking of Catarí at all. L.S.: *Letras Secretas, Luigi Salvatore, Lux et Spiritus* ..., it was raging in his head, while he rushed off from the wood path to the coastal road. Don Lois and his spiritual enlightenment. That's how they wanted to sell that good old Dux to him, the whole Do Mar clan, including la Dolores and Marcella, *and* Roberto Marquez, the sturdy Prof with an LS obsession. To complete the show, they had engaged *the* heavyweight of Marcaio: don Moragues, the commercial jack-of-all-trades, who joined in their project, according to the gentlemanlike principle he used to cherish: live and let live, if only Marcaio (and himself) benefited from it. *Señor Dux, time for our action has come.' Pull the other one!*

They had a nerve, those fellows, wanting to hitch him to their carriage, while they had kept him dangling all the time, under the misapprehension that he was played on by a mob-like gang! Well, now they were going to learn to know him in his true shape, that little Dukie whom they had chased to and fro across the island like a marionette. Like some chased animal.

Chased? One moment all his feelings halted, his frantic rage, his bottled-up frustration from the past days. This was not going to be another red herring, was it, an umpteenth insipid dido to divert them from the right track? *Damn, why have I left Catari behind to that presumptuous bunch - the 'desposyni', phew, whatever!* But on the other hand, it could not all just be co-incidence? The fact that they wanted to make him, celebrated glory of the white screen, a signboard of ...

Yes, of what? Dugal jammed on the brakes, as if some giraffe or rhino were crossing the road, whack in front of him. For a while he was simply gazing in the void: *shall I turn round or just drive on, straight*

313

to the goal: the lair of the Chest? Just then he heard the beep tone of his mobile phone. Probably it had been whinging for some time without him noticing: the leitmotiv of the Walkyrie, played by a barrel organ. '*Catarí*', the personalized calling-list on the little screen said! Quite a reassurance anyway, for she wanted to call her madman to order: hey, idiot, where are you hanging about?

"Yes, baby, sorry that I dashed off like that. Now I'm here at …"

To his own astonishment he found himself to be already quite a distance up the Col de Fanabia. It had all gone so fast.

"Hello, Mister Maïks," said a harsh voice. "Your baby can't answer at this moment, because she is sitting here with us, handcuffed, a wad in her mouth. Normally, nothing will happen to her, if you stay reasonable and return nicely … to your safe homestead. In fact, we have a bone to pick with you …"

"Don't believe them, those louts want to blackmail you …"

It seemed to come from very far, but that muffled voice ‒ it couldn't be but Catarí's. Dugal snapped the phone shut, the rest did not interest him at all. No conditions, no identification, no why. Catarí, his life, his only sense of living was at stake, that's what counted! With a tug at the steering-wheel he turned the car round, in the opposite direction, heading down at full throttle. If possible, he would have flown through the bends and over the rocks. *Who was that, what do they want from us, how much brass, or is it again that stupid L.S. connection they are after?* Innumerable questions were scurrying through his mind, while the Venta Morena, the old tavern in the last hairpin bend, came rushing up to him …

Of that last part of his crazy ride he had no remembrance at all. The track to Ses Taca through the wood had seemed endless, though. Each tree was drawing up to him threateningly, as though behind all those stems a gnome were waiting for him, to treat him to a sawed-off specimen: bang, plop on his little Seat, and they could drag Dukie away, as far as his pinioned Cathy. But he had got through it, and there he was, standing still on the yard in front of their house. Nothing, a deadly silence. He saw no other car, no single trace of any burglars.

No time for circumspection, he thought, for each second could be of vital importance to her. He still saw himself ramming his shoulder against the front-door, and in there a blinding intense light was shining that suddenly seemed to give immense dimensions to the hall: a celestial light source ~ which painter had he got that from again: Altdörfer, Grünewald, or was it a Fra Angelico adept after all?

Dugal's eyes were blinking rapidly while he stared up in disbelief: where was the ceiling? Then it struck his eyes, a gruesome sight: there, at an invisible thread, she hung, in a long white dress. Or not quite ~ "Stop, don't move, Duke, or they push me off!" Catarí shouted, in a strangled voice. She was standing on a board that had been laid across a cupboard, jutting out over the banister. Only now he noticed the figure standing behind her. A big bloke in a black suit, but his face was not quite distinct because of the strong lighting.

"Hey, Zorro, what do you want?!" he heard himself calling loudly, but that did not seem to make much impression on the sinister figure.

"Finalmente, señor Maïks. Bienvenido!" he said, while he held Catarí at the throat before him, arm stretched.

"No time for pranks, bastard!" Dugal shouted, but the strength of his voice was inversely proportionate to his inner calm. "Take my wife away there and I'll do what you want. What are your conditions?"

"Oh, oh … His Lordship is already coming down a peg or two! That's what I like to hear. Well, I'm telling you in advance: if *I* jump off this board, it will knock over and … goodbye, Missis Maïks! So, our little transaction is to happen hic et nunc. You understand? Here and now, pronto!"

Dugal was standing there helplessly. What he should avoid now, was nettling this weirdo. The only thing he could do was nodding: *go ahead with your claims ~ what do I care? Even if I have to appear on the cover of Playgirl or get my last penny out of the safe … I'll do it all. I've no choice anyway. You, Catarí, are my everything, my only poss-* … He had almost thought 'possession', but in all the misery of the moment he imagined with a grin how furiously Cathy would react to that.

"Well then, Mister Maïks, we've got just one condition, one demand: your L.S. documents."

Dugal swallowed. He had reckoned with anything, but this … "That … that won't work. I can't … I … I haven't got them."

The lugubrious figure took a deep breath and said grumblingly: "Oh really? You can't. You don't have them. More 's the pity … Then this act makes no more sense either."

He lifted one leg, ready to jump, and Dugal already saw Catarí going up and down like on a springboard.

"No! I will try to gather the copies, but I cannot promise that I …" he shouted in despair.

"Mister Maïks," said the man firmly, "for us there is no 'but'. We have warned you often enough. This is the limit, our patience is exhausted. Adíos!" And while he was tilting his weight on one side, the board canted over frightfully and Catarí slipped away. "NO, NO!" he was still able to scream …

"NO NO NO!" he had bounced up in his bed, with pounding heart. His bed? Utterly stunned, he was looking around. There they were, all of them, in a semi-circle: Dolores, Roberto, Marcella, the old do Mar couple, and Catarí alongside, her hand resting on his right shoulder. "Easy, easy now, everything's going to be fine!" she spoke soothingly.

"Is going to be fine. Fine," he echoed, parrot-like. "What's wrong with me then?" *Am I paralyzed or have I lost a leg?* "Why can't I …?" he groaned, in a spasmodic attempt to sit up.

"Relax, señor," a nurse now interfered. "You are altogether healthy, but as a result of the smash …"

"Smash? What happened then, did I fall? But no, impossibly, it was you who tumbled down, Cathy, I still wanted to intercept you and then …"

"An evil nightmare, darling," Catarí said apprehensively. "You crashed into the façade of that venta …"

"La Morena. Bumped up to it, so to say," Roberto now completed. "You know yourself, eh, amigo. All aflame and ablaze, you certainly wanted to grab along half the stock of hierbas there," the professor said with a wink.

"You only have a few broken …"

"Fractures?!" he shouted, and promptly got a sharp twinge in his chest.

"…ribs," said the nurse. "Therefore you've got a sedative injection, lest you should move too much."

"With the result that you were raving on quite a bit," said Catarí, stroking his forehead. "Raving? Talking gibberish, yes," Roberto poked fun at him. "You were knocking together a whole scenario, you know!"

They were all laughing pleasantly together, but Catarí's watery eyes told him it had not been funny at all. "But how?" Suddenly it came back to him again: that phone-call by Catarí's kidnappers, and how he had raced back home like a rabid dog. And then that scene with that board and …

"You did not get back home at all, Duke" said Catarí. She looked at him pityingly, the way you do with a beloved who starts seeing the most extraordinary things. "Hey, I'm not going crackers, and I'm not hallucinating," he protested.

"Of course not," she appeased him, looking round at the others. This time la Marcella came to her aid: "Really, you didn't get any further than that last bend in the descent. A little later I myself passed by that place too. By chance those wooden benches in front of the venta happened to break the brusque contact with the wall there."

"And those dreamlike fantasies must have been a projection of suppressed fears from your subconscious," also Dolores Francisquita contributed her bit at last.

Grimacing with pain, Dugal managed to lean a bit on one side: "Thanks, professor Jung," he groaned, and I am Freud, I guess?"

What's going on here? he thought. He was definitely certain about that alarming message, that gruff voice, and the fact that his Cathy had tried after all to warn him. Or … had it been a trick to calm him down and lure him back home, after that tantrum of his? Out of the question, wasn't it? Suppose they, the whole lot of them here, had been in league with … Catarí! And then it had all got out of hand, because he had, once again, been panic-stricken. With this fatal result in the end …

"Is this a conspi- … racy maybe?!" he exploded again, but had to throttle back at once because of a twinge, after his impulsive outburst.

"Mister Maïks, you must absolutely relax. And avoid any excitement," the nurse interfered again. She injected a solution in his drip and some minutes later he was overwhelmed by a sense of heaviness that took all resistance out of him.

As his eyelashes started to tremble again with the first sunrays, like the wings of a butterfly, and a whole bird orchestra besieged his eardrums with an exuberant twitter, Dugal felt at a total loss. *In what century am I awaking? Have they administered a truth serum to me or dumped me in some lunatic asylum, in the dunce's corner of the civilized world?* Half numbed, he turned on his side and then he saw Catarí. Hanging a bit aslant in the armchair near the window, she had dozed off herself, her mouth slightly opened. How cute, he thought: a watchdog that has passed into dreamland.

"Hey," she smiled, stretching her limbs with the limberness of a purring cat. "Welcome in the realm of the lotus eaters. You've slept around the clock, you know." At once his brain began to spin around feverishly again and he wanted to ask her hundreds of questions at the same time. Yet his lips seemed to be glued together with sticky silicone and his throat was as coarse as sandpaper. "Calm down," she said. "You've got to restrain yourself for some time, after all those ventures."

Dugal took a deep breath, with closed eyes, as her hand stroked his cheek. Lucky dog, he praised himself, that he, of the entire male gender, was granted this preferential treatment, and by such a guardian angel at that: the wet dream of his whole kind. Concurrently though, some scalding suspicion arose in him again. Suppose his mad race had really ended against the façade of the Venta Morena, and all the rest ~ that abduction and the macabre execution ~ had all been just a nightmare … Why then did that panicky voice keep echoing in his mind: *Don't believe them, they want to extort you* … For that had been unmistakeably Catarí's voice, and that phone call, *that* was actuality, right before he had flung himself down that mountain pass with such a contempt for death.

Catarí was likely to feel what was he brooding over. He could derive it from the wrinkle that drew a bow between her eyebrows. *On that most ravishing forehead in the whole history,* it ran through his mind. For which Caesar would have betrayed Rome and even Hector his Troy. But wasn't it precisely those beautés naturelles who managed to utilize their pretty face for personal purposes ~ the Cleopatras and Helens on whose behalf history had made such shenanigans?

She was just going to bend over him (for a little mea culpa after all?), when the door opened and one of the white coats brushed her off: "Señora Ionès, would you just …?" As she looked round in the doorway, the man got a stethoscope and a pressure gauge out of his pockets and talked encouragingly to him: "Just some test measurings, señor Mikes."

Measurings? And what then about all those wires and contraptions he was connected to? Still, the fellow carried on, meanwhile probing Dugal's memory: "And sir, do you remember some more things already?"

"What should I remember?" Dugal joined in the game, and all that the doctor was angling for, he rebounded with another empty question. *"Docky,"* he thought, *you're not going to take me in, not even in a thousand years. This is no hospital, but a psycho ward. Damn, they've dumped me in a nut-house!* On the spur of the moment, his hand reached out and he gave that psychic a slap, right on his small specs. At the man's confusion, Dugal slipped out of bed, pulled the wires and all along, flung the door open and took to his heels.

He could not have got much farther, for a few minutes later he came around, status-quo in the same bed. Still a bit groggy due to the effort, he saw a behemoth of a lout coming up to him. "That's just Roberto," said his Catarina, holding him by his arm, as if she were afraid he would tear off his cannulae once more.

"Where's that false doc?" he said and Catarí had great difficulty to get it through to him that this poor soul was not a disguised shrink at all who had to declare him loony. "Darling, what crazy things are you doing?" she sighed and for a moment he even felt sorry for her.

"Dear chap, you whacked that poor fellow nearly into afterlife," the Chest now also drew up to him. "But you were certainly thinking: I'm just doing a rehearsal now for the oncoming scenario about 'The Dux and the Duke'." Prof. Marquez shook his head, with pursed lips and that commiserating look that would make Dugal freak out at times. And he told him he had been obliged to use all his influence to keep him out of range.

"No police, eh? Don't blazon it, eh?" Dugal suddenly bounced up in bed, with a snappy, ferrety phizog. Roberto straddled beside him on the bed. "No," he said, closing one eye, "you don't think that I ..., that we ...?" And he turned towards Catarí: "Would you believe our lordship here suspects us of ..."

"...of hoodwinking me with a rehearsed act?" Dugal balderdashed in between. And now that he thought of it: hadn't he first heard the cracking of a recording that was turned on? Simultaneously that scene sprang to his mind ~ apparently from his nightmare, while he had been lying there senseless ~ and suddenly he thought he recalled from very far that threatening voice. Darned, it had sounded so much like Roberto's!

The worried wrinkle on Catarí's forehead made him almost ashamed of his own assumptions; fallacies, weren't they? Her very way of nodding: *What brings him to these ideas?* was enough to make him waver. To his, and Catarí's, great surprise, however, Roberto Marquez all at once nodded affirmingly: "Well, in some sense you are right, amigo. At least regarding that menacing call on your mobile. That voice recognition is correct. As far as Catarí's voice is concerned."

"What's all this about?!" Cathy looked totally dumbstricken. Dugal gazed from one to the other, without knowing what to think of it all. *Are you going to let down each other so soon?* he wanted to sneer, but the Chest muzzled him quickly. "Now listen for one time, Mister Duke! Whilst you were dozing and raving here after your failed F1-zigzag race along the flanks of the Fanabia, some people here on our banana island, as you like to call it, did not keep lying on their backs."

Roberto's unusual apodictic tone made Catarí and Dugal watch each other glumly. "I wanted to withhold the report from you, to spare your concussed portion of grey cells a bit. But now that I see you are your own rabid self again ..."

He produced his cellphone from his pocket and went up to the window, while making a few calls in the purest, unpolished Marcaín. *Who the devil is that gorilla calling together?* the Mikes signalled to each other behind his back. Suspicious though Dugal remained about a possible game of those two behind his back.

"That's it, my dear," the professor turned to him again, to pat him on his shoulder. "In an hour they will come and update your memory. In that way you needn't hear it all from me, because ..." he winked at Catarí, "the nearer the Church, the farther from God."

49

He must have been dozing off for a while again and when he awoke, he was sitting in an arm-chair, in a sterilely furnished room. His first idea was: *Ses Taca, they have pillaged you, say it is not true!* All tinted grey, the colour he and Cathy hated so much. *Those maniacs who change the world into a lab, I'll wring their necks!* In an urge he wanted to jump up and vent his rage on the first thing that came in his hands: a metal chair, a glass bowl with plastic flowers ... But he was not able to. His legs refused and on further consideration he proved to be buckled at his waist. In a wheelchair!

Damn it! They've diddled me! The next thing that entered his mind, was: *a confinement cell, they've dumped me in a lunatic asylum!*

On Dugal's thumping a little nurse hopped in, Mister Maïking a bit panickily. "Qui-iet, Mister Maïks, qui-iet!" and right behind her came another white smock-frock, allaying Dugal by his own calm demeanour. "Mister Mikes, you are still residing in our hospital, you know, so there's no reason to get agitated. But we thought you would already be able to receive your visitors in a wheelchair, in a somewhat more comfortable environment than your room. If you are feeling well, you may take the pains to try. What do you think?"

What do you think?! How could he know what was coming up to him, but dumbly nodded and watched the nurse, who positioned herself at his side: en cas que. Then 'the visit' was shown in. Catarí and Roberto ahead ~what did you expect? And behind them a sturdy figure, but without the whole retinue of Doloreses and Marcellas he was reckoning with.

"Señor Maaaïks!" bawled the third man, heading straight for him, arms wide open, and now in the light Dugal recognized him. Señor Moragues, don Carlos ... The tycoon of Marcaio! So that's what he looked like in the flesh: all vitalism and charismatic appeal, thàt one had to grant him.

Before he could overwhelm Dugal in a billow of rhetoric violence, the

321

latter took away his breath. "Aha, that's what the new Rey de los Bailares looks like!"

Adeptly the big man made a 360 degree rotation and asked theatrically: "And? What about this view?"

"Well … A little less enlarged than on the telly, I should say. But still enough imposing!"

Señor Moragues guffawed uncontrollably and unaffectedly. His buxom figure suited him as well as the striped costume in which he could have staged a publicity shoot for Armani. And that's what Dugal told him. Whereupon the big ship-owner burst into   Homeric laughter once again and then chortled in his turn:

"And I see the viceroy of Marcaio is still alive and kicking. Apparently that car skid did not scathe his mental resistance at all. Still blessed with gift of the gab, that's how we know him, hmm?"

From the others don Carlos got sufficient acclaim, but Dugal did not pass up the opportunity either: what was it then that urged His Highness to pay him a visit in his humble cell? "I know that complacent look," he said to his small public. "Almost like a pre-electoral triumphalism exhibited by a president to announce, in the middle of the balloting fever, that he has caught the last terrorist."

"One to one! Shall we leave it at that?" don Moragues reached out his hand to him.

"A draw. Why is that so hard to believe for me.?" Dugal could not help driving his counterpart out of his corner. What prevented a born winner like don Carlos to give a bozo in his situation, already smacked quasi kayo before he could become a threat on his territory, the coup de grâce?

"Do you remember," Prof. Marquez interrupted their sparring match, "what I told you earlier?" Dugal gazed at him with a glazed expression: *you have been puking so much bunkum already*. But then something began to dawn on him, like: *in an hour you'll know more*, and he would be astonished about that bloodcurdling call. At once all his pugnacity arose in him again.

"If that voice wasn't yours, Roberto … Then, then …" Dugal's eyes flared at don Moragues. He also descried how the latter and the professor touched each other's elbow, as a commiserating signal: *please, you tell him*.

Two uncles who ignore how to elucidate to their nephew, just waking up from a coma, that all the while his wife has got another lover.

"Now we can assure you with certainty, señor Maïks, that we've got him!"

"Whom? Black Peter?" Dugal acted Simple Simon. But when he saw Marcaio's big man showing a painful grimace, he felt sorry for him.

"My menfolk managed to spot the instigator behind all those hmm … occurrences. Look, we think that you thought that … we thought that your phantasy would run up in a stampede. That, with all those threat letters and false messages, you were going to suffer from paranoia. And admit it," he said with a broad grin, "you began to suspect all of us a bit, didn't you?"

"Your menfolk?" Dugal igored the question. "Like those chopper pilots and paramilitaries?"

"You can regard them as some personal militia, yes," said Don Carlos in a chivalrous tone. "I know that, as a true-hearted democrat, you detest that. Godfather methods, I understand you. But you may be reassured, they are boys from FC Marcaio, the club that I sponsor. In their spare time they do some detective work. The way volunteers do so for the Red Cross, they play Interpol, the hidden camera on this island, on behalf of the real sleuths. A severe selection done by myself, believe me."

"Wow, and what did Mister Double-Check find out that can put himself and Professor Chest on the leeward?"

Dugal saw that his irony ricocheted on the man. Señor Moragues in his turn left the honour to Roberto, this time. Dugal had never seen him so serious before. "Brace yourself, Duke! The chap they arrested, the pivot of the whole action, is someone you would have expected the least."

Dugal's eyes swerved from one to the other. *Are you playing an 'ad absurdum' game with me, to see how daft I am?* But the professor didn't twitch a muscle: "Not just on suspicion of, or with downright evidence. He did confess!"

"He?" Dugal did not notice any trace of sarcasm yet on Roberto's face and he asked whether and where he could see 'him' then. "At the central police station maybe?"

But the Chest rattled on: "You'd better prepare for that confrontation, amigo. It's almost like your alter ego, someone you believed you can hold on to through thick and thin. A rock: Peter, but who was to disown him thrice before the rooster crowed."

Peter? He did not know of any Peter, Dugal still acted a bit indifferent, but actually he already burned with curiosity. "Take me there. Come on, straight to that charge room or jail cell. I want to see what you have contrived."

"Hmm, you needn't appear at a police office for that," said Mr. Moragues, and all at once Catarí interfered in the debate. Obviously to avoid another miscue of her chickadee.

"That man is in our home now, at Ses Taca."

"Fettered and all, rest assured," Roberto agreed with her, for the consternation on Dugal's face told him enough.

"My men are there with him, mister Maïks. We wanted to settle this in all discretion, so as to avoid any needless hoo-ha. Every further decision is up to you. Therefore we are glad that you want a complete clarification about this case so soon."

All of a sudden things went full tilt. After a last 'veterinary inspection', as Roberto remarked facetiously, they headed per wheelchair for don Carlos's discreetly aligned cohort opposite the Palmera municipal hospital. Four armoured cars, beside which a few decent-looking fellows were waiting. Roberto and don Moragues all but jumped over each other to help Dugal out of the wheelchair, under Catarí's vigilant eyes.

During the whole drive Dugal kept sitting there feckless, staring blankly. He'd rather have soared over the Sierra Fanabia in a supersonic jet plan, landing in the trees around Ses Taca by parachute. The sooner he would get that bloody bastard in his hands, the better.

Catarí anxiously kept an eye on him and in front the professor nodded at her encouragingly in the rearview mirror: *all's going to work out fine.* But her heart shrank when she thought of the moment they would be driving up their drive. Dugal did not want to wait for the wheelchair and stumbled to the door leaning on her arm, but there Roberto already had to come to his aid. That bushed he was after that short effort. "Just take it easy. You've just been patched up, my dear. And please show now that you're that cold fish they all take you for."

Fishy he did not feel. Rather oafish and helpless. With limp legs Dugal faltered in through the hall, backed up by his two male bodyguards. But cool-blooded? He tried to recollect a shibboleth from a historic movie in which he had to give the heroic incitement: 'Whatever emerges there, brace yourselves!"

But the conjecture of who was actually in there, his tormentor, manacled at that, did not give him any combativeness at all. Hadn't Catarí been there with him, maybe he would have backtracked to no avail.

In the first salon, still in the rural style of yore as Catalí d'Omar's tavern used to be here, there was nobody. From that rather dark room they moved to their favourite parlour and through the half-open doorway they already heard the small company congenially laughing.

The kind of chiaroscuro in which the room was enveloped by the softened light, gave the scene an unreal effect. Was that the pre-trial custody they had promised Dugal for sure: with a bunch of thoroughly plastered security agents clowning around and sipping a dram with the bloke who had been browbeating him all the time?

"Well I never!" There they were, don Carlos's praetorians: caught in the act, cheerily toasting with their tumblers! And in their midst the villain in charge, relaxed and altogether uncuffed, over a few of their bottles of hierbas and paló. How dare you …! Dugal was about to kick up a row, when the man rose up so that the light fell fully on his face "Hello, Mikes!"

Dugal felt like hit by a stroke. "You, … Cormick! The last one I had expected. You, gallows-bird ~ how can you!" If possible, he would have throttled him, lynched, clapperclawed him … Kkkrrr …

And then, Dugal passed out once again. Just a few moments, this time. He still heard everything they were saying, but from very far, without him being able to react. *An ambulance …! Is there no doc around here …? His blood pressure, it's definitely just a syncope …*

Quite soon, though, he came to himself again, looking around, a bit dazed, at the two angels at his side.

Then, as his sight was sharpening again, he recognized Catarí, who was holding his hand, and at his other arm was Manolita, fumbling with a pressure gauge.

Where are you coming from, all of a sudden? he wanted to ask, but their maidservant said: "You're getting much better again, eh, Mister Mikes? Ten over seven. Pretty normal, such a drop in blood pressure, after what you've been going through."

"Our Manolita has got a professional training. Fortunately she happened to be just around the corner," Catarí hastened to stand by her, so as to remove Dugal's suspicion. And that's what the pretty lassie did look like: *professional, above all,* Dugal simpered.

Queer, wasn't it, how those Do Mars popped up wherever you did not expect them? "Mister Mikes is now fit enough for a short talk. But please, take it easy," said the youngest scion of the clan to someone at the rear.

And then, that blighter came and bowed over him: "Hey, it's me, Carmichael. You still remember me, don't you, old buddy? We both used to form quite a close-knit team. An unmatched twosome, that's how the bosses of the film biz often called us, eh?" The way one talks to an old schoolmate one meets again after half a century, in the old people's home. Senile and a bit dozy. That's how Dugal stayed there for a while, staring vacantly, as if the man in front of him were an exanimate dummy.

Wouldn't I recall you, 'buddy'! he thought. Carmichael Ducrichon - Cormick, or Doug, for loyal chums, sometimes also snidely nicknamed 'Duke Richton', by some envious confreres. How often hadn't they tagged along together? Carmichael as a scriptwriter, producer or stage director, in so many a project, and changing shapes every now and then. Doug and Duke, they had been called in one breath at every turn. Each other's antipode, but in many respects also each other's complement. Not that they formed an inseparable duo, à la Selznick and Cukor, or Gilbert and Sullivan. Sometimes they would chew each other out, yet they were to cross paths over and over again, due to common interests. In a sense, Cormick was Dugal's alter ego: where one tarried, the other persisted; what one of them squandered, the other managed to rectify.

And now this harbinger of script and screen would like to diddle him. He of all men, and not the Chest or don Carlos; not to mention Marcaio's obscurantist sodalities. But perhaps this too was just the umpteenth red herring.

Don't react to it, he thought. *I let you squirm a bit, my friend, and then, you'll have to come up with more sensible arguments.* He enjoyed putting his old pal on the rack and at the same time he felt sorry for him, the way he was wriggling to get through to Dugal. Pathetic, actually.

"Would you leave us alone for a while?" he rasped, ignoring the two men's raised eyebrows, as well as Catarí's surprised look, giving her the feeling he could also miss her assistance. "For a private talk with this character, please. Just between myself and Mister Corps Diplomatique here: Cormick Doug," he had to add on behalf of Moragues's watchdogs, who were reluctant to just buzz off without a sign of their patron.

After all of them had got out, unwillingly ~ Catarí last of them, her burning eyes shooting rockets at Ducrichon: *hands off my hubby, or else you'll have to deal with me* ~, Dugal said gelidly: "Well, CD? What about it?"

To an outsider they would have seemed a queer couple: a somewhat lanky but portly figure, leaning forward and putting himself out in humility vis-à-vis that convalescent man in his wheelchair.

"You are not going to believe this, Duke. Yes, those Moragues blokes have snapped me. An underhand pack that work for an astute magnate, you daresay. And okay, I've set op all those actions. That is … not altogether. I've only coordinated them. In other words, used them in order to accomplish my goal. I … I wanted to draw you out, tear you away from that darned inertia. Man, this life is not meant for you, here on this drowsy island. Okay, perhaps nice for sun worshippers and retired pen-pushers, but not for someone of your calibre, Dukie." He hesitated for a moment as Dugal watched him with a dirty glance: 'Dukie'?

"Yes, I know. You were to throttle back a bit, flee the hurly-burly. But that was

basically Catarí's idea, wasn't it? To be honest, such a romantic whiff: both of you in a nostalgic hacienda, a life in the Land of Cocaigne, without any paparazzi around every corner … Wonderful to relive your honeymoon once, but damn it, man! There's still so much to do for you. And for Catarí …"

Dugal let him run to and fro, his arms drawing circles in the air, and he gloated over the man's excitement, as though the ultimate deadline of life were at stake. *Rave on, boy! I know you've something more on your mind.* And out it came all at once.

"Okay, Duke, perhaps you start displaying some forebodings of dilapidation. In the end, there is that small age gap between you. But that's no reason to detain Cathy in your antique cage here, in such a remote hole. Or are you afraid her success might exceed yours? The first diva who trespasses the unwritten cinematographic law that actresses will get on the

327

breadline as their external beauty is losing its prime time value. Whereas your own status would sink to category B-movies, with high wrinkle level.

That one hit the mark! Normally Dugal would have ripped such a braggart's throat straight away, or at least verbally smothered him. But he knew what was the only way to tackle this specimen: in cold blood, as he was gasping for breath. When there came a gap in Doug's torrent of words, Dugal clapped his hands: "Bravo, maestro! Couldn't be better. You would have made a first-rate lawyer. But it's no use trying, I know the real motive for your whole scheme here."

He waited a little: the lethal moment before the matador will give his fatal blow. But CD too was fully immersed in his victim role, staring at him with a question-mark between his eyebrows: *oh yeah, and what do think that is?*

Now he was about to give him the broadside, but Dugal was astonished about his own equanimity while doing so. "Jealousy. Envy of my career, my flukes in the film biz. My windfall at material and private level. And most of all, because I scored better with the other sex."

Carmichael kept gazing at him, with dilated pupils and his mouth wide open. His head was turning red and any moment Dugal expected a fit of rage. Suddenly though, his old chum burst into laughter. An irrepressible, uncontrolled laugh, lasting for minutes, it seemed. Until at last he went pale and had to clutch the table. Dugal scrambled to his feet and started patting him on his back, as if Cormick had swallowed a hot potato that had to get out of his oesophagus at any price. "Sit! Calm down! Breathe quietly!" That's how Dugal stood there, clearly in panic all at once, lest Ducrichon should be choking.

50

I think you've always envied me, buddy. For my successes, the laurel wreaths that I got and you covertly aspired; all the Oscars that I notched and you failed to hook. Oh yes, the critics used to laud you, your vision and your facile pen. But the awards you did snatch away, were mere crumbs, peanuts in comparison. From your own point of view. While I was walking on the red carpet, with the most gorgeous actresses at my side, you were doing the honours along the side-line. Falling in with shabby art buffs and wrinkled governors with their spruced-up ladies-in-waiting.

All sorts of things ran through Dugal's mind as he was standing next to the panting, prolapsing Carmichael, uncertain what to do. He had already patted him on his back several times. All in vain. He was just about to call for help, when all at once the man started to cough and at last he came around. "Eh, eh," he groaned, making some grating guttural sounds. "You see, Duke, nothing's so dangerous as a fit of laughter. Now we are quits, I think."

For a while they kept chuntering, Dugal a bit warily after seeing his old chum gasping for breath. And the latter was glad he could now get a bit closer to Dugal. "Yes, Duke, I admit I perhaps overstepped the mark. But no pain, no gain. You know how we sometimes think, you too. In our branch there are moments when you take life for a screenplay. When I started at it, I thought you were going to find it wacky, afterwards, yet brilliant material for a smasher. Come on, man, I wouldn't want to do you any harm. Never."

"Now drop that sentimental twaddle, Doug," Dugal rebuffed, "or tears will come to my eyes. You'd better tell me how you got to it, and from which moment onwards."

Dugal listened to the braggart with the necessary scepticism, as usual when Carmichael Ducrichon, alias Doug Cormick, got on his soapbox.

He swore up and down that one day he had disembarked on Marcaio, totally unwitting, just to drop by and, okay, in passing pick up a gratuitous vacation in a historic frame. Quite a windfall, eh? But the first thing that struck him, on his way from the airport to Palmera town, was the paper the newsvendors were wielding in between the cars, at every traffic light crossing. "Letras secretas, publicación por Señor Maïks en el Diario!"

"What? So you don't question the authenticity of those letters?"

"Not at all! I wouldn't dream of doubting about that. Dugal, do you believe I could regard you as a forger?" Or ...?"

"Or what?" said Dugal, dewy-eyed. But he could imagine Cormick's discontent that Dugal would suspect his old mate of that. "Do you really believe I hid those letters in there?"

"All right," Dugal parried. "But what would you believe in the end, if they spread such a net around you? For a blood-curdling scenario you would toss someone to the lions, wouldn't you?"

"You don't believe that yourself, do you?" the other grumbled. "You know, while I was reading the first instalments, I saw at once it was bound to become big stuff. This could be no mystification, as your literary friends themselves recognized the hand of the master in it. I gathered that you would throw yourself on this unique piece, with all your ardour. And that you were bound to meet with a lot of resistance ..."

"...which you could readily exploit. Poke it up, 'co-ordinate', as you like to call that. Macchiavelli games."

"Ah, let's be modest. It wasn't so difficult after all. At the hairdresser's, the baker's, in the estancos, at the counter of a bar ..., everywhere it was the daily topic of conversation. Barfly wisdom, you'll say. But on Marcaio you pick up a lot in that way. For a dram of hierbas or a glass of beer you can find out many a state secret, you have no idea."

"Just a moment," Dugal interrupted him and returned to the door in his wheelchair. "Here's someone who wants to make a public confession," he shouted, "and I want some witnesses, for I'm not going to put this on record."

Catarí ushered the others in, saying: "Dugal, there's someone else here who may be interested in this." Manolita made a sign from the portal and there came señor Rainieri, flanked by his wife and Dolores. The whole Do Mar-clan, Dugal sighed.

It took a while until everybody had drawn up to the table and got a drink. "You stay here too," said Catarí, holding Manolita back by the hand. "All right," Dugal said, "Mister Ducrichon is all yours. Please, shoot your arrows at him!"

"Ouch, should I feel like the worst doping sinner now on granny Winfrey's lap?" the latter chortled and at once the ice was broken. Cormick did not wait till Dugal or don Carlos started shooting with live ammo. "In Dugal's view I'm Judas now," he said. "I confess everything."

And the infamous scenarist set off telling spontaneously: from his arrival up to the point when he got into action himself, under the spell of what his old buddy was contriving again. Without any lucrative intentions, he assured. Just for the story of that unique LS figure behind it. "And the remarkable link with this Duke," he added. His first informers had been common people: manual workers who had got wind of something along the edges of the 'milieu". Mere small talk for pub crawlers, as he said before, but it had led him to some clear traces.

"And señor Carmichael will not withhold those sources from us, that's for sure," don Moragues hampered his statement, and Cormick sighed almost obsequiously: "I can hardly escape from that, can I?"

At first he tried to explain why actually he had the same aim in mind as Marcaio's tycoon himself, but the latter's ironic cough stopped him again. "Those groupings, eh? Hmm, yeah, I don't know them so exactly by name. Actually they were three of them. One politically biased: an extreme rightwing party, I think; one of rather religious inspiration, equally conservative, it seems; and a cultural organization in between the two others and using them for its own purposes. Very language-minded and all that ..."

"Let's say separatist," old Do Mar now spoke for the first time.

"But he does know them, I can tell you," don Carlos now stirred him up. "You were in contact with them anyhow, weren't you, my friend?"

"Yes, hmm ..., well, not really, only indirectly," Cormick Doug shirked out. But with so many pairs of eyes burning at him, he was compelled to give a detailed explanation. Via his contact persons ('bar counter friends', he called them) he had got every leak seeped from one group to the other. "Those first, stark nationalistic activists - it sounded somewhat like Cuba Libre ..."

331

"Bailares Liberades, the autonomists," don Moragues said drily, "right-wing, of course, but radical? Well …"

"Those, oh yes. They went off the deep end at once ~ hmm, which led to some material damage …"

"My cabriolet, dammit!"

The smirking twist to Doug's mouth showed he was somehow enmeshed in it. "Sorry, Duke. I had recognized your car there near the lib. and showed it to such a seeming Rosicrucian: *Look how the king of Marcaio drives!* How could I know the building yard nearby belonged to a fanatical native? A bit of dust or mud I would have liked to see on the coachwork of your car, just to tease you a bit. But something like that, no!"

Why, he had only encouraged the 'cross-breeding' between those two reactionary pillars, Dugal sneered. And he hadn't by any chance made common cause with a pseudo-professor, a Schnabbel, who had to come and sniff around here in their very own house?

"Allegedly of the Viennese university? Let's keep that one under wraps!"

Mister Ducrichon had to admit that sneak had hoodwinked him. His research work was simply meant to exhort Dugal, but that little fellow raked in the payola to resell his precognition underhand to a third party. However, these blokes turned out to be pretty xenophobic, targeting at all that was Anglo-Saxon. Fortunately they had failed to hit Dugal, but all but blasted away a copper. Oh dear, Doug couldn't mask his secret pleasure: he had seen that vehicle himself from afar, completely buried under the pulp ~ the second 'error' committed by those fellers. "Hey, do you know who that bumped car belonged to? To the mayor of Palmera!"

For a moment Dugal had to contain his laughter, but at the same time he felt like grabbing his old pal by the throat. Who could guarantee him Carmichael had not pushed on those free radicals so as to discombobulate that little Yankee … If need be, make him a head shorter? "Do you know what *I* think, Dougie? That you were not just standing alongside there by accident, as an amused spectator. No, it was you who shoved that pack of paparazzi on my neck, drove all those guards of the holy L.S.-grave bananas by way of the rumours about don Lois's alleged saviour's role. Oh yes, and then there was that resurrection theory with regard to his beloved Catalí ~ that was pure grist to your mill, wasn't it? It enabled you to exasperate those rogues and thus crank up the agitation. How far would they go to put me through the hoops? Toss my car down from the Col de Fanabia; put a little bomb at Plaza de Llosera, under the car behind ours. And who would tip the journal section of Radio Marcaio, with a deliberate false message, you guess? *After the detonation of the explosive Dugal Mikes is said to have been carried off by his scurrying wife.* You don't say so. I see little Cormick sitting behind the window in the nearest bar, laughing up his sleeve!"

"Oh oh, take it easy! You're seeing ghosts everywhere or are you really getting paranoid?"

"Do you know what I think, my friend? That you threw gobs of moolah at those yobbos to knock me down a peg. But rotten luck: again and again it was a fall-through. Even with Marquez junior as a crash pilot in charge you tumbled out of the prizes. But ran into extra expenses. And what about Jordi Martell's death? An unfortunate incident, that was. A rope dancer should beware of a fatal outcome, shouldn't he?"

Now it was Doug Cormick's turn to freak out. "That takes the biscuit! Are you going to tell me I'm after everybody's blood, merely for a screenplay about a forbidden, class exceeding romance from the good old days? As though I had staged it all in advance. Putting a film crew at every corner, in order to register each of your movements, every scrimmage with fictitious extremists. Look …"

What Doug wanted them to see, was to remain unknown, for at that very moment a servant of the Do Mars' dropped in out of the blue. "Look, there's an extra broadcast with La Marcella on Canal Balear." He carried a laptop in his hands and pointed at the screen: Catarí hurried to the TV set so everybody could watch it on a bigger display.

After a few seconds there she was, Marcaio's infamous hostess, in a flimsy blouse. In the pre-announcement they must have mentioned the Archiduque and now Marcella sent the fox in to count the chickens: " …today's special guest: señor Mortado, who has come to lift a corner of the veil about the LS file. Señor, you seem to have more inside information. Is it possible that you have led the other people involved up the garden path?"

That grin on the face of that typographer seems familiar to me, Dugal grunted. "How dare you think anything like that, madam? You surely know a number of Archiduque fans are listening now, like the Do Mar family, Messrs. Mikes, Marquez and Moraguez …, Ducrichon ‑ welcome, gentlemen. And the ladies too. I also know it's the job of a TV presenter like you to rake up rumours. And journalists like myself? They must dig up extra facts so as to shed light on unsavoury practices. In this case the machinations of extremist groups eager to exploit the LS-connections, so that …"

Bang! A loud blow at the rear of the studio made the two speakers duck down. Automatically also the watching guests at Dugal's side jumped back. *What's going on?* They saw a few masked men running up to the camera, Mortado was overpowered and one lifted La Marcella up in the air. She was kicking around, just in front of the camera, so everyone could see her scanty thong. Then a leptosome lout nestled himself in front of the mike and took off his balaclava.

"Aldorfo! Esto bandido!" Moragues and old Do Mar had leapt to their feet, with wide-open mouths. Dumfounded, they were watching how the bony bloke started to deliver his tirade. In pure Marcaín, utterly Delphic to non-indigenous fellow-countrymen. Just here and there the Mikes were able to pick up a few words, enough though to understand their seditious verve. " …discharge the autonomous government … blow up the regional parliament … occupy the radio and TV broadcasting stations … install a revolutionary council …"

"Stark raving mad," Roberto muttered. "They want to liquidate everything. Proclaim a right-wing free state 'Bailar', how daft one must be!"

"That's going to end badly," señor Do Mar whispered, and when they asked him whence he knew that rogue: "Aldorfo? A great-nephew of ours who called himself that way. After the Conde de Altdorf, you know. He fancies being the real heir of the Archiduque. They ought to …"

But before this, otherwise so dignified, gentleman pronounced his curse, they saw another armed gang dashing into the studio. There were some mean blows and some gunshots. Then a flickering screen image and after that no more. A black screen, silence, nada. "An assault on the broadcasting station, oh no, Marcella, poor thing," Catarí screamed. "And Miguel," sighed Roberto.

A few seconds later the screen flashed on again, as quickly as it had evanesced. An ordinary lady announcer was sitting at her desk, but in another studio, as if nothing had happened. But the nervous twist about her mouth spoke volumes. "Queridos spectadores," she said, whilst trying to smoothen her ruffled head of hair, "please excuse me for this short disturbance, but a deplorable incident occurred at our studios …" *As if we didn't notice,* Dugal jibed, but 'Shhh, did the others. The nice beaut drudged to minimize things, but by and by she was spilling the beans. For the sake of her objective reporting, which otherwise would be spurned anyway.

"A small group of extremists invaded a few of our filming studios today, in an attempt to hijack our staff and master our broadcasting station. In vain, as it turned out, for they had been signalled and a bit later they were overpowered by the guardia civil, backed by the security agents of señor Moragues. All of our co-workers got off unscathed. Only Miguel Mortado, who happened to be in our studio just now, was taken to hospital with minor injuries. Hmm, just now we …"

The news anchor looked aside at a paper that was handed to her. "We … have just been told now that another assault, a … small putsch was attempted on our Marcaian parliament. Just after the capture of our broadcast station a few gang members tried to commit a coup d'état by force of arms. Soon however this resulted in a scuffle with the guards, resulting in a few injuries. When an intervention team got into action, a barrage fire broke loose, with casualties on both sides. Two of the raiders managed to escape and intruded into the conference hall. Reportedly they …"

After another short hesitation the presenter reported grenades had been thrown, causing total panic among the parliamentarians present at that moment. All in all, the damage turned out less bad than was thought at first sight, as did also the number of injured, since the politicians were able to seek cover. One terrorist was in a critical condition, as a grenade went off in his hand. The other, eliminated by his pursuers, had a list in his inner pocket, containing the names of envisaged targets, among whom …"

Like petrified the Mikes and their guests were staring at each other. Each of them heard his or her name on the wish list of the extremists, as the news lady read them out without blinking. After that another guest speaker sat down beside her, in Mortado's place. "Marcella's husband," Catarí cried out. And that's how he presented himself: "I'm taking over Marcella's chore for a while and I'd like to wind up tersely señor Mortado's research."

He summarized the actions and motives of the radical gang in one apodictic upshot: "They have only one aim: fight everything that could profile don Lois as a cosmopolitan, pan-European pacifist." Therefore, he concluded, everyone who confirmed that image of the Archiduque, was a thorn in their flesh and … had to get out of the way. One could just hope that now this nightmare would come to an end.

"Amen," said Ducrichon, jumping in front of the screen, and he looked at them all. "Hey, this is really a bridge too far. What if this scenario is another mere frame-up?" Like a bat out of hell Roberto and Moragues pulled him away there: "Stop play-acting, you dimwit!"

Promptly the news anchor took over from La Marcella's husband again, but faltered just as quickly. She glanced perplexedly at the computer screen at her side, turning to a co-worker who handed her a page. "Dis …, disculpe. I've just received some very inconsistent messages here. One announces that the LS-centre, Son Maraitx, was bombarded, but hmm …"

Dugal was now eyeball-to-eyeball with the speaker. *Need I pull it out of you?* All at once she rattled on, as if she heard it: the second message explicitly gainsaid it all. The local live cams in the museum, dedicated to the coryphaeus of Marcaio's cultural élite, proved there wasn't a cloud in the sky. And then …, the police had just apprehended a cybercrime gang specialized in computer simulations. Apparently they had put up the whole scheme to mislead the public opinion. Perquisitions and arrests had been carried out and, according to researchers from don Moragues' retinue, the whole network had been rounded up.

The young lady turned a quadrant with her swivel-chair, as if she were looking at another camera. With a roguish smile ghosting around her mouth, she said: "And now we have a big surprise in store for those who don't believe in the resurrection: the come-back of an alleged victim of this entire LS-operation. May I present to you? Mr. Jorge Martell!"

51

─◆─►◄─◆─

There they were sitting once again on the back terrace of the old taverna, high up, below the crest of Col Fanabia, bedazzled like a couple of blowflies that have been chased persistently with a swatter for minutes on end. The Conca de Llosera deep below was bathing blissfully in the deep afternoon glow. Eyes half-closed, Dugal tried to fancy a haze of Botticelli's gracious oyster-shell as if any moment his Venus could emerge from it. But only Catarina's yawning mouth was floating on his retina, behind his cocktail glass. Not filled with hierbas or ice-cubes this once, but with ordinary mineral water from the nearby spring. The maidservant had added a sprig of rosemary in it. "For the fragrance," she winked. *Hmm, yummy.* But was he dreaming or had this rosemary a suspicious taste of Xoriguer, the local gin?

"Hey, here's your Aphrodite." How Catarí managed to read his thoughts over and over again! At the same time her gaze strayed off to the villages scattered around in the side valleys behind Llosera: Binaritx, Forlunaix, Higueras … Mere miniature houses in a puppet museum. Even the church of Llosera looked like a youth sin of a Gaudí adept, with her somewhat capricious façade: a pretty-pretty toy for a bored god.

"It' all so unreal," she mumbled. "Indeed," he sighed, a bit groggy, due to the aftermath of the recent ventures rather than that bit of 'spring water'. Catarí, looking pretty wan herself as she was sitting there, sipping at her straw, as if that draught of horchata made of chufas could pep her up in a jiffy, squinted aside lest that whole mountain flank should tumble over them. What else could one expect? After half a morning of checkups at the hospital and then lying on the physiotherapist's rack. "You are fit for service again," that fellow had said jokingly. *Doesn't he really recognize me or as is he doing as if? How evanescent global fame can be,* had crossed Dugal's mind. However, upon parting that bit of a masseur asked Catarí for an autograph. Therapists? Ravers, that's what they were, and Casanovas! And what nerve that chap showed while opening the door for her with an elegant gesture: "Take care your husband doesn't exert himself!" But okay, he was so lucky he could walk again without a crutch or rollator. Contrariwise, Catarí would have been stuck with a cripple for a lifetime. You'd better not think of it.

Thence off to a reunion with the whole LS-clique. All of them were present: Roberto, Dolores and the Do Mars, la Marcella, Carlos Moragues, Mortado and, last but least, Jorge Martell. In a cosy, old-fashioned bar near the Moorish palace, papered all over with pictures from the good old days. Among which the Archiduque did not fail, of course. There even hung quite a batch of LS-images and sketches, and oh yes, a couple of Catalí-pics as well.

Roberto Marquez welcomed them with professorial phlegm, but it was don Carlos who said: "In this very tavern my bisabuelo and His Highness met several times. It was don Lois's favourite haunt, so to say." And indeed, he also showed them a few drawings of his forebear.

The patrón with his eye-catching whiskers sent for some huge, paunchy wicker-bottles. It looked like a scene from Murillo's epoch or a painting by Ribera Gomez, for the two daughters were graciously hip swaying along them, as if they figured in some zarzuela, two big steins of Bavarian beer in each hand. Perhaps nicked by a trainee at the HB or some other Munich beer temple? Not that the tongues needed loosening ~ they had already set about blabbing blithely without one drop of the exquisite liquid. And soon the high-spirited ambience was growing into a real cacophony. The way they were all talking off their heads, it was hard to believe that a few weeks ago the whole island was going berserk. Jorge Martell was not lagging behind either. Again and again he was congratulated with his resurrection. It was not until they got seated for a few tapas that señor Moragues could becalm the tempers.

"Dear friends, I consider myself lucky to welcome all of you here for this little Round Table. Contrariwise, we should now be bemoaning the absence of one or more of these invitees." *Straight to the point*, Dugal smirked, and from the corner of an eye he saw the Do Mars furtively looking at each other.

With wide strokes Professor Marquez depicted the course of the recent LS-intricacies and all the rumpus about the Dux's manuscript scrolls. "We should try to apprehend the sensitivities the publication of these articles caused in certain layers of our community. Exasperation sometimes, disgruntlement because of the alleged lack of respect. Anxiety too about the uncertain destiny of their own parentage ..." *I daresay,* they saw honourable mister do Mar sigh affirmingly. But he nodded at don Carlos and the latter expressed his relief that the storm had abated at last and now the old tranquillity of mind had spread again like a comfortable blanket over the island.

"If there's one thing we've learnt from this adventure, it is the way this deep-rooted solicitude can be misused by certain opportunists. So far we have been living in the fallacy that it's still nice to dwell here peacefully, on our Isla de la Calma. While the crazy world around us seemed to be ablaze, we remained spared from the turbulences in this era. Terrorists, suicides with bomb belts, desecrators of monuments and ruins ..., it was all so far-flung. Such crackbrained firebrands fitted in the jumble of New York or Paris, but here? Our jolly old-fangled Palmera seeming a mere loafing site for wobbly retired pen-pushers. And our creeks and beaches, they are painted red by grizzled beatniks and nostalgic daydreamers. Nobody ever thought any kind of sinister specimens could mix with us, islanders, and our guests, sneakily hatching their evil schemes. How naïve it is, in fact, to believe in our immunity against microbes that infect our whole globe! Now it's like awakening from a bad dream.

A world fire is raging around us and we see the smouldering sparkles blowing over to our archipelago. Never will our fragile little world be the same again. But mind it, didn't our ancestors think the same, as far back as don Lois's days? Why did he go into hiding here, why did he experience a romance here which the fine de fleur in those days could not grasp?"

"Yes," Roberto Marquez set off again in his turn, "and then a Marcaio worshipper blows in from across the Big pond; quite soon a fistful of cryptic manuscripts turns up and there the ball starts rolling again. And to cap it all, right after that some dodgy scriptwriter lands down on a hilltop ..."

Everyone was sniggering about the way the professor portrayed Ducrichon's cunning: his slick method of pitting the various camps against each other, the ultimate aim of which was a docusoap in which the actors are unaware of their role in the game. And thus he literally dragged Jordi Martell into the affair, the seemingly dead graphic and forger, suddenly rising from his ashes.

Reluctantly Martell came to the fore. *Welcome to my resurrection.* "Apparently everybody was taken in," he laughed peevishly, but apologized excessively at once. "I couldn't but perform a suspended animation. Otherwise it would have grown much worse. Then also our peaceful island would have suffered a real carnage."

After a firework of questions he confessed his plot with Carmichael Ducrichon. Lately Doug had turned up out of the blue with a darned scenario. It all looked so innocent after all, turning around the illustrious, venerable Duque *and* with Duke, that deuced actor. Two controversial, yet celebrated he-men ~ who could take offence at that in a time like this? Besides, that naughty approach appealed to him. A cross between hidden camera techniques and collage effects.

Quite something for a copyist like himself, with a hidden agenda and a box of tricks. They also knew that Duke at first would be furious, but afterwards be over the moon with the result.

But they had not reckoned with their host: Aldorfo, the self-declared heir of don Lois. But in fact no more than a wicked wretch, surrounded by a horde of rough rowdies, eager to beat up all that did not fit in with their way of thinking ~ a rectilinear brotherhood with an explicit loathing of differentiated opinions and particularly of morbid spirits with an IQ beyond 80.

With Jordi's help Doug had explored their natural habitat: dusky pubs where those heavy thugs could carry out their favourite hobbies. There they would be hitting the bottle all day long, venting their wrath about that tourist cattle of palefaces who were making their beaches unsafe. If it were up to them, Marcaio would before long be a paradise free from bonobos and honkies. In the face of that raffle it was no good option to flaunt one's curiosity. Such blokes had a sense for it, when it was blatantly clear you wanted to pump them.

Jordi and Doug proceeded pretty cautiously, but evidently one of their infiltrators had sneaked. The payola won't have been big enough, Jordi grinned. Another informer had suddenly done a moonlight flit. Slain or sent up in smoke? One could make a guess at it ~ anyhow, both of them had sniffed the miscalculation in time.

"Consequently we simply had to back down. As quick as lightning the scriptwriter in Ducrichon had devised an emergency action: I was to feign a stroke, by means of an old home-made herbal concoction, and he had to perform a metamorphosis with a false beard and another passport. My artificial coma was nicely provoked by a doctor Alarò, by means of some micrograms of deadly nightshade, opiates and God knows what kind of alchemistic hocus-pocus; afterwards sneakily adjusted by an antidote from belladonna or so. De verdad, the man's great-grandfather had already been the Dux's personal physician. And señora Catalí's too," Jordi added with a significant wink. "And yes, everyone walked right into it. The 'coroner' and the undertaker themselves too were close friends who were in on the game. And before I realized it, I awoke from my suspended animation on a pleasure yacht that took me and Doug to the neighbouring island Meniza under a starry sky. There we went into hiding with the Capplèr family ... Kindred to the Kappelers from Galileio."

However sophistical, Jordi Martell's report hit home. There was nothing else they could do but take it for granted. Doug's devious vanishing act at their house had already given them a sample of his cunning. All of the whole company were eager to know what that slyboots still had in store.

Promptly Jordi produced a smartphone from his trouser pocket and let them listen to a recorded message: "Hi, this is Carmichael Ducrichon. I think I owe you an explanation ..." What nerve he's got, each of them thought, but after the message they heaved a sigh of relief. Doug had gone with the wind, to Madrid, and there he had handed over all his takes to an impresario who was soon to deliver them personally at Ses Taca. Ensuring it would exclusively remain an embellished documentary about the Dux and Catalí in which their 'amour secret' was treated with wariness. And on the assumption that Duke too was bent on stashing the LS-documents safely, in the same spirit, where they belonged: in Marcio's collective patrimony. "No speculative suggestions, no roguish sensationalism, no theatrics whatsoever ... Promised. Herewith I confide everything to the parties involved. And to the sound judgement of the finder and owner, Dugal Mikes."

No speculative intentions, no sensationalism ... What a swanker!

While Catarí was standing near the iron fence, at the brink of the ravine, overlooking the Conca and the villages deep below, Dugal was staring ahead, absorbed in thought. How that whole company had put up with Doug's gimmicks just like that! One great relief, as if all objections had been swept away, without any further consideration. Carmichael the repentant managed to take them in with one mea culpa: he had taken calculated risks, but underrated the local zealots. And apart from that? No sweat at all. How could you let yourself be buttered up like that? As Roberto Marquez had phrased it: the genie was back in the bottle.

"…in, or out of the bottle?" At first he thought it was Catarí, but it was the bar girl who was leaning over him with the hierbas jar in her hand, a little worried about the guest's hazy glance. Had he been grumbling to himself so openly?

"Oh dear," Cathy came and sat down again, "my husband is a little frustrated about the outcome of the Archiduque's intimate secrets, you know." On that, she gave him a stroke in his neck, the way one does to a boy whose toys have been taken away.

"Those hidden letters from Don Lois' cañas? Wonderful! Never have I read anything like it." Catarí en Dugal looked at the girl with growing amazement. Were those ardent eyes of hers just sparkling with adoration for the celebrated star? *Or for both of us*, Catarí thought. Or was there more behind it?

"You needn't regret anything, señor. A secret can bestow deeper richness and inner satisfaction upon us when we share it with only a few people, but rather in spiritual affinity, that is. Come and have a look, I have something else for you."

After a moment of hesitation they followed the bright cutie. *Does she remind me of someone or is that sheer imagination?* it ran through their mind. She took them along behind the counter, under a door lintel. *Mind your heads*, she pointed. After four, five steps they were standing in a mezzanine, soberly but cosily furnished with a three-quarter bed, covered with a lace bedspread, a polished escritoire, a large closet and a showcase full of old books. They stood there, facing each other with uplifted eyebrows. The young lady nodded: *up there*. Inside, above the beam, there was a small painting. "A sopraporta", said Catarí spontaneously, as they appeared in many palacios. *The Col de Fanabia*, they suddenly realized. That was here!

Not just a landscape, no, but this very spot where they were standing now. In the middle a transcendental light shone that pulled your sight to the central point of the picture. And there ~ it made their hair stand on end with dismay ~, there was the little house, their locanda, the wine bar. But if you looked closer … They were standing right under it now: the outer wall seemed almost vitreous, so translucent, the way the artist had painted it. Bit-by-bit it was shimmering through, this room in which they were standing now! Here! The girl pointed at the signature underneath. "Can you read it?

Dux … Duci. "Ducin …," she helped them. *Duc in … altum!*

With a broad smile she congratulated them. "He painted this himself, with a clear wink at their private secret." Now that sympathetic damsel was getting just a bit too mysterious to their taste and the ambience in the small chamber sweltering. *The Dux himself? To be sure.* They knew, as everyone did, that Don Lois was a gifted draughtsman. Hundreds of pen drawings he had made, to illustrate his botanical descriptions by which he had mapped out the local Mediterranean flora. A natural talent, according to some biographers. But that this deuced homo universalis had also made paintings? "Once in a while, as you see," the lassie smiled.

With ever intensifying interest they looked around in the room. "Did he sojourn here in this pied-à-terre? Stayed over, wrote things …?" From the writing table and the bookshelf with thick leather tomes ~ the Dux's complete works ~ their gaze swerved back to the narrow bed. The bar lass could read their thoughts. *And he, did they … here ?* "On Catalí's part for sure," she said. "In hard times, you see." An allusion to the non-official post-mortem version. Now she went to the bookshelf. One push on the hidden handle underneath and the shelf made a half-turn round. From the opening behind it she took a wooden box and put it before them on the little table. LS, was engraved on it. ""The magic box," said Catarí. An irresistible force urged them to open the wooden lid. Then, in disbelief, they stared at its contents: exactly the same kind of paper scrolls as in the Dux's cañas. But these ones were tied up by means of a silk ribbon. *No, don't say these are no copies of …?*

"Go ahead," said the girl, and with trembling hands Dugal picked out one. A triplet of sheets, he noticed, as he unfolded the specimen in a trice.

For a moment he watched the two women with bated breath and then he began reading:

> *Caro mío,*
> *I have received your first letter from Bohemia. I was so much seized by emotion that I ...*

52

Dugal rubbed his eyes. He could not grasp what he was seeing. An answer to the letters *written in exile by a tormented mind?* What every right-minded person was apt to regard as an elevated form of soliloquy, self-consolation, would not have a schizophrenic dimension after all, would it? He cleared his throat and read aloud:

> *Caro mío,*
> *I have received your first letter from Bohemia. I was so much seized by emotion that I could hardly open it at first. And now, a long time after reading it, the images are still floating through my mind. Your description of the arums in the first place and the way you compared me to my favourite flower. Ah, which woman would not feel dignified by so many words of praise? Too great an honour in fact for a common girl like myself. Yet, somehow that fits in with your raving about my homeland, does it not, of which I and Ses Taca make part, in your view. But it does you honour, the way you put our 'natural nobility' above the high claims of the aristocracy. To me that proves so well your aversion to the arrogance of the beau monde.*
> *   As far as your demure confession of your own shortcomings as a lover is concerned … However sincere that compunction may sound, such pangs of conscience are thoroughly unfounded. After all, as you got your eye on me, and on Ses Taca, I knew what was in store for me. In the end the same happened to me: the first moment we exchanged glances, the soil seemed to sink away under my young feet. Had the moirae, those fortune spinsters whom you did not*

believe in, chosen me for a hopeless, whimsical love game? In my maidenhood I dared to fancy anything, save that at this moment of recognition our path had already been outlined ...

Dugal lowered the letter in his hand, staring ahead, visibly flustered. Catarí could guess very well what was going through his mind. At first she wanted to stir the girl of the venta by her elbow, to suggest: *this is getting too much for him at this moment, forgive him - you see, he is not so tough as he would like to appear.* But as she watched the lassie from aside, she saw in those young, perfect traits an unexpected apprehension, as though such a damsel could read her hubby's mind just as well. And suddenly it occurred to Catarina what Dugal and she herself had sensed a while ago, in a 'moment of recognition': *this maestra, like two peas in a pod, really looks like ...*

"Señor Mikes ...," said the girl and he had the epistle taken gently from his hand. With a commiserating smile she led him by the arm back outside, on the terrace, where the bulbous hierbas bottle looked at them like an angel that awaits us at the heaven's gate.

In perfect unison they were all three of them caught up in listening to the warbling of the birds, while in the gardens, some levels below, a student-guitar-player was violating a piece by Granados.

"If you want to read the rest of the letters ... You're always welcome," the young lady said. "But I have the feeling that our ideas about this forbidden romance have much in common. Probably don Lois and Catarí would have felt their secret safeguarded with us. Or am I wrong?"

Dugal was looking at her as if he came back from another reality. Had he actually heard the bodega lass or was he so absorbed in his own thoughts that it did not register with him? "Yesss," he lingered to say and to Catarí's surprise he put his hand on the new maestra's shoulder. Why didn't she feel a shade of jealousy this time? This was a totally different Dugal speaking. Even for her, who knew him from the in- and the outside.

"Of course they would. These scrolls change everything. They give the mysterious, sometimes passionate letters by the Dux quite a new dimension. They put his views in a different perspective. And you are right, Cathy. That's how it is, isn't it? Or shall I say ... Catalina?"

The young lady nodded cryptically: "As you say: Catlina. But then …, you both agree with me?"

Then they huddled around the little table, holding each other's hands. *A peculiar everlasting alliance,* each thought to himself. So few words and yet so much unanimity. This find, this extraordinary batch of letters, in response to the ostensibly anguished effusions of a soul consumed by nostalgia, gave the LS-affair a completely unexpected turn. What shortly before still seemed a bizarre game of blackjack, a soliloquy of a schizophrenic spirit, in which the bewailed beloved levitated over the island like a sylph … ~ that literary unicum suddenly lost the magic of its frenetic, eccentric goad. Catalí's writings provided the clear proof that the Dux's confessions were no psychotic dreams of an old fool. No more than these replies gave a message from the hereafter. Whoever read them, at once felt the lively testimonial power of a smouldering passion. Those words debunked the picture of don Lois as a demented weirdo, withering in the web of his own imagination.

"Without you, and without the contents of this box, Dugal would never have given up," said Catarí to the reticent Catlina. "To him don Lois's spiritual legacy hidden in those cañas, was a piece of heirloom Marcaio and the whole world were entitled to. And now …"

Well, now, Dugal could merely nod, now it was absolutely private matter. The perquisite of two people who, under the wrong constellation, in the wrong epoch, had endeavoured to break the chains of prejudices and caste norms. A tantalization, as they were to find out to their own expense. Yet it had not prevented them from braving the crosscurrent, even if the whole establishment shed all its anathemas over their heads.

"I'm so pleased with your understanding, señor," Catlina said with an ironic smile. "Though it must be a pity for you to let this artistic project slip by."

"I daresay," he affirmed. But what was most important ~ that a jewel remained in possession of the one it was meant for, or of a descendant, or that it was up for grabs to voyeurs and old biddies? Dugal now realized that the LS-vibe had unchained a storm and had staked quite a lot of human lives. A scandals section à la Choderlos de Laclos or the rebuked idyll between Madame Sand and her Polish protégé was small beer in comparison. It just showed the moral sensitivities had not changed a bit with the hoi polloi in a hundred years. Still the same prejudices and hypocrisy they had already fallen victim to themselves. It is just that the part of class-consciousness was now surpassed by the yellow press. That was always sure to find some harmless victim who would get crushed under the wheels of the rumour mill. Even a princess of Wales or a first lady, all the same. "As long as it provides food for scandalmongering. Some people gloat over aggravating attitudes that are unpalatable to a number of their contemporaries. But are they really aware what extreme reactions that may trigger?"

Each of them recalled the scenes of carnage the papers were bulging with, the last few years. The further our technical development was spreading, the more the world was exposed to ribald fanaticism. Here, on this archipelago, it had always seemed so far-off. Fundamentalists, terrorists? Anywhere but here. The Bailares remained an oasis of common sense, an outpost for reasonable, good-willed people. Nothing of the sort! All that time there had been brewing a kind of petty intolerance. And what was worst of all, somehow Dugal had to agree with the sceptics. By what right had he attempted to deprive them of one of their greatest paragons, a cornerstone of their spiritual heritage? As though one wants to dig out a saint in order to see if he lived up to rules of asceticism, or retrieve a pharaoh from his place in the sign of Orion.

"Perhaps it was a bit amiss to sneak into don Lois's life like that," Dugal mused. "Oh, a bit, just so" Catarí winked to Catlina. They couldn't help grinning about it. Had it been that clear then? Dugal got to admit meekly that he had fallen into the trap of his own empathy. Really, that nasty quirk of the impassioned actor to live in the skin of his persona! Victim of his professional misshaping, so to say. With some highly motivated theater fleas that imitation virus had so strong an effect that even in daily life they kept playing their impersonated character. "Just fancy: they get wrapped up in their role so much so that in the end they start to believe they are a president or an investment guru themselves. Or Napoleon, or the first lady's bodyguard," Catarí taunted. "Yes, or a Russian woman spy, homicidal showgirl, an Interpol lady sleuth … Even a movie star!" retorted Dugal.

But they were both used to that kind of teasing. But ah, their dramatic zeal had never taken them that far. Neither of them could blame the other for showing any signs of a manic obsession or being imbued with schizophrenic inclinations. Professional attitude, it was called, and that presupposed the spiritual resilience to disconnect in good time. Dropping one's persona on the bedroom rug. But whether it would be so easy for Dugal this time as well? "Me identifying myself with the Dux? Come on."

Of course you wouldn't, Catarí clicked her tongue. Duke and the Dux, they did not have much in common, did they, except for the likeness of their nicknames? "Indeed," he admitted frankly, "I 'm no match for him." Such a universal spirit, with that versatile knowledge … Who could compete with that in this age of levelling superficiality? The ladies were jointly snickering at Dugal's overt raving about his idol from bygone times.

The adoration was as thick as butter. Catarí was quite aware that he also realized how difficult it would be to give up his dream. Comparable to an inventor who is reluctant to renounce his invention, even if it is contestable and proves to have evil consequences. So, against his better judgement.

"Do you allow me to abduct you to the cellar for a moment?" Catlina suddenly distracted their attention with a roguish laugh. And as they looked up in surprise *(what, another LS-secret?)*: "No earth-shattering discovery, you know. Although …"

The Mikes exchanged such dazzled glances that the lass did not unnecessarily want to keep them in suspense. "Our clandestine home recipe," she grinned. "Hierbas."

They all three of them burst into a hearty laughter. On the I.o.Marcaio that was a current practice. Every family used to prepare its own herbal liqueur, in some hidden shed or shanty. And each boasted his 'secret', as a matter of fact endless variations on the same theme. But an anise drink, that was as vague a term as beer or tea. The tastes varied with the medley of plants they used for distilling that concoction.

Closing his eyes, Dugal sniffed up the fragrances ascending from the dale alongside the terrace. The scent of lemon balm and angelica, of fennel and mint, of chamomile and wormwood, of orange blossom and aniseed, all those essential substances were mingling to an undefinable conflation in his nostrils. What qualities were attributed to their mysterious elixir! Digestive, stimulant, sedative, heart-fortifying, … The panacea that survived dynasties. *And dispels chimaeras*, Dugal chortled. While the ladies were going downstairs, arm in arm ahead of him, he took a last glance at the world above: a captain who overlooks the upper deck before moving below decks.

Duc in altum. What else had he expected to find on the upper threshold of the cave door? It was engraved there in a handwriting that looked suspiciously much like don Lois's. A kind of Sütterlin of whatever it was called. Tilting his head with a grin, he ducked under it. *Maybe His Excellency once did so on his way down, to subject the Do Mar home recipe to his well-trained palate.* The winding staircase was electrically lighted, but by apposite torches mounted on wrought iron fittings. Here one was led down by the nose following a steadily intensifying liqueur odour. And there they were already waiting for him, a little tasting glass at the ready: his Catarí en 'Catlina'. The duplicate of Manuela, their stand-in housekeeper, or of the deceased Catalí? No oak barrels here, but glass distilling flasks – neatly labelled with date and name: Catlina, do Mar, Rainieri, Catalí …

Compliantly he had his glass filled with a little dash of the stuff. Swirling the glass in slow motion, eye-lids closed, he sniffed up the inebriating aroma. *Mmm, exquisite.* But before he could utter a word, when lifting his head, he found himself gazing mesmerized by the vaulted wall behind the shelves with the big phials. *There, look!*

"What's the matter?" The two lasses were staring at him commiseratively, like at a beloved who one thinks shows the early symptoms of altzheimer. His wifey came to stand by his side and while watching with him, she started kneading his neck. "Duke, there 's nothing on that wall That's imagination. Due to the heat outside and eh …, then that cool draught here. Isn't that so, Catlina?" Catarí looked at the young lady with an imploring glance: *say it isn't true.*

But he seized Catlina by the arm: "But you see it, don't you? You know what is scrawled there: *Isch furkte misch* … Just read!" With an apologetic nod at Catarí, the girl said: "Si señor. I do know." And she explained: behind the craquelé paint effect on the stucco there was a cached text, hardly visible to the superficial onlooker. But someone who scrutinized this place on the wall, could discover the enveiled message underneath. The magic-eye reading technique, as they called it. "But you need a bit of imagination for it," she laughed. Catarí too made an attempt, half closing her eyes like in a hypnosis session, and after some time a kind of text seemed to be getting through. A piece of poetry maybe?

"A favourite poem of the Archiduque's, and one by his namesake at that: Rainer Maria. Ich fürchte mich so vor der Menschen Wort," Catlina cited, in what sounded to them like a quasi unaccented German. Promptly she began to translate, obviously a rehearsed exercise.

> *People's words imbue me so much with fear.*
> *They denote things by so distinct a sound:*
> *this is a house and that is called hound,*
> *and the front is there and the end is here.*
>
> *Also their mind does scare me, their mocking goal,*
> *they know all that was and will once come;*
> *no more mountain enraptures their soul,*
> *their garden and lot verge on god's kingdom.*
>
> *I like to hear the singing of things so much.*
> *I will always warn and avert: do not touch.*
> *you stir them : they turn rigid and mute.*
> *You spoil all things down to the root.*

Motionless the Mikes kept standing there, staring at that wall. Each verse, each word that the young lass had scanned, empathically and yet a bit aloof, was still ringing in their ears! The way one lets a nip of hierbas act on one's tongue, drop by drop. "Walls can speak," Catarina whispered.

Catlina left the couple to their thoughts for a while. As she returned with a bowl with olives, she found them as tacitent as before. Somehow though she felt Dugal had gone through a complete metamorphosis. "Finally I've grasped it," Dugal mumbled. "Here lies the Duke's testament. This is it. This very place. Mister Raniero do Mar was right: we had better respect his own choice. Slipping out of time by his own decision, to escape from the here and now. Not just a simple vanishing tric. What idiots we've been."

"You shouldn't put it that sharply," Catlina comforted him. "Don Lois's unseen return must have been emotionally inspired, as this letter proves." And as for this anonymous cover address of maestra Catalí, it was undoubtedly a symbol of their secret 'conspiracy'.

Whether she herself was not so opposed to the LS-marketing, he sounded her. Oh, it did not seem really desecrating to her. It might even open up respectful people a little more to the Duque's motives and his personality, she thought. If that could be a consolation to him.

The aroma of the elixir and the bitter aftertaste of the black olives still in their mouths and nostrils, they continued for quite a while chatting on about the significance of that intimistic moment.

Wavering between admiration and regret Dugal had to acknowledge: "I couldn't do it. That total self-restriction, absolute abstinence from power and career ..." He did not notice the mocking twinkle in Catari's eyes: really, couldn't he? No, for that matter he was too much apprehensive about so many questions as far as the late Duque's choice was concerned. His latent aversion from his own kind, his contempt for the pick, however comprehensible it seemed, was an easy pose after all, wasn't it, seen from his high-rank comfort zone? As an heir of the Ancien Régime he had taken a counter-stance in all matters: anti-establishment, anti-protocol, anti-elitist. On the other hand, this exponent of the spiritual nobility had preferred a passive attitude, yet without ostentatively rebelling. Due to his rejection of a leading role, he had kept on a sideline: thanks for the honour, I'd rather live up to my own standards. That freedom, however, could also be interpreted as weakness. Or was it hopeless inertion, cowardice? What common citizen could afford such aloofness? It was precisely owing to his origin that he kept for himself the luxury of pulling out and leading his own bought-off life on the lee side, far from the epicentre of power. True, particularly for that reason Dugal had admired him. At the same time, however, one consideration kept slumbering under his skin: whether all that had not been a galant way to shy responsibility? In the end, what with his contacts and his spiritual authority, don Lois had the potential to bundle all pacifistic forces of his time, get the champions of a humanitarian Europe on the same rail. The way he had backed up world exhibitions and scientific congresses ... He was close to the source so as to launch a counter current against the hawks. To add a new verve to humanism, as it got three centuries before. What if he had used his inner strength for that higher purpose: 'duc in altum'?" With a little more backbone the Dux could have put himself forward as the saviour of the Occident, à la Napoleon, yet not 'de manu militaris'. Nor for the sake of restoring absolutism, in the Metternich fashion …

And … would you have done so? Catarí did not even need to pronounce that moral issue, her eyes said enough. *We know each other that well*, Dugal smiled. *Even without any words we can guess what's going on in the other's mind.* Oh yes, she was right. To be honest, he would have thanked for the honour himself. The Dux figuring as the first Mister Europe avant la lettre? Too nice a notion, taking into account the balances of power in that juncture. "I wouldn't like to be in the imperial shoes," don Lois was said to have confided to niece Lizzy once. That powerless omnipotence - or almighty impotence ?- outweighed any human heart or brain. History surmounted the will and goodwill of enlightened spirits, ground down by the wheel of fate.

Yeah, and look at me, he grimaced, *Duke the Great*. What had he achieved, for Heaven's sake? What had he moved in this stormy age? Besides a handful of trophies and awards, his name would remain linked to the genre for ever. So what? Had mankind benefited from it in any way, had he added one ounce to making this planet more humane in this whirlwind of times?

"One can't compare different eras after all,"said Catlina. "Besides, doesn't history largely develop independently from the will of reformers, no matter what mountains they moved?"

Thank you, nice attempt, my child, Duke smiled resignedly, but now he felt need of another dram of solace. With something more than some befuddling essential oils. Once back above-ground, he sucked the purifying mountain air into his lungs, as if it could give him the catharsis the Archidux too must have yearned for. He sighed aloud: "Ay, dear friend, tell me how you found peace with yourself here." Because *can anyone who does not find peace in himself, pass it on to others?* Socrates couldn't have put it any better, he chuckled, but would the world take any advantage of all those reflections? Duke could imagine what the ladies downstairs thought about it and, frowning, he gazed into the narrow vale, to see if he could not get an answer from the thrushes and the rustling of the trees and little waterfalls between the hills.

Personal note

As an inveterate Belgian, predisposed to be trilingual from the cradle - Dutch-French-German - and so, innately, presupposed to be entangled in petty communal hassles, I have, for an eternity, fostered a deep affinity for that somewhat cryptic, quaint figure: 'el Archiduque'. This stateless world-citizen knew thirteen languages, spoke them and wrote books in them, among which even pretty queer ones, like Friulian. Narrow-minded nationalism was strange to him.

L.S., an aristocratic outlaw, though scion of the highest lineage, was a pot full of paradoxes. To some maybe one of the last polymaths, to others a mere oddball, this 'last archduke of stature' flouts all tedious biographies. A non-conformist avant la lettre, he cannot be fitted into any category. An anti-imperialist peer, anti-globalist cosmopolite, an environmentalist technophile, a progressive conservative ... He reconciled all those opposites with his down-to-earth common sense. Ineluctably, that harbinger of the pacifist movement was precocious for his epoch. Nowadays he would make a pragmatic ecologist, imbued with the spirit of technological innovations, yet at heart a forthright conservationist.

For all those reasons, such an elusive maverick stands out as a unique character for a novel, rather than as a suitable subject for the biographer. To make him look even more intangible, I slightly veiled his personalia: name, sobriquets, character traits, idiosyncrasies as well as other realia concerning local topography and persons. Even more so the particulars of his local mistress, 'Catalí'. Equally swathed are the data of his modern counterpart and near namesake, a Dougal Mikes ('Duke'), plus the latter's spouse, Catarí, who play the leading role in the contemporary scene: accidentally embroiled in LS's track, they will get more and more enthralled by their predecessors' personalities, unwillingly identifying with the couple and their mysterious life path ...

As for my own nullity, I crossed that Excellency's path long ago, passim, as some will sail the Med in the wake of Ulysses. Later on I lost a bit sight of him, as I got more absorbed by different occupations. Until one day the fascination for that extravagant peer caught me again, unawares. Old love does not rust.

Julian Vandenbroeck.

Lightning Source UK Ltd.
Milton Keynes UK
UKHW011202091120
373077UK00001B/107